Tangled Webs

Beth Strauss

About the Author

Beth Strauss is an educator, nurse, freelance journalist, and novelist. She is the author of the mystery/romance *Tangled Webs*. After spending her career in academia and the health sciences, she decided to pursue her first love: writing. Beth completed her Master's degree in Journalism at Harvard and published stories in local papers as well as an academic article in the *Journal of Advanced Nursing* before she realized she preferred the freedom of creative writing over the regimented styles of academia and journalism. Growing up in Southern California and enjoying her college days in Berkeley, Beth became accustomed to an active and athletic lifestyle. She eventually headed east to Philadelphia and now bounces between both coasts. When she is not writing, she enjoys pottery and photography, as well as taking hikes with her rescue pup, Maddie.

Tangled Webs

Beth Strauss

Bella Books, Inc.
P.O. Box 10543
Tallahassee, FL 32302

First Edition - 2025

Editor: Heather Flournoy
Cover Designer: SJ Hardy
Author photo credit: MODA Photography

ISBN: 978-1-64247-694-1

PUBLISHER'S NOTE

Acknowledgments

The world is a better place when people are willing to share the gift of their time and expertise. I'd like to acknowledge the people who helped make this novel possible. A huge thanks to Detectives Amanda Wenrich and Holly Halota. Your patience and willingness to handle banal and rudimentary law enforcement questions, as well as identifying police procedural errors I missed, were indispensable. To Sheri Kolb of the Davis, California Evidence Response Team, Alameda County Deputy Sheriff Stephanie Beasley, and Forensic Pathologist/Medical Examiner of San Bernardino County's Sheriff Department, Matthew Miller, MD. You all infused my characters with authenticity and helped them follow strict protocol while handling the crime scene and visiting autopsy. Simply put, you made them shine. To DA Hartman and Sally Nottage for your time and honest advice. No finished manuscript succeeds without the work of an editor. And when you are lucky enough to have a fabulous editor, well then, your finished product glistens. Thank you, Heather Flournoy, for all your hard work, kindness, and a sense of humor that made the process enjoyable. To Katherine V. Forrest for your mentoring and tireless commitment and suggestions to help this manuscript sparkle—you are a gem. I am eternally grateful I had the opportunity to work with you. And finally, to my parents, who enrolled me in my first creative writing class—Quills for Kids—at age 12. You opened the door. I finally walked through.

Dedication

To my parents. You taught me strength, tenacity, and persistence.

CHAPTER ONE

Karen Cappelletti visualized the Glock cradled in the palm of her hand, contemplating her next step. She felt her index finger resting on the thin, cool metal strip. Felt the firm tug as she pulled it back. The jolt of it firing. The lingering smoky, sulfurous aroma. A hot metallic slug whizzing through the air, penetrating that thick, insensitive, self-absorbed brain.

Her foot slammed onto the brake pedal—following an abrupt refocus to the present—saving her vehicle from hitting the car ahead of her, still stopped at the green light. Clutching a travel mug filled to the rim with coffee and billowing steam, the scalding liquid flew onto her wrist, just missing the cuff of a freshly pressed white button-down. *Damn it, Capp! Get your shit together. You're a goddamn detective. Act like it.*

Karen berated herself, perturbed for allowing her muddled thoughts to create such a distraction—a distraction created by that early morning text. *A text. Not even the courtesy of a phone call.* She glared at the innocent electronic device sitting on the passenger seat. *No phone call, no apology, just a fucking text.* Her mind drifted back to earlier that morning. It started out like a punch to the gut, sucking the air right out of her at a time when she felt most vulnerable. *Follow through*, she fumed. *Be reliable. Act like you care, for once.*

Torn between frustration and rage, depression and defeat, she eased her way through the intersection. The effortless five-minute drive from home to work took her through Parks Ford's business district, past the quaint shops and mom-and-pop restaurants on Market Street. Moments later, she turned onto the curved driveway of the town's police station. A grassy area surrounded the driveway and buildings, a pleasant, peaceful appearance, not to mention a delightful scent of fresh-cut grass every Thursday. This day was different, though.

Today, she was met with the sight of a raucous crowd gathered outside the county courthouse, a mere half block from Karen's office. They packed the parking lot shared by both the town and county municipal buildings and spilled into the open space in front of the police station, leaving Karen circling to find a parking space. Finally parked, she headed to her department's building, elbowing her way through the noisy throng just to get to the front doors.

As she pushed through, she noted the signs protesters elevated in the air. Residents of this small town outside of Philadelphia were vehemently opposing the release of a prisoner in the county's jail. She passed by television cameras, listening as town residents spoke to reporters of Kenny McPherson's drunken rages and numerous minor assault charges. They spoke of his wife's bruises. Reporters looking for a tasty soundbite found residents expressing fear over what Kenny might do once he was free. This sleepy suburban community—hard-working and close-knit, a town where you grew up learning right from wrong quickly—never wanted to see Kenny again.

In an even, deliberate fashion, Karen proceeded up the cement steps of the old, two-story stone building. The multipaned colonial-style windows along the left side of the building spoke to its nineteenth-century roots. She slipped through the glass double doors of the police station, the sound of the crowd fading as the door clicked closed. A palpable stillness surrounded her.

Standing in the silence, she felt a knot twist deep in her gut. Kenny McPherson. The man Karen herself had arrested ten years prior. Her mind revisited the news anchor's comments about Kenny's crimes. Felony assault after attacking his wife with a knife. She recalled how the assault left a gaping, three-inch wound across the woman's left cheek. This news felt personal.

With a deep sigh, she trekked down the hushed hallway to her office, the thud of her Blundstones bouncing off the linoleum flooring. A clear picture of what her day would likely entail illuminated memories of Kenny's arrest, the scar on her right forearm a grim reminder. Her uneasiness felt like a black cloud forming in the cloudless sky and abundant sunshine beaming through her office window.

For the past year, this four-point-two-square-mile town had been dealing with a flurry of banal but annoying issues requiring police activity and worsening during the summer months with children out of school. And even though Parks Ford was the county seat, their pocket-sized police department only had twelve patrol officers.

With Labor Day complete and early October beckoning, the town had returned to a peaceful calm, unpleasant for a single divorcée detective with empty-nest syndrome in need of a distraction. She sat in the silence of her office watching the second hand perform laps on the wall clock.

Breaking her vacant, mesmerized stare, her hollow gaze pivoted to the corner of her desk and Caiden's graduation picture. Her precious little girl, her head full of loose, auburn curls. She had desperately hoped Caiden would stay local for school, but a lucrative scholarship to the Fashion Institute of Technology had pulled her away from a town that no one ever left.

She sighed over the original reason for the emptiness at home and in her life. The predictable demise of her eight-year marriage and now—after fourteen years of dating rather aimlessly—another dysfunctional relationship, this time with a thirty-four-year-old physician's assistant, ten years her junior, who had opted for travel work assignments. Miles had promised to return home after Caiden left. His one-line text message stating he was extending his current work trip an additional three months left a sickening pit in her stomach. Another letdown. One of many.

Her tidy, sunlit office was a far cry from the mess swirling inside her head. Even after the morning's disappointment, she felt reluctant to throw in the towel on yet another relationship. She took pride in her ability to persist through obstacles. It served her well in her career—surely it would be a useful skill in fixing her dysfunctional relationships.

The chief of police lumbered in, interrupting her faraway trance.

"What the hell?" Karen motioned to the crowd outside.

"You've heard?" Chief Walden said, his wide-shouldered, six-foot frame taking up the entire doorway to her office.

She nodded. "Hard to believe it's been ten years."

"Town's been causing a stir. Even signed petitions. Might see a protest at the prison tomorrow." A routine even-tempered look came over his aged, pale face, complete with graying chin whiskers and a maze of wrinkles, each with its own story. "They don't want him out, and they don't want him here."

"Can you blame them? You know this town. They remember his shit."

Walden let out a muted snort. "Only place I've worked where children grow up and leave home to move a few blocks away. It's incestuous."

"People here may know your business, but they don't judge." She felt a need to defend her lifelong residence. "You're judged on your character. Kenny's being judged on years of atrocious actions."

"Just read through the old file. He sent his wife to the hospital."

"Yup. Ambulance and several squad cars got there ahead of me. I remember coming down the street as they were loading her into the bus."

"One of his drunken rages?"

Karen shrugged. "Marianne said he waved a knife at her. Neighbors said she ran outside, blood streaming down her face... screaming. Kenny staggered out next. Apparently, a neighbor kept him back with a baseball bat."

"Lucky you didn't end up with her in that bus."

Karen groaned.

"Heard you took it on the arm."

"Forearm. Ruined my favorite button-down." A laugh quivered in the back of her throat. She felt a phantom ache deep in her arm.

"How'd it happen?"

"Rookie officer was with me. His sloppy procedural move." She glanced away, her chest tightening. "Let down his guard while cuffing him. Turned Kenny around, right where the knife was on the counter. I was reading him his rights." She snorted. "Couldn't handle a woman collaring his misogynistic ass."

Walden scowled. He scratched his thinning hair, shaking his head. "Lucky it wasn't worse."

"No kidding." She felt her eyes widen as she nodded. "Marianne never returned to their house. Moved in with her cousin."

Walden shot her a grim look. "What about the kids? He hurt them too?"

"Marianne took the brunt of the abuse." Her gaze drifted. "Tammy was the youngest. Heard she moved away when she turned eighteen. Bobby was in his early twenties. He's still in town."

"In that house? How do you stay with such horrific memories?"

Karen nodded, staring straight ahead.

"Well, I think Kenny may be a different man now."

Karen always admired her chief's even-keeled, optimistic outlook. Her jaded view—not to mention the scar on her left forearm—left her skeptical. Eighteen years his junior, she wondered if her cynical outlook would ever mature into his.

"Up for a drive? See if Bobby's there. Nothing pressing here."

She grimaced. "His father's release could bring up a ton of shit."

Walden gave a single nod, then pivoted, heading down the hall to his office.

Karen grabbed her blazer. A trip across town to the old McPherson house. It was a place she hoped to never see again.

As Karen drove her black police SUV, she ruminated over the town to which, twenty-two years ago, she had sworn an oath to serve and protect. At just over eleven thousand residents, Parks Ford's population swelled to nearly sixteen thousand as people came into town to shop, dine, or work in the business district. The business district—the main hub—consisted of one main street packed with shops and restaurants. She knew the street's history. Originally named High Street, owing to its early eighteenth- and nineteenth-century British heritage and occupancy, it was renamed Market Street by nineteenth-century residents because all the shops and markets existed on that one street.

Present-day Market Street hadn't changed much, as if stuck in the nineteenth century. Most businesses were still situated there, and a trolley continued to chug up and down the street. The police station sat a block off Market, nestled in between the library and other municipal buildings. A small volunteer fire department building was a block away, not far from the expansive Central Park. An art center, several blocks from Market, served as the heart of the town's thriving artistic community.

Karen headed south and west toward the McPherson house, making her way from the business district past modest two- and three-bedroom homes built in the mid-twentieth century. Postage-stamp-sized yards had children's toys scattered about. Most front yards proudly displayed American flags, or less proudly housed a decrepit, broken-down vehicle in the driveway. Mowed front lawns had weeds cropping up along the perimeter of chain-link fences.

She drove down streets with trees still bearing the leaves of an early autumn day. In another three to four weeks, the foliage would light up the sky with oranges, reds, and yellows, before free-falling to the ground—a beautiful fall ritual.

Within the span of five minutes, Karen moved through a section of older row homes and twins, built during the first quarter of the twentieth century, to the far western edge of town. Here, newer single-family homes lined the streets of a blue-collar area—simple, small homes with minuscule front yards and modest backyards. If a homeowner wanted to expand, they would have to go up, not out. Owners took pride in their homes and labored to keep up their properties. Referred to as Garden Valley, this was where the McPherson house was located.

Her black SUV wound around the twists and turns of streets all too familiar. Ten years. The scar on her arm. A lifetime ago. She felt an inexplicable sadness come over her as she drove down Hillside Street.

She recalled arriving to see Kenny stumble back into the house. No one had known if his children were inside or if anyone else had been hurt. She'd only briefly spoken with Marianne when her attention was diverted to a dark sedan pulling into the driveway. It was Bobby. As he rushed toward the house, officers slowed him and Karen stopped him. She had no idea what condition Kenny was in and, with the injured Marianne pressing charges, the house was now a crime scene.

Kenny had been slouched in a chair in the kitchen, disheveled and reeking of alcohol. His sweaty, dirty, white ribbed tank top hung over his flabby torso. Blue jeans spotted with blood. Remnants of the dinner Marianne was preparing sat on the countertop, along with the bloodstained knife. Splotches of blood dotted the path from the kitchen to the doorway, onto the front porch, and down the steps.

Now Karen's tires crackled on the beat-up asphalt street as the SUV eased to the curb in front of the house. She gaped, struggling to recognize it. Instead of the eyesore in virtual disrepair, the house boasted a renovated, freshly painted front porch. A row of angel coneflowers lined the walkway, their delicious fragrance filling her nostrils. New siding covered a home once marred with peeling paint that fell onto weed-filled grounds. The old chain-link fence surrounding the lot had been removed, presenting an open, welcoming appearance.

Neighbors peered out from behind their blinds as Karen stood on the walkway and looked around, admiring the azalea bed framing the porch, bursting with deep-pink blooms. As she strolled up the wooden porch steps to the front door, the local regional commuter train rumbled off in the distance. She tapped on the door. The pit in her stomach grew.

The door creaked open a few inches with a tall, dark-haired man peering through the opening. It was Bobby. The minute the slender and muscular young man saw the detective, a smile erupted.

"Detective." His voice was soft. His youthful, handsome face glowed. "It's been a long time."

"Hi, Bobby." She returned his smile, noting how well he looked.

"It's good to see you. What brings you back out this way?" Bobby motioned for her to come inside. His head was a wavy mass of thick brown hair, his jaw chiseled and clean-shaven.

Karen sucked in a deep breath. "Listen, Bobby, I'm sure you know." She stood in the foyer of the one-story bungalow. "Your dad's getting out tomorrow. I just wanted to reach out…check in."

Bobby's gaze lowered to the hardwood flooring. His shoulders and upbeat mood sagged as if all the air inside had escaped. Looking up, he expelled a long breath. "Life's been calm. Peaceful. I don't want him here."

"Look, Bobby, I have no idea where he's planning to go or if he's even thinking of coming here. I just felt you should be prepared."

"Yeah, yeah. That's cool. I appreciate it." His eyebrows pulled together—a portrait of tension. Unease. Emotions likely not this intense for a decade.

Karen studied the change in his demeanor. She had come to know him through the years. A kind soul. She recalled his compassion toward the homeless population at the end of his block, opening his wallet even when down to his last dollar. "You okay, Bob?"

His jaw tightened. "I spent a shit ton of money to keep this house…not to mention all the repairs." His body grew animated. "I worked two jobs to keep things together. Why should I welcome him back?" A rhetorical question. He looked as if his mind was filled with marbles that were about to perilously scatter to the floor.

Karen moved toward him to lay a comforting hand on his shoulder. From down the hall, a slender woman with cropped, tousled sunny-blond hair headed toward them. The notable lightness of her step contrasted with the mood in the room. Fearing she had interrupted Bobby and this blond-haired woman, Karen turned back to the door.

"Kare, do you remember my little sister, Tammy?"

Tammy, alert and curious, scrutinized the detective's face as she approached. It was a gentle, almost seductive look that made Karen feel incredibly transparent—like cellophane. Yet she had never established that level of familiarity with Tammy, which caught her off guard. At the same time, she felt a touch of flattery, causing her to consciously force back the smile she felt beginning to take form.

As Tammy approached, Karen felt her eyebrows arch and eyes widen. She looked at the woman now in her early thirties. The Tammy she remembered had a shy, rough-around-the-edges tomboy appearance and straight, plain, sandy-brown hair. Back then, Tammy had pretty much stayed out of sight and Karen had rarely dealt with her. *Is this really the same person?*

Tammy bounced down the hall toward her, beaming with a bright smile that lit up her entire face and a personality visibly steeped in charm and confidence, extending her hand.

"Hi, I'm Tam."

Karen was taken aback and a touch flattered by the eagerness in Tam's tone and the brash nature of her eye contact. If she hadn't known better, she'd have thought she'd caught a sparkle in Tam's eyes that spoke to an interest beyond just friendly and casual warmth. "Hi, Tam. I…I'm sorry, I don't remember you from when I was out here making calls."

Karen thought back on how Tam was so shy. Now, she appeared beyond assertive, almost aggressively so. *No…confident. She's confident.*

Bobby stepped in. "Tam moved to New York before the abuse got bad and you were here all the time. She wasn't around when Dad got arrested."

"Ahh." Karen nodded. "So, back for a visit?"

"Nope." Tam's tone was light and airy. "I'm back!"

"Really? Didn't like the big city?" Karen asked. It was the same city her daughter had just relocated to.

"I didn't like the crazy cost of living. I'm an artist. Couldn't make ends meet."

"I understand." Would this be the plight of Caiden, her artist daughter? "What kind of art do you do?"

Tam beamed. "I'm a ceramicist."

Karen squinted.

"I make pottery." Tam flashed a gentle smile.

"Oh...great...cool." Karen attempted to sound a touch less ignorant.

Tam's face was gentle but animated. Alluring. Fantastically, inexplicably charismatic. Not at all what Karen would have expected from the unassuming kid she'd seen run around the neighborhood. She couldn't help but think how Tam was so willing to return to Parks Ford, when someone like Miles, who had proclaimed his love for Karen, refused to stick around for more than a month at a time, let alone lay down roots.

"What's goin' on?" Tam said to her brother, who was disconsolately leaning against the wall. "You look like you just lost your best friend."

"Nothin'." The word was barely audible.

"You're full of shit."

Bobby looked up at his sister. "What if Dad does come back?"

She winced. "Can he just come back and take over the house? It was your money."

"After he went to jail, I made him sign a quitclaim."

"Will that work?"

Bobby shrugged and looked at Karen.

Karen fought to keep her emotions at a distance. "Listen, I don't think your dad will cause problems. He'd be a fool. But if you need anything, just call me." She had no idea how her positive words were being received. After all, she had her own gnawing discomfort about Kenny's release.

"See? We have someone to help if there are any problems." Tam looked at her brother, his head lowered as he picked at the cuticles on his thumbs—a nervous habit Karen remembered from his adolescence.

"Bobby, we can call our detective." She shifted her gaze from Bobby to Karen. "I really appreciate you offering to help us. You're very kind." An enigmatic smile touched her lips. "Maybe we could get to know each other better...that is, when you're not working."

Bobby shot his sister a contorted side glance.

Tam whispered something to her brother, but all Karen could overhear were the words *she's hot*. There was a glint in Tam's eyes.

Christ. Am I invisible?

Bobby rolled his eyes and shifted the subject. "I just don't want him here."

"You don't owe him anything, Bob. Just call Kare here if he stops by." Tam turned and looked at Karen with a wide grin. "Thank you for your offer."

"I'm not gonna bother you." Bobby looked at Karen. "You have more important things."

"She told you to call." Tam's voice was smooth and reassuring. "You have her number, right?" Leaning over to her brother, she whispered in his ear again.

"Leave it alone. She dates men," he said in a hushed tone, gritting his teeth.

Karen's chest grew tight. Her eyes darted, landing everywhere—anywhere—to avoid eye contact with Tam. She felt a vaguely familiar, warm sensation run up her neck, flooding her cheeks as her hand rested on the doorknob.

Tam gave Bobby a playful punch in his shoulder. "I was just joking, dumbass. When did you lose your sense of humor?" She shifted her attention to Karen with a smile that practically lit up the entire room. "Seriously, thank you for stopping by and looking out for us. I'll help my brother through this."

Karen nodded. She couldn't tell if Tam was being earnest or facetious but figured Tam likely didn't feel the same level of concern as her brother. Having been removed from the turmoil and chaos for so long, Tam could embrace a light and airy tone. *Probably good for Bobby to have her here. She's confident. Easygoing. Positive.*

Karen pivoted to leave. "Bobby, you've really done a great job here. It's nice to see you again." She felt tenderness for him and how difficult this moment must feel.

"Thanks. Life is good now." His even-tempered, soft voice had a slight lilt as if welcoming her soothing words.

Karen nodded and headed back out to the porch.

"I'll walk you out," Tam said, running out behind her.

"I'm good." Karen trotted down the steps and back to the street.

"Hey, Kare." Tam raced toward the curb.

Karen tilted her head, wincing at the familiarity with which Tam addressed her.

"Hey. If my dad comes back. If he causes problems, ya know, like, how do I get ahold of you?" Tam gave a sheepish grin.

Karen cringed, sure that Tam was just shy of flashing a wink. Right there, on the street, with neighbors peering out their windows. Karen yanked out her business card. "There's the number where you can reach me." Her tone was crisp.

Tam brushed Karen's thumb with lingering fingers as she grasped the card. "I hope we can get to know each other. My friends are all strong, professional women. Like you."

Karen hopped in her car and accelerated away from the curb.

Tam's presumed advances annoyed her. Working in a male-dominated profession, it was incumbent on her to maintain a strong, tough exterior—which she did. But she often wondered what people thought. Did people equate that tough exterior with being lesbian? Tam's public display of interest only elevated these concerns.

At the same time, she felt flattered by the attention—something sorely missing from her life. The sheer thought of her longed-for closeness being furnished by someone of the same gender, someone with such an attractive personality, caught her breath short. It was one thing to worry about what people thought of her tough exterior, her choice of profession, her inability to hold a man. But dating a woman? She was certain gossip and suspicion would harden into judgment.

But I'm open-minded. Or am I just open-minded when it involves other people? She vigorously shook her head as if to shake away the contradictions.

Turning the corner off Hillside, Karen chuckled to herself, recalling the first woman she experienced feelings for: an instructor at the academy. The flush of flattery she felt when the instructor admired her work. A crush, she told herself. Yet she couldn't get the woman off her mind. She had always chalked it up to admiration, then briskly dismissed the feelings.

Karen arrived back at the police station minutes later to a handful of messages resting on her tidy desk. She stared at the words hastily jotted down on the top message: *Please call.*

Shit. What on earth could have happened?

She picked up her office phone and stood rigid. The call picked up on the first ring.

"Kare?"

"Yes. It's Detective Cappelletti." She enunciated each word. "Got your message. Everything okay?"

"Yeah. Everything's good," Tam said, almost gleeful. "Bobby's off with his friends tonight. I'm still pretty new in town..." An empty buzz filled the phone line as if waiting for Karen to respond. "I don't know the local joints...ya know, like where to get a drink or the good restaurants—"

"Seriously?" Karen felt her eyes narrow. Her tone was acid. "You're calling the police station to request recommendations for a good bar or a diner?"

Tam's laugh danced through the phone line, an infectious laugh that drew an involuntary soft chuckle from Karen. Immediately disarmed and not quite sure why she was entertaining this young woman's ridiculous request, she cleared her throat to mask her amusement.

"If you don't mind driving out of town, Michael's still has the best steaks," she said, referring to cheesesteaks. "In town, can't go wrong with Pat's or Coco's. The Geneva Diner on Market...same quaint feel...excellent food. Lots of bars, but Grimaldi's is about a half mile from your place."

"Cool. Thanks." Tam seemed to be waiting for something else. "Hey, Kare, listen—"

"Detective Cappelletti."

"Oh. Apologies." Tam paused. "Look, I know you're busy. I shouldn't have bothered you. I guess...I just don't have any friends here yet. I'm feeling a little lost."

What if this was Caiden, a stranger in New York City, with no friends to speak of yet? I'd want someone to extend a welcoming hand. "All good, Tam."

"I'm sorta used to just putting myself out there and meeting new people. That's pretty much what I've had to do since I moved away. I'm really sorry if I overstepped."

"No worries. Go grab a bite and a beer. Enjoy your evening."

Karen paused before putting the receiver down. Something about Tam. She was self-assured. Upbeat. *I don't remember her being this assertive as a kid. Nice change. Guess moving away was good for her.* And as much as Tam persisted, she seemed to recognize when she neared Karen's boundaries. *A little unexpected attention. It's kinda nice.* Karen shrugged and let out a soft chuckle as she hung up the phone.

She glanced down at the other messages: a reminder about the police academy graduation celebration that weekend. *Yeah, I'll be sure to be busy that night.* The last message drew a blank stare. A neighbor of hers had found a rat in her toilet. She rolled her eyes. "That's an Animal Control issue," she muttered under her breath, aware that her elderly neighbor, Marge, might just be hallucinating.

She sat at her desk, staring into space. The barren squad room only exacerbated her feeling of hollowness. Grabbing her phone, she snatched her steel-gray blazer off its hook.

"Hey, Jake," she called to a patrol officer down the hall. "Headed out. Call if you need me."

"Sure thing, KC."

Heading out the front doors, a vibration came from her leather bag. A pleasant surprise illuminated the phone in her palm. Judy, her childhood friend and neighbor. Even though Judy lived at the end of her block, she hadn't talked with her all week. A text message.

Hey you! Judy had typed.

Hey Jude. Karen grinned; she loved that Beatles song. *When's our next Friday girls' night?*

No night out with Miles?

Karen growled as she typed. *No. Extended assignment. Again.*

Next Friday?

Sold. Karen typed with emphatic eagerness. *C u then.* She tucked the phone in her bag and headed home.

Beginning the slow traverse up her rounded brick walkway, she stopped to gaze at a front lawn in desperate need of mowing, looking forward to a month from now when the mower could be put away for the winter. Gingerly, she put her key in the front door, dreading what awaited on the other side. It seemed like an eternity before she finally gripped the handle and entered the vacant space.

Karen rummaged through the refrigerator for something that might constitute a dinner. A leftover half of a cheesesteak and a beer. She could have walked down the street to her parents' house for a healthy meal. But, oddly, she preferred solitude.

She sat in her sparsely appointed living room—frozen—startled by the stillness surrounding her. An empty silence—an unfamiliar "sound." A cavernous void enveloped her as she felt the absence of her vibrant, bright, and talented daughter. Leaning her head back on the sofa cushion, she could hear Caiden's clogs clunking down the steps. The slam of the refrigerator door. She envisioned the half-eaten container of yogurt left behind on the countertop as Caiden rushed out the door, yelling reminders of what to pick up at the grocery store. The house was never quiet with Caiden around.

She glanced at her phone—a blank screen. Nothing from Caiden. Recalling the constant "just checking in" phone calls she received from her parents when she first started at the academy, she swore she wouldn't bother her daughter. Nothing from Miles, which left an odd sensation of relief. A sudden realization: she really didn't want to chat with him or hear him go on and on about himself. Yet, she craved hearing his voice—any voice—to break the silence. Her thoughts drifted. Drifted to Tam. Tam's upbeat laugh. Her insouciant eagerness for attention.

The ring of her phone penetrated her rambling thoughts. *The Brady Bunch* ringtone. A warmth of relief.

"Hey, Dad. Thought about you guys tonight. Almost headed down for dinner."

"We had your mom's baked ziti. Plenty left. Want me to walk some down?"

Karen smiled. "I'm good, Dad. Already ate. How are you and Mom?"

"Good. Well, we're concerned about you."

"Me?"

"That character getting out of prison tomorrow."

Character. What a way to describe Kenny McPherson. A chuckle seeped out. "I'll be fine, Dad. He's not gonna hurt me."

"That's what you thought the day you arrested him—"

"I'll be fine. Promise."

"We'd feel a lot better if Miles were there."

The comment landed like a lead weight. "I'll be fine." Her stoic, independent nature came out in full force. "Maybe I'll even swing by for some ziti tomorrow night. Gotta busy day tomorrow. I'm headed to bed." A lie. She just didn't feel like chatting. Something was gnawing at her. Kenny? Miles? Caiden? Not Tam. *No way.* She chuckled to herself.

In bed, she stared at the blank ceiling, wide awake. The house felt somber. She kept waiting to hear Caiden get up and shuffle to the kitchen for a late-night snack. She longed to see the blue light peeking through the cracks of her bedroom doorway as Caiden sat up late at her computer. The house was pitch black.

She tossed and turned, working to push aside the void left by Miles's protracted absence. Shoveling away the detritus of personal failures—a personal skill set. Yet even in the face of growing evidence, she couldn't convince herself to toss Miles on the debris heap, much to the dismay of family and friends. Lying in a pervasive stillness, haunted by loneliness, she wondered whether the best choice would have been to give up her career to save her marriage.

C'mon, Capp. Let it go. She stared at the ceiling and sighed. She needed rest—for her mind to rest. A storm was brewing. The next day held the potential for enormous stress. Tomorrow, Kenny McPherson would be a free man.

CHAPTER TWO

As usual, Karen was in her living room by 7:30 the next morning, enjoying steaming coffee and the *Delco Times*. Her phone disrupted the peace. Officer Jake Roberts. Kenny had been released.

"Know where he went?" she asked.

"A dude named Jack Doyle picked him up."

Karen cringed.

"Apparently, he's gonna stay there, temporarily—"

"Jesus. Jack Doyle?" Her voice grated through the phone. "What the hell is Kenny thinking? Couldn't have started his new life with a better influence?"

Roberts remained silent.

"Okay…thanks. I'll be in shortly."

Driving to the station, her phone rang again.

"Detective," the front desk clerk said. "A call came in for you from Bobby McPherson. He said, and I quote…" The papers near the receiver rustled. "'Tell her Kenny McPherson is back at 351 Hillside.'" Her words flowed like bubbling Jell-O.

"Thanks, Blanche. Headed there now." Shaking her head, she tapped the red disconnect button and pressed down harder on the accelerator.

Turning onto Hillside, Karen could see a car she recognized: Jack Doyle's dinged-up white sedan in front of Bobby's house. A scruffy-looking man, weathered in appearance, stood at the edge of the walkway.

Karen got out of her SUV to see the pot-bellied, gray-haired Doyle leaning on the hood of his car, laughing and clapping his hands as if egging Kenny on.

"C'mon, Bob. How 'bout showing a little love for your old pops?"

Bobby's face contorted. "You destroyed our lives. I got nothing to say to you."

"Bob…I'm still your father." He reached for Bobby's shoulder.

Bobby swatted his arm away. "Go away!" His voice quaked as neighbors peeked out their windows.

"Go away? It's my house, son."

"Not anymore. You signed that paper, remember? If it weren't for me, this house wouldn't even be here." Bobby's words howled through the still morning air. "Leave us alone." His eyes moistened, upper lip twitching.

Kenny reached for his son again. Bobby's hands balled into fists, the edges of his knuckles whitening.

Karen stepped in, turning first to Doyle. "Doyle. Back off."

Kenny and Bobby continued to verbally spar.

"Kenny." Karen's commanding voice echoed. "This how you want to start your new life?"

Tam rushed outside, her bright smile and cheerful eagerness as her eyes landed on Karen utterly inappropriate for the moment. In a split second, her expression changed as she seemingly took in the scene. She raced down the porch steps toward Karen, feverishly reaching out in what Karen construed as panic. Again, Kenny extended a hand to Bobby. Chaos erupted. Karen had seen and heard enough.

"All right," she shouted, holding up her arms and stepping into the center of the melee. "Jesus fucking Christ! *You!*" She pointed at Tam. Her deadpan glare and steely tone matched the intensity of the moment. "Back in the house. Bobby, get to work. Kenny, if you're smart, you'll walk away and go to Doyle's house. Probably not a good idea to be making waves your first day on parole, ya think?"

Tam's head dropped like a wilting sunflower, a mix of disappointment, concern, and surprise. She receded without another word. Bobby stalked off, slamming his solid frame into his black Mustang, and backed out of the driveway, his tires screeching as he accelerated down the street. Doyle snickered, leaning back on his car. Kenny walked back and joined him. Karen shook her head. *Such a scumbag. What's Doyle gonna push Kenny to do next?*

Kenny flopped into the passenger seat while the stubby-legged Doyle strutted back around to the driver's side. A folded pamphlet fell out of his back pocket as he waddled away. Karen watched as they disappeared down the street, a cloud of debris and dust in their wake.

She scooped up the pamphlet. *What the hell are you doing, Kenny? Letting Doyle lead you right back to prison?* She stomped back to her car, chucking the pamphlet announcing the Lehigh Valley Knife and Blade Show into a neighbor's garbage can.

Opening her car door, she noted a thin man in threadbare clothes sauntering down the street, his teeth like weathered boards on an old picket fence as he smiled at her. The man hobbled as he walked with shoes so worn that half his toes were sticking out. Maybe six feet tall, very thin. His skin was dry and brittle, like a leather hide left out in the sun. His smile shone through scraggly facial hair well beyond a five-o'clock shadow.

"Gotta smoke you could spare, ma'am?" the man asked as he shuffled by.

"Nah, I don't smoke. You okay?"

He glanced down at the badge on her belt, nodded, and smiled. "Just goin' for a walk, ma'am."

Karen smiled back, wrestling a bill from her wallet. "What's your name?"

"Cliff, ma'am."

She handed him a five-dollar bill. "Cliff, get yourself a cup of coffee and a bite to eat. And stay out of trouble."

He held the bill in his battered, dirt-stained hands. "Yes, ma'am. Thank you, ma'am. Thank you." Gratitude seeped from his gentle, hazel eyes. "God bless you."

Karen got back into her car. "I'll take it. I can use all the blessings I can get," she muttered.

Two weeks flew by—uneventful and quiet. Tam left a handful of messages for Karen at the police station, persisting as if hoping for something. Anything. For Karen, Tam was the furthest thought from her mind. The town started letting go of a bit of anxiety and animosity toward Kenny, but Karen wasn't yet ready to let her guard down. Beyond his first day out of prison, Kenny had remained out of the public eye. No old antics. No hanging out at bars causing disagreements and altercations.

On Friday, Karen was ready for a "girls' night" with Judy. The two women frequently gathered on Friday nights: Judy with a glass of red wine, complete with ice cubes, and Karen downing a few beers.

Judy was often the eyes and ears for Karen when she couldn't make it down to check on her parents, who lived in the same house Karen grew up in. Judy, post divorce, lived in her childhood home right next door.

Karen tossed a plastic container of leftovers in the microwave and threw aside the work week. At seven o'clock, she walked down the street to Judy's, arriving in faded blue jeans and a light, well-worn sweatshirt. Judy, on the other hand, greeted her looking like she was going on a date—a flowing yellow sundress, dangling earrings, and makeup. The six-foot-tall divorcée had barely an ounce of fat or muscle attached to her slight frame. She sported a black bob that framed angular facial features—a perfect match to her quirky personality.

"Don't you ever just throw on jeans or sweatpants?" Karen asked with a grin.

Judy laughed. "You never know who might come to the door."

They headed to the back deck, drinks in hand. It was a beautiful October East Coast evening: low humidity, cool temperature, a pleasant breeze.

"Yeah, well, I'm all about comfort. No need to impress anyone," Karen said, continuing the conversation.

"Maybe that's your problem."

"What? That I won't go overboard to impress a man?"

"Yeah. Why don't you try a little harder?"

"Jude, I've been trying my whole life…to move up in my career, raise a daughter, have a nice home, help my parents. I don't have extra to play that game."

Karen had friends and tons of acquaintances. Heck, the whole town knew her and often treated her like their best friend. Finding men to date was never an issue. Yet each time she brought a man into her life, the lonelier she seemed to become.

Looking off across the manicured backyard lawn, she reflected on past choices and decisions. As she'd moved up the law enforcement career ladder in her late twenties, her then-husband, Lou, had grown insecure with her accomplishments and accolades. When he pushed her to tone down her career, she pushed back, and off he went.

"Geez, girl. If I had your long dark hair, that toned body, and beautiful Italian skin, I could have any guy I want," Judy said.

Karen came back to the present as if taking an eraser to the memories. "Ya know, Jude, it's just sex. That's all it's about for men. They just want you for sex."

Judy shrugged. "What's wrong with that?"

"I want more. A connection." She looked away. "Someone I can count on. Someone that won't go away when I'm not in the mood for their fucking dick." Her female friends, including Judy, described sex with men as a spectacular fireworks display. She had never experienced that. She shook her head, a quick refocus. "Wouldn't hurt to walk into the department Christmas party with a man on my arm for once, though." The thought of, once again, attending the holiday party alone caused her throat to tighten. Fears of what people would think haunted her. She swallowed the knot away.

Judy let out a soft chuckle. "You take relationships too seriously. I enjoy the sex with no other expectations. I get my 'connections'"—she made air quotes—"from my friends. I lean on them. Stop taking men so seriously. Enjoy the sex and move on."

That's the problem. I don't enjoy it. "I don't think I can do that. Not now…not at this stage. I want more."

"Pining over Miles?"

Karen looked at her feet. She fiddled with her beer bottle, the drips of condensation running down her fingers. *Should probably be toasting to his absence.* She felt her fierce independence beginning to surface.

"You sure you're not missing him just because you're lonely?"

It was a thought Karen had briefly considered, then whisked away. *I do have feelings for him, don't I?* "After this assignment in Paducah, Kentucky…intentionally choosing to stay there three more months…I should've known. I mean, like, who the hell stays in Paducah for six months?"

Judy laughed—a deep-in-the-belly, throw-your-head-back laugh. "Paducah's not that bad, is it?"

"No idea. Never been there. Hell, I didn't even think it was a real place. Just figured he was BS-ing me so he could go away again." Karen stared off into the distance.

"Can't he get a job here?"

Karen shrugged. "Probably. Likely. I know the money is better with traveling."

"Have you considered maybe 'here' is just convenient?"

It was a question Karen had refused to consider. "Somewhere… deep down…I know he's never gonna change."

"They never do." Judy's tone was soft, gentle. "Do you…are you…in love with him?"

"Love? Like my parents? No. I don't think I've ever felt that… for anyone."

Lightning bugs sparkled over the lawn. Karen gazed off across the lush greenness as Judy refilled her wineglass. The early-fall gnats danced through the air in the distance. She thought about what she truly desired—craved. *Why do I keep settling for Miles?*

"What are you looking for, Kare? What would make you happy?"

Judy's words startled her as if she had just read her mind. Karen answered her seriously, describing a desire for someone to be there for her. Someone who wouldn't fear her accomplishments or feel threatened. Someone to support her work and her achievements. Judy listened, her eyes intense with patience.

"I want a connection. Chemistry, ya know? Someone to sit up with 'til three a.m. and talk about…shit, anything." Karen heard yearning in her own voice. "I want someone to lift me up after a rough day. Be my rock during the hard times, not a rock to crush my dreams." Karen took a final slug of her beer. "Someone who will love me just as I am."

"Someone who will hold on to you, even when you push them away?" The therapist-like tone of Judy's words stung. "Why do you gravitate toward men that are unhealthy for you?"

Karen stared as if the answer were somewhere in the space between the deck and the end of the lawn.

"You pick emotionally unavailable men. Broken. And you're hell-bent on fixing them. It's as if by fixing *them*, you'll heal the scar that Lou left behind."

"That's ridiculous. I got over Lou a long time ago."

"Bullshit. You kept it bottled up inside you as if putting the cork back in a bad bottle of wine could magically turn it into an incredible cabernet someday."

Karen continued to stare off at the starlit sky.

"And when you do find someone available, you wall them off. It's like you feel that if you don't have to overcome obstacles, then they're just not worth it."

Karen couldn't argue. It was almost as if she sabotaged her relationships—as if she didn't want them to succeed. She never seemed to be into guys that had their act together. Yet professionally, she made quick decisions and had rapid answers—kept her emotions steady to make those prompt assessments.

The two women continued down the road of dating, partners, and life in general for hours. And then, as if to end the therapy session, Karen glanced at her watch. "Well, look at the time. We've been out here for almost four hours."

"Hmm," Judy thought out loud. "Maybe *I'm* your ideal partner."

CHAPTER THREE

Karen's phone chimed, startling her out of a deep slumber. Her room glittered with morning sunshine.

It's seven…on a Saturday, for Christ's sake.

The *Dragnet* ringtone. Alarm bells went off in her cloudy mind. Half awake, she groped for her phone.

"Good morning, Chief. What's up?" Her voice sounded like it had run across gritty sandpaper. Her brain, sloshing in a rough sea.

"Detective, we have a homicide. The call came into dispatch this morning," Chief Walden said. "Officers dispatched…confirmed the DB. Apparent stabbing. No weapon located at the scene." Walden let out an audible sigh. "I need you over there."

"Of course, sir—" she said, sitting up on the edge of her bed.

"Ten-twenty, 351 Hillside. Caller identified as a Ms. Tammy McPherson."

Karen's eyes closed. Her head drifted back. A queasy sensation gurgled up from her stomach to her chest. "Victim ID?"

"No word yet."

"I'll be right there."

She grabbed a pair of black slacks and threw a black brushed cotton jacket over her white button-down shirt.

Who's in the driveway? If it was Kenny, Tam would have said so. Thoughts raced through her mind as if her head were a pinball machine. *Where's Bobby?* she wondered and worried. Tam's fourteen-year absence made her a virtual outsider. Growing up in a house full of violence and abuse, she'd never had many friends to start with. She'd have no one to turn to now.

Karen strapped on her belt and holster and attached her badge. Within five minutes of the call, she was en route to the police station to pick up her department vehicle and crime scene kit. Anxiety filled every bone in her body.

On Hillside, squad cars lined the street along with gawking neighbors, most still in their pajamas and robes. The sun had crept up just beyond neighborhood roofs, casting shadows across the cordoned-off crime scene and causing Karen to squint as she eased her way down the street.

Yellow police tape fluttered in the light morning breeze as it dangled across an area encompassing Bobby's house and the house immediately to the left. The crumbling cement sidewalk and the first few feet of the asphalt street in front of both houses were also roped off with tape attached to trees and utility poles.

Karen wedged her vehicle in between two squad cars, facing Bobby's house. She spotted patrol officers scattered about, talking with neighbors. With only a dozen patrol officers in her entire department, it appeared that almost three-quarters of the force was at the scene. Approaching the driveway, she worked to mask emotions threatening to surface.

A thin man lay motionless at the base of Bobby's driveway in a puddle of what was most certainly blood. He wore dirty, torn blue jeans and a white long-sleeved T-shirt, now mostly crimson. His shoes, tattered. Stepping closer to the edge of the police tape, she recognized the victim—the same man she slipped a five-dollar bill two weeks before. The homeless man who had once walked through the neighborhood was now a lifeless body lying on the cold, hard cement.

"Who's first responder?" Karen called out before venturing closer. She held her breath, praying the first responding officer was not Officer Brennan.

No response.

"Weapon?" Karen threw out to any officer who could hear her.

The only officer within earshot was Officer Mott, standing in the street behind his squad car entering information on his iPad. He looked up and morphed from deep concentration to eagerness, racing over to Karen.

"No, Detective. We're searching the perimeter now."

"Has the county been notified?"

"Yes, ma'am. Coroner is on his way. The county's crime scene team should be here shortly, ma'am. Sheriff asked if you'd contacted Detective Riley."

"Doing it right now."

She turned her back to Mott, shuffling a few steps away, and phoned Detective Camille Riley, the County Detective Liaison assigned to her. In a case of this nature, the county's more expansive services would be heavily relied upon. With the homicide in Parks Ford, Karen would serve as lead detective. Riley would assist and streamline access to crime specialists and the forensics lab housed in the county buildings. Her department's proximity to the courthouse and sheriff's office meant an effortless walk across an expansive parking lot from the Parks Ford police station.

Karen turned back to Mott. "Let me know when she gets here."

She turned her attention to the horrific sight before her. A cracked, gray, cement sidewalk outlining an aging asphalt street was splattered and stained scarlet. Food wrappers were scattered about, probably remainders from the last garbage pickup. A couple of smashed Deer Park plastic water bottles and dumped cigarette butts comingled with dirt-stained wrappers in the street. Even though it was likely garbage, it would all be collected as evidence.

The overgrown, weed-filled area between Bobby's house and the one to the left looked like it hadn't been mowed in over a month. Bobby's black Mustang sat in the driveway. A red Mini Cooper was parked at the curb in front of the house, yellow tape draped around its perimeter.

"All of you," Karen bellowed to her colleagues. "Where have you been? Where did you walk?" She paused. "What did you touch?"

Before an answer came, Officer Brennan appeared at the top of the driveway. His linebacker frame ducked under the yellow police tape, heading straight for Karen. She winced, watching him lumber through the immediate crime scene—an area that could contain minute, precious pieces of evidence—in absolute disregard for proper protocol.

And he wonders why he didn't get the detective role. She mentally rolled her eyes. "Watch where you walk." Her tone was quiet.

Brennan shrugged. "You know as well as I do it's already contaminated."

Knowing Brennan's vindictive nature and being in no mood to argue, Karen sought whatever information he'd gathered so she could begin her process free from his destructive ignorance. This was now her scene, and as much as it grated on him, she would be taking control of it.

Whatever damage he did was done. She bit her tongue. "Whadda we got?" She glanced at officers taking preliminary statements from neighbors and potential witnesses.

"Not much. Blood trail starts back there." Brennan pointed to the house to the left of the McPherson's. "No murder weapon…maybe the perp took it with him. Blood spatter's mostly dry. The blonde over there…" He pointed at Tam standing on the porch of her house. "She's the one that found the body."

Karen looked over at Tam—pale face and swollen eyes—pacing and biting her fingernails. Bobby sat on the top porch step, his face in his hands.

"She's a little…" Brennan circled his index finger around his ear.

"She found a fucking dead body…on her driveway. How would *you* feel?" Karen gave him a hard glare and threw words at him like tiny shards of glass. "How do ya think your wife would feel?"

She scanned the surrounding area for anything unusual—anything out of place. "What else? Anything unusual?"

"Nah. Looks like someone's got an issue with a homeless person."

Karen fumed. *What a piece of shit conclusion.* "Over there." She pointed at a spot of liquid on the asphalt. "Did you check that?"

He scoffed. "Someone's car leaked oil—"

She cut him off with a dismissive gesture. "Hmm…maybe the guy that drove up and killed our vic?" She shook her head. *No damn wonder he's stuck in patrol.*

"Ya always gotta cop an attitude, don't ya?" he snarled.

Karen turned away, centering her attention on potential tire tracks to go with the apparent oil stain.

"I'd focus your attention here." Brennan pointed to the slain victim.

Karen fought an eye roll. She knew protocol. She would start by taking in the entire scene as a whole, then, beginning at the outer edge, work her way in. The area farther away could yield clues as to how the killer entered and exited the scene. "Don't need to draw any early, faulty conclusions," she said with satisfaction-laden words.

"C'mon, Capp. This isn't a time to go by the book. This scene's a ticking clock. The more time you waste, the colder it's gonna get."

Karen trooped away, looking around and assessing the crime scene perimeter. After her initial walk-through, she established entrance and exit points, preventing officers—Brennan included—from traipsing willy-nilly through the scene. Scene integrity was her top priority now. She continued, tucking her hands in her pockets and looking for the route least likely to have been taken by the victim and attackers. That would be her point for accessing the scene.

Waiting for Riley to arrive—a welcome relief from Brennan's snarky attitude—she grasped for more information.

"Any witnesses?" she asked anyone in earshot.

"No, ma'am," Mott responded.

"Okay. Talk to every resident on this street." She grimaced at the sight of neighbors already gossiping with one another. "Mott," she barked. "Keep these people separated before you all get to them." She looked up at the porch. "And those two," she said, pointing at Bobby and Tam. "Keep them apart until I get there." She knew that the more the neighbors talked, the more inaccurate the interviews would become.

Karen directed Mott to have officers include the homeless people in their interviews. Did they know anyone who might have committed this murder or anyone who may have had a beef with the victim?

She took a deep breath. "How many neighbors and how many homeless people are we dealing with?" she asked, trying to assess the number of interviews she could expect. Without waiting for an answer: "Did anyone hear anything last night? See anything?" She paused. "Any Ring cameras?"

Mott perked up. "We have two neighbors with cameras." He popped with enthusiasm. "We're checking them."

So efficient…so pleasant. Always one of her favorites, Mott came across as somewhat of an outcast among his colleagues. His stocky frame was less fit than other officers. His mild-mannered temperament and pudgy midsection matched boyish facial features. Karen thought of him as a Pillsbury Doughboy in a uniform.

She nodded approval. "Any evidence markers placed?"

"No, ma'am. The technicians just arrived."

"Okay." She pointed to a slender, baby-faced uniformed officer with jerky movements and a wide-eyed expression standing at the crime scene entrance. "Rookie?"

Mott smiled and nodded. "Officer Perkins."

"Watch him. He probably has no clue what he's doing." She wondered how much of a clue any of them had about a homicide of this nature. A rarity in this town.

Even with the county's crime scene photographer on site, Karen still chose to snap her own images. After photographing the entire scene, she began her midrange shots. She had a keen eye for detecting anything remarkable or out of place. A piece of clothing. Anything that could have been dropped by the perp. Something that could have fallen out of a pocket or a car. Her eyes searched the area. Focused. Intense. With Bobby's car parked at the top part of the driveway, the base of the driveway was wide open for a deceased victim. Neither his vehicle nor the Mini was warm or leaking oil.

Her attention shifted to the area farthest from the victim. A long swath of bloodstains spanned the distance of the house to the left. She assessed the degree to which the blood had dried, hoping to pinpoint an approximate time of the assault in advance of the coroner. The manner in which the blood landed on the surface would help paint a picture of the attack. Most importantly, testing the blood would be critical in identifying anyone else injured during the attack.

She identified the first spots as passive drops falling freely from the bleeding source. All the initial drops were low velocity, indicating she wasn't dealing with a struggle or anything along the lines of a gunshot wound. The drops continued along the light-gray sidewalk, going from easily discernible spherical drops to drops accumulating on top of each other, creating palm-sized puddles and satellite stains.

The bloody puddles were approximately thirty feet from the initial blood spatter, with the victim's body only five feet farther. She sketched out a rough diagram. The bloody trail extended through the span of a single residential property. She knew that meant he succumbed rapidly to his wound or wounds. She tracked the drops, discerning the victim's movement through the scene. *How many other people were here? And who?*

A yellow-and-black bandana was lying to the right of the blood trail near where the first drops were spotted. She delineated it on her sketch, then signaled for an evidence marker to be placed. It appeared to be soiled—some sort of dirt. It was positioned close enough to the blood trail that Karen presumed it fell from the victim's pocket during the altercation. She reminded herself it could have just as easily been dropped by the attacker. Dirt samples from both the area near the blood trail and the area where the homeless people lived would be collected. The Pennsylvania State labs would be tasked with determining a match with the dirt on the bandana.

Karen continued, identifying large bloody footprints on the sidewalk that spanned the bloodstained path, moving parallel with the sidewalk and ending at the driveway. They seemed to match the size of the victim's shoes. She would know definitively after the evidence was meticulously scrutinized at the crime lab.

The lifeless body was lying in a moderate puddle of red liquid, the edges of which had already dried to a blackened, gelatinous state. Estimated time of death would be determined once the coroner arrived, but so far Karen was viewing a relatively blank slate. Nothing pointed to the victim putting up a struggle. He almost looked at peace in his demise, rather than alarmed, frightened, or surprised.

A handful of items caught Karen's attention: the bandana where the attack appeared to have started, the fist-sized puddle of liquid on the asphalt directly across from the victim, a matchbook on the driveway about three feet above the victim's head, and two turquoise-and-purple mint candy wrappers two feet to the left of the matchbook.

She instructed the crime scene photographer, busily capturing images to the right of the driveway, to snap a few shots of bystanders milling around. Karen knew if the perpetrator returned to the scene to observe, these images might produce a crucial lead.

The crime scene team had arrived and immediately began the arduous process of setting up their computerized "Total Station" instrument. The device, once used in reconstructing vehicle accidents, was now a key tool in mapping out crime scenes. The computer eliminated the time-consuming process of taking meticulous measurements of key pieces of evidence and their relationship to one another. *Sure beats manual triangulation.*

Painstakingly, she gathered her own images, covering the area over and over, each time moving closer to key aspects of the scene, potential evidence, and the body. Graduating from midrange to close-angle shots, she arrived beside the motionless victim.

Karen turned back to the street to spot Detective Riley driving up. Waiting for Riley to grab her bag and join her, she homed in on the immediate area, gathering her thoughts. Riley trekked over, following along Karen's identical path to the body. A relatively new detective with the county sheriff, Riley was sharp and intuitive, having honed her investigator skills with various departments over the decades. While Karen had the build of someone in law enforcement, Riley was much more petite—a thin Black woman whose hair was a sculpture of long, tight, cornrow braids. She was five feet, four inches of solid, compact muscle. Riley's quiet personality was in direct contrast to Karen's. They complemented one another and worked well together.

"Morning, Riley." She looked down at her colleague, dressed more casually in black utility pants and a camouflage jacket over a charcoal-colored fitted shirt.

"Morning. What do ya got so far?" Riley was a straight shooter. No wasted small talk.

Karen looked around once more and shook her head. "Not much. Officers are doing prelims…we can check those back at the station. We still have homeless people who hung out with the victim to interview. Area's sealed off…still searching for a weapon. I'm heading over to talk with the woman who called it in."

Riley nodded, visually processing the scene herself. The sun had burned off most of the morning dew, leaving a faint scent of grass and damp dirt hanging in the air, along with the coppery odor of blood.

Standing next to the body, Karen noted what appeared to be a linear pattern of blood drops directly across from where the victim had landed. Smaller than all the other drops, Karen determined they were medium-velocity drops that didn't free-fall from the victim like the lower-velocity drops. These would have been propelled at a faster rate. The line of drops was perpendicular to the long blood path, instead of in the same direction the victim was moving.

Karen pointed to the blood pattern. "Cast-off pattern?" she said, referring to a pattern created by blood being thrown, or cast off, from a weapon. The drops created a straight line, which would point in the direction the object was traveling when the blood flew from it.

Grim-faced, Riley nodded. "We have a blood spatter expert we can call in."

While Karen craved working a case independently, the reality was that homicides didn't happen in Parks Ford. She would need to defer to the specialists who did this type of work all the time. And, if this case ended up in court, they would be relying on an expert's testimony.

"Yo, Brennan," Karen called out. "Have your guys expand the perimeter to go all the way back to the woods." She pointed to the weed-ridden space between the two homes that extended back to a wooded area butting up to neighbors' backyards.

Given the linear direction of the cast-off pattern, Karen knew that if the weapon had been thrown, as the pattern suggested, the direction pointed straight toward that open space. Without additional cast-off patterns, she believed they were dealing with a single blow that occurred approximately thirty-five feet back, and a potential discarding of the weapon near where the victim lay. Wherever the first blow landed, it appeared severe enough to cause rapid blood loss, leaving him to collapse only a short distance farther.

The detectives simultaneously noticed what appeared to be a bloody partial shoe print also perpendicular to the blood trail and in the same area as the cast-off pattern. Karen gathered close-up images, noting the lack of clear distinguishable marks usually found with shoe prints.

She pointed to the print, which was only the top two inches of a singular shoe and noticeably smaller in width than the other prints. "Hard to imagine our perp was the same height as the victim."

"We'll know more when we get our vic's actual height at post." Riley said.

Karen scanned the man's lifeless body, tucked in a fetal position on his left side in a burgundy puddle. Without moving the corpse or touching him, she squatted down, taking a close look at his fingernails. Dirty, but nothing else visually to note, at least to the naked eye. At the postmortem, his nails would be clipped and sent to the lab for microscopic scrutiny.

The victim's arms were drawn close to his body, his hands gently fisted, making the underside of his fingers and hands impossible to examine. Identification of scratches, cuts, or defensive wounds would have to wait until the coroner arrived. Hunched over, Karen examined Cliff's hazel eyes—partially open with a faraway stare. His jaw looked relaxed, leaving his mouth slightly ajar.

The crackling of tires on asphalt signaled the coroner had arrived. Karen scarcely dealt with homicides, so she rarely crossed paths with the man, but Warren Bettenkoff's attitude was known throughout the county: "As soon as a person is determined dead, hands off. It's *my* body." Karen and Riley had their chance at a preliminary "hands-off" examination and would now step aside.

Bettenkoff arrived at scenes dressed in suits straight out of an episode of *Perry Mason*, which puzzled Karen, since he would be donning protective equipment. *Why the extra fuss with a nice suit? Coroners in other counties just wear class D utility uniforms.* He also wore a scowl across a face filled with wrinkles and age spots.

Bettenkoff headed toward the victim with a stiff, hasty gait, his greasy comb-over holding firmly in place. He wasn't one for pleasantries, especially with female law enforcement personnel. Pulling off his suit jacket, exposing his suspenders and firearm, he loosened his tie and snapped on a pair of heavy-duty surgical gloves.

"He wears a gun?" Karen whispered to Riley.

Riley smiled. "In some parts of this county, homicides are gang related. Gang members return to destroy evidence."

"Highly doubt this is a gang thing here in Parks Ford."

Riley smirked. "Better to be safe."

Wasting no time, Bettenkoff enclosed Cliff's hands with paper bags and zip ties and checked the body's temperature—an attempt at establishing a preliminary time of death. As the investigator of the death, he would also examine the blood trail to determine where the attack may have occurred, how far the victim got, and finally, the place of his death.

People around town joked that the county's coroner was "three days older than God." While he was crusty, he was sharp and had decades of training under his belt. Even so, questions about the number of wounds and wound angles would have to wait for the medical examiner's expertise. Karen hoped this information would offer clues to the attacker's height. For now, the two of them yielded to the coroner.

"Don't expect him to willingly share information with us," Riley whispered.

Karen shot her a look of incredulity.

"It's fine. I'll pepper him with questions after he finishes." Riley smiled.

Karen briefed Riley on the scant information she'd obtained. The focus was on finding the murder weapon, securing evidence, and conducting the balance of neighborhood interviews, including the two people she dreaded the most—Bobby and Tam. Looking over, she noted a quiet, somber Bobby sitting on the steps of his porch, still in pajamas. Tam had retreated into the house. Using extreme caution, Karen walked toward the exit of the cordoned-off area and toward Bobby, careful not to contaminate any evidence as yet uncovered. She motioned for Riley to join her.

As the two women approached the porch, Tam came running out the front door like a bronco storming out of the gate, screaming.

"*Karen! Karen!* Oh my God…I can't believe this. Who would do this?" Bordering on hysteria, she ran toward the detectives.

Karen held up both hands, commanding Tam to stop and calm down. She felt her own emotions balancing on a seesaw between feeling sorry for Tam and, at the same time, being irked by Tam's continued familiar tone with her. Officers held Tam back as the detectives approached.

Karen's demeanor morphed into intent. She had to get Tam to focus and recall details without distractions. With the coroner on the scene, that would be a monumental challenge.

"Okay. Tam…I need you to catch your breath. Calm down."

She found herself addressing a completely unfocused, frazzled, spinning-out-of-control young woman. Karen introduced Riley, but Tam's eyes zeroed in on the end of the driveway and the coroner.

"Why don't we step inside where it's a little quieter?" Karen pulled Tam back inside the house. They headed to the right toward the kitchen. Tam was caught between catching her breath, trying to talk, and outright sobbing.

The kitchen looked the same as it had ten years ago when Karen arrested Kenny. Simple white cupboards lined the walls around the sink and a window to the side yard. To the left of the cupboards, a tall pantry with a two-foot-wide hallway to the back door separated the pantry and sink area. A teeny breakfast table stood with three chairs around it. The scent of morning coffee lingered.

Karen began in a sympathetic tone. "Tam, I'm going to be investigating the incident that just occurred. I need to talk with you for a few minutes." She motioned for the three of them to sit at the dime-size wooden table.

Tam slouched down into one of the metal chairs, barely looking up from the table in front of her.

Karen continued, "I understand this is traumatic and there's a lot going on." She paused, her eyes steady on Tam. "Thankfully, this is not a common occurrence in this neighborhood. When things like this do happen, we understand it kinda rattles everyone. Bear with me and be patient." She leaned over and looked into Tam's bloodshot eyes. "There are some questions I have to work through with you." She pulled out a small notepad and pen.

Tam nodded. Karen already had Tam's full name and address, so she proceeded to her date of birth and phone number. Simple questions that Tam could easily move through. As Tam got her bearings, Karen advanced to more specific questions about the homicide.

"Tam, tell me what happened this morning. What time did you walk outside?" Karen leaned onto the wooden table with her elbows, giving Tam a deep, intense stare.

Tam looked up, then over at Riley, before answering. "It was around 6:40, I think. I woke up really early and couldn't fall back asleep."

"What time did you first wake up?"

"Maybe around six."

"And what did you do then?"

"Stayed in bed for a while. Finally got up around 6:30. I decided to make some coffee and sit out on the front porch." Tam's shoulders began to drop. Her torso became less rigid. "I went outside around 6:45, cuz it's usually quiet out front at that hour…especially on a weekend." Her timeline was now off by five minutes.

Riley sat silent, arms crossed on the table, void of expression.

Karen nodded. "Did you happen to glance outside and notice if the body was there before you went outside?"

"No. Just made my coffee and walked out."

"Okay, Tam. What time did you discover the body?" Karen's tone held empathy.

Tam looked at her with deep-blue eyes in a complete state of vulnerability. She gave a slight shrug and answered in little more than a whisper. "About a quarter to seven."

"What did you see? Tell me what you were doing when you found the body. Walk me through exactly what happened." Karen pelted her with the questions, poised with pen and steno pad.

"I came out front to sit on the porch with my coffee…enjoy the morning sun. I stepped onto the porch and saw a man lying on our driveway. I thought it was just one of the homeless guys…passed out or fell asleep. I was pissed."

"What did you do then?" Riley asked, in a flat tone.

"I yelled at him—"

"What did you yell?" Riley interrupted.

"I can't remember."

"Then what?" Karen leaned in a little closer to Tam.

"I was annoyed. I walked down to the driveway to wake him up." She paused.

"Continue," Karen said. Her stern tone coupled with a deadpan stare was aimed squarely at a vulnerable Tam.

Tam's eyes welled up. Karen softened her tone. "Please… continue."

"I saw blood. A lot of it. I walked closer…more blood. I freaked." Tam's tears started to flow again. A growing red outline framed her ink-blue irises.

"What did you do then?" Karen maintained her calm, gentle composure.

"I called out to him—"

"What did you say?"

"I don't remember."

"How close did you get to him?" Karen persisted in as patient a manner as she could muster, wondering exactly how far she could push Tam before she crumpled again.

Tam gave her a puzzled look. "Close enough to see a lot of blood and that Cliff wasn't moving."

"How close?" Riley enunciated each word, urging a more precise answer.

Tam shot her a cold glare. Karen noted the tension.

"Tam." Karen nudged. "Do you remember how close you got to him?"

"No."

"No, you don't remember or no, you don't know?"

Tam took a deep breath. "No, I don't remember."

"Did you touch him?" Riley was abrupt.

"No. I didn't touch him. He wasn't moving. I freaked and ran inside to call you." Tam turned to Karen with a deer-in-the-headlights look. "I grabbed your card and called the number."

It was a Saturday morning, so the station would have been empty. A department that size would have all its officers out on patrol, so the off-business-hours call would have been rerouted to 911. The 911 dispatcher would have notified patrol officers, who responded to the scene and made the decision to notify the chief.

"You mentioned the name Cliff. Did you know him?" Karen asked.

"Sorta. Bobby pointed him out to me. So, yeah, I sorta knew him. I'd say hi when he'd walk by the house."

They continued to press Tam for specifics, but she struggled to recall details of the motionless body. Her memory was vague, disorganized, and unreliable, and Karen knew that pressing her further would yield few meaningful results. The one odd detail she *could* recall was a partially opened Grimaldi's Pub matchbook lying on the driveway. Karen remembered the matchbook next to an evidence marker. Just as Tam remembered, it was about three feet from the body. This meant Tam at least got that close. Karen reminded herself that every time someone entered the scene, they altered it in some way. *How could Tam have altered the scene when she ran to the body?*

Scribbling notes, Karen asked, "Where were you last night?"

Tam wrinkled her nose and squinted as if offended. "Home. I don't go anywhere. I don't have people to go out with."

Karen nodded. "I understand—"

"Do you? You're, like, Miss Popular in town. Nobody thinks shit about me."

Riley rolled her eyes at Tam's pity party. Glancing at Riley, Karen bit her bottom lip to stave off a laugh.

In a softer tone, Karen continued, "What time did you go to bed last night?"

Tam looked up with doe-like eyes and shrugged. "I'm not sure. I know it was before midnight." She paused. "Bobby was still out with his friends."

"Was the body on your driveway when you went to bed...did you notice?"

Tam shot her a quizzical look. "You think I would have gone to bed with someone lying on my driveway?"

Karen's glare bore through Tam's eyes. "I'm trying to establish a timeline. Would you please answer the question?" She watched Tam pick at the cuticles of her fingernails.

"No. I didn't see anyone lying on my driveway before I went to bed." Tam rolled her eyes. "You should probably talk to Bobby. He was out last night partying."

"I'll talk to Bobby in a few minutes. So, you went to bed around midnight. Did you happen to look outside and notice if there was anything unusual before you went to bed?"

"No."

"No, you didn't look outside, or no you didn't see anything unusual?"

Tam's frustration grew visible. The tears had subsided and now she donned a miffed expression. "No, I didn't look outside. Why would I?"

Karen shot her a tense, blank stare. "When was the last time you had a chance to look out front and see that everything was normal?"

"I got home last night around seven. I didn't go back outside after that."

"Do you know whose red Mini is parked in front of your house?" Riley asked.

Tam seemed to sparkle at the question. "It's mine." A smile emerged.

"So you got home last night around seven, parked your car out front, and never went out again?" Karen asked.

Tam nodded.

"So it's safe for us to say Cliff ended up there somewhere between seven last night and 6:45 this morning."

"Yeah, I guess. I think my brother would've seen him. He got home after I went to bed."

"Do you know what time he got home?"

"No. I was sound asleep."

"You didn't hear him come in?"

Karen continued, keeping her questions neutral and nonaccusatory—focusing on what Tam saw or heard, her timeline, and her pattern of activity. She also sought information about Bobby that she would look to corroborate with him.

"Do you remember hearing anything unusual last night?" Karen asked.

Tam began to decompose again. "No. Nothing. My bedroom faces the back of the house, though." A river of tears emerged.

"Did you hear *anything* last night?" Riley pressed one last time.

Tam shook her head.

“Could you verbally answer the question?” Patience exuded from the pores of Karen’s face.

Tam compliantly responded, “No, I didn’t hear anything.”

“Okay, Tam. Thank you.”

The detectives walked down the hallway and back outside to get a glimpse of the view that Tam would have had from the porch. Tam followed close behind. Karen turned back and thanked her again, handing her a second business card and encouraging her to call if she remembered anything else.

Now it was time to talk with Bobby.

CHAPTER FOUR

Karen stood on the porch next to Bobby and looked down at the driveway, envisioning how it must have appeared to Tam. Riley snapped additional shots from the porch before heading down the steps for close-ups.

"Want me with you?" Riley asked.

"Nah. I got this." Karen maintained a solid tone, but deep down she dreaded this interview.

Envisioning the mild-mannered Bobby as a suspect felt like a stretch, and it saddened her to imagine him going through this horrendous event after everything he'd endured in his past. She counseled herself to keep an open mind. *Treat this interview like the others.*

Based on information from Tam, Bobby was potentially closest to the vicinity within the time frame of Cliff's murder. She sat on the top step next to Bobby and sucked in the cool morning air as if it would act as an elixir for the angst coursing through her veins. Bobby was planted on the steps, head buried in his lap, his dark-brown curls a tangled mess following a night of sleep. Having Tam inside was ideal. Karen needed to hear his story separate from hers and out of earshot of one another.

"Bobby, can you tell me what happened?" Karen spoke in a semiwhisper.

He shook his head as if lost in a maze of disbelief. "I was out cold last night. The first thing I remember this morning…Tam was screaming something. She was calling the police. When I got out of bed, she pointed to the front yard."

Karen leaned in, jotting notes.

"I walked outside as police were pulling up. I stepped closer to the guy on our driveway…an officer pushed me back. I looked back… realized it was Cliff." Bobby's eyes became moist.

He knew the victim, too. She would return to this later. Continuing down a similar line of questioning as she had with Tam, she worked to establish a timeline. With Bobby, questions focused on where he was last night, when he left home, and the time he returned. Bobby was much more precise and direct, answering without effort: His friend, Vince, picked him up around 8:30; they went to the Stewart James Saloon and grabbed a light dinner; then, they headed to Grimaldi's Pub around eleven; there, they had an altercation with Frank Ryanard. She scribbled every detail.

"What time did you leave Grimaldi's?"

His forehead wrinkled. "That part's kinda sketchy. I was pretty hammered. Vince drove." He scratched his head. "It wasn't closing time. I think it was a little after midnight."

"I'll need Vince's full name, address, and phone number."

Bobby nodded.

"Do you remember seeing anything unusual as you arrived home? Anything out of the ordinary on the street?"

Bobby shook his head and grimaced. "Nothing. But even if something was going on, the street was pitch black. We don't have streetlights. At that hour, everyone's porch lights are off."

Karen recalled walking home from Judy's last night, the street dark and deserted as if it were in its own deep slumber. Only a glimmer of light from a dim, clawlike sliver of a crescent moon lit the street. "What do you remember seeing when you got home? Anything in your driveway?"

"No. I was pretty drunk. Vince pulled up right behind my car." Bobby referred to the twenty-two-foot cement driveway in front of the house. "I remember his headlights seemed really bright. I was worried it would wake my neighbors." He shrugged. "We would've noticed if someone was on the driveway."

With information from both siblings, Karen knew Bobby arrived within hours, maybe minutes, of when the stabbing occurred. Which meant Vince was also in the vicinity. Once the autopsy and blood spatter analysis were complete, they would have a more definitive time of the attack and possibly additional DNA evidence from others present.

"When you got out of Vince's car…when you walked up to your porch…did you see or hear anything? Did you see Cliff out walking?"

Bobby dropped his head to his lap. "No. Barely made it up the steps."

Karen would confirm the details with Vince. "When you got inside the house, what did you do?"

"Went straight to bed. Just peeled off my clothes and landed."

"Did you hear anything after you went to bed? Your room is closer to the front."

"Kare…I was tanked. I passed out. Didn't hear a damn thing 'til Tam started screaming."

At that moment, it occurred to Karen that she never minded Bobby's affectionate tone with her. It was a special closeness and trust established ten years ago. Nothing had changed. "Do you remember seeing your sister when you got home?"

He groaned. "Turned on the hallway light…felt bad when I realized how it lit up her room."

Karen felt her eyebrows rise waiting for the rest of his answer.

"Sound asleep. She didn't even move as I stumbled by."

Karen nodded. "Do you know if any neighbors have cameras?"

He gave a half-hearted shrug. Karen sensed his growing weariness and frustration.

"You knew the victim, correct?"

"Knew him? No. But I'd wave when I drove by. He went by Cliff. Walked down our street every now and then. Always said it was one of the few where he felt safe."

Karen continued writing, keeping her face neutral, expressionless.

"Last question, Bob. Do you know anyone who had an issue with Cliff? Anyone who would want to hurt him?"

Bobby's face tightened. "Lots of people in this town are nasty to those poor people." He waved a hand toward the end of his street. "Asshole Frank Ryanard had plenty of hate last night."

Karen's mind flashed to the numerous times she had dealt with Frank. A bitter man in his midsixties, practically bald with a thinning head of short gray hair. She pictured his constant scowl and basketball-sized belly protruding from behind his usual summer attire: Bermuda shorts and a Phillies T-shirt. Frank had lost his wife to cancer years ago and now lived alone, complete with a miserable attitude and negative outlook on life.

Karen stared at Bobby, waiting for any scrap of information—a tiny detail—he could offer, other than conjecture.

"If you're looking for someone who hated those people, you'll be talking to half the town. But no one on our street had issues, I can tell you that."

That was helpful. It corroborated the neighbors' statements and alerted Karen they would need to find a different motive or cast their net farther.

"Cliff was well-liked. Always nice to everyone. Even Tam tried to get to know him."

"Did she?" Karen felt her head tilt.

"Yeah. Thought she was trying to feel included in the neighborhood scoop. But she'd say hi to him. Ask me if that was Cliff when he'd walk by." Bobby looked up at the street and winced. "No...no one had a beef with him. Not that I know of."

Karen allowed a long pause to saturate the air, using it to formulate her thoughts, or rather, her next question. "Any reason to suspect your father?"

"There's always reason to suspect that bastard," he growled. "But honestly, it's more likely some drunken fool that had an issue with the homeless and decided to do something after leaving the bar."

"Someone in particular?"

"No. Like I said, could be any one of a hundred people that sit around and complain." Bobby's face drooped. A heavy, dejected load weighed down his cheeks.

Not the portrait of a killer. Karen glanced down at her notes. "Okay, Bobby. Thank you. If you think of anything else...anything...give me a call." Karen stood and obligatorily handed him her card.

Tam stood by the front door, appearing eager or maybe agitated. Karen's mind was elsewhere and turned away from Tam to focus on the scene. She joined Riley a few yards from the base of the porch, examining the porch steps for any potential clues connected to the scene.

"Wait…where are you going?" Tam blurted out, pursuing Karen down the steps.

Karen and Riley exchanged blank looks.

"I can't stay here alone. Will you stay here with me?" Tam's plea bordered on pathetic.

Karen reined in her frustration. "I understand. I've got work to do. You'll be safe."

Tam cowered like a frightened puppy, complete with droopy, pouting eyes. "Can't you just stay here with me?" she pleaded. "I'm scared."

"Tam, I get it. But I've got a killer out there somewhere and I've got a lot of work to do to find him." Karen worked to push her irritation aside. "Tam, your house is a crime scene. We've got damn near every officer in Parks Ford over here. No one's gonna hurt you."

Tam visibly fought back tears. Karen tilted her head. *She seemed like such a strong person. Now she's like a scared child.* Then she saw the connection. *Growing up…so much violence. Maybe this is like PTSD for her.*

"Look, I'll swing by later to check on you." Karen found her tone more fitting of a big sister than a police investigator. She felt her maternal instincts kicking in.

Tam nodded, wiping away a handful of tears. As much as Tam appeared to desperately need Karen to console her, that would be the most she would get for the rest of the day.

Karen sketched out the position Tam claimed to have been in when she saw the body. She scanned the entire area. *Did Cliff call out for help? Maybe no one saw him, but how did no one hear him?*

From a distance, she scanned the trail of blood. A straight line. Her mind recreated what potentially happened. Cliff was dying, yet he walked in a straight line until he landed. The partial shoe print. Right where he landed. *Did the attacker stay with him, or is that a bystander's shoe?*

Bettenkoff finished pronouncing the victim, and the corpse was bagged and awaiting transport to the morgue. Karen and Riley watched as he entertained the seasoned officers, cracking jokes with Brennan.

"Dude, how do you tolerate decomp?" Brennan referred to deceased bodies in a state of decomposition.

A straight-faced Bettenkoff matter-of-factly replied, "Gas mask. Best forty dollars I ever spent."

Karen shook her head. Surely, there had to be something more meaningful these men could be doing, let alone be more respectful of the victim.

Riley flagged down Bettenkoff. "Anything we need to know? Any defense wounds?"

Bettenkoff's scowl became more pronounced. "No cuts on his hands, wrists, or arms. Appears to be a single wound…upper abdomen."

"Any signs of tampering? Any reason to believe we're dealing with more than one attacker?"

"A well-positioned blow…likely aorta. Only takes one good pop from one person." Bettenkoff's smug attitude permeated the hushed environment. "Lividity's consistent with the vic landing right where you found him."

"Aorta's a large vessel. I'd expect more blood." Riley's brows furrowed.

"With the aorta? Mostly internal bleeding. Not like a surface artery."

Karen listened in. *The man may be ancient, but he knows his stuff.*

Riley nodded. "Estimated time of death?"

"Rigor mortis just starting to set. Dried blood spatter." He paused as if mathematically calculating. "Likely within the last seven to eight hours…not much longer."

The coroner's determination fit well within the timeline obtained from Tam and Bobby. They needed more, which potentially wouldn't happen until the postmortem. In the meantime, they could follow up on interviews.

Patrol officers were meeting with the homeless people, so Karen and Riley scanned notes of preliminary interviews conducted with neighbors. One by one, they thumbed through statements:

"Didn't hear a thing."

"We don't have issues with the homeless."

"Didn't see anything unusual."

"I can't imagine who would do this."

One neighbor went so far as to suggest, "That house must be cursed."

They walked down the street to follow up on the officers' preliminaries of the four to five members of the homeless entourage. Karen scanned neighborhood yards—anything out of the ordinary—

possible footprints. She searched for yards that were fenceless and provided easy access from the wooded area and the street. Perhaps their attacker didn't walk down the street or drive. Perhaps they got to Cliff in a different manner.

They arrived at an abandoned storefront parking lot with makeshift tents of old tarps and sheets nestled between the street and the wooded area. Karen obtained a similar chorus of answers:

"I didn't see anything."

"Didn't hear anything."

"Everyone liked Cliff. No one had a reason to hurt him."

"We've never felt frightened in this neighborhood."

Only once did someone remember Cliff having an altercation. A young homeless man, a self-described friend of Cliff's, recalled a time when a man drove up and initiated a shouting match. According to the informant, nothing came of it and Cliff walked away.

"Do you recall when this happened?" Karen looked down at the man's wrist. No watch and clearly no calendar—basically no semblance of time.

A quizzical look came over his hardened, weathered face. "Several months ago?"

"Can you describe the man for me?"

"Yeah. Tall, bald white guy. Old, beat-up white car…Jersey plates," he said. "We just figured it was a pissed-off dude from town. We're used to that shit."

It seemed the altercation had been chalked up to a disgruntled resident having an issue with the homeless. Karen knew no one would be alarmed by the New Jersey plates. There were plenty of those around.

Occurring so many months prior, Karen wasn't overly alarmed by the incident and didn't feel it warranted immediate attention. She made a mental note to circle back if needed. *If there was bad blood between Cliff and this bald guy, why wait several months to come after him? Why now?*

Karen's stomach groaned. It was now pushing one in the afternoon, and she hadn't eaten since last night.

"Head back to the station?" she said to Riley. "We can review notes and create a plan."

They would also wait for news of additional evidence and potentially the discovery of the murder weapon by the crime scene technicians. Critically important, they needed a definitive identification of their victim. Identification would guide their next steps and initiate the process of notifying next of kin. Karen made that a priority, as much as she dreaded it. Family members were often a gold mine of information.

As she drove back to the station, Karen's mind shuffled through the possibilities of motive. In every instance, it came back to people with a violent temper or an issue with the homeless—or both. Frank Ryanard was top of mind. A man with nothing but caustic words for the homeless. But then, he was caustic to just about everyone. People in town who had filed continuous complaints about the homeless were possibilities, but would they go this far…and why? Kenny crossed her mind, but what would be his motive? It could also be some sick person who felt like harming someone—and Cliff was an easy target.

Hypothesizing served no purpose. The "wait game" had begun. Waiting for more evidence. Waiting for forensic examination. The postmortem wasn't scheduled until Monday morning. The town expected answers. Just because it was Saturday didn't mean the detectives would be sitting on their hands. Making matters worse, a storm was headed up the coast, requiring the crime scene team to move quicker than usual. Processing the scene before the rain arrived would preserve precious evidence; rushing the process would risk overlooking or missing evidence. It felt like a catch-22.

Parks Ford expected their police department would be working nonstop to find the killer lurking within their tight community. With pressure mounting, Karen pulled into the circular driveway of the station. It was time to dig in and create a plan.

CHAPTER FIVE

The two detectives reconvened at Parks Ford's police station. Karen knew Riley was accustomed to the county sheriff's office with people scurrying about like ants, even on weekends. In the police station, she could have rolled a bowling ball down the hallway leading to Karen's office.

"Coffee?" Karen asked. "It sucks, but I'll gladly grab you a cup."

Riley chuckled. "I'll grab a Wawa when we head back out," she said, referring to the area's local convenience store.

Karen poured herself a cup of the sludge and took the edge off its bitterness with a hefty dose of creamer. Riley settled into a stiff wooden chair, its legs creaking under her muscular frame. A stillness surrounded them. The only movement was the lithe black second hand gracefully doing its laps on the wall clock. Together they compared initial impressions.

Karen shot Riley a grim look. "At this point, all we've got is a homeless man who went by Cliff. He appeared to've been stabbed to death between the time he was last spotted alive on two cameras, at 2:13 in the morning, and the time Tam claimed to have found him, around 6:45. That's a lot of time."

"Here's the interesting part," Riley said. "The cameras also caught a single vehicle driving down the street at 1:06 and driving away at 1:09. No other individuals or vehicles were recorded on the street around that time."

"Our killer, or killers, entered the scene either from a house on the street, a side yard closer to the attack, or from the one a.m. vehicle." Karen scowled. Her last observation pointed directly to Bobby. *Was someone else with him? Someone he's protecting?*

"Based on our prelims, no one in particular stands out as a suspect. And everyone that knew the victim stated he had no enemies," Riley said.

"Last night was clear. Limited light from the moon. Bobby said the street was dark." Karen paused, replaying possible scenarios in her mind. "From your experience, Riley, what do you make of a victim with zero defense wounds? It appears Cliff didn't put up a fight."

"Could be he was completely caught off guard. Could be he knew his attacker."

"It's usually not a stranger that commits a murder." Karen drummed her pen on the desktop. "Stabbings are intimate. Cliff had to trust his attacker enough to let him get that close, or didn't see or hear him." An awful feeling began to wash over her.

"We're likely dealing with a fixed-blade knife. A switchblade would have made a sound. Startled the vic."

"Makes sense. But how did the attacker conceal such a large blade?"

"You said it yourself," Riley said. "The street was dark."

At the scene, they had identified scattered plastic water bottles, food wrappers, and cigarette butts, all of which looked like they had been lying near the street for several days. Karen had noted a soiled bandana lying on the sidewalk immediately to the right of the blood trail. They had a baseball-sized puddle of fluid on the street across from the body, a matchbook from Grimaldi's Pub on the driveway, along with two Glitterati mint wrappers to the left of the matchbook.

"I'm guessing the matchbook fell out of Bobby's pocket when he got out of Vince's car," Karen said. "But these candy wrappers. Ever heard of Glitterati?"

Riley shook her head.

"That's not a candy you find at the local Wawa. Might be something unique to our perp."

Riley gave a slow, seemingly thoughtful nod.

They also had a long trail of blood that spanned two homes, approximately thirty-five feet in length, with a solitary cast-off pattern perpendicular to the trail and directly across from their victim. No murder weapon had been found yet, and there were no footprints in the grassy area between the two houses.

"Between the cast-off pattern and the lack of footprints in the grass, if a weapon is found in that area, it was more than likely thrown," Riley said.

Karen nodded. "We've got large bloody footprints moving parallel to the blood trail. Crime lab should be able to match those to the victim's shoes once we get his personal effects at the post."

"But this partial print," Riley said, pointing to a picture of the two-inch top section of one shoe found across from the victim and next to the cast-off pattern. "Not moving in the same direction as the others."

Karen visualized how the attacker potentially discarded the weapon. "The perp stepped forward to discard the weapon, accidentally stepping into blood?"

"Agreed. And it couldn't have been someone who walked up later."

Karen nodded. "The partial print was made in fresh blood. If someone walked up to Cliff this morning, the print would have been made in congealed blood. Has to be from our perp."

"Absolutely," Riley said. "And no discernible marks on this shoe print. No tread. No brand. Most shoes have marks of some kind."

"The width appears notably smaller than the other prints. Can we assume the attacker was smaller than our victim?"

"Not always. Some attackers try to disguise themselves by wearing shoes smaller than their normal size."

Karen stared at Riley, trying to imagine an attacker going to these lengths. She reminded herself that with the victim being about six feet tall, an assortment of people would fall into the "smaller" category. "Let's wait for the lab. Maybe they'll pick up something we're missing."

The blood trail revealed that the stabbing occurred to the left of Bobby's house with the victim able to stay on his feet until he got to Bobby's driveway. No other drops of blood were found beyond where Cliff landed. Karen also noted that nothing was found on the walkway or steps to Bobby's house.

"Vic didn't get very far," Riley said. "Bettenkoff thinks the attacker punctured his aorta." Her dark brows furrowed. "I've seen stabbing victims run a lot farther before succumbing to their wounds."

"Cliff was pretty frail. Not much fat or muscle to protect him or help him fight off an attacker. Damage to the aorta would've led to a rapid, large loss of blood." Karen looked across the room in thought. "Cliff knew Bobby. He felt safe with Bobby. He landed on Bobby's driveway…not in the street…not on the grass…not the next house over. Think he was trying to get to Bobby's, or was it just a coincidence that he landed there?"

"Or, was he intentionally left on Bobby's driveway, and if so, why?"

Karen felt the hairs on the back of her neck begin to bristle. She hadn't considered that scenario. Images of Kenny flooded in. *Was Kenny, or Doyle, trying to frighten Bobby? Maybe scare him to drive him out of the house?* "If Bettenkoff's time of death estimate is correct and Cliff was on camera walking at 2:13, then it must have happened shortly after."

"So, Bobby was home when the attack happened," Riley said.

Karen rifled through her notes. "According to Bobby, he was home and had already passed out in bed…well before Cliff walked by the Ring camera. Through his stupor, he noted Tam was sound asleep."

"We need to corroborate the exact time he arrived home." Riley's voice and expression were void of emotion.

Riley's demeanor was curt, a style that Karen had grown to understand and appreciate. She recalled how, early on, she viewed Riley's personability as a slab of cement. No small talk. No sharing anything personal. It was all business. Now Karen felt sheer relief to have that intensely professional approach beside her.

Karen knew they had considerable time between the completion of processing the scene and the crime lab's initial interpretation of the evidence. The potential discovery of a weapon and identification of their victim also loomed as the clock ticked.

"Let's corroborate Bobby's story and time frame. Divide and conquer. You head to the Stewart James and research those odd candies. I'll hit up Grimaldi's and stop by Vince's," Karen said. She threw back the last of the room-temperature mud in her cup, frowning as the liquid rolled down her throat.

"Meet back here?" Riley asked.

Karen gave a single nod.

Karen pulled into the asphalt lot of Grimaldi's, practically empty at the three o'clock hour. Windows crowded with neon signs were barely visible in the daylight. She made her way to the entrance, tugging on the steel handle of a thick, wooden door.

At the far end of the walnut horseshoe bar, a muscular bartender leaned on one elbow, making conversation with the lone patron. His tight-fitting gray T-shirt enhanced his physique. The minute he spotted Karen, he wiped his hands on a bar rag and walked down to greet her.

She navigated around high-tops framing the room's perimeter and headed to the bar in the center. The smell of stale beer permeated her nostrils.

"What can I do ya for?" the bartender said with a smile, tossing the damp rag aside.

"Joe, we had a homicide…not far from here."

His eyes widened. "No shit."

"You work last night?"

He nodded. "So this is a business call?"

Karen returned the nod.

"Suppose I can't grab ya a beer."

She allowed a smile to escape before pulling out her notepad and pen. "I need to ask you a few questions about customers who were here last night."

"Shoot." He chuckled. "Not literally."

"Do you remember seeing Frank Ryanard?" She kept her tone neutral, even though she wanted to snarl and say "loathsome Frank Ryanard."

Joe let out a snort. "Same old, same old. Sitting right here. Hunched over his brew."

"Did he talk to anyone?"

"As always, everyone avoided him. Never arrives with friends. No one thinks he even has any."

Karen fought back a smirk.

"Spent most of his time complaining to the other guy on duty last night. You know the deal. We listen. Give routine nods."

"Remember seeing Bobby McPherson?"

"Sure. Was sitting right over there with a couple of his buddies." He pointed to the opposite end of the bar where he had been standing moments before. "The bar was half full. He and his buddies were cracking jokes. You could hear them laughing throughout the place. All good. Made the place more lively at that hour."

Karen looked up from her notepad. "Do you remember the hour?"

He scratched his shaved head. "Think it might have been around eleven. No, 10:30." He shrugged. "Somewhere between 10:30 and eleven."

"He wasn't sitting near Frank?"

"Nope. But all their joking got to him. He grumbled and sneered each time they laughed." He wiped his hands on the nearby towel. "Started yelling at Bobby. Asking him about the deadbeats in his neighborhood."

Karen recalled Bobby's words about Frank's hate toward the homeless.

"You know…the homeless. Frank hates those people."

Karen scribbled notes. "Remember what he said?"

"Something about bringing down property values. He started to get real confrontational."

"What did Bobby do?"

"Nothin'. Just stared at his beer. You know Bobby. He's the last person to get into a fight."

Karen allowed a faint smile to rise. "Did his friends say anything?"

"Yeah. His buddy Vince started punching back, ya know. Telling Frank those people are almost a half mile from his place. Told Frank to give it a rest."

Karen held her stare firm on Joe. Silent. Waiting for more.

"Bobby looked uncomfortable. And you know Frank. He's the last person to give something a rest."

She nodded, envisioning Bobby—simple and unassuming, his solid five-eleven frame likely dressed in jeans and a long-sleeved T-shirt—trying to blend in.

"The boys made jokes about Frank's 'tude. It was kinda funny."

Karen smiled. *'Tude. Something Caiden would say.* "Was Frank's bitterness more palpable than usual?"

"Nah. He's more bark than bite."

She knew that was the general belief but had no idea how far Frank's hatred would go.

"Frank wouldn't stop, and Bobby looked nervous. That's when I stepped in. If he was gonna harass my patrons, he had to leave. Eighty-sixed, again."

Karen knew it wasn't the first time the ornery man would be pressed by a bartender. He'd be asked to leave, spout off that he'd never patronize the bar again, and show up the next week causing more problems. An endless cycle for a mean-spirited, broken man. "What did Frank do?"

"Threw a few bills on the bar and stormed out, muttering obscenities the entire way. Bobby's friends laughed hysterically."

Karen stifled a chuckle. "Know what time they left?"

"One of the guys left with his girlfriend. Maybe 11:30. Bobby and Vince didn't leave 'til after midnight. The place was pretty packed then. I think it was around 12:30."

Karen stared at the shimmering top of the walnut bar before thumbing back through her notes. Bobby's story appeared accurate and truthful but also proved he was in the neighborhood at the time of the murder.

Karen thanked Joe and tossed her card onto the bar. "Call me if you remember or hear anything else."

"Detective, what happened? Is Bobby in trouble?"

Karen smiled. "I'll keep you posted on anything that affects this area." She pivoted and walked out to the parking lot.

Next stop: Vince Arenado's.

Karen drove the short distance past Bobby's neighborhood and pulled up to the front of Vince Arenado's modest brick twin framed by a three-foot black wrought iron fence. Leaning on the gate to look for the latch, it gave way with her weight. She strode up the uneven brick walkway and the three steps to the porch. Glancing to her left, she noted an older red sedan in the driveway, making a mental note to check for any leaking oil. Her knuckles rapped on the front door.

She scanned the yard, waiting. A second knock. *That's gotta be his car. Where is he?* She peered through the window of the aging wooden door beyond lacelike curtains. No signs of movement. She rapped again—with more force—and waited. Nothing appeared unusual. Carefully placing her hand on the doorknob, she subtly gave it a brief, gentle twist. Nothing.

Karen headed down to the driveway and placed her hand on the hood of the sedan. Cold. Squatting down, she spotted a puddle of liquid accumulating under the engine. She grabbed a container from her crime kit, then wedged her torso under the car to get a sample of the fluid. She was so focused, in fact, she forgot that she was wearing a white shirt. *Fuck!* Futilely, she tried to brush the driveway debris off the front.

A click, then a grinding noise, caught her attention. Turning to her right, a thirty-something, muscular man appeared on the porch.

"Vince Arenado?" she asked, flashing her badge.

He nodded. "Bobby told me you might be stopping by."

Walking toward him, she pointed back to the driveway. "That your car?"

"Yeah."

Vince stepped out of the way and motioned for Karen to come inside. As careful as she had been collecting her sample, a greasy residue coated her hands. She rubbed them together, trying to get the debris off while carefully scrutinizing her surroundings. Vince's minuscule living space had little furniture, and what he did have was simple and tidy.

"Not many guys your age keep a house this clean," she said with a grin.

"About a decade ago…I was in the military. You just learn some things there that never wear off. Please, have a seat."

Karen nodded and sat at the edge of a small beige love seat. Although impeccably clean, it had seen its fair share of use. A hand-me-down, she figured. Still, she didn't want to dirty it with her greasy hands.

"You wouldn't happen to have a paper towel I could use?" She held up her hands.

"I'll do ya one better." Vince reached for a red-and-black bandana. "Just went through the laundry."

Karen forced a smile. Inside, her stomach turned. She wiped her hands and pulled out her pen and steno pad. "That car out front, was that the one you all took last night?"

"Uh-huh."

"Who else was with you?"

"On the way out, three of us. Bobby, me, and Bruce."

"Bruce?"

"Yeah. He's one of our friends. Met up with his girlfriend and cut out early on us."

"So he wasn't with you when you dropped Bobby off."

Vince let out a snort. "He wasn't with us past ten minutes at Grimaldi's." He shook his head. "Women." He blinked, then looked at Karen. "Sorry, ma'am. Didn't mean no disrespect."

She smiled and nodded. "None taken. Do you happen to remember what time you left Grimaldi's last night?"

"Can't give you an exact time, but it was a little before one a.m."

"Do you know what time you dropped Bobby off?"

He looked at his hands as if in deep thought. "Well, we went straight to his house, so…I suppose…a few minutes after one?"

Karen understood the uncertainty. No reason for them to be checking their watches. They were friends out having a good time. But his timeline matched the camera footage. "Do you remember seeing anything as you drove down Hillside last night?"

"Ma'am, it was pitch black. Only saw what my headlights lit up." He paused. "I remember pulling into Bobby's driveway right behind his car. His sister's car was by the curb." He chuckled, then caught himself as if realizing this was no joking matter. "I'm sorry, ma'am… I'm just remembering how drunk Bobby was. He couldn't even get his house keys out of his jacket pocket. We were both laughing."

She returned a faint smile. "Did you watch Bobby go into his house?"

"Yup. Made sure he got in okay, then took off."

"Remember what time you picked him up that night?"

Vince shrugged. "We decided to head out at 8:30 and I'm pretty good about being on time, so I figure it was right about then."

"You pulled up into his driveway?"

"No, ma'am. Just pulled up in front of his sister's car and waited in the street."

"So you remember seeing Tam's car?"

"That hot little red Mini? Yeah. Hard to miss." Vince's sandy-blond-framed face lit up with a boyish smile.

Karen grinned. She scanned the coffee table and other countertop surfaces for any purple-and-turquoise wrappers. None.

"Heard you talked with Frank Ryanard last night."

Vince smirked. "No one talks to Frank. Such a bastard. Oh… sorry, ma'am. He's not a very nice person."

She muffled a chuckle. "Got into an altercation with him?"

"Nah. He was complaining about those homeless people on Bobby's street. We were kinda laughing at him and poking fun, ya know?"

Karen scribbled notes.

"Bartender kicked him out." Vince chuckled. "Surprise, surprise."

"Remember what time that was?"

"Early on when we got there. Maybe 11:30?"

Karen paused, mentally calculating the times being presented. "What time do you remember getting home last night?"

Vince shrugged. "I came straight home, so…maybe…1:15?"

"Your neighbors have any cameras?"

"Yup. Woman next door."

Perfect. That will give us a definitive time. "Have any problem with me checking under your car for leaking oil?"

"Go right ahead. You'll find it. Needs some repairs."

"Any problem with me taking a sample of it?"

"No, ma'am. Would you like me to get you a baggie?"

Karen fought back a smile. It was hard not to like this guy. "I've got evidence containers."

"Evidence?"

"Could be." She really had no reason to suspect Vince. Pausing, she reflected on the bandana he offered. *Anyone could have one of those.* "Any problem giving us a blood sample?" she asked with a soft voice.

His smile faded. "No, ma'am. No problem."

"I'll let you know if we need it." She offered a reassuring smile.

Karen thanked him and handed him her card before heading back outside. She trotted next door to the neighbor with the house camera. As with most twins, the front doors between both houses were a mere twelve feet apart. In less than a minute, she was standing at the woman's door. The main door was wide open, allowing Karen to flash her badge through the storm door window.

The neighbor was eager to help and supplied access to her camera footage. Vince was pretty close on his timeline. His car drove up at 1:16 that morning and had not left the driveway since. Vince's alibi seemed confirmed. He stated he drove straight home from Bobby's, and his car looked similar to the model on the Hillside camera footage. That vehicle was filmed coming and going at 1:06 and 1:09, respectively. It was likely Vince's car and he was dropping Bobby back home.

Riley texted that she was about a half hour from the station. With time to kill, Karen decided to venture over to Fran Murphy's house. Fran was the cousin of Marianne McPherson, Kenny's ex-wife, and it was Fran's house where Marianne had sought refuge after he attacked her. She had no idea if Marianne would be willing to talk about the old neighborhood, but she needed to try.

Perhaps Marianne knew of history in that neighborhood that might point to a person capable of brutally attacking a homeless person. Perhaps, after all these years, there were things about Kenny—kept locked away—she would now be willing to reveal. A Pandora's box that Marianne would now open. Perhaps.

CHAPTER SIX

With the sun hovering at the tree lines to the west, Karen pulled up to Fran Murphy's house. She admired the open and inviting front lawn that looked as if it had just been mowed and trimmed. Making her way around the quarter-circle paved walkway, green grass tucked neatly within its boundaries, she arrived at the single step to a pristine cement porch.

With trepidation, she paused before pressing the well-worn, dime-sized doorbell. Her shoulders tensed as Fran arrived at the door.

"Detective. This is an unusual surprise. Come in."

Karen returned a gracious smile. She spotted Marianne in the living room to her right. After so many years, the woman hadn't changed, except for a handful of additional facial lines. Same dirty-blond hair. Same chopped pixie cut. Karen silently marveled how Marianne's weight had also remained the same: a bit chunky, but evenly carried on her now sixty-year-old medium-height frame.

"Thanks, Fran. I was wondering if I could have a word with Marianne."

Fran motioned to the living room. Marianne quietly rose from a chair by the window. Her shy affect also remained unchanged. And, even after all these years, the scar on her left cheek was still pronounced.

"You look well, Detective," Fran said.

Karen shrugged. "Can't complain."

"It's been a long time. What brings you out here?" Fran's tone seemed guarded.

Karen refrained from answering, instead diverting her attention to the pale-faced Marianne. She offered a faint smile, knowing her presence was likely drumming up difficult and terrible memories.

"Hello, Marianne. You look well."

Marianne finally spoke. "I suppose you're here about Kenny."

"No, no. Not at all." Karen felt a sense of relief, even though the topic she needed to discuss wasn't any more pleasant.

Marianne stared as if guarded or simply confused.

"Marianne, something happened at your old house last night." She paused to gauge Marianne's reaction. None. *Jesus. Did she have a lobotomy?* "There was an incident, and the victim was found on the driveway of your old home…dead."

Marianne's eyes widened. She morphed from expressionless to complete shock. "That neighborhood? No. It can't be. It's a good neighborhood. People take pride in their homes…their neighborhood." A horrified look washed over her face.

Finally, Marianne expressed emotions. Karen took a deep breath and felt her shoulders drop. "Yes…a homeless man was found dead. We've talked with Bobby and Tam—"

"Tam? In New York?"

Surely Tam's been in touch with her mother. "No. She's here. She moved back."

Marianne looked like a wounded child, gazing down at the worn carpet of the entryway. So this was how she'd learned of her own daughter moving back into town.

"Have you been in touch with Tam…at all?" Karen kept her voice soft. She felt like she had slapped the poor woman in the face by breaking the news.

"Not since she moved north. Part of me resented her for that." Marianne continued to stare at the threadbare carpet, then looked back up at Karen. "But she was off to follow her dreams…can't blame her for that."

"Marianne. Can we sit and chat?" Karen glanced at Fran, still standing by the front door. "Would you mind giving us a few minutes?"

Fran headed into the kitchen. "I've got dinner on the stove to tend to."

All Karen had consumed that day was coffee. She struggled to refocus as her mouth watered from the smell of whatever was cooking.

"Please, let's sit here." Karen motioned to the chairs by the window. "Marianne, you know your old neighborhood and your neighbors. I'm just looking to gather information."

The broad window opened to a peaceful neighborhood. Children rode their bikes up and down the street, and basketballs rhythmically pounded off the asphalt. The two women sat. Quiet. Marianne stared at her lap.

"Neither Bobby nor Tam heard or saw anything last night. I felt I needed to close the loop…see if you know of anyone who would have a reason to hurt anyone in that neighborhood."

Marianne returned a mesmerized-like stare. Seconds ticked. The silence grew uncomfortable. Just then, Fran's son, Joey, walked in and answered the question for her.

"Yeah, I'll tell you who. That bastard Kenny," he blurted.

All eyes turned to the scrawny Joey. He projected a tough persona but likely couldn't hold his own in any altercation. He stood in the entryway, covered in white, chalky debris, his beat-up leather work boots caked with the same detritus. Karen shot him a cold glare, annoyed by his eavesdropping and interruption.

Undaunted, Joey continued, "Nothing happened there 'til Kenny got out, ya know? Now look…already problems in the old hood." Joey wrinkled his nose as if smelling something disgusting. "You don't need to look any further. You got your killer."

Karen mentally rolled her eyes at his makeshift detective work. *Killer? How does he know it's a homicide? I said there was an incident and a man was found dead.* She carefully studied Joey as he spouted out his verdict.

"Joey, we're checking everything out. Do you have any evidence that might lead us to suspect Kenny?"

A scowl wrinkled his pale, thirty-one-year-old face. "You know what he did to Marianne. He's violent. He had all sorts of weapons at that house."

Not a shred of evidence behind his assertions, but Karen couldn't help but perk up at his last comment. "Weapons?"

"Yeah. A huge knife collection and God knows what else."

Alerted by this information, she turned back to Marianne. "I'm sorry…I know this is difficult…but were there weapons at that house? Anything that might be used to hurt someone?"

Marianne squirmed in her armchair, pants swishing as they rubbed up against the upholstery. "Kenny did have a knife collection." Her voice was quiet. "The only time I saw him pull one out, though, was one time when he went hunting. He never used a knife on me," she said without even a flinch.

Karen fought to conceal an eye roll. *Is she really coming to Kenny's defense? After everything he did to her?* It never ceased to amaze her how some women could still support their abuser, even when they had destroyed every aspect of their lives. Karen knew Marianne had primarily suffered wounds from Kenny when he struck her with his hands, but the act that sent him to prison was completely different. *Has she blocked that from her memory?*

It didn't matter. What mattered was his apparent knife collection. Karen struggled to recall a knife collection that would have been in view when she stopped by the house years back. There was nothing resembling that in either of her recent visits.

"Marianne, do you have any idea what happened to that knife collection?"

Marianne squinted in concentration, then shook her head.

Fran emerged from the kitchen. "Joseph Brendan, how many times have I told you not to track your dirty shoes through the house? Look at you. You're filthy."

"Jesus, Mom. I've been working all day. Can't help it."

"You can use the back door," Fran said, raising an eyebrow.

Joey thrust his shoulders back and lifted his chin in defiance. Fran held her stare. He conceded, leaving the room with a recalcitrant stomp.

"Never seen so much goddamn dirt. Bad enough I had to wash blood from his clothes this morning," Fran said.

"Blood?"

"Cut himself on something at work."

Karen forced a smile. "How much blood?"

"Oh, just a few spots on his pant legs. All clean now." Fran trooped away.

A few spots. I think we'd expect more. Karen made a mental note. "Fran?" Karen called to her back. "Was Joey home last night?"

"Of course. Where else would he be?"

Karen held her stare. "That dirt…looks like chalk dust or lime."

"He works at the quarry down in Delaware. Next to White Clay Creek Park."

Karen chuckled. "Guess that's how the park got its name."

Fran shook her head and retreated to the kitchen.

"Marianne," Karen said, "when was the last time you saw Kenny's knives?"

Marianne's shoulders rose as she stared out the window. "It's always been there."

"Where, exactly, do you remember them being stored?" Karen vaguely recalled a display case in the living room a decade ago, but nothing resembling that now.

Marianne gave her a quizzical look. "Why, they were in the living room. In his display case." It was as if she couldn't believe Karen hadn't seen it for herself.

"Is there any other place he stored his knives?"

Marianne shook her head.

"Do you know if Bobby did anything with them?"

Again, she shook her head.

"I apologize, but can you give me a verbal answer?" Karen's voice was soft.

As if coming out of a trance, Marianne looked up. "No. No. They were in the living room. I don't know if Bobby did anything with them."

Karen nodded. "I need to circle back to my first question."

Marianne tilted her head.

"Do you know of anyone who would want to hurt any of the homeless people in that neighborhood?"

Marianne answered in a voice so quiet that Karen struggled to hear. "No, everyone looked out for each other." She shook her head as if trying to shake away an unfathomable concept.

"Okay." Karen closed her notepad. "Thank you for your time. I'm sorry if this brought up difficult memories. Please call me if you need anything…or if you remember anything that might be pertinent." Karen handed Marianne her card and took a quick glance around the living room. She spotted a candy jar sitting on the coffee table. "May I?"

Marianne smiled and nodded.

Karen looked into the jar. Nothing resembling the wrappers at the scene. She grabbed a candy anyway and headed back outside. This wouldn't be her last call to this house. Joey seemed to have a bit more information than she was comfortable with.

By the time Karen made the five-minute drive back to the station, Riley was comfortably planted in her office, her black leather work boots propped up on the corner of Karen's desk. They reviewed and charted timelines and alibis. They also addressed their inability to locate the mint candy wrappers.

"Did some research. Those candies aren't carried at local grocery stores. But…you can get them on Amazon. Also sold at Walmart."

"So that opens it up to just about anyone." Karen shot Riley an exasperated look.

Karen continued, updating Riley on her conversation with Marianne, including Joey's accusation that Kenny had a substantial knife collection.

"What happened to the collection?"

Karen shrugged. "Beats me. I'll follow up with Bobby. Don't remember seeing anything earlier."

They both laid out a timeline based on interviews: Tam went to bed at midnight and Bobby returned home shortly after one a.m. Vince dropped Bobby off and was home by 1:16, based on a neighbor's camera. Tam found the body at 6:45 that morning.

Karen envisioned it playing out. There was no doubt in her mind that Tam didn't touch a body lying in a puddle of blood. "She doesn't recall how close she got but remembers seeing the matchbook, which was only three feet from the body."

"She didn't mention the mint wrappers," Riley said.

"Not surprised. She seemed rattled. Likely remembered some things and forgot others."

With their review complete, the office was silent with an occasional tapping on a keyboard or turning of a page to interrupt the constant hum of the air vents. Karen scowled, looking through preliminary interviews—nothing of value. A camera only caught the victim. The victim appeared to have no enemies. Breaking the silence and jolting Karen out of an intensely focused stupor, her office phone rang.

"Detective Cappelletti."

Riley leaned in to try and catch a few words.

"Got it. Thanks." She hastily jotted down the information. "We have an ID."

"Intake complete?"

"Just finished. Printed at the morgue. Nail clippings sent off to forensics."

"And?" Riley's ebony eyebrows raised.

"Victim is Cliff Stephenson," she read from her notes. "Thirty-eight years old, originally from Salem, New Jersey. Moved to Pennsylvania six years ago to work at the refineries near Marcus Hook. Survived by a brother, who still lives in Salem, a sister, married and living in North Carolina, and a mother, Sandra. The mother lives in a nursing home in Voorhees, New Jersey. They're getting the address now."

An officer appeared in the doorway with a sheet of paper.

Karen took and scanned the document. "Right around the time our victim moved to Pennsylvania, his parents were involved in a serious automobile accident on the New Jersey Turnpike. Father died. His mother was left partially paralyzed, requiring her to be cared for at a nursing home facility."

"I think I remember that accident," Riley said. "It was awful."

Karen contemplated the family tragedy. "Three surviving children—Cliff, Keith, and Margaret." Karen looked up at Riley. "Sound like the accident you remember?"

Riley gave a brief nod.

Karen expelled a sigh. It was one thing having a gruesome murder, but now the revelation that the victim was mere years from her own age. *What if something like this happened to me…and someone had to notify my parents?* The burden of notifying Sandra, after sustaining so much loss and grief, felt like an unfair piling on of rocks made of tragedy. She was about to add a boulder to the heap.

"Want me to go with you?" Riley asked.

"Nah, I got this one. Go home and rest. I'm gonna need you tomorrow." Karen got up and grabbed her jacket. "We'll pick up where we left off tomorrow morning. Oh-eight-hundred?"

Riley nodded.

On her way to the parking lot, Karen dropped off the oil from Vince's car at the crime lab. She knew she had to plug away long into the night. She knew her town. They would expect the department to be working nonstop to find the killer.

CHAPTER SEVEN

Never a big fan of the notification process, this one felt worse than the others. It was one thing to notify a parent of their child's death. But after this poor woman had already lost her husband and life as she knew it, this felt like a cruel sucker punch, with Karen delivering the blow.

The thirty-minute drive to Voorhees felt like thirty days. Her mind meandered back to when she became a newly minted investigator. Her mentor referred to a homicide investigation as different, due to the deeply serious nature of a murder and the wide-ranging impact on those involved. She remembered him saying that because life is our ultimate value, murder is the greatest crime that can be committed. And for the victim's survivors, it is likely the worst day of their lives, akin to an atomic bomb being dropped on them. Her mind shifted to Cliff's mother, feeling grateful she chose to forgo casual jeans for a more formal appearance.

She pulled into a half-empty parking lot. The air hung—a hushed stillness. The only perceptible movement was the faint rustle of a few leaves on the strategically placed trees of the landscaped grounds. The lush flowerbeds of petunias mixed with rich tones of mulch made the environment appear pleasant and inviting. Still, Karen knew this was the last place most people wanted to live.

Strolling from her car to the facility entrance, Karen caught a whiff of antiseptic as the sliding doors swooshed open. The lobby had a feel of faux hominess: welcoming but with an air of medical sterility amid the appealing ambiance. She felt surrounded by a quiet void. Glancing around, she searched for signs of life. The sound of her loafers rubbing along the surface of the thin lobby carpeting seemed to echo in the stillness. *Lord, this is the last place I want my parents to be.*

Finally, a human being. Behind an oversized laminated fake walnut desk, a casually dressed woman looked up from her phone and smiled. The woman's name tag bore the name of the facility, but she wasn't wearing medical scrubs or medical attire of any sort.

Karen flashed her badge. "I'm here to see Sandra Stephenson."

The woman scanned her computer screen, then smiled. "I'll get someone to take you to her room."

Karen nodded, then turned to take in the view of the enormous front lobby. It looked inviting, yet nobody was lounging in any of the luxurious chairs or sitting at the tables with magazines. The piano in the corner sat silent. Finally, a woman in white medical scrubs appeared.

"Sandra Stephenson? That's who you're here to see?" The stocky redheaded woman sleepily popped her gum as she addressed Karen.

"Yes. Please."

Karen was nonchalantly escorted to Sandra's room by the emotionless medical assistant who seemed interrupted from a nap. Every step toward Sandra's room grew heavier and heavier.

The assistant gestured toward a room with an open door. Karen made her way across the meagerly furnished room to the bedside.

"Mrs. Stephenson." Karen's voice was buttery soft. "My name is Detective Cappelletti." She presented her badge. "I'm a detective with Parks Ford police department, in Pennsylvania." She paused to take in a deep breath.

Sandra stared at the space between the detective and the door, her eyes blank.

"Unfortunately, ma'am, I'm here to deliver some difficult news."

Sandra turned her head on her pillow and focused her faded blue eyes on Karen. No words emerged from her mouth. She squinted as if bracing herself.

"Ma'am, early this morning, your son Cliff was attacked. I'm very sorry, ma'am, but he succumbed to his injuries. He died this morning." Karen held her breath. No matter how much experience she had amassed, there was no predicting the person's response.

Sandra stared at Karen, her pale face blank, seemingly trying to register what she just heard as if Karen were speaking a foreign language. When the woman's eyes moistened, she knew Sandra had registered the information. Her heart broke for this woman—a virtual stranger.

A few tears cascading over mottled cheeks became a full sob. Karen dragged a chair next to the bed and sat, reaching across the pressed white sheets for Sandra's hand.

Plastic flowers in a vase sat on the windowsill. A pile of sterile-looking pillows sat at the other end of the room on another chair that looked straight out of an office supply catalog. On a table were pictures of various people. She made a mental note to ask Sandra about the individuals and where they were now.

"What happened to my boy? Do you know?" Sandra asked from beyond her tears.

"Yes, ma'am." Karen sucked in a deep breath. "He was stabbed. We have no motive yet and we're diligently searching for suspects." She studied Sandra's face. "Do you know of anyone who would want to hurt your son?"

"No, no, no." Sandra's tears seemed to emanate from her throat, muffling her words. "He was always well-liked. Such a good-natured, sweet boy."

"Ma'am, were you aware that he was homeless…living on the streets?"

"I was." Sandra looked away as if hiding guilt. "So unfortunate. He got a wonderful job. Working at one of those refineries in Pennsylvania." She shifted her gaze back to Karen. "Two years in, he lost his job. Company layoffs."

Karen nodded, pulling out her notepad and pen in a discreet manner.

"I couldn't do anything to help him, you see. I get very little from the state. But every now and then, I'd have his brother drive over and give him some money I tucked away."

Karen held her gaze. "Can you tell me about his brother?"

"An older brother. He still lives in our old house in Salem. His sister is in North Carolina. Husband...kids. Haven't seen her in months."

"Ma'am, I don't mean to pry, but why wouldn't Cliff just go home to Salem?"

Sandra shook her head in disgust. "Keith wouldn't allow it. Jealousy. You know...his kid brother scored a big job and left home. Once Cliff lost his job, he refused to let him come back."

"Keith. That's your other son...Cliff's brother?"

Sandra nodded, her cinnamon-and-sugar hair rustling along the pillow.

Karen scrawled the information onto her notepad. "Do you know the last time Keith saw Cliff?"

"Can't ever be sure. I sent him to give Cliff money a few months ago. It was all I could do. I feel so helpless." Sandra's eyes welled with tears as she began to weep again.

Karen could only imagine her pain. But she needed to press.

Sandra shared scattered, sometimes disjointed, thoughts while Karen feverishly jotted everything down. It became evident that bad blood existed between the brothers, which now warranted a visit to Keith. The sister remained absent from any family business and barely bothered to visit her mother. The whole situation nauseated Karen.

Karen walked through the pictures sitting to the right of Sandra's bed, making notes on the physical descriptions of each person as well as any commentary Sandra offered. It was a small and fragmented family.

"Ma'am, when was the last time you saw Cliff?"

"Oh my...it's been years. He had no car, and I can't leave here." Sandra looked lost in a fog of empty despair. She stared into an empty space beyond the edge of her bed. "I've missed his gentle smile...his sweet face. He's a good boy, Detective."

Then, as if moving on to a new stage of grief, she perked up. In an almost clear-eyed fashion, she began to question the accuracy of Karen's assessment. "Are you sure it was Cliff? Maybe you've got the wrong person. There are a lot of homeless people out there. You could have the wrong person."

"Yes, ma'am, we're sure. Apparently, he was fingerprinted. A requirement for his refinery job. Those prints are in a national database. We matched them and made a positive identification." She took a deep breath. "I'm truly sorry, ma'am."

It wasn't the first time she had seen a family member react this way, but this time it felt different. Maybe it was knowing that her own daughter was now away from home—away from her protective house and arms. Maybe it was that Cliff didn't seem to have enemies, making the homicide even more unjust. Maybe she was getting too old for this job. Karen rubbed her eyes as she closed her notepad.

She couldn't help but imagine herself in Sandra's position. Trapped in an impersonal facility that was being called home, having lost her husband in a horrific accident, never seeing her daughter, having not seen her youngest son in years—this must have been one more blow to a decade marred by family tragedies.

"Ma'am, is there anyone I can call for you?"

Sandra shook her head.

"I really think it would be good to have someone with you."

Sandra let out a sound that resembled a snort muffling a sarcastic laugh.

"Can I call your daughter? Maybe Keith?"

Sandra smiled. "I'll reach out to them. Thank you."

Karen felt uncomfortable leaving this woman alone. She felt a need to reach out to someone to stay by her side, but she could only offer.

"If there's anything I can do to help…please." Karen dropped her business card on the bedside table. "Please reach out to me."

"Detective," Sandra called out as Karen was two steps from the door. "My boy…he was a sweet boy."

Karen nodded and forced a faint smile.

"Please find out who did this."

"Yes, ma'am. We'll work diligently to find the person responsible." Karen took a deep breath. "You have my word."

By the time Karen left the nursing facility, she was not only physically exhausted but emotionally drained. She pulled out of the lifeless, sterile parking lot and turned her car to the west.

It was pushing eight p.m. by the time she hit Pennsylvania soil. Having barely consumed a few bites of a hoagie from earlier, she was famished. She so desperately wanted to head straight home. But the thought of Tam crossed her mind.

How frightening that morning must have been for her. Exhausted and ready for a beer and some sleep, she decided to follow through on her promise and make the trek back across town to Hillside Street.

Maybe Tam had already headed to bed. If so, she would leave her card and head home. Deep down, her fingers were crossed, hoping no one would answer the door when she knocked.

CHAPTER EIGHT

At Bobby's house, Karen rubbed eyes that felt gritty and eyelids that seemed to weigh ten pounds. Yellow police tape still fluttered in the soft night breeze. Karen waved to the two officers protecting the wide swath of cordoned-off area still under investigation. She plodded up the four wooden steps to the porch. Her hand in midknock, the door sprang open to Tam's bright smile.

"Oh…hey." Karen's words felt awkward slipping from her lips. "Just stopped by to check on you." Her eyes felt weary as she steadied them on Tam's refreshed face.

Tam gave a cheerful smile. "Thank you." She stepped aside. "Come on in. Can I get you a beer?"

God, that sounds good. Karen gave a barely perceptible grin. "I really can't stay. Just wanted to see how you were doing." She looked past Tam to see if Bobby was around.

"Oh, one beer won't kill you. C'mon…it's a beautiful night," Tam said, motioning to the kitchen and back door.

"You go ahead and enjoy. Technically, I'm still on duty." Karen felt herself struggling to maintain her professionalism and set clear boundaries. *Why am I here? Tam looks fine. Just check on her, like you promised, and get going.* Karen stood in the entryway, glancing at Bobby straight ahead in the living room, lounging on the sofa watching TV.

"You look really tired," Tam said in a soft tone. Her smile faded. She appeared genuinely concerned.

"I am. Last stop for the day." *My God, how bad do I look?* "I really can't stay."

"C'mon. Just one drink. It'll help you feel better." Tam headed down the hallway to the kitchen.

Karen followed, giving Bobby a quick nod as she walked by. Tam pulled two beers from the refrigerator.

Karen shook her head. "No." Her tone was firm. "I'm still working. I'll take a water." She looked around the room where she sat in twelve hours earlier with a Tam who looked and acted one hundred eighty degrees different.

Tam gave a sheepish grin but honored Karen's request.

"It's amazing how the inside of this house looks exactly as it did ten years ago," Karen said as they walked out the back door to a slab of cement that Tam referred to as "the deck."

Tam made a sour face.

Probably not a time she wants to remember.

A faint breeze whispered through the trees of the wooded area behind the yard. A mild night—temperatures in the low sixties—with a touch of lingering humidity in advance of the storm racing up the mid-Atlantic coast.

On the minuscule cement slab sat two plastic chairs and a round plastic table. It wasn't luxurious and it certainly wasn't how Karen's deck looked, but she felt immense pleasure in just sitting without any pressing obligations. It was the first time she felt her senses relax in over twelve hours.

Karen gazed out at a backyard filled with clumps of crabgrass, dandelions, and other lawn weeds. Hostas surrounded the cement patio, and a handful of overgrown white azaleas dotted the flower beds around the back of the house. Most adjacent yards had no fences. The exception was an occasional three-foot chain-link fence here or there, usually at homes with dogs.

Just beyond the back property line was a wooded area with overgrown vegetation. The only time residents could see through to the other side was when the vegetation disappeared during the winter months. Now, the foliage was green and lush, typical of a summer finale in Pennsylvania. In another month, the air would grow colder and the leaves would turn a brilliant array of colors before falling to the ground, leaving the trees bare. The grass would fade to beige, then brown. By late November, most people would hibernate inside, not seeing their neighbors for the next three to four months.

"How's the investigation going?" Tam asked, twisting the cap off a Yuengling beer bottle.

"I actually can't talk about the investigation. But I can say, it's been a very long day."

"I'm sorry."

"How are you doing? You seemed pretty distraught earlier."

"Better. Trying to push it out of my mind."

"I understand."

Karen was trying to be considerate but found it hard to find anything to discuss with Tam. She couldn't discuss the case, and she had no history with Tam. She wasn't artistic. The two had nothing in common. Still, she felt drawn to the young woman—her charisma and her seemingly fearless individuality.

In the silence, Karen fumbled for something she could ask and genuinely care about. "Putting aside this morning, how does it feel to be home?"

Tam looked at her sweating bottle and gave a faint smile. "Okay. It's brought back a lot of memories, though."

Karen grimaced as Tam went on to share memories of her father coming home drunk. She spoke of a time when she was a child hearing her mother cry out while she was in bed. Karen sensed Tam's fear and helplessness as she shared the details.

"I remember tiptoeing into the living room. I hid behind our old, overstuffed chair." Tam took a swig of beer. "It was the first time I saw him hit my mother."

Karen felt a deep sadness seep into her chest, almost suffocating her. "What did you do?"

"I just froze."

"What happened?" Karen asked, sensing Tam needed to talk through it with someone.

"My mom never fought back. No matter what."

Karen winced. She knew the narcissistic man and the destructive personality disorder he subjected his entire family to.

"I always wanted the love and attention I saw my classmates get at home." Tam looked off into the darkened sky. "I got it when I moved to New York."

Probably heard her story and felt sorry for her.

"People valued me for who I was. I was pretty smart. I knew how to survive. I think people saw that."

Karen tried to listen and nod. She sincerely felt bad for Tam and wanted to connect with her, but she was also fighting an all-encompassing fatigue that felt like a hundred-pound lead balloon weighing down her eyes and her mind.

"I remember one night. My father stumbled in…drunk…again. Everyone was asleep. I snuck down the hall and peeked into the kitchen. He was down on his hands and knees at the pantry. Just sat there, grumbling. It was weird."

"What was he doing?"

Tam shrugged. "Never found out."

Karen changed the subject. "Tell me about your time up in New York."

Tam delivered story after animated story, sharing all the things that were so different in New York City compared to the small town of Parks Ford. She perked up—bright and vivacious—carrying the conversation effortlessly. Karen experienced a frivolity absent from earlier and found herself quickly relaxing and feeling at ease despite her bone-deep exhaustion.

Karen polished off her water just as Tam finished describing her life as an artist in the big city. She stood to leave.

"Do you have to go?" Tam said, not budging from her chair.

"Yeah. I'm exhausted. If I sit any longer, I won't be going anywhere."

"That's fine with me." Tam smiled in a manner that Karen read as flirtatious.

Karen couldn't help but smile. A subtle laugh slipped out. "I have to go."

Karen stopped at the entrance to the living room. Bobby was still sunk deep into the well-worn cushions of the tired mustard-yellow couch that had seen better days, seemingly lost in a television program. As tired as she was, she felt compelled to follow up on Joey's comment.

"Bobby, did your father have a knife collection?"

He grimaced. "Yeah. Hated it." His faded, sunken eyes looked at Karen. "It was always his big, proud display," he said as if mocking his father's need to equate the knives with his manhood.

The topic seemed to infuse life into his lounging body. "Months after he went to the clink, I pawned 'em off. I wanted them the hell out of here…and I really needed the money." His gaze was half on Karen and half on the TV.

Joey was right. Karen walked into the living room and pushed for more information. "How many did he have?"

"Shit, I don't know. Enough to fill an entire display case in here."

She nodded to herself. Indeed, she had seen a display case back then, but did she ever see the knives? Her memories were vague. "Do you remember how big the display case was?"

"No." His succinct words punctuated an apparent lack of desire to discuss the matter further.

"No, you don't remember, or no, you don't know?"

He stared at Karen.

"Bobby, I know this is uncomfortable, but I really need an answer," Karen gently prodded. "This information is important."

"No, I don't remember." Bobby shifted his attention to the aging shag carpeting, carpet twists interspersed with carpet pills.

"Did you get a fair amount of money for them?" Karen attempted to help him relax and be more forthcoming.

He half shrugged. "I got money. It helped pay the bills." He stared down straight ahead. "Did I get what they were worth? No idea." He glanced up and met Karen's eyes. "Some of the knives were apparently collector's items, but I honestly couldn't tell you which ones."

"Do you remember where you pawned them?"

"The Darby Pawn Shop, just outside of town."

Karen squatted down to meet Bobby's eyes. "Did you pawn all of them, Bobby?"

He met her gaze. "Every fucking last one." He enunciated each word. "You can search this entire house if you want. They're all gone. Have been for years."

She felt Bobby getting defensive and irritated. Tam looked noticeably uncomfortable and concerned.

"No. No need for that." She gave an affirmative nod and smiled.

Bobby's uncharacteristic reaction gnawed at her. She turned toward the entryway.

"Hey, do either of you have any mints? Need something to keep me awake to drive home."

"I have gum." Tam perked up. "Will gum help?"

Karen muffled a snort. "Sure. Thanks."

Tam ran off to her room and bounded back, producing a pack of cinnamon Trident.

Not even mint. Through her fatigue, she forced a smile. "Thanks, Tam."

Tam walked Karen to the door. "Thank you for stopping by. I know you're tired, and I really appreciate it." Tam gently tugged Karen's arm, pulling her closer. She gave her a soft peck on the cheek.

A tingling sensation shot through Karen's chest as she stood, perplexed. There was nothing in the Detective's Manual on how to handle this. Maintaining her composure, she turned to Tam and smiled.

"Thank you," Tam said again. Her eyes looked serious, her tone sincere. "You really helped put me at ease."

Outside, with her colleagues nearby, Karen sighed with relief when Tam stayed on the porch instead of following her to her car. At her car, she gazed back to see Tam's stare fixed on her. She looked away and shifted her attention back to the case.

That Bobby seemed so agitated with her questions about the knives was puzzling. She pulled out her notepad and jotted down the pawn shop information and other details he had shared.

Then there was Tam. In private, the attention from Tam felt delightful—something she craved. The brashness with which Tam moved through the world without a second thought about revealing her sexuality—or expressing her interest—caused a fluttering of excitement and nerves deep in the pit of Karen's belly. Yet she cringed at the thought of Tam making those advances in front of her colleagues—hell, in front of anyone. Her ambivalent reactions felt like a runaway horse she was struggling to harness. And ethically, she knew she had no business getting involved with anyone involved with the case. Still, surges of warmth pulsated from her stomach to her chest, and back.

Heading home, a smattering of raindrops dotted her windshield as she passed through the business district. By the time she reached her neighborhood, raindrops had wet the roadway, leaving a subtle sheen. Sunday was forecasted to be an entire washout with the nor'easter bearing up the coast. She and Riley would need to plug away. To make headway. At this point, she was pushing a fifteen-hour day. Dinner no longer sounded appealing.

As much as she craved the inside of her home and her bed, she parked in the driveway and sat. The only sound, a periodic pattering of drops hitting her windshield and car roof. Her vision blurred as her mind drifted into thought. *What's going on?* She had dreaded going back to see Tam, yet acquiesced and stayed for almost an hour. She was stirred by the gentle kiss, yet flustered by what this woman was doing—and she was eternally grateful it all occurred behind closed doors. *Must be because I'm lonely.*

An emptiness flooded over her as she plodded up her walkway. The house was dark. Still. Quiet. The drapes across her bay window were still wide open. Her only thought was to drop her keys and head upstairs to bed. Lonely or not, her bed was an enormously inviting thought.

She examined her weary deep-brown eyes in the bathroom mirror, brushing back the layered strands of hair from her face. After a steaming, hot shower, she sank onto her soft cotton sheets and felt the void next to her. Rolling over, she tugged up on the covers.

By midnight, a steady rain began to fall across the area. A lone wall clock in Karen's bedroom rhythmically ticked with the background sound of rain pecking at her windows. The enormity of her new case had leveled her. She fell sound asleep.

CHAPTER NINE

When Sunday morning rolled around, Karen sat up in bed, rubbing her eyes into responding. Her body felt as if it had been pummeled for fifteen rounds. Throwing back the covers, she plodded to her bedroom window and scanned the deserted neighborhood outside. Sheets of rain pelleted the sidewalk and streets, coming down in thick horizontal layers. The wind whipped through the tall oaks and maples, leaving debris littering front lawns and sidewalks. With rain forecasted for the next two days, any evidence overlooked at the crime scene would be destroyed by now.

With her first cup of coffee in hand, she sat below her bay window and watched the torrents of rain pound the side of the house. She loved this kind of weather—perfect quiet time, an opportunity to sit and sort through thoughts. The rain matched her mood: empty and lonely. She sat motionless, staring outside as if mesmerized, melancholy thoughts drifting in. Her blurry stare refocused as her phone chimed off in the distance. *Shit, how did I forget my phone?* She shook her head at her fatigue-related absent-mindedness.

She trotted back upstairs to her phone. A voice mail. She held her breath. Missed call. Riley. Bright and early at 7:45 on Sunday morning. The county detective was ready to get going and was checking on Karen's ETA. She groaned, realizing she had a work partner holding her feet to the fire.

When Karen entered the stone-quiet police station, Riley was already sitting in her office. She glanced at Riley's beat-up work boots, baggy black tactical pants, and fitted long-sleeved shirt, admiring her partner's rock-solid physique. Her long braids were now pulled back into a tight ponytail. *A get-down-to-business look, if I ever saw one.*

Karen grabbed a cup of coffee that tasted more like wood and sat down at her desk. They needed to get a handle on this case fast but so far had scant leads to work with.

"No clear signs of struggle." Karen flipped through her notes. "We'll get more tomorrow at the post, but right now, looks like a single wound and he didn't get that far after the attack."

Riley raised her eyebrows. "I remember a case I had a couple years ago…gang dispute. A guy was stabbed, then ran through several yards, through a house, up a flight of steps, and down a hallway before the blood trail ended. That was a shit ton of evidence to collect."

Karen felt uneasiness wash over her. Riley had so much more experience with these types of crimes. Parks Ford didn't have gang-related violence, let alone homicides.

"Well, that's not what we're looking at here." Karen at least felt confident she knew her town's dynamics. "And robbery was clearly not the motive."

Karen filled Riley in on her visit with Cliff's mother.

"In her room, there was a picture of a tall guy with a shaved head. It was her other son, Keith. Apparently, the brothers had a long-standing, jealousy-fueled dispute."

Riley raised her eyebrows.

"We need to put this Keith guy on our list of possibles," Karen said, referring to possible suspects.

Riley pointed to a sheet of paper on the corner of Karen's desk. "That was here when I arrived."

Karen snatched up the paper and gave it a quick scan. "The lab." The information had come back faster than she had expected. "The only blood found at the scene was that of the victim."

Riley cast a dejected look.

"The oil sample I dropped off…it matched the oil in the street. Guess I was hoping to hear something else." A wisp of air escaped from her balloon of hope.

"Well, we pretty much ruled out Vince."

"True. Would've been better to identify oil from a different vehicle. Maybe give us a lead." Karen looked up. "Okay, let's go over the people we have so far. Starting with the McPherson family. Thoughts on Kenny?"

"History of violence. That's no secret. Did he have a beef with the homeless people? Maybe he didn't care about the homeless but saw it as a way to try to scare Bobby, or possibly frame him for murder."

"A way to get him out and get his house back?" Karen asked. "But he got out of prison with nothing but the clothes on his back. Seems unlikely to have his shit together so quickly to pull it off." She paused, then continued, feeling her stomach begin to tense as she thought about the next possible on her list. "Bobby."

"To frame his dad?" Riley said.

"The whole framing thing seems too simple and convenient. But he did have a house filled with his father's knife collection. Told me last night, he pawned them all."

Riley looked up. Her eyes grew larger as her dark eyebrows rose toward her forehead.

"Why would he kill a homeless guy he liked?" Karen added.

Riley half shrugged. "Tam?"

"Just returned to town two weeks ago." Karen heard her own voice—steeped with incredulity. "Absolutely no motive that I can think of. It's not like Cliff had something she wanted." Karen paused. The room fell silent. "No access to a knife…and no money to buy one."

Riley pursed her lips and nodded. "Joey Murphy?"

Karen caught her reflection in her office window, her forehead wrinkling like ripples on a pond. "He hates Kenny. Would've loved to implicate him. He knew Kenny had a large knife collection."

"What about Jack Doyle?" Riley said without hesitation. "He's still a slimy dick."

Karen looked up from her notes, amused by Riley's definition of Doyle. She thought back on the brochure that fell from Doyle's pocket and shared the incident with Riley.

"Maybe he purchased the knife for Kenny. And like I said, he's a slimy dick." Riley seemed unable to resist the last comment.

Karen chuckled.

"Seriously. Could Doyle have been cooking up something to scare Bobby? Help his buddy?"

"To help Kenny?" Karen was skeptical, but it was possible.

"And...he can't stand those homeless people. So, for him, it's a win-win," Riley added, leaving Doyle a clear possibility. If nothing else, he would certainly be on their future interview list.

"Frank Ryanard," Karen tossed out.

"Another dick. Hated the homeless."

"He's likely to be more bark than bite."

"True. But he's a whack-job," Riley said. "Remember when his daughter bought the whole family an Ancestry and Me DNA kit for Christmas? They had to trick him into giving his saliva? He turned around and tried to press charges against them. His own family. Who *does* that?"

Karen chuckled, marveling at how easy it was to work with Riley. Effortless. This was a difficult case, one that had the whole town on edge. Yet, Riley made it a pleasure to sort through facts and explore answers.

Riley never brought her personal life into her work, so Karen knew little about her besides her professional accomplishments. No wedding ring, and she never discussed a husband, partner, or any children.

What she did know was that Riley was determined. Professionally, she had worked through gender and racial barriers to become one of the county's detectives. Karen knew she was confident, tough as nails, and didn't get rattled. To Karen's delight, Riley also expressed a preference for working with female, over male, colleagues.

"How 'bout one of the homeless people?" Riley asked.

"Possible, but they all seemed to look out for one another. Can't see a reason for a dispute."

Karen continued panning her notes when her office phone blared like a bullhorn through the deserted police station. She picked it up and listened, nodding periodically and scribbling down a few details before thanking the caller.

"We have a weapon," Karen said, scrawling additional notes. "A knife was found yesterday evening between the two houses, approximately one hundred feet from the victim. Human blood on it. Waiting to hear if it matches our victim."

"Prints?" Riley's tone was hopeful.

"None. But the angle at which it landed in the ground suggests it was thrown from the front of the house. No footprints were found in the vicinity. Supports our earlier assessment of the cast-off pattern."

Chief Walden entered, his hefty black shoes soaked from the rain. Karen looked up, surprised by his presence on a Sunday. But in a town of this size, Walden always wanted to be on top of everything going on—"no Monday morning surprises" was his motto. He indicated he was aware of the recovered knife and expected more information shortly.

"If the knife was a hundred feet away and the perp threw it," Karen said, "we're looking for someone with enough strength to throw that far. Not to sound sexist, but that pretty much rules out a woman."

"Yes." Riley nodded and, after a short pause, said, "You *do* sound sexist." She flashed Karen a knowing smile. "I could probably throw a knife that far. Just sayin'."

"C'mon, Riley. You're built like a brick shithouse. Most women aren't like you."

Officer Roberts appeared in the doorway and tapped on the door, passing Karen a memo. She scanned it before handing it to Riley.

"The knife—an Ek Commando Presentation Knife." Riley read the memo out loud.

"Ever heard of one of those?"

Riley popped open her laptop.

"Ahhh, Detective Google." Karen chuckled.

"Okay." Riley read from the screen. "That type of knife has a six-and-a-half-inch blade. Apparently, it's functional, but, true to its name, it's usually purchased for presentation or display purposes."

Karen winced as Riley shot her a curious look.

Riley continued, "These knives run between two to three hundred bucks each. The cost alone limits our suspects."

"Not if they bought it at a pawn shop," Karen murmured.

"True."

"It's an expensive knife to just throw away." Thoughts bounced through Karen's head. "It wouldn't have been grabbed in haste. If someone had planned to kill this man, why pull out an expensive knife to just discard it?"

"Guns are expensive, too, but people throw them out after they're used to kill someone."

"I get it, but the sheer expense would eliminate some people from being able to access the weapon, no?"

"People access weapons in all sorts of ways…legal and not," Riley said.

"No fingerprints. Looks like the perp had a plan in place to commit the murder and conceal their identity."

"Or, they were wearing gloves." Riley stared into space, her mind seemingly chugging through possible scenarios.

Karen broke through Riley's trance. "We know Kenny had a large knife collection displayed in the house. Bobby confirmed that. Said he pawned them all off."

"If Bobby pawned one of those knives, we would have a record of it," Riley said.

"We *would* have—but not after ten years. The pawn shop may have their own records."

Karen began creating a to-do list. "It's Sunday. Pawn shop is closed. I'll make it my first stop tomorrow, after the post."

"How about we head back to the scene?" Riley said. "We can reinterview neighbors. Tomorrow, I'll go back and talk with Bobby… get another perspective on his demeanor."

"You sure you're up for that? You can always go to the pawnbroker."

Riley paused as if facing an uncomfortable moment and took a deep breath. "Capp, this really isn't my business, and your personal business is your own…" She hesitated. "Bobby's sister. She seems a bit too close to you, ya know? A bit…attached. It might be good if I go over there. That way, there won't be any blurred lines anyone can point to."

Karen avoided Riley's eyes. A slow heat rose inside as she felt herself growing flustered. She knew there was nothing between her and Tam. To her, she had effectively warded off Tam's advances. Yet, Riley's comments felt like a cold splash of water thrown onto her face. She resented what she perceived as Riley's assumption.

Karen opted to bite her tongue and go with Riley's suggestion. *No fuss—no appearing insulted.* She would hit the pawn shop on Monday while Riley questioned Bobby further about the knives in his father's collection.

For now, they would both revisit a soggy crime scene. Although the odds were slim, they could check for anything potentially missed the day before. As they headed down the long hallway to the front door, two drenched patrol officers walked in, leaving a puddle of water in their path.

"Yo, Capp. Got a handle on this murder yet?" Brennan yelled out.

"Making good progress." Karen's eyes darted for the exit.

"Town expects an arrest soon—"

"We're on it, Brennan." She felt her jaw tighten.

"Excuse me, Detective..." Officer Roberts interrupted.

Karen spun around, glaring at Roberts. His eyes became wide, his face ashen as he hesitantly handed her a document. She snatched the paper from his hands. Taking a deep breath, she looked up and thanked him. It was the information they had been waiting for.

Karen started the SUV and put her head back on the headrest, closing her eyes.

"What's up with you and Brennan?" Riley asked.

"Twenty-plus years of bullshit. He's still pissed I beat him out for the detective position."

Riley semistifled a laugh. "That lug? He thinks he's investigator quality? Please."

Starting at the bottom of a male-dominated profession, Karen had worked through the academy, her penance as a patrol officer, and eventually the selection to her current position. Uncovering the mysteries of various crimes was a challenge and intriguing to her. To Brennan, she was a woman who had no business in the important role of investigator. It didn't help that the misogynist had been jousting for the same position. And in Parks Ford, there was only one investigator in this speck of a department.

"When I was still in patrol with Brennan, there was an incident." Karen stared out the windshield. "A guy claimed the town manager came on to him in the men's restroom. Brennan reported it."

Riley groaned.

"It was a big deal back then. The investigation got turfed to the county." Karen looked down at the steering wheel. "Apparently, the guy that reported the incident was a friend of Brennan's. Rumors were they were both out to get the town manager...set him up."

"What ended up happening?"

"Never got resolved. The town manager resigned." Karen put the car in gear. "I think Brennan thought he had the investigator spot in the bag after that."

Riley chuckled. "He probably didn't get the position because he sucks at getting his reports done. Besides, you got it all over him."

Karen felt herself relax. It was as if Riley saw a sister in trouble and was there to offer support. Riley shared with Karen that even though she dealt with racism throughout her career, in her opinion, the obstacles were more about sexism than racism.

"As women, we're always outnumbered. We have to fight just to be seen and heard in our departments. Black, Brown, and white guys…they always get ahead faster than women," Riley said.

Karen admired Riley's resilience. She turned and looked at her colleague. "We for sure got the murder weapon. The blood was a match." A calming sigh followed. "That was the information Roberts was chasing me down for…and I bit his head off."

Riley chuckled as Karen sped off.

At 351 Hillside, yellow tape was still in place, dripping with water. Two squad cars remained. A river of muddy water poured into the street from between 350 and 351—the area where the knife had been discarded.

Karen looked at Riley. "We haven't got a chance in hell of finding anything at this point."

The rain pounded the windshield. Karen examined the photos of where the knife was discovered. Pictures from a mudless afternoon yesterday made the current landscape look foreign.

They donned their rain gear and sloshed through the soggy soil between the two homes. Any faint footprints would have been washed away by now. Still, they scoured the area, looking for anything the perpetrator may have dropped or accidentally discarded. At the back of Bobby's house, Karen looked at the cement slab where she and Tam had sat the night before. The plastic chairs had toppled over. Water dripped off the edge of the table like a waterfall.

Finding nothing of value, they trudged back to the street, where Karen officially released the crime scene. The yellow tape came down and the last remaining officers were dismissed. Karen positioned herself in the spot she believed the perpetrator may have been when they discarded the knife. Indeed, it would have required a fair amount of strength to throw an object that far.

The women divided up the street and circled back to residents, hoping someone would recall seeing or hearing something now that the shock of the incident had subsided. One by one, door after door, residents shook their heads.

The two headed back to the station to dry off and create a plan moving forward. All they had was the murder weapon and the victim's identity. After the autopsy, they would have access to anything on Cliff's body. Did he have anything in his pockets? A large wad of cash—unheard of for someone in his situation—would certainly raise red flags. Was anything on Cliff's hands or under his fingernails? Clawing the attacker in self-defense could lead to a gold mine of information—information Karen was banking on.

The agenda for Monday was set: Karen to the postmortem at eight in the morning and Riley back to Hillside to follow up with Bobby. Riley would then head to Jack Doyle's to conduct a preliminary interview with Kenny while Karen checked out the Darby Pawn Shop. They would reconvene at Hillside around noon.

Karen's house was dark when she got home, everything gloomy and dismal with the rain, but the emptiness of her home was like salt to a gaping wound. After changing into flannel pants and a T-shirt, she cracked open an ice-cold Yuengling and clicked on the TV. A midseason football game served as background noise, dulling the exhaustion and frustration of a long weekend of work.

Her blurred, trancelike stare was interrupted by the sound of her phone. Caiden's name on her caller ID was a joy and relief.

"Hey, babe…how are you?"

"Great, Mom. I absolutely love it here."

Karen smiled, hearing the joy in her daughter's voice. She sat back on the sofa and felt the rigidity in her body dissolve. For the first time in several weeks, her heart felt full again.

"I'm so glad to hear your voice. I've been—" Karen hesitated, wondering if she should express the anxiety she'd been feeling.

"I know, Mom. You've been worried. I'm sorry it took so long. I've just been super busy."

"It's okay, babe. I'm glad everything is going well. Thrilled to hear you're enjoying yourself." But Karen missed her little girl. Desperately.

"I heard jackass stood you up again."

Karen sighed. She knew Caiden couldn't stand Miles. "Yeah. He extended his assignment." She could hear the disgust in her own voice.

"You okay, Mom?"

"Yeah. Got plenty of things to keep me busy."

"Really? This is usually the slow time at work."

Karen wondered how to broach the subject. "Well…we had an incident this weekend. A homicide—"

"What?" Caiden's voice jumped an octave. "When? Where?"

Karen explained the bare minimum details and assured Caiden that the case would likely wrap up by the end of the coming week.

"That's my mom. You're such a stud-ette." Caiden's jovial voice was like sunshine. "Finish up the case and go out and celebrate. Maybe you'll meet someone new."

Karen rolled her eyes playfully at her daughter's optimism. Deep down, she believed her age and career choice posed enormous threats to landing a successful relationship. But she wouldn't throw water on Caiden's positivity—the very thing she needed the most.

After a light and carefree phone conversation, Karen threw aside the heaviness of the weekend. Tomorrow would be stressful. She needed all the calm and positivity possible to start the week.

CHAPTER TEN

A dreary Monday morning saw the slow tapering of the stormy weather. At 7:30, Karen was on the road and headed to the county medical examiner's office.

Heading down the aging hallway of the county building—still quiet at this hour—she heard only the dampened tap of her shoes on the muted jade linoleum flooring, its hazy surface showing every decade of wear and tear. It always amazed Karen how a facility of such importance could become so outdated. The last time it underwent a revamp was in the late 1970s…and it showed.

Toward the end of the hall, light from a room illuminated a small section of the hallway. As she neared, the smell of coffee hit her senses along with the drone of a singular male voice. She peered into the room. The chief medical officer was "giving report" to his pathologists and technicians at the shift change. An investigator from a neighboring town caught her eye and waved for her to come sit with him. She shook her head. The other investigators seemed to share her negative sentiment, their heads buried in their cell phones.

Report ended with a scurry of activity. Karen chatted with the two detectives she recognized before continuing down the remainder of the hallway and through the steel doors into the autopsy room. She was immediately assaulted by the arctic chill of the room. The forensic pathologist was waiting inside as the technician wheeled in Cliff's body.

Sterile. Cold. These sole thoughts enveloped her. Steel countertops and tables with wheels. Sinks and an assortment of tools and chemicals in containers. Drains peppering the tile flooring. The pungent odor of formalin. The tables, countertops, and sinks glinted in the fluorescent lighting.

The technician clipped off the tag on the plastic white bag, unzipped it, and moved Cliff's body onto the metal table. The photographer began the methodical and arduous process of taking dozens of pictures, both with clothes and without. Cliff's body was washed, and the process was repeated.

Blood-saturated clothing went to a drying locker. A handful of nickels and quarters and the single scratched red plastic lighter found in his pockets were bagged and tagged as evidence and now Karen's responsibility.

Cliff's shoes would be examined and, presumably, matched with the bloody footprints at the scene. His clothing would be carefully scrutinized for fibers, hair, fluids, and dirt. If foreign DNA, perhaps from blood on Cliff's clothing, could be found, Karen would have a critical link to a suspect.

The forensic pathologist, dressed in navy-blue scrubs and light-blue booties over her clogs, donned a light-blue disposable gown and gloves. She conducted her actions with grace and swift precision. *I love it when a woman is professional and competent.* An internal smile emerged.

She glanced over at Karen with a gentle smile. "I've read Bettenkoff's report." She had a soft, almost melodic tone. "What assessment did you make when you examined the scene? Anything I should know?"

Christ, this woman's seen a million homicide victims. Don't sound ignorant, Capp. She reviewed what she and Riley had observed at the scene. "The victim didn't get very far. I've seen scenes where stabbing victims have run across yards and through homes before collapsing." A lie. She was using Riley's story from Saturday.

The pathologist solemnly nodded as she surveyed the grayish-white body, dictating into her recording device. "Poorly nourished white male. Seventy-two and one-quarter inches in height." She paused, glancing at the illuminated red number on the scale built into the metal table. "One hundred thirty-four pounds." Her eyebrows raised as she looked over at Karen, who grimaced.

"A single perforation in the skin corresponding to the single puncture in the victim's shirt. Edges of the wound are sharply cut, indicating a perpendicular entry located just below the xiphoid process and eight and one-sixteenth inches superior to his navel. The tissue is dented from the force. Hilt marks are absent." The pathologist looked away from her recording device, making eye contact with Karen. "The aorta is deep, but a long blade could have punctured it. We'll know more shortly."

"The knife we recovered…a six-and-a-half-inch blade."

The pathologist raised her eyebrows. "That would do it." The lines between her brows deepened, resembling a pitchfork. "Anything else you know about the victim? Any medical history?"

"In his late thirties. From Salem, New Jersey," Karen said. "We believe he's been homeless for a couple of years."

Karen shifted her stance, trying to talk but focusing on breathing through her mouth instead of her nose. She hadn't been to a postmortem for a while but never forgot the odors. "I know he's a smoker. Have no idea about alcohol or drug use."

The pathologist nodded. "You'll have a full tox screen in about ten days." Her smile put Karen at ease.

"Can the angle of the stab wound help determine the attacker's height or handedness?" Karen asked.

"No." A definitive answer. "Nor can we determine from the wound where the attacker was positioned during the attack."

Karen forced back a look of surprise and disappointment. "But I've read articles—"

"No." The pathologist cut her off. "There are too many unknown variables."

She picked up her scalpel and demonstrated different positions and different ways to hold a weapon. The victim or the attacker could have been standing or kneeling. "Too many variables and possibilities."

The metal doors whooshed open again. A second technician wheeled another body into the bay about fifteen feet away. The two investigators Karen chatted with earlier followed. When the body was put on the table, it became evident it had been found in a decomposed state. The stench of decay was horrific, an acrid charnel smell that was sickly sweet. She was glad to be a good fifteen feet away. Still, the odor was inescapable.

Karen listened to the constant chatter between the other two investigators, the technician, and the pathologist working on their putrefied victim. A gunshot victim. Multiple wounds. The pathologist carefully drew a diagram of the victim and the location of each wound while the investigators jabbed at him about his lack of artistic abilities. Karen wished she felt that level of comfort to casually crack jokes. She caught herself. *No, not professional. You're here to get information, not to joke around.*

Karen refocused on her own victim. Full X-rays of Cliff had already been taken. His fingernails had been clipped and sent to forensics for potential trace evidence. The pathologist now began her lengthy and meticulous internal evaluation, masking before executing the classic Y-incision—a bilateral incision from the shoulders, progressing down from the breastbone to hip bone.

Karen leaned against the wall of the room, as she had done ever since her first postmortem. It led to a rush of memories. During her detective training, she'd heard stories of her male counterparts passing out after the procedure began. It wasn't so much the sight as it was the smell. She had sworn it wouldn't happen to her. To guard against that, she had leaned up against the wall. Gradually, her body had slid down that wall. *At least my first autopsy failure was more subtle.*

"Postmortem injuries identified as a singular stab wound to the chest at the midline proceeding at an oblique angle upward and a slight left-to-right angle." The pathologist methodically dictated her findings without even a glance at Karen.

"The victim sustained extensive intraperitoneal hemorrhage. Approximately three and a half liters were lost, consistent with wounds to the abdominal aorta and inferior vena cava. He would have bled out quickly, with death likely occurring within minutes. COD: exsanguination due to a singular stab wound to the anterior chest."

The wound was irregularly shaped. Since the weapon didn't have a jagged edge, it was believed to be caused by a twisting motion. The pathologist was unable to definitively say whether the attacker twisted the knife or whether Cliff twisted during the attack.

Karen always hated the high-pitched whirring scream of the Stryker saw. *Nothing in this part of his body will help our case.* She justified her decision to bow out before Cliff's cranium was opened, thanking the pathologist.

The building was bustling by the time Karen headed back down the hallway. Even though it was only ten in the morning, she felt like an entire day had elapsed. She walked away with about the same amount of information, except this trip contained a box of evidence bags to take to the crime lab.

She headed home to take a shower and change clothes. In a steaming hot shower, she doused her entire body with a heavy lemon-scented shampoo—especially her hair. She knew of people who went so far as to eat horseradish, then strong peppermints, to rid their sinuses of the autopsy smell.

Clean and refreshed, Karen made her way to the pawn shop. The rain had almost ceased, but the sky was still a morbid gray. Or maybe it was just gray, but after two hours in autopsy, it just felt morbid.

A blaring red-and-blue neon sign of the Darby Pawn Shop blinked on and off—the store was open for business. Before getting out into the damp dreariness, she texted Riley, eager to hear about any revelations from her visit with Kenny and Doyle and equally grateful she didn't have to be there.

Riley's response was simple. *No answer, no cars around.*

Try again this afternoon or tomorrow? Karen replied. As much as she dreaded it, she would have to face the inevitable confrontation with Kenny. At least Riley would be with her.

Headed to Hillside now, Riley texted.

Karen responded with a thumbs-up before throwing the phone in her bag and getting out of the SUV.

A small bell jingled inside a dingy glass door covered with security bars. Karen entered the cluttered shop, scanning the shelves and countertops full of other people's property. An entire back wall was lined with hanging guitars. Below the varied string instruments, electronics and camera equipment were mixed in with tools and leather handbags. An L-shaped glass counter expanded across half of the building. Below the countertop, jewelry, fine watches, and rare coins were secured.

She glanced at the antiques stacked along the walls to either side of her and the garment racks of clothing. The musty smell of old cigarette smoke hung heavy in the air. Making her way to the counter, she walked across thin, decaying gray carpeting spotted with stains that had likely been there for ten to twenty years. *Would there even be records of pawn tickets a decade later?*

A man with greasy gray hair framing his large bald spot appeared from a back room. His belly protruded from behind an untucked flannel shirt draped over baggy blue jeans. "Help you, ma'am?" the clerk asked with a voice that sounded as coarse as sandpaper.

Karen pulled out her wallet and flashed her badge.

"I'm Detective Cappelletti. Parks Ford PD." She glanced around her. "I'm inquiring about a large lot of knives that were pawned here—" She took a breath. "About ten years ago."

The man let out a snicker, his belly bouncing with each laugh. She returned his chuckles with an intense stare.

"We're only required to keep records for three years—" he said defensively.

"I understand." She cut him off. "I'm investigating a case that involved a certain knife…an Ek Commando Presentation Knife. I'm trying to see if it was pawned here by a man named Bobby McPherson."

Much to her surprise, the pawnbroker did remember Bobby. He remembered a large batch of knives pawned by a young man who didn't fit the bill for a knife collector. Unlike most brokers, even though the pawn ticket had long expired, he kept personal records that went back decades. He raised a pudgy arm covered in rolled-up flannel and gave a waving motion to Karen as he turned and walked to the back. She followed, walking behind the counter and down to the basement. At the base of the worn wooden steps, the man crossed his arms and looked over at Karen with raised eyebrows.

"Knock yourself out." He pointed to stacks and stacks of cardboard boxes.

"Do you also have records of the items you've sold?"

He stared at her. Again, he pointed to the boxes. "It's all there."

He pivoted and waddled back up the stairs. She surveyed the boxes. Approximate dates and years were scribbled in thick, black Sharpie ink along the sides. She pried open one of the cardboard tops. Inside were stacks of binders filled with handwritten documents. She realized she would need a more specific timeline from Bobby.

Karen texted Riley.

He's headed to work. Do my best, Riley tapped back. *Will talk with Tam, too.*

Tam wasn't living there then.

Want to check on other things with her.

Tam had seemed guarded with Riley. Her colleague was a no-nonsense, get-right-to-the-facts detective, and Tam likely needed a bit more coddling. But she decided not to push back.

Karen located two boxes that contained records from around the time she arrested Kenny and informed the pawnbroker that two boxes, placed by the base of the steps, would be picked up by an officer. Heading back outside, the little bell chimed behind her. The damp, mildewy smell from the building lingered in her nostrils.

CHAPTER ELEVEN

Karen headed across town to meet Riley. As she made the turn onto Hillside, she glanced at a handful of homeless people gathered in the lot near their pitched tents. A thin, short, dark-skinned woman stood off to the side wearing a crimson-stained khaki jacket. Karen slammed on her brakes and made a sudden U-turn.

The woman in the khaki jacket gave her a wide-eyed stare and started to run. Driving closer, Karen confirmed her initial suspicion. The front of the jacket was stained with what appeared to be blood. She continued the pursuit by car until the woman veered off into the weeds and brush.

"Yo…" Karen yelled, now on foot. With each passing second, she lost ground. *Damn it.*

The woman was agile and navigated the rough terrain with ease.

Karen slowed, gasping for air. "Police. Stop." She bent over with hands on her knees when a flash appeared from the corner of her left side.

"I got this." Riley sprinted by like a gazelle, closing in on the woman who was also winded and slowing.

Karen watched as Riley grabbed hold of the woman's shoulder, putting an end to the pursuit.

"Fucking middle age," Karen muttered. "Where—" she said, sucking in oxygen as she caught up to the two of them. "Where did you get that jacket?" Her words came out staccato as she worked to slow her breathing.

"I didn't steal it," the woman said, glancing at the badge on Karen's belt with a panicked look. "It was in the bushes. By the fence." She pointed to a weed-filled area on the opposite side of a chain-link fence separating the homeless tents from the wooded area.

"Listen," Karen explained, finally regaining her breath. "We're not accusing you of anything. We need to examine this jacket…and to ask you a few questions. In town. Okay?"

"I didn't steal no jacket."

"When did you find it?" Riley asked.

"Couple days ago." She looked away. "Cliff used to wear it."

Karen shot Riley a look.

"He left it on the fence when he wasn't wearing it. It started raining…" The woman looked down. "Well…Cliff wasn't gonna use it no more. So I got it for myself. Found it on the ground…other side of the fence."

Officer Mott pulled up. Karen informed him she needed the woman transported to the station for questioning and the jacket preserved as evidence.

"Before you go," Karen said to the woman. "Show us exactly where you found this jacket."

The woman walked the three of them back to the lot with tents. She pointed out where Cliff would lay the jacket on the fence and then pointed to an overgrown area on the opposite side where she claimed to have found it.

Karen nodded to Mott. "Get her something to eat. We'll be back shortly."

Karen and Riley examined the overgrown area where the jacket had been found. Discarded garbage, a few car tires, and a handful of dirty, torn articles of clothing were strewn about.

"Clear to see how someone could have found a perfectly good jacket out here," Karen said.

"But she *knew* it was Cliff's—knew exactly where he left it," Riley said.

"Can't say that makes her guilty of murder." Karen tried to envision this woman, around Riley's height, thrusting a six-inch knife into a six-foot man.

Back at the station, the afternoon crept toward evening. Riley plopped her solid frame on a chair in Karen's office. They'd spoken with the woman who found Cliff's jacket, and with her statement complete and signed, she was driven back and the jacket was en route to the crime lab.

"I don't get it," Riley said. "Let's assume the stains on the jacket are blood. Then what? Our perp killed Cliff and then took the time to pry the bloody jacket off him and walk it back to the homeless area to discard it behind the fence?"

Karen pulled off her reading glasses and tossed the woman's statement onto her desk. "If that were the case, we'd have more than one partial footprint. The perp would've stepped all through the area where Cliff was lying."

A slow, methodic nod from Riley.

"There'd be no other way to get the jacket off him," Karen said.

"So, our attacker couldn't have removed the jacket."

"Or anyone else. And there was no damage to the jacket. If Cliff was wearing it, wouldn't there be a hole or some sort of cuts on the front where the knife penetrated it?"

The two stared at each other and then spoke in unison. "Let's wait to hear from the lab."

The next morning, Karen arrived to see Riley sitting across from her desk, bright and early. "Christ, she must've been in the military," she grumbled, realizing her day was off to a shotgun start.

In reality, Riley had never been in the military, but she did come from a military family. Her father and two older brothers served, which led to a childhood of regularly relocating throughout the country. Karen believed this enabled Riley to feel comfortable moving from police department to police department throughout her career while she, in contrast, felt nauseated at the mere thought of leaving Parks Ford.

Karen forced a smile. "Understand we've had a number of cranks admitting to it."

Riley chuckled. "Not one of them knows we have a partial footprint without key distinguishing marks. Without that, we know they're full of shit."

Karen let out a light chuckle. "How'd it go with Tam yesterday?"

"Talked with her after Bobby headed to work..." Riley paused. "Does she even work?"

Karen answered with a nonchalant shrug.

"She held to her earlier statement. Didn't hear anything after going to bed."

Karen sat, silent, waiting for more.

"Checked out her bedroom. From her window, there's a clear view of the area between the two homes, but no view of the front of the house or driveway." Riley frowned. "I guess I'm not completely comfortable with Tam not hearing anything."

Karen fiddled with the pen on her desk. "The weapon was thrown. What would she have heard? A thud?"

Riley nodded with an expressionless face.

"So, what now?"

"Wanna give Kenny a try?"

"Let's do it."

Pulling up in front of a dilapidated house in the middle of a quiet, unassuming, middle-class residential neighborhood, Karen and Riley strolled past the cracked, weed-clotted concrete driveway to the left of his slovenly front yard. This time, Doyle's white sedan was sitting on it.

Doyle grizzled as he peeked through the front door window to Riley's and Karen's badges.

"I'm guessing he's not very welcoming of police," Riley said with a grin.

"Plus, not one, but two women...one being Black."

"I love bigotry. Bring it." Riley flashed a confident smile.

Karen chuckled. "You'll pick away at Kenny and Doyle like a Thanksgiving turkey after the meal is complete."

Riley fought an outright laugh, but a snort still managed to escape.

Doyle scowled, stepping aside to let them in. The heavy odor of cigarette smoke hung in the air, wafting over dated furniture and aging spot-ridden brown carpeting.

"We're here to speak with Kenny," Karen said.

He clumsily shuffled into the kitchen, his pot-bellied torso stacked on top of legs befitting a football linebacker. Kenny sat at a scuffed-up wooden table, a sour look pasted across his pale face. Doyle plunked down on a wooden chair next to Kenny.

Karen scowled. "We need to talk with Kenny alone."

Kenny shrugged as if not desiring any unnecessary issues with the law. He waved a hand. Doyle had been dismissed.

Karen noticed how weathered and fatigued Kenny's face had become. His graying dark-brown hair desperately needed a cut and styling.

"Kenny," she began. "Can you tell me where you were Friday night?"

"Home. Both me and Doyle. We was right here." He sounded annoyed.

"Why are you so angry with that question?"

"I've been staying out of trouble. I'm moving on with my life." His flabby belly jiggled as he protested.

"Kenny, a man died on the driveway of your old home late Friday night."

"I don't want no trouble. No drama." Kenny's voice was a bellow.

"Any idea who might want to hurt someone in that neighborhood?" Karen studied his face. "I know it's been years, but you know the neighborhood."

He shook his head and began fidgeting in his chair.

Doyle walked back in. "It was a homeless guy, for Christ's sake. No one likes 'em. Plenty of reasons for someone to go after one of them. As far as I'm concerned, one less homeless dude pissing all over the hood is a good thing." His tone, gruff and assaulting.

Karen and Riley exchanged looks.

"Like maybe you, Jack?" Riley said. Even someone husky like Jack Doyle didn't intimidate her. She was tiny but tough.

"Me? Fuck no. We're almost a mile from there."

"You have a car," Karen said matter-of-factly. "Why so much hate toward those people?"

"They're lazy. Make that neighborhood look bad."

This, from a man with a rusted-out, broken-down vehicle in his front yard trashing up the neighborhood. It was clear to Karen that Doyle was a man filled with a boatload of hate who attacked anyone different from him. Adding on to this, his use of projection served to divert attention from his own flaws. It shocked her that he hadn't taken shots at their gender or Riley's race. *Probably knows better.*

"Jack, you just said you live a mile away, so why do you care how they live or how that neighborhood looks?" Karen asked.

"I got friends there. They all hate 'em."

That countered everything the people on Hillside had said. Karen noted Doyle's apparent familiarity with the neighborhood and the supposed "friends" he had there. But for now, they needed to talk to Kenny.

"If you can't allow us to talk to Kenny without interruptions, we'll have no choice but to bring him into the station."

Something on Kenny's face prompted Doyle to back off. With one childlike huff, he pivoted and left the room.

"Kenny," Karen said. "Do you have any idea who may have hurt someone in that neighborhood?"

"Youse know I haven't lived there in ten years. Don't even know who's over there no more."

"Your friend Doyle says he has friends there. How 'bout you?" Riley jumped in.

Kenny let out an exasperated snicker. "No one there wants nothin' to do with me no more."

"What about the homeless people…did you ever deal with them when you lived there?" Karen probed.

"Weren't there then. And that lot they're squatting in used to be a store…a nice store…with an owner that kept up the place, ya know. That neighborhood's gone to shit."

"When was the last time you were there?" Riley asked.

Karen was pleased with the question. She couldn't ask it because she had been there the day he stopped by. She noted his uncomfortable and agitated mannerisms.

"Last week. Day I got released. Ain't been back since."

"Okay. How about the Stewart James or Grimaldi's? Been there lately?" Riley knew these were the two local hangouts close to that neighborhood.

"How the fuck is that your business where I go? My parole says I'm allowed to live my life."

"It's a simple question," Karen said.

Kenny dropped his head and stared at his lap. "Don't drink no more. I'm stayin' out of bars."

Has he really changed, or is this just a distraction?

"Your buddy Doyle seems to think those homeless people have no right to live in that neighborhood—or maybe he thinks they have no right to live at all. Is that your opinion, too?" Karen's question brought a glare from Kenny.

"I'm just trying to keep my nose clean. I don't got no opinion."

"But you just said those homeless people living there have made the neighborhood go to shit…your words, not mine."

"Just think it can't be good." Kenny softened his tone. "I don't got nothing against them. I don't know 'em. Just think it's not good for the neighborhood, ya know?"

"Okay, Kenny." She handed him her card. "Thank you for your time. If you hear anything, we could use your help. Give us a call, okay?" She glanced around the slovenly kitchen, dirty dishes and containers comingled with mail and newspapers, trying to make out any Glitterati candies amidst the debris.

"Yo, Doyle. Same thing. You hear anything, you let us know." She handed him her card.

Doyle scoffed, snatching it from her hand. He tossed it on the cluttered countertop, then wiped the same hand on his pant leg. Karen smirked, letting him know she had noticed.

Back at the car, Karen turned to Riley. "Thoughts?"

"Doyle's still a nasty jerk and hates the homeless. Motive? Maybe. But we'll need a whole lot more," Riley said. "Said he has friends in that neighborhood. Seems too coincidental to me."

Karen tilted her head, looking out her side window. "It's a small town, Riley. People know people everywhere."

At the station, the clerk at the front desk promptly handed Karen a message before she made it five steps into the building. New information from the Trace Evidence Unit. The detectives' presence was requested.

The forensics lab was housed in the county building, a short walk across the parking lot from the station. The detectives hustled over. The stains on the khaki jacket were, indeed, human blood. And the blood matched their victim. Blood from other sources was not found.

A synthetic fiber was identified, a single, yellow-brown nylon strand. Hair samples were also found. That information was not as clear-cut. Some hair fibers matched the victim, leading to the question: who was wearing the jacket when Cliff was killed? Cliff wasn't wearing it when they found him. It appeared evident that the only way massive amounts of Cliff's blood could saturate the outside of the jacket was if the perpetrator was wearing it.

Two additional hair samples were found. At some point, other people had worn this jacket. The second hair sample was identified as belonging to the homeless woman wearing it the day before. The next step would be a DNA analysis of the third sample. But even with an intact hair fiber sample, finding a DNA match would be challenging and time-consuming. Unlike TV shows or movies, this was not a process that typically happened in a matter of minutes, or even hours.

Karen pivoted to head back to her office.

Trace scientist Adam Carver called out, "I have more."

Karen and Riley froze midstep. Carver had information about the white long-sleeved T-shirt that Cliff was wearing when he was attacked. The T-shirt had one ripped opening in the front, consistent with where the knife would have penetrated it. There was also a tear, approximately two inches long, where the collar met the top of the left shoulder. *Was the attacker on the left side of Cliff and pulling at the shirt?* The cast-off stain and the partial footprint had all been on the right side of the bloody path. *Two attackers? One grabbed Cliff on the left and one delivered the fatal blow on the right?* The next piece of news leveled Karen.

"On the left sleeve, Serology identified blood from a second individual," Carver said. "It's been sent to Biology for a potential match."

The news she had hoped for. Find a match and they had their suspect.

"There's more," Carver continued. "Embedded on the left sleeve of the shirt were two silver specks. One layer contained polyurethane, melamine, and styrene. The second layer consisted of acrylic, melamine, and styrene."

Karen shot Riley a blank stare.

"Automotive paint?" Riley asked.

Carver gave her an admiring, definitive nod, then launched into a detailed dissertation on auto-body paint. "The paint chips can vary but are usually comprised of four layers. A typical automotive paint-layer system contains a topcoat of clear and base color layers in addition to one or two primer layers between the base coat and sheet metal."

Karen felt her head begin to swirl. *I don't recall this in the Detective's Manual.*

"The first primer layer is a clear acrylic coat that includes polyurethane, melamine, and styrene. It's directly applied to the metal. The second primer layer consists of acrylic, melamine, and styrene, providing a smooth surface layer for the paint layers. Then, there's the color coat and the final layer…a clear protective coat. In auto-body work, microscopic abrasives containing silica, rust, and methylene chloride from sanding coat-painted surfaces exist." Carver finally took a breath. "The specks we found are consistent with paint chips with only a partial-layer structure—the two primer layers."

"So, our victim worked in an auto-body shop?" Riley's rhetorical question was bathed in sarcasm.

"It certainly appears that, at least in some capacity, he worked with automotive paint," Carver said.

"He didn't work," Karen said. "He was homeless. Nothing but a handful of change in his pockets when he died. Could those paint specks have been transferred to the victim's clothing during the attack?"

"The specks were embedded in the fabric. The attacker would have had to have direct contact and vigorously rub against the victim," Carver said. "I can't rule it out, though."

"When do you think we'll get a match on the blood on the sleeve?" Karen asked.

"Hopefully, by tomorrow."

"What about the single partial shoe print?"

"Not enough to work with. Barely two inches on the print and absolutely no distinguishing marks to create a potential match."

The obscure second shoe print had been to the right of Cliff's shoe prints. The blood on Cliff's sleeve was on the left. If they could match the second shoe print, they might be able to identify an additional attacker.

Riley let out a sigh. "Looks like we have more than one attacker."

"It definitely looks like more than one person at the scene with Cliff," Karen said.

"Doyle's issue with the homeless and his supposed friends over there…" Riley said. "Looks questionable."

"One of them work in auto body?" Carver asked.

Karen shrugged. "Let's wait for a match on the blood. Anything else?"

"That's it." Carver's wide Cheshire cat grin punctuated his statement.

It was enough. They headed back to Karen's office—silent—with a torrent of new information.

Riley broke the silence. "What do you make of the specks of automotive paint?"

"Can't figure it." Karen felt a need to tread carefully with her next few words. "Bobby works at an auto-body shop. But if Bobby was the attacker, wouldn't he have been wearing the shirt…not Cliff?"

"That's the part that doesn't add up," Riley said.

Karen flopped into her desk chair. "We still need to reach out to Cliff's brother, Keith. And those Glitterati wrappers. Everyone we've interviewed…those candies are practically nonexistent."

Riley shrugged. "Are we sure our perp dropped them?"

"They were right in the middle of our crime scene, feet from the vic's head…"

"Yeah, yeah, I get ya." Riley paused. "Look, we've still got people to interview. They could still pop up. And we're also waiting on that bandana."

Karen groaned. She knew that forensic geology results took weeks to months.

Riley headed back to her office at the county courthouse while Karen culled through the boxes of pawn shop files. She pulled out the binders, one after another, with their lingering cigarette stench. Sifting through the pages of notes and receipts, she was certain her office was beginning to smell like a smoky pool hall, or an ashtray… or both.

Identification of the second bloodstain on the T-shirt—it'll break the case wide open. She stared at her office phone as if willing it to ring.

Karen realized it was time to stop avoiding the inevitable—time for a visit with Bobby. As an added perk, she might even get to see Tam. She realized she was starting to enjoy the attention that Tam showered her with in private. But, first and foremost, she reminded herself, she needed to confront Bobby.

CHAPTER TWELVE

When Karen's SUV glided to a stop on Hillside, Bobby was sitting on the front porch, nursing a beer.

She joined him on the top step of the porch. "I need a little more information about the knives you pawned. Any idea when you pawned them? A month? The year?"

"It was ten goddamn years ago. All I remember is it was shortly after Dad went to jail. I had to pay the mortgage."

Karen listened intently, pulling out her notepad.

"You gonna charge me for selling off my father's knives?"

Karen fought back a grin. "I need this information to check the pawn shop records."

Bobby stared straight ahead.

"Did you ever go back? Ever get any of those knives back—"

Bobby's grimace cut her off midsentence. "I did not go back. I did not get one damn knife back. I hated them."

The pale-blue sky morphed into shades of yellow, orange, and pink as the sun began to set.

"A few more questions. Do you remember picking up a matchbook at Grimaldi's the night you were out with your friends?"

He shrugged. "Possible."

"Where would you have put it?"

"My pocket, I suppose."

"Pant pocket, jacket pocket?"

"Most likely my jacket pocket."

"Do you still have it?"

"There's nothing in my jacket. Just cleaned out my pockets yesterday." He looked at Karen. "Nothing there."

Could've been there. Fell out when he got out of Vince's car. She reprimanded herself as she struggled to stay neutral.

"Bobby, could I look at your jacket?" She knew if the matchbook fell out of his pocket during an attack, traces of blood would likely be on the jacket—or a clear attempt to clean it.

"Yeah, it's in the laundry basket. I'll go get it."

The laundry basket. Clean or dirty? This is critical. Please, Bobby, have it still be dirty.

When Bobby returned, it was evident it hadn't been laundered. It smelled of his cologne and had dirt stains on the elbows. She examined it and considered taking it as evidence. But unless there were clear signs of blood spray or spatter—even a small drop—he couldn't have been wearing it and brutally stabbed someone. Nothing. "Thanks, Bobby. Appreciate your help."

Karen stood up. "Is Tam home?" The question came out before she could catch herself.

Bobby motioned with his head toward the front door. "It's unlocked."

Karen walked into the entryway and called out to Tam. From the kitchen, Tam bounded down the hall, sporting an alluring smile the entire way.

"Hey. Just stopped by to ask your brother a few questions. Thought I'd pop in to see how you're doing."

"I'm good. How are you?" Tam gave Karen an A-frame hug. "Want a beer?"

"I'm good. Need to get home…but since I was out here, I wanted to check in on you."

"One beer," Tam insisted. "I promise…just one."

Karen smiled. "I'm still on duty."

Tam rolled her eyes. "Water it is," she said with a joking annoyance. "Wanna sit out front? We can watch the sunset."

"Let's just sit in here." She motioned to the kitchen table. "How much do you remember about your father's knife display?"

"I remember seeing them. Bothered me, but not like my brother."

"Did you ever touch them or play with them?"

Tam wrinkled her nose. "Ew, no. Besides, my dad kept a lock on it. Bobby must have broken the lock after Dad was gone."

Karen kept her notepad tucked away but mentally noted Tam's comment. She shifted the subject. "Have you given any thought to what you're going to do next?"

Tam squinted. "Next?"

"Yeah. After New York being too expensive. Are you planning to stay here? Will you get a job in town? What are your plans?"

"Kare, I'm an artist. I make pottery and sell it."

"Yeah, I got that…sorta. Where will you sell your work? Will you stay here and do that?" She had no idea what it was like to work at something other than a typical nine-to-five career job.

"For now. If it works out for me here, yeah…I'll stay here." Tam's eyes met Karen's. A charming smile rolled over her face.

"Have you sold any of your work here?"

"Geez, what is this? The grand inquisition?" Tam's tone held a lighthearted sarcasm. "I feel like I'm one of your suspects."

Karen rolled her eyes. "You wouldn't know what it's like to be one of my suspects. You don't know the half of it."

"True. And I hope to never find out." Tam grinned. "You're a hard-ass."

Karen chuckled. "I'm just wondering if you have a plan for yourself. Eventually, you're going to have to do something."

"I know. I will." Tam's smile disappeared.

How did she make it in New York without a steady source of income? "You must have done well for yourself in New York."

"Pretty well."

"Well, clearly you did well. You have a nice Mini Cooper. You don't buy those on *my* salary." Karen's tone sat somewhere between jest and jealousy. "I must've gone into the wrong line of work." She shot Tam a smile.

Tam fidgeted and avoided eye contact.

Not my business. Karen got up. "Lucky you, my bottle is empty so the grand inquisition has concluded."

"I promised I'd let you go after one drink, and I'll be true to my word." Tam paused as if hoping Karen would change her mind.

Let me go? I'll damn well go when I want. Karen nodded and headed for the door.

At the door, Tam reached up and gently grabbed Karen's cheeks with both hands. In a flash, it was over before Karen could react. A simple kiss. Nothing passionate. But it was something Karen had never experienced before. Soft lips. No facial hair. Gentle.

She felt something, but not anything she could articulate. Something she couldn't understand or rationalize. She longed for physical intimacy, but this was not what she imagined. She didn't feel that kind of draw to Tam. *Or do I?*

Karen reached for the doorknob. "Have a—" The words gurgled in the back of her throat. She cleared it and tried again. "Have a great night."

"You, too." Tam seemed suddenly subdued.

In her car, Karen threw her head back and closed her eyes. *What the fuck are you doing?* Her heart raced. Her mind skipped around, chasing emotion after enigmatic emotion. Tam's kiss felt nice. But something was off. She struggled to put her finger on it. The attention from Tam was delightful. She loved her personality. So, what was bothering her?

Is it that she's a woman? Caiden had lots of gay and lesbian friends. *I loved every one of them.* She started the car. *Am I only open-minded when it's about other people?* The thought embarrassed her. *No, I just don't have feelings for Tam...I think.* She put the car in gear and headed down Hillside.

She knew she enjoyed the attention that Tam showered on her. After all, she wasn't getting those needs met with anyone else. As much as she was flattered, she also knew there was no way in hell anything could happen with Tam—for professional reasons if nothing else. *Keep your professional boundaries clear.* She nodded to herself at that final thought and headed home.

Thursday began with hope for DNA results, either from the third hair sample on the khaki jacket or the blood on Cliff's sleeve. Those hopes were quickly dashed. Karen moved on to researching Cliff's brother, Keith.

Based on her conversation with Cliff's mother, she knew Keith was aware of Cliff's hardships and had stopped by at his mother's behest to bring Cliff money. Recalling the pictures, she understood Keith to be about Cliff's height, with a shaved head. He was a muscular version of Cliff, with the same smile that Karen vaguely remembered. Cliff had an altercation with "a tall, bald, white guy," and Karen suspected it was Keith.

With her office phone silent, she grabbed her blazer and headed out. Passing through the noisy squad room, she glanced at the young rookie officer from the crime scene. Officer Perkins. She noted his lackadaisical manner, tipping his chair onto its back legs while holding his balance with his fingertips on his desk. *Is this what he thinks police work is…a chance to lounge around and get paid?* She shook her head with irritation, feeling the urge to tip his chair over.

Perkins beamed. Bright brown eyes popped out of his ghostly pale face. "Good morning, Detective."

Passing his desk, she stopped in her tracks. In slow motion, she pivoted. Stone-faced, she stared. His wide smile faded.

"You eat these mints?" She pointed to a palm-sized pile of purple-and-turquoise wrappers scattered on his desk.

Perkins beamed as if relishing the recognition Karen was giving him. "Yes, ma'am. Ever since I gave up smoking. Would you like one?"

"Were you eating these on Saturday at the crime scene?"

His chair teetered, almost toppling over. He gathered his balance and sat upright. "Maybe."

"Where did you put the wrappers?"

"My pocket." His voice quivered.

Karen's jaw tensed. "You sure? Cuz we have two of those wrappers. They're marked as Evidence Marker Twenty-two and Twenty-three."

He flushed as she leaned onto his desk and lowered herself eye to eye with him. "So, either you contaminated my crime scene, or you're our perp."

He sat frozen. The room became deathly silent.

The sound of her fist echoed as she slammed it onto his desk. "Fucking idiot. You contaminated my crime scene, you goddamn rookie." She fought to bite her tongue. "Get your shit together."

His pale face splotched with patches of rose.

"You goddamn well better hope you didn't leave any prints or hair fibers. You'll be my number one suspect." She took three steps from his desk and turned back around. "And get that smug look off your face."

Fuming, she stormed out to the parking lot. Her cell phone vibrated as she hit the steps. She was too irate to deal with it. *What a fucking moron. No one told him to keep his hands in his pockets? Why would anyone have to? Did he sleep through his training?*

"Goddamn it! We've been spinning our wheels over those goddamn wrappers. Idiot," she said to no one in particular.

Climbing into her SUV, she caught her breath and pulled out her cell to check for a message.

A text from Tam. *Jesus Christ. This day is going down the shit chute.* In an earlier moment of concern, or weakness, or both, Karen had given Tam her personal cell. Tam was now taking advantage of Karen's professional lapse. It was a friendly text—just a quick good morning—but Karen was in no mood. She threw the phone onto the passenger seat.

It would be less than an hour's drive to Keith's house in Salem, New Jersey. A pleasant drive past miles of South Jersey tomato farms, produce stands, and the Heritage family vineyards and wine-tasting room. Karen was finally getting her emotions in check when Riley touched base.

"You're driving," Riley said. "Where ya headed?"

"Beautiful Salem, New Jersey," Karen said with sarcasm. "Cliff's brother, Keith. Something I should have done earlier. Any news on your end?"

"A couple of hits on people who purchased our knife. So far, they're all willing to show proof of possession. Any news on a DNA match?"

"Not yet. But I do have a hit on the Glitterati wrappers."

"Really?" Riley's tone perked up. "Where? Who?"

"A fucking moron rookie cop at the crime scene that morning. He dropped his wrappers on the driveway."

"How'd you discover *that*?"

"Walked by his desk this morning. He's all chipper, just hanging out in the squad room. Noticed the wrappers…right there…in the middle of his damn desk." Karen cringed at the animosity she heard in her voice. She had been a rookie—decades ago—and recalled how it felt. She had been brutally unkind to the officer and even more unkind describing him to Riley. Something else was grating at her to cause this level of reaction.

Riley could no longer conceal her laughter, which helped Karen.

"So, needless to say, we don't have to keep searching for those mints," Karen said.

"The DNA and hair fiber evidence will be much more fruitful. Trust me," Riley said. "I'll keep plugging away on my end. Let me know what you come up with in Salem."

As noon approached, Karen pulled onto the packed gravel that served as a driveway. The air was still. Silent. Barely a leaf moved on the surrounding trees. She walked across the gravel to the weathered front door, tapping on it three times. No sign of movement inside.

She walked around the tattered three-bedroom rancher, eyeing the peeling white paint on the wooden window frames. *Sad. This house has seen better days.* The house was wrapped in white six-inch aluminum siding, popular in the 1950s. Now, that stylish siding had dents, scrapes, and stains. Aging red shutters framed the windows, one in the front dangling by a single nail. A five-foot square cement pad created a patio to the side of the front entry, with a plastic chair and a rusting table topped with an ashtray overflowing with cigarette butts. The gutters of the one-story home had weeds and tree seedlings growing out of them. Hard to imagine anyone lived there except for the fresh nature of the cigarette butts.

At the back of the house, an old three-hundred-gallon oil tank sat, presumably filled with oil to heat the house. At the far back of the yard was a dilapidated storage shed perilously leaning to one side. Karen completed her full walk around the house before peeking into the front window. A queen mattress took up the entire living room with two other mattresses leaning up against the wall. Piles and piles of books, pictures, and knickknacks lined the walls. Someone definitely lived there, just not in the manner she was accustomed to. A chill ran up her spine thinking about sitting inside to conduct an interview.

Homes in the area were spread out over large lots. An old brick house sat a good two hundred feet to her right. To her left about fifty yards away, and across the two-lane, forty-five-miles-per-hour highway, was a farmhouse with produce growing in the back fields. She left her car in Keith's gravel driveway and trekked to the farmhouse. She wondered if the neighbors remembered the Stephenson family back when they all lived there.

The farmhouse was in much better shape, as were most of the other homes in the area. Same era, but better maintained. The Seventh-day Adventist Church sat just down the street from Keith's place and the farmhouse.

The church was probably the only thing that resembled a typical setting in Parks Ford. Homes in her neighborhood were packed closer together with a suburban feel. She couldn't recall one home in Parks Ford that didn't have a paved driveway. She tapped on the front screen door of the farmhouse. A middle-aged man, overalls covered in dirt, walked to the door. *Lord, I'm definitely in the sticks.*

"Ma'am," the man said before Karen could pull out her badge. "Oh, Officer."

"Detective."

He nodded.

She inquired about Keith Stephenson.

"Yep. A man named Keith lives there. Whole family used to be there." He glanced away. "Sad what happened." Other than the family history, the farmer didn't have much to share.

Karen walked around to the handful of other houses dotting the highway. They, too, knew Keith, and some neighbors vaguely remembered Cliff. They all knew the family history. Not to her surprise, people at the church had never seen Keith attending services. The best information she obtained was that Keith usually didn't arrive home from work until after six in the evening.

Back at Keith's house, she wedged her card between the front door edge and the doorjamb. In her car, her cell phone blinked with a number of new texts: one from her mother, one from Judy, and three more from Tam—just saying hi. She tossed the phone onto the passenger seat. The messages could wait. More importantly, she needed to decide how to deal with the one-liners coming from Tam—a woman she had no business socializing with, at least until this investigation was complete.

She drove past the farmhouse, the scent of manure hitting her nostrils. As much as she could never see herself living in this area, there was something special about the virtually empty two-lane roads, the open fields of farm produce, and a meandering stream here and there. It infused her with a sense of peace as she drove along.

By late afternoon, Karen was back in her office banging out the pawn shop receipts. She sneered at the worn binders annoyed over their never-ending stench. After a few hours, she reached for a diversion with her cell phone.

"Hey, babe. How's it going up there?"

"It's cray! I love this place. I'm meeting so many amazing people."

Karen could hear the exuberance in her daughter's voice. She beamed with pride.

"How's everything there?" Caiden asked.

"Still not many leads. It's been a grind."

Caiden groaned. "Mom, you've totally got this. You'll figure it out. You always do." She changed the subject. "I heard Judy's got a new guy…anyone new for you?"

Karen was silent.

"Mom, I just think it would be great if you could get out and just meet more people. I know you…you start in on a case, and your whole social life goes in the toilet. Just think about it. It's not like a date would kill you."

Karen found her mind floating off in a direction that caught her off guard. "There's a woman from here that used to live in New York City. She's an artist. Maybe you can meet her when you come home." The words escaped with immediate regret setting in. *What am I thinking? There's almost a sixteen-year age difference between them.*

"Why do you always change the subject when I bring up dating?"

"I didn't. I just thought—" *What* was *I thinking?* Karen fumbled. The suggestion of dating had made her think of Tam. *Oh, God.*

"Thanks, Mom, but I'm good." Caiden started to giggle.

I miss that giggle. Karen heard a doorbell in the background.

"Gotta run. You take care, okay? And get out and date someone."

She stared at her phone, then glanced at the stinky binders. With a queasy feeling, she dialed Miles's number. After four rings, it went to voice mail. She struggled to discern her feelings. Anger? Yes. Sadness? A little. And a little relief, too. *Relief?*

She threw the binders back in their yellowed cardboard box and headed home. *Please, God, give us something to go on tomorrow.*

CHAPTER THIRTEEN

The next day, Karen and Riley scoured the last of the pawn shop records. Not one of Bobby's pawned knives matched their murder weapon. Another dead end—no different from how the week began.

"The question is, did Kenny not own an Ek Commando and, therefore, Bobby couldn't pawn it, or did Kenny own one but Bobby hung on to it?" Riley said.

"Why on earth would he hang on to that particular knife?" Karen said, exasperated. "For what reason? He hated those knives."

"If Kenny owned that knife, then we know Bobby kept it."

"Or got rid of it somewhere else. And we know Tam didn't take it. Her father was still in the house guarding his precious collection before she moved." Karen heard the defensiveness in her voice. "All right. I'll swing by Bobby's this afternoon. Show him a picture of the weapon. See how he reacts."

"We need to do the same with Kenny."

Yes. The man with the violent past. He's more likely to be the one we should suspect.

"Any word from Keith?" Riley asked.

"Of course not. Didn't expect him to call. You should've seen his place."

"That bad, huh?"

Karen shook her head. "Joey Murphy. Still a little guarded with the preliminary. Too eager to pin everything on Kenny…knew of the knives at Bobby's house. His mother said he had spots of blood on his work pants."

"Let's plan another trip to his house. See what he says," Riley suggested.

"About the blood?"

"The blood and a potential alibi for Friday night."

"He's suspicious," Karen said. "Not sure I see him as a suspect, though."

"We can rule that out after we speak with him."

Karen gave a nod to Riley's blank stare and matter-of-fact tone. "Next steps?"

"Figured I'd give it a go with Frank Ryanard. Wanna join, or should I go solo?" Riley asked.

"If you're good going alone, I'd appreciate it. Want to wrap up these files."

"You got it. Call you when I'm done."

Karen rubbed her forehead and reviewed the global shots from the crime scene. A detail caught her eye. She had disregarded the possibility of the yellow-and-black bandana being dropped by the perpetrator, leaning into the assumption that it belonged to Cliff. It was filthy. Completely covered with debris. Looking at her own photographs, she realized how far it sat from the blood trail. *Too far. A good three feet from Cliff's shoe prints.*

"That was definitely dropped by our perp," she muttered. "Why did I dismiss that?"

Grabbing her office phone, she dialed the forensic geologist in State College, Pennsylvania. Geological studies typically took weeks to months, but she needed the information now. *This is critical. It could blow things wide open.*

Six regional forensic labs existed in the Commonwealth. Luckily, the one in southeastern Pennsylvania was situated right across the parking lot. But geological studies had to be sent to State College. She urged them to rush the processing of the bandana.

Karen kicked her drawer closed and hoisted her foot onto the corner of her desk. Mulling over potential suspects and motives, she found her mind curiously drifting to Frank Ryanard. Deep down, she didn't see a bitter, sixty-eight-year-old man going after a homeless person so viciously. Joey. She remembered his eyes revealing an odd nervousness when she was at Fran's house. Both men were suspicious, but she couldn't wrap her head around calling them potential suspects. Then there was Doyle. He was the one who ate at her. *Friends in that neighborhood? More than one attacker?*

Her thoughts wandered. Emotionally, she knew she was battling loneliness. At the same time, she felt an odd draw to Tam in a way she couldn't understand. Definitive answers hallmarked her career. It also spilled over into her personal life. With Tam, she had nothing close to definitive.

Karen glanced at her watch. *Bobby should be home by now. If not, Tam will be. She's always home. She doesn't work, as Riley so bluntly pointed out.*

At Bobby's place, the door sprung open with Tam's bright face greeting her. Karen fought back a smile.

"Is Bobby here?"

"No, but I am." Tam took Karen's hand and guided her into the house. "He's still at work."

"I need to ask you a few questions, Tam."

Tam's face tightened. "Why do you always have to talk about the case? Why can't you just stay in the moment with me?"

Karen felt her jaw drop, completely caught off guard by Tam's brazenness.

Tam motioned for Karen to follow her to the kitchen. She reached for the freshly brewed pot of coffee. "You look like a tough, no-nonsense cop who takes her coffee black."

"Guess I have a soft side with a touch of nonsense. I'll take mine with cream." Karen smirked.

Tam returned with two mugs.

"You spoil me," Karen said as she took a sip.

"This? This isn't spoiling. Now if I brought you breakfast in bed, that would be spoiling." Tam winked.

Karen almost spit out her first sip.

Her gaze shifted from Tam to texts from Riley. "Excuse me." She held up a finger and put on her reading glasses.

Tam pursed her lips, her mood clearly soured. With each text, Tam became more agitated. She gazed up at the ceiling, then propped her head up with her fist. "You're never present for me when you come over. It's always talk about the case."

Karen stared at her, dumbfounded. "Tam. That's what I do. Why does it bother you so much?"

"It frightens me. Hearing the whole murder thing over and over. It's nothing for you—" She threw her arms in the air with futility. "But I've never dealt with anything like this before."

"Give me a minute." Karen finished texting Riley.

Tam snickered.

"What?"

"You wear reading glasses."

"Yeah. It's an age thing."

"It looks cute. But I like this better." Tam reached over and removed the glasses. "Your eyes are too pretty to hide."

Karen felt a novel and strange sensation run through her body. A warmth she couldn't articulate. She looked up at Tam, her face profiled as the sun hit a low angle through the kitchen window. It had been so long since someone had flirted with her—had fought to capture her attention or had fussed over her.

Her heart rate accelerated as she struggled to shift the conversation. Yet, aside from an unexplained draw to Tam, nothing flowed. An odd feeling: not really wanting to be there but also not wanting to leave. *Is this just a symptom of loneliness and enjoying her attention?* She floundered, unsure how to react.

"I read about your police department having a big fundraiser for the homeless," Tam said.

"Yeah. We do. Every year. Around the holidays."

"Well, I thought—especially in light of everything—I might donate one of my pottery pieces. It could be auctioned off. Seventy to eighty dollars."

Karen smiled. *She really is a good person.* "That would be nice. Thanks, Tam."

Bobby walked in at that moment, his shirt and face covered with work debris. His shoulders sagged at the sight of Karen.

"Sorry to pounce on you the minute you walk in the door," Karen said, "but the sooner I ask my questions, the sooner I'll be on my way. Deal?"

Bobby shrugged, walked to the refrigerator, and grabbed a beer. Twisting off the cap, he leaned against the countertop.

She pulled out the picture of the murder weapon. "I just need to check. Does this knife look familiar at all?"

Bobby looked at the picture. A long, hard look.

"It's really hard to say. To me, they all looked the same. I know some were supposed to be collector's pieces, but I wouldn't know one from the other."

He was answering her questions with calm ease.

"When I brought them in, the guy gave me the same price for all of them. But at that point, beggars can't be choosers, ya know."

She turned to Tam. "Do you recall any of your father's knives?"

Tam took the sheet of paper, squinting. "This doesn't look familiar at all. But like Bob, I really didn't spend time looking at them."

"Thank you…both…for your help."

"You any closer to finding the guy?" Bobby asked.

"We hope to make an arrest soon." Karen's autopilot response. She couldn't talk about the case to him, or anyone. Her pat response seemed to suffice.

"Bobby. You always get that dirty at work?" Karen looked his clothes up and down.

She patted his back. Dust particles flew off, illuminated by the sunlight. *Cliff's shirt. Specks of paint.* She grabbed a paper towel and wiped the hand she used to pat Bobby's back, then tucked the paper towel into her bag.

Tam laughed. "You can throw it in our garbage can."

Karen smiled. "All good. I'll chuck it when I get home." She headed for the front door.

Tam followed like a toddler following her mother. She grabbed Karen's upper arm and drew her close. Her soft lips landed a kiss on Karen's mouth.

Karen twisted out of Tam's grasp and offered a strained smile before escaping out the front door.

Back in her car, Karen tried to make sense of everything. *She's harmless. You're just frightened.* Her thoughts froze on this concept. *Am I frightened of the unknown, or is this really heading down a road I don't want to be on?* Her thoughts were interrupted by a call from Riley.

"What happened with Frank Ryanard?" Karen asked.

"He was about as helpful as a stubborn mule. He's such an ass."

"A very bitter man."

"Yes. A bitter man who hasn't changed. Even his house hasn't changed. Like something out of the seventies."

Karen chuckled. "What's wrong with his house? The outside always looks nice."

"Lord, the man's still got mustard-gold shag carpeting. Nasty."

Karen let out a laugh. Even during the most frustrating times, Riley found a way to bring in some humor.

"He was at Grimaldi's the night of the murder. Eighty-sixed," Riley said, referring to him being tossed out of the bar.

"We have that corroborated."

"Yes. Said he went straight home."

"Doesn't guarantee he didn't go back out."

"Are you seriously suspecting Frank?"

"He's got a lot of hate. Besides, a really good and experienced investigator taught me…everyone is a 'possible' until ruled out." Karen could envision Riley beaming—her white teeth sparkling, framed by her rich, onyx complexion. "We're back to square one. Any thoughts?"

"How'd it go at Bobby's?"

"Nothing. Neither of them recalled seeing the knife at the house." She carefully chose her next words. "Bobby came home from work covered in dust. Got a sample of it. We'll see what the lab says."

"Think it will resemble the specks on Cliff's shirt?"

"Possible. He works in an auto-body shop. I'll drop it at the lab." Karen paused. "I'm going to give Keith another try before heading home."

"All right. See you Monday. Have a great weekend."

From Bobby's house, it was a quick seven-minute drive to the Commodore Barry Bridge and over the Delaware River to New Jersey. After an additional half-hour drive, Karen's hopes of speaking with Keith were quickly dashed. She left her card—again—and headed back to Pennsylvania.

Karen's thoughts immediately turned to Tam and the tornado of emotions she had experienced earlier. She needed to sort through everything and knew the perfect remedy. A detour on her drive home.

Karen crossed back into Pennsylvania and found a spot along the banks of the Delaware River to sit and quiet the chaotic thoughts running rampant. A familiar scent hit her. The brackish blend of fish and sea life mixed with petroleum. The whir of traffic on the interstate behind her created an unusual calm.

People stood along the shore, peacefully casting lines from their fishing poles. She watched the water in a hypnotic and meditative manner. A breeze came off the water, slapping her face and whipping her hair around. A barge chugged by at an ant's pace, making its way north to the Philadelphia ports.

The river sloshed against the bank of jagged rocks. Between her confusion over Tam, a virtual dead end with the case, and her uncertainty over Miles, her head felt like a cluttered mess. She replayed the plethora of disappointments from Miles. *Will I ever shake him?* That thought caused the turbulent mess in her head to swirl faster.

Recalling the earlier events with Tam, she pulled out her phone and pecked on "Miles Stillwell." His rugged, unshaven face appeared on her screen.

"A FaceTime call from you. What a surprise." His monotone voice was less than convincing.

Karen felt a weak smile form at hearing his baritone voice and seeing his face—his usual five-o'clock shadow draped over his chiseled facial features. Handsome features framed by dark, wavy hair just beginning to show a touch of gray along the sides.

"How are you? I've missed you." She struggled to get the words out, not sure they were accurate.

"Yeah. Miss you, too." He looked away from the screen.

"Is this a bad time?"

"No, I've got a minute."

A minute? She gathered her thoughts. "I don't want to bother you if this isn't a good time."

"I'm headed out in a few minutes. How are things with you?"

She felt a palpable distance. It was as if their words were forced—scripted—mechanical. "Busy. Looking forward to the weekend." She heard a doorbell in the background.

Miles's gray eyes shot from the screen. "Hey, my ride just showed up. Any way we can catch up this weekend?"

"Sure. This weekend. Call when you have time." *You can't tell your ride to wait and talk for a few fucking minutes?*

She shook her head. Seeing his face—hearing his voice—it didn't bring joy. Instead, she felt apprehension.

CHAPTER FOURTEEN

Monday morning, Karen was ready to get back in and make headway on the case. As usual, Riley was sitting across from her desk when she arrived. She threw her gray gabardine blazer on the hook when the chief appeared in the doorway.

"Got something," Walden announced. "The blood on the victim's shirt came back from CODIS. We got a partial."

The Combined DNA Index System—an FBI database referred to as CODIS—had identified a partial match from the offender index. That meant the partial match came from someone already convicted of a violent crime.

"A close match to none other than Kenny McPherson," Walden said.

Karen felt her chest tighten. Her breathing slowed. "A partial match? Not identical?" An exact match would put Kenny square in the crosshairs of their investigation. Depending on the degree of match, a partial meant a blood-related family member.

"Not identical. Fifty percent match. A male."

Strongest possibility—a parent-child relationship.

"Like his son?" Riley said, quickly, almost obligatorily adding, "Or full brother?"

Karen felt her body tense. *Almost positive he didn't have siblings.*

If the blood on the shirt matched Bobby, and the dust she collected also matched, they would be miles closer to solving the crime, but not in a manner Karen anticipated. *What the hell? Bobby?*

"Can we get an officer to bring Bobby in?" Riley asked. "We'll see if we can get him to consent to a DNA sample."

"Capp?" Walden looked at Karen, eyebrows raised. "It's your case." His deep, almost parental voice permeated the room.

"Of course," she said in just above a whisper.

She looked at Riley, fighting her emotions and the moisture in her eyes.

"I'm sorry, Karen. I know you didn't want this to be the outcome," Riley said.

Karen shook her head. "Still need to keep an open mind."

Bobby arrived at the station an hour later, eyes wide and darting about. Karen watched as the officers had him sign a voluntary consent and a technician swabbed the inside of his mouth. The informed voluntary consent program, a relatively new program at Parks Ford police, used the RapidHIT ID system to create a faster DNA turnaround time. The purpose of the program was to avoid incarcerating the wrong individual. But in this case, it could lead to the match they had anticipated. Identifying an exact match would take about an hour and a half. In the meantime, Karen would use that time to convince Bobby to come clean.

In the sole interview room, Bobby sat at the metal table, head down, elbows on his knees, and hands clasped. Watching him, Karen opted to give him a little time to sit and think and, perhaps, stew. She found herself stewing, as well. Her heart felt like a sack of lead.

After an hour and twenty minutes, Karen entered the room with Riley close behind. They had their results—a perfect match. Bobby sat with his head down, very much like the morning of the murder when Karen sat next to him on the porch steps. His right arm dangled in his lap while his left forearm rested on the table.

"Bobby, you remember my partner, Detective Riley?" Karen said.

He looked up with a solemn expression and nodded.

"Do you know why you're here?" she gently asked.

He gave a slight shrug. "You got something on me…but I have no clue what." His voice cracked.

Karen kept her tone steady and measured. "Bobby, we found your blood on the shirt Cliff was wearing the night he was killed."

His body shot up straight. "What the hell are you talking about?"

Riley pulled out a picture of the long-sleeved T-shirt Cliff had been wearing and the close-ups of the various areas stained with blood smears. She placed them on the table and pointed to one with a close-up of the left sleeve. "Right here. That's your blood. We have it confirmed."

Bobby leaned forward and studied the pictures. His eyes squinted as he leaned even closer, then looked up with a shocked expression.

"That's my shirt," he said.

"What?"

"That's *my* shirt."

Riley let out an exasperated sigh. "C'mon, Bob. We're trying to help you."

He looked up wide-eyed at Riley, then Karen. "I'm telling you… that's my shirt." He tapped his finger over and over on the pictures.

Riley appeared agitated, almost impatient. Karen remained silent, staring at an indignant Bobby.

He leaned forward, rapidly jabbing his index finger on a photo showing the shirt's entire left side. "Right there. That tear. My shirt tore at the shoulder."

"Tell us about it, Bobby," Karen said in a calm and even fashion. "How did you tear your shirt? Lots of people have tears on their clothing."

"Vince and me…we were horsing around, got to wrestling. He tore my shirt. Right there." Bobby again pointed to the two-inch tear on the left shoulder. "I wore it to work the next day. It was already ruined, so it didn't matter. After work, I was bringing home a piece of scrap metal…cut my thumb on it." He held out his right thumb.

Karen looked at the digit with no signs of an injury. She shot Riley a glance. Riley looked skeptical.

"My thumb was bleeding. I kept wiping it on my shirt as I drove home. When I got home…there was blood…all over my sleeve. Figured the shirt was toast."

"What did you do with it then?" Karen asked.

"Tossed it in the trash," he said with a shrug. "Just chucked it on top of the trash bin lid before I walked in the house."

"When was this?" Karen asked.

He rubbed the back of his neck. "I don't know. Like, end of July. Maybe the beginning of August. A while ago. It was hot. Humid."

Karen stood up and excused herself.

"Stay here," Riley instructed Bobby as she followed Karen into the hallway. "Capp, stop. I know you don't want to believe Bobby did this—"

"It's not that. We can check how old that stain is."

Karen broke into a jog, darting across the parking lot and into the county building and the trace evidence lab.

"Carver, what's that test you do that can check for how old a bloodstain is?"

"Raman spectroscopy?"

"Yeah, that's it. I knew it sounded like Asian food. Can we use it on one of our pieces of evidence?"

"The blood needs to have been less than two years—"

"It's around two months."

Unlike most other tests, this particular one would take seconds. Karen headed back to the station and stood silently with Riley in the hallway. Riley leaned against a wall, her head down, arms tightly folded in front of her.

For a quick test, it felt like hours passed. Karen began to pace. She and Riley hadn't spoken a word. Finally, Carver appeared, ambling toward them in his odd, stiff gait. He stopped in front of Karen and held up a sheet of paper.

"Your Asian food…delivered."

Karen grabbed the report and rapidly read through the results. Without turning, she handed the document to Riley.

The bloodstain had been created well before Cliff was killed. Cliff likely found the shirt and took it to wear. Karen knew that Bobby wasn't necessarily exonerated, only that there was nothing to tie Bobby to the attack via that bloodstain. They were right back at the beginning.

Karen reentered the interview room to a frightened and exhausted-looking Bobby. "Thank you for your patience, Bob. We'll have an officer promptly get you back to work."

Back in her office, she collapsed into her chair, part relief and part frustration. "What the fuck are we missing?"

"If I had that answer, we'd both know." Riley smiled.

Karen shot her a sardonic look. "We need more from the lab. I still need to get in front of Keith."

"Then let's get busy."

As the early chill of late October beckoned and homes were adorned with Halloween decorations, Karen plodded along. The case was nearing two weeks old with no resolution in sight. Karen knew the longer the investigation went, the colder the trail would become. Her frustration elevated. Rubbing her aching eyes, she found her thoughts drifting to Tam. Amused, she allowed herself a momentary distraction.

Plucking at her computer keyboard, she searched for information about Tam's addresses in New York City. *Anywhere near Caiden?* She was also curious about Tam's relationship history. *Was she living with someone? Maybe that's why she ran back here. A relationship gone bad.*

She scoffed as she stared at the lines on her computer screen. Her last location was Manhattan, but before that, she spent years in various locations throughout northern New Jersey. Hoboken. Teaneck. Hackensack. *Close enough. Maybe she wanted to impress me.* Karen shook her head as a smile warmed her face.

An incoming email flashed across her screen. The forensic geology report from the state lab. *Yes!* The bandana contained dirt consistent with the samples sent from the neighborhood. The study also found traces of kaolinite, ultisol, and silicon dioxide. She shot Riley a quick text.

Moments later, they were both staring at Karen's computer screen.

"Silicon dioxide," Karen said. "That's glass."

"Vineland, New Jersey. Big glass manufacturing industry there. Where does Keith work?"

"Vineland, but he's a truck driver."

Riley stared out the window. "It's also used in automotive paint."

Karen stifled her groan. "What do you make of the kaolinite and ultisol?"

Riley stood, reading the report over Karen's shoulder. "Have no idea what ultisol is. It says that kaolinite is a mineral typically found three feet or more below the surface. Think we're looking for someone in construction?"

"Did a search while you were heading over. Ultisol is a dirt indigenous to this area. Kaolinite is predominantly found in Georgia.

Locally, it was at White Clay Creek, now a state park in Delaware." Karen tapped on her keyboard and studied a map of the White Clay Creek area. "Shit."

"What?"

"Joey Murphy. The quarry in Delaware. It's right next to White Clay Creek. When I was at Fran's, he walked in covered head to toe in a white substance from work. I assumed it was lime."

Riley's ebony eyebrows arched. "Head to the quarry?"

"Let's go to the house. When he gets home, he'll be wearing his work clothes. Too many coincidental pieces with that boy." Karen hopped up, infused with energy.

Finally. A lead.

Joey stood in the entryway preparing to head up the stairs when he caught sight of the detectives. Karen walked toward him, studying his clothes. Sweat stains on his gray long-sleeved shirt with areas of dark-brown debris. Her gaze met his shoes.

"What?" Joey said. His eyes darted between the two detectives, his posture rigid.

Why is he already defensive? "Joey, this is my colleague, Detective Riley. We'd like to get a sample of that dirt." She pointed to his boots.

"Why are you bothering me? Kenny is the man you should be after."

"Joey, it's a simple request. Why are you so angry?"

He stood, silent and staring at Karen's face, then his eyes shifted to Riley.

"You have a tremendous amount of hatred toward Kenny," Karen said.

"Wouldn't you, if he did what he did to your family member?"

Karen gave a single, slow nod. "You work at the quarry. With kaolinite?"

His face contorted. "What's that?"

Riley walked over. "Better question is, what's on your shoes?" She pressed. "The white dirt, Joey. What is it?"

He fumbled with his words. "Uh...lime...I think."

"Then you won't mind giving us a sample of the lime on your boots," Riley challenged him.

"You two are trying to frame me." His gaze bounced between both detectives.

Karen frowned. Joey's shoe size appeared eerily similar to the partial print they found at the crime scene. He had every ingredient of being a suspect. But they had zero evidence to tie him to the scene.

Karen cocked her head. "May we get a sample of the dirt, Joey?"

He shrugged in surrender. "What do you need me to do?"

Joey paced in his socks as Riley placed the dirt sample into an evidence bag and took measurements of his shoes. She finished with photographs.

"The Friday before last, your mom said you came home with blood on your clothes. Mind explaining?" Karen asked him.

"Cut myself at work. No biggie. Didn't keep me from goin' out with friends after work."

Karen felt her eyebrows raise. "What time did you get home?"

"I dunno. Like, eleven. Maybe midnight."

To Karen, that was late enough to require an alibi. "Who saw you come home?"

"Nobody. Everyone was asleep. I try to be quiet when I get home that late."

Riley chimed in. "So, no one saw you come home." It was a statement.

Joey shook his head.

"Did you go back out?" Karen asked.

"No. Why would I?"

Karen didn't answer. "If need be, will you consent to a blood sample?"

Joey's eyes became wide. "Um, I guess. Why?"

Neither Karen nor Riley responded. But as far as they were concerned, Joey had no alibi for the night of the murder.

"Thank you for your cooperation, Joey. We'll keep you posted," Karen promised, noting his deer-in-the-headlights look.

In the car, Karen's turn signal was the lone sound. Finally, she spoke.

"Thoughts on Joey?"

Riley let out a snort. "I know we need to do our due diligence." She paused. "I just don't see the kid attacking and brutally stabbing a six-foot-tall man…no matter how frail Cliff was."

Karen nodded. The car was silent again.

"Riley. I have an idea. We're not getting a hit from CODIS for the hair fiber. Remember that case in California? They got that police officer for murder and kidnapping. The Golden State Killer. I forget which database they used, but it was one of those genealogy databases."

Riley seemed reignited. "GEDmatch. I think that was the name. They compared DNA from crime scenes with the GED database and narrowed their field of suspects."

"Well, whad'ya think? I know it's a shot in the dark, but it's worth a try."

"Let's give it a go. That hair fiber could be key," Riley said.

"Great. I'll get on it." Karen pulled into the station feeling an adrenaline rush.

She felt lighter. Hopeful. Her change in mood prompted her to do something she had been mulling over. To visit Tam. Off duty. Just relax and enjoy her company.

Previous visits had always started with Tam offering a beer and Karen accepting bottled water. To Tam's outward delight, caps were being twisted off bottles of Yuengling. Tam shared fascinating stories about her work as an artist and experiences in New York—a world completely foreign to Karen, who had spent her entire life in a small town, committed to career success and raising a daughter. At times, Tam's stories brought Karen a pang of jealousy, wondering what life would have been like had she left this peanut-sized town.

Tam continued talking while Karen received work-related texts. Tam persisted and, at one point, took Karen's phone and placed it on the table. For a brief moment, she would succeed, only to have another text reimmerse Karen in the case.

Finally, Tam erupted. "It's always about your work. You never take an interest in mine."

Karen was thrown—less by the tone of Tam's outburst, which was understandable, than by its content. *Tam doesn't work. What is she talking about?* She stared blankly at Tam.

"Why don't you come experience what I do? Come to the pottery studio. See what it's like to do what I do."

Karen laughed at the absurd suggestion.

Tam gave a sheepish smile. "C'mon. Come throw pottery with me."

"You're not serious, are you? I'm not artistic…at all."

"That's okay. I'll teach you." Her charismatic smile lit up her face.

Karen finished her beer and got up to leave. “I’ll think about it.”

Tam shot her a miffed look.

“I’ll *think* about it,” Karen reiterated in a softer tone.

Tam beamed. “Great. Pick you up at ten, this Sunday.”

Karen grinned and shook her head. Tam had a way of taking her boundaries and annihilating them.

She sauntered to her car, her head floating in clouds of pleasant confusion. *Stop questioning everything. The woman likes you and wants to show you her world. What’s so wrong with that?*

CHAPTER FIFTEEN

Karen stood in front of the bathroom mirror Sunday morning staring at herself. *What the hell were you thinking? You can't do this.* A blank look stared back at her. She frowned, contemplating what she had gotten herself into. She knew she should have never agreed to a personal outing with Tam, for professional reasons if nothing else. But something else about spending time with Tam was irking her, even though she still felt drawn to the young woman. She couldn't put her finger on it but knew it was there. And now it put her into a foul mood. Still, she headed out the door at the sound of a tooting horn.

"Good morning." Tam sat in the driver's seat, overflowing with excitement. "I texted you the YouTube link." An instructional video demonstrating how to center clay on the potter's wheel. "Did you check it out?"

"Yeah," Karen lied. She didn't feel like conversing. Curt, zestless responses followed Tam's questions and comments.

Like a huge scoop of ice cream slowly melting down the cone, Tam's excitement seemed to wither. Her attempt at conversation devolved from there.

They continued to the studio, a two-minute drive from the police station. Even though Karen had lived in the town her entire forty-four years, she had never graced the art studio.

Tam drove up the narrow, ascending driveway to a stone building that looked more like a mansion. Her Mini pulled into a virtually empty parking lot surrounded by tall junipers, isolating it from a nearby highway. She energetically hopped out and grabbed a bag of tools and a twenty-five-pound plastic bag of clay. Karen watched, dumbfounded.

She followed Tam down a hall that smelled like wet earth. Each side of the hallway was framed by rows of wooden cubbies, each with pottery tools, clay, and a completed piece here and there. Her acrid mood remained unchanged.

They entered a room labeled "Wheel Room." Virtually empty, except for a lone potter sitting at a wheel, covered in a long denim apron spotted with wet clay. The potter sat focused on an intricate platter she was creating from an alabaster-colored porcelain. The only sound in the room was the spinning of her wheel. Karen glanced past the slender potter and eyed the room. In a J-formation, potter's wheels lined the wall from one end of the room to the other.

Tam took a spot three wheels to the right of the other potter and directed Karen to sit at the wheel next to her. Glumly, Karen plopped down on a two-foot-high stool and stared at Tam as she pulled out her tools and efficiently marched over to the sink and filled two one-gallon buckets with water. Tam was clearly in her element.

Tam produced two round sponges about the size of Karen's palm. She opened the bag of clay and with a long, thin wire cut off two chunks about the size of a softball, pounding each chunk into a perfectly round sphere.

Handing Karen one of the balls, she said, "Just like the video, throw it onto your wheel."

Karen took the clay and wound up like Nolan Ryan, firing the innocent sphere onto the steel wheel head. It hit with a splat nowhere near the center of the wheel.

"I said throw it *onto* the wheel, not *through* it," Tam jokingly berated her.

The potter three wheels to their left let out a giggle but kept her head down. Strands of sandy blond hair fell forward, coming loose from her ponytail.

Tam scraped the clay off the wheel and pounded it back into a ball. "Try it again. Preferably close to the center."

Karen took the ball and gently tossed it onto the wheel, amazingly, right in the center. She sparkled with pride. It was the first joy she had felt all morning.

"Great," Tam said perfunctorily. "Now, you need to use a lot of water." She dipped her hand into Karen's bucket and tossed handfuls of the liquid onto Karen's ball of clay. "Okay…start your wheel."

Karen located the pedal that put the wheel in motion. *Hmm. It's like a sewing machine pedal…sort of.* She pressed the metal pedal vigorously down to the floor. The wheel flew into a full-speed rotation. Water sprayed off in varying directions, covering the two of them, and the little ball of clay flew from the wheel and into the plastic splash pan surrounding it that served to collect water and clay debris. The clay pounded against the pan's walls. *Thunk, thunk, thunk.*

Karen saw a gentle smile emerge on the face of the other potter, partially concealed behind the strands of hair. The woman kept her head down and avoided eye contact, for which Karen felt eternally grateful.

Tam sighed. She reballed the clay, cleaned off Karen's wheel with a hand towel, and instructed Karen to try again. Just then, her cell phone rang.

"You brought your phone in here?" Karen said with annoyance.

"Wait…you're complaining about *my* phone when that's all you do when we're at my house?" Tam looked at the caller ID. "I gotta get this." She hustled out.

Karen sat on her stool and stared at the innocent ball of clay in front of her. *What the hell am I doing here?* "This is bullshit," she said under her breath.

The potter sat up and looked at Karen, offering a sympathetic smile framed by rosy cheeks dotted with a smattering of freckles.

"I can't believe I'm doing this." Karen scowled. "I can't believe I fucking let her talk me into this."

The potter's soft voice emerged. "Ah, c'mon. It's fun. And it's very therapeutic."

"Oh, great, that's just what I need…therapy."

The potter laughed. "Would you like some help?"

Karen stared.

"I'm offering you help. And it's expiring in five…four…three…" She slowly counted down, grinning.

"Okay, okay. Yeah…I could use some help." Karen rolled her eyes, feeling it was beyond obvious that she needed help. A lot of it.

The potter rinsed her hands in her water bucket, wiping them on her apron. She made her way over to Karen's wheel, grabbed Tam's stool, and over the next handful of minutes, gave Karen the CliffsNotes version of how to center a ball of clay on the wheel, complete with how to position her hands, the appropriate pressure points for each hand, and correct body position.

"Now," the potter said. "Start your wheel…*slowly*."

Karen gave a side glance as the potter let out an amused giggle.

She couldn't help but chuckle herself. Slowly, she set her wheel spinning and placed her hands into the position the potter had instructed. The potter tossed a handful of water onto the spinning mud and guided Karen on how to press each hand onto the clay. As Karen started to struggle, the potter got up and walked behind her. She reached around Karen's body and placed her firm hands over Karen's.

"It's all about feel. I want you to feel how the clay responds as you work to center it."

Wild. I've never done anything quite like this. This is wild!

The potter gently pressed on Karen's hands, kinesthetically urging them to give the clay more pressure. Karen couldn't help but notice the potter's strong, toned forearms as they worked next to hers. As Karen started to move her hands toward the clay, the potter reminded her to keep her left arm locked into the side of her left leg instead of moving it forward.

"Then how do I press forward onto the clay?" Karen asked with a genuine interest in mastering the technique.

"You lean forward with your upper body," she said. The potter pressed her chest into Karen's back to mimic the position.

Karen felt the potter's breasts push into her back, urging her torso forward. What began as an instructional exercise was slowly morphing into a sensual experience. *Focus, Capp.* The feeling reminded her of the other attractions she had felt toward women—what she had always deemed an admiration, of sorts. The feelings would be acknowledged, then dismissed.

As they worked the clay in unison, their hands became saturated with wet mud. The wetness allowed both of their hands to flow effortlessly on the clay and onto each other. After several minutes, the ball stopped wobbling and became steady. A calm mass of mud on the wheel below their hands.

The potter slowly pulled her hands off Karen's. "You got it. You did it," she said.

Karen pulled her hands back and sat upright in amazement. She turned to look over her left shoulder at the potter. Their eyes met. Gentle, warm blue eyes. Deep indigo blue, like spilled ink.

"You got it," the potter said again, this time in just above a whisper.

Karen's head spun as she gazed at this woman—this stranger. Lost in the woman's gaze and as if guided by a force outside herself, she reached up and gently placed a muddied hand on the woman's face, pulling her closer. Their eyes locked. The room sat silent except for the whirring of the wheel head, still spinning.

"Is that a thank-you?" the potter asked, smiling.

Mortified, Karen pulled back and looked away. "Um…yeah," she muttered. *What the hell am I doing?* She had no idea where her actions had come from. Her mind spun, whirring just like the wheel in front of her.

Then it hit her. Like someone had opened the blinds and let the sun stream through, illuminating everything in its path. Everything came together. Her previous interactions with Tam—all the tension that had built up—had brought out feelings long tamped down. She had no way to release or express them. She needed to experience them, to liberate them—but not with Tam. There was something about *this* woman. Something Karen had never felt with Tam. With this woman, all the pent-up emotions flooded out like a dam breaking.

Tam burst back into the room, startling the potter and leading her to stumble backward, tripping over Tam's stool. Tam crossed the room and glanced at the potter, at the clay covering the left side of her face.

"What the hell happened to you?" Tam scoffed at the woman's apparent messiness.

The potter sputtered, "Oh…uh…ya know, how, like, when you have an itch on your face…and you forget you have clay on your hands?" She let out a giggle.

Karen felt a sudden warmth pour over her face.

"We have to go," Tam told Karen.

"What? This was supposed to be our day doing what you wanted to do."

"We have to go—"

Karen cut her off. Proud. Beaming. "Look what I did." She pointed to her perfectly centered mound of clay.

"We have to go. That was Bobby. My dad is back at the house." Tam started throwing her tools back in her bag and sponging off her wheel.

"Have him call the police. That's really who should be responding. Not you. Not me." Karen had grown weary of the drama over at Hillside. But she also didn't want to leave—leave the presence of the woman who had just broken her world open.

"Let's go." Tam tossed both buckets of water into the sink and scooped up Karen's "accomplishment" and tossed it back into her bag of clay.

Goddamn you, Tam.

Karen rinsed her hands in the sink and followed Tam toward the door. The potter looked up silently as Tam walked by, then Karen. When Karen got to the doorway, she stopped. Looking back at the potter, their eyes met. One last look. *Those blue eyes. Mesmerizing.* A perturbed Karen walked out, feeling an unexpected disappointment set in.

For the first time since she met Tam, she had clarity. Tam was the last person she wanted to be with. She enjoyed the attention Tam doused her with; she was drawn to her charismatic personality. Her maternal instincts led to feeling an angst for what Tam had endured in her childhood. But right now, she felt done. She didn't give a damn about what Kenny was up to. This wasn't her drama. She wanted out. But she'd invited it in when she welcomed Tam into her personal space. *Mistake noted. Now I need to fix it…pronto.*

When they pulled up to the house, Kenny was standing at the base of the front porch.

"Detective, this is my house." His voice carried more of a pleading tone than anger.

This was the last way I wanted to spend my Sunday. Professionally, she knew she needed to take control of the situation and pulled Kenny aside calmly, recommending arbitrating the matter in family court. To her relief, he agreed and left.

She looked up at Bobby standing on the porch. "You okay?"

"I'm gonna lose this house, aren't I?" His eyes welled with tears.

"I don't know, Bobby. But this needs to be resolved so these altercations don't continue. I'm in your corner." She placed her arm around his shoulders.

"You wanna come in?"

Oh, hell no. That's the last place I want to be. I can't get away from here fast enough. She bit her tongue. "Nah, I'm good. I'm just gonna…I'm gonna head home."

When she reached the end of the block, she felt like she'd just executed a grand escape. Tam had not pursued her. She sat on a curb waiting for her ride, picking away at the dried clay that covered her jeans and sweatshirt and replaying the events at the studio. *What a messy hobby. I'm covered in this shit.* Her mind drifted to the potter with her apron covered in the same clay mess. She found nothing endearing about making pottery. *At least I finally got that goddamn ball to do what it was supposed to do.*

Then she berated herself. *I never should have left this morning.* She paused with the last thought. A reality surfaced. *If I didn't go with Tam this morning, I never would have met that potter.* "Doesn't matter. I didn't even get her name," she muttered, then let out a snort. "What would I have done with it if I had?"

At home, Karen relaxed on her back deck. Her thoughts kept drifting back to the art studio. Something extremely powerful had happened with that potter. Something electric. Identifying it—putting a label on it—felt foreign.

It wasn't anything she had ever felt for Tam, or really for anyone. It was an epiphany of sorts. Her uncomfortable reactions to Tam's advances had nothing to do with her gender or sexuality after all. She just wasn't attracted to her. It became abundantly clear: She needed to establish firm boundaries with Tam…not a task she looked forward to.

CHAPTER SIXTEEN

The week started with a whirlwind of activity. Karen found two genealogy services willing to assist law enforcement with DNA identification. She reached out to the county's family court services to address Bobby's situation. Phone calls and two additional trips to Keith's house were completed. The fact that he wasn't responding and was never home brought an uneasy trepidation. *Why is he avoiding me?*

Things with Tam had already gone well past the point of drawing the line, and by Wednesday she knew she had to explain to Tam what she needed to do on a professional level. Her preference was to perform this chore in a public setting to decrease the risk of an emotional outburst or manipulation.

Tam called and texted incessantly, creating additional turmoil.

Karen finally responded. *Meet you at Grimaldi's for a drink? Tonight at 6?*

Tam responded immediately. *C U at 6.*

At the end of the day, Karen headed to Grimaldi's and chose a high-top table away from the few customers gathered at the bar. The jukebox was blessedly silent. Tam arrived with her charming smile and bubbling personality, prompting several men to pause conversations and look her way. But Tam's eyes were focused in one direction.

"Tam, I've allowed things to get way too close," Karen said without preamble. "I'm knee-deep in a murder investigation. This is totally against protocol."

Tam's beer bottle landed with a clunk as she erupted into an emotional meltdown. "Why are you so engrossed in this case? He was just a fucking homeless guy." Tears filled her eyes.

Karen looked at Tam, stunned. Gathering her wits, she spoke in a hushed tone. "He was a human being. Someone's son…someone's brother." She stared at Tam. "He was a human being."

Tam childishly rolled her eyes.

"Yes, he was without a home or a job, but he was a person. He had just as much a right to live as you, me, Bobby…anyone." Karen felt like she was counseling a child on how to play nice.

The news landed like a steel weight. As Tam acted out, Karen struggled to believe she was a thirty-two-year-old woman. Nonetheless, she held firm, standing up and bidding Tam good night without looking back.

Serves you right, Capp. What were you thinking, getting that close to her? She had her answer. Emptiness in her personal life had been quickly filled by a very attractive and charismatic person. She was lonely. It was hard to turn away from Tam's attentiveness. But she knew that she could no longer compromise her boundaries, both personal and professional, just for the attention of a person who would clearly never respect them and likely trample all over them. That said, the voice in the back of her mind told her there was still another reason for creating a firm boundary with Tam.

The next day, Tam continued to pepper Karen with voice mails and texts. But Karen's mind was elsewhere. Unable to shake other thoughts from Sunday, she debated talking with Judy about the potter and pondered her best friend's reaction. *How much can I share? What do I hold back?*

Sitting in the still of her office, she found her mind drifting to the gentle, encouraging voice of that potter. Feeling the woman's toned arms wrapped around her as she helped Karen with the clay. The feel of the potter's breasts pressing into her back. But more than those stirring mental souvenirs, she simply couldn't shake the memory of the women's radiant eyes that held hers as she softly smiled when

Karen mastered the clay centering technique. It reminded her of that all-encompassing excitement and elation, the torrent of warmth surging within her, when her academy instructor—the one she had a crush on—complimented her successes.

But with the potter, she cared little about the success. It was more about the interaction and the instantaneous connection she felt. She recalled the flutter she felt in her chest as her eyes drifted to the woman's lips, and how she forced herself to turn away, afraid she might do something that would mortify her. *What the hell, Capp?*

A tap on her office door interrupted her thoughts.

Officer Roberts stepped two feet inside her door and put his head down. He seemed nervous. Uncomfortable.

"What's going on?" Karen gently pried.

"Tam McPherson. How much do you know about her?"

Christ. Why is he asking me this? What does he know? "Why?"

"Thinking of asking her out on a date."

Karen choked on a snicker. *Oh my God, he has no idea she's gay.* She smiled. "Go for it, Roberts. I think you should go for it."

"You think?" His face lit up.

"Sure. Why not? You're handsome. Got a good job. You're a great catch."

Roberts's smile widened. "Thanks, KC. Appreciate if you could put in a good word for me."

"Roberts, she's an informant for this case. I can't get involved with personal conversations with her." Her face felt hot, as if she had a red sign on her forehead flashing: Liar…Liar. "Just ask her. I'm sure she'll be flattered." *Maybe then she'll leave me the hell alone.*

"Yes, ma'am. Thank you again."

Karen smiled as he left. A short burst of amusement to ease a difficult day. She tossed her pen across the desk and turned off her computer. It was time for a heart-to-heart with her bestie.

Surprising Judy with a visit, Karen arrived in a rollercoaster mood. Judy shared details about her weekend and then asked, "So… what did *you* do last weekend?"

A tightness filled Karen's chest. *Well, she keeps wanting me to move on from Miles.* It was hard for her to fathom what she was about to share. Taking a deep breath, she started with a blow-by-blow description of how she'd gone to the studio with Tam to learn pottery. How Tam took a phone call and left her to fend for herself. Then how a wonderful artist stepped in to help her.

That was the easy part.

She felt a queasiness as she proceeded to tell Judy how a moment of innocent instruction and assistance mysteriously turned sensual. Judy stared at her in silence. *Shit. Silence is the tactic I use.*

Karen took a deep breath. "I have no idea what she felt, but it was incredibly powerful for me."

Judy's plain stare evolved into a smile. Karen knew that all Judy wanted for her was to be happy. She probably couldn't give a damn who it was with, as long as they were good to her. Having Karen pull away from Miles would just be icing on the cake.

"Jude, I don't know what's wrong with me. I can't get this woman off my mind." Karen felt flustered. "I don't even know anything about her. I don't even know her name, for Christ's sake."

"Well, go find her," Judy said casually.

"What? How?"

"You're a detective. Go find her."

Karen envisioned herself going to the studio. "I guess I could go back, show my badge and—"

"Or…you could just be a civilian. Be honest and explain you met her and want to reconnect."

Are you fucking kidding? Karen settled her frantic thoughts. *It'll probably be easier than finding our goddamn killer.* She couldn't help but smirk. "You're okay with this?"

"I'm not surprised, if that's what you mean," Judy said.

"What do you mean? I've always dated men."

"But you've had attractions to women."

Karen shot Judy a look.

"Remember that female officer that took your place when you got promoted to detective?" Judy asked.

Karen shrugged. "Yeah."

"You two were tight. I always assumed you two were together." Judy was matter-of-fact. "Bottom line. I don't give a shit. As long as you're happy."

"Thanks, Jude."

"Keep me posted. I can't wait to hear more."

Karen left Judy's feeling lighter. *Jude didn't bat an eye. So, what's my problem?*

Heading back to the station, she passed the art studio, a place she never gave a second thought to. Sitting at a stop sign, she glanced at the long driveway heading up to the studio. She paused, her gut roiling with anxiety…or fear…or apprehension. Accelerating through the stop sign, she proceeded forward and back to the station.

At her office, AncestryMatch had agreed to an expeditious processing of the DNA for their third hair fiber. And now, a familiar alert sound chirped on Karen's computer. Incoming email.

She glanced at Riley before pulling up the report.

"Patrick Miller, twenty-four shared segments, shared DNA six-point-four percent, estimated relationships: great-uncle or great-nephew. Jessica Kelly, fourteen shared segments, three-point-seven percent shared DNA, estimated relationships: first cousin, once removed or second cousin…"

"You're fucking kidding, right?" Riley's irritation saturated the office.

"Hold on…" Karen scanned the document. "Here. Twenty-eight percent DNA shared. Estimated relationship: brother." She looked up at Riley. "Joseph Ryanard."

"You shittin' me?"

"It gets better. Barbara Masterson, fifty percent DNA match. Mother." She scanned further. "Here we go. Our third hair fiber matches…Frank Ryanard."

"Frank?" Riley asked, in amazement. "I know he's a bastard…a real piece of work…but—"

"He's been very outspoken about the homeless down on that corner—"

"I know. But they're not even in his hood. What, did he drive over there? I just don't see it."

"Agreed," Karen said. "But we can't ignore this. This is huge."

"If he drove over, there'll be traces of blood inside the car."

"Let's get some answers first…not spook him." Karen stood up and grabbed her blazer.

"You got it, boss."

Frank Ryanard worked for a local delivery company, so he wasn't likely to be home at the midday hour.

"Know where he works?" Riley asked.

"Yeah. A delivery company run by a real chauvinistic jackass. Dolly Delivery."

"You're kidding. A chauvinistic delivery company with a woman's name." Riley seemed amused.

Karen laughed. "I think 'Dolly' refers to that thing with wheels that moves stuff."

"Ohhhhh."

Five minutes later, they arrived at Dolly Delivery only to learn that Frank was on the road with an overnight assignment and wouldn't return until tomorrow. Things were back on hold.

Karen headed home and passed the art studio again. *Christ…I never even noticed this building until now. Driven by it a million times.* She glanced to her right at the long driveway and continued driving. At the next stop sign, she turned right and circled the block. Judy's words reverberated. *Go find that artist.*

After coming full circle, she turned right and headed up the long driveway.

CHAPTER SEVENTEEN

The ascending one-lane driveway reminded her of a narrow country road with foliage on each side and trees bowing over the asphalt. Several cars filled the lot this time. At the door she entered on Sunday, a half-balding man sat smoking a cigarette, right ankle resting on his left knee. Sweaty salt-and-pepper strands of hair framed a patch of bare scalp.

Karen strolled over and pulled out her badge. "Approximately five foot six, dark-blond hair, possibly pulled back in a ponytail. She's fairly thin but has a strong build. I don't have a name."

He looked up and tilted his head.

Probably wondering what the hell the police are doing here. She realized the foolishness of her charade.

"Think you're talking about Ali. She's over there." He pointed to his right, his cigarette casting ashes as he extended his arm.

When Karen arrived at the far edge of the studio building, she spotted an enormous brick kiln in front of her. She proceeded around the corner, catching a glimpse of a woman standing by the kiln loading ceramic pieces into plastic bins. It was her. The potter.

The potter seemed completely immersed in her work, focused and oblivious.

Moving through her feelings of awkwardness, Karen stopped about four feet away and spoke in a hushed voice. "Hey."

Startled, the woman turned. Her face lit up with immediate recognition. A smile blossomed below toned cheeks framed by dark-blond hair pulled back in a tight ponytail.

"Hey. You back for more?"

"Uh, no. I just, uh…I wanted to stop by and, uh, thank you. I wanted to say thank you for all your help on Sunday."

Karen felt like cellophane—as if the woman could see right through her. The woman nodded at Karen and continued to smile.

"I didn't think I'd see you again," the potter said.

"Yeah. I figured that. So I thought I'd stop back by…to, ya know…thank you." *God, I sound stupid.*

"I hope you at least had a little fun."

Karen half laughed. "I did."

She saw a slight blush creep up the woman's face. Breaking her gaze, she walked over to where the potter was packing up her completed work. "Wow, you make all this?"

"Yup." Her soft smile exuded pride. Her eyes twinkled.

Karen picked up a tall coffee mug glazed in soft yellow tones with a medium-blue glaze falling over the rim. "This is beautiful."

The woman's smile was gentle. "Take it. A gift from me. So you can always remember your experience here."

Are you kidding? I've fucking relived every goddamn minute over and over. "That's okay, but thank you." Outside of her element, Karen felt an uneasiness pour over her. She abruptly shifted the subject. "Ya know, I never got your name."

"I'm Ali. Alicia Barnes." She handed her card to Karen.

She's a professional potter. Holy shit. "Hi, Ali. I'm Karen." They exchanged firm handshakes. "It's really nice to meet you." Nerves raced through her like surges of electricity.

Ali gave her a coy look, glancing at the badge on Karen's belt. "You're a cop?"

Karen chuckled. "Yeah. A detective. Definitely not an artist…but I guess that was obvious." She pulled out her card and handed it to Ali.

Ali grinned. After an uncomfortable moment of silence, they both started to talk at the same time, stepping on each other's words. Karen nervously laughed as they both fumbled to create something meaningful to say. Ali yielded.

"So, again…I just stopped by to…to say thank you." Karen heard her own words, blurted out so awkwardly.

She started back to the parking lot. Her face felt flushed. After walking about five yards, she stopped. Turning around, she drew in a deep breath. "Would you like to grab a drink sometime?"

Ali answered without hesitation. "Sure. I'd love to."

You would? "Great. Do you know where the Stewart James Saloon is?"

Ali chuckled. "Yeah, my cousin works there on weekends. I know it well."

"Oh. Okay. Tomorrow night, say, seven p.m.? We'll beat the Friday night rush."

Ali nodded. "Sure. I'm looking forward to it, Karen."

My name. It sounds magical coming off her lips. Karen felt a queasy excitement. *It's done. No turning back now.* She had no way of knowing if this was considered a date or just drinks with a new friend.

"Okay. So, I'll see you tomorrow night." Karen turned to walk away.

"Karen," Ali called out. "You've got my number. On the card. Give me a call if anything changes."

"Sure thing." *Nothing's gonna change.* Her thoughts caused an uncontrolled smile to surface.

Karen felt as if she were floating down the long driveway. Light. Giddy. She felt twenty years younger. A girlish giggle escaped her lips. She had a date. She also felt petrified, unsure of her footing in this novel arena.

But she had a date.

The next day, Karen walked through the main glass doors to a booming voice echoing down the hallway.

"Detective Cappelletti."

She froze midstride and turned to acknowledge Chief Walden. "Yes, sir."

"Tammy McPherson…"

His baritone voice attached to Tam's name startled her. She felt a surge of dread. "Yes, sir?"

"She just donated two beautiful pieces of artwork…for our holiday auction."

A half-smile rose on Karen's face. She fought to push it back.

"She's a good egg."

"Yes, sir. She is." Relief washed over her.

"Hard to believe Kenny's her father," he said. "Looks like the rest of the family turned out pretty good."

Karen nodded, this time allowing her smile to show.

"When you see her, tell her thanks. Very generous of her."

"Yes, sir. I'll do that." *When I see her. Was hoping that wouldn't happen for a while.*

Karen entered her office to find Riley seated, her feet on the corner of her desk. "Make yourself comfortable."

Riley flashed a wide smile.

They decided to start at Frank Ryanard's house first. Karen parked the SUV in front of Frank's perfectly manicured postage-stamp-sized lawn. His neighbors' yards were covered with falling leaves, but Frank's had been raked into pristine piles at the curb. The street was practically void of life except for a handful of squirrels eagerly digging little holes and burying acorns in his yard.

"Think Frank yells at the squirrels?" Karen joked.

Riley snorted. "This walkway is bad feng shui," she said matter-of-factly.

Karen shot her a disparaging look.

"It is." Riley's tone bordered on giddy. "It goes straight from the curb to the door. It needs to curve…to break up the rush of energy."

"For God's sake. Can you stay focused?"

Riley chuckled as Karen reached up to knock on the door.

Frank stood at the front door in a wrinkled T-shirt, his baggy jeans held up under his belly by a wide leather belt. He grumbled and scratched the overgrown gray whiskers on his chin.

"Why're youse bothering me? I got nothin' to do with nothin'."

"We have a few questions," Riley said. "Is there someplace we can sit?"

He motioned to the back of the house and waddled away from the door.

"Frank," Karen said as they sat in his small living room, "as you're aware, we're investigating an incident that took place on Hillside several weeks ago."

"Yeah, a homeless shit got what he had coming."

Karen inwardly cringed. She hated it when people expressed this mentality against fellow humans. "I think it's pretty well-established,

Frank...you have an issue with the homeless people over there." It wasn't a question.

"Yeah. So what?" he bellowed.

"How often do you get out that way?" Karen asked.

"I don't. Besides, what's it to you?"

"What's it to us?" Riley said. "We're investigating anyone who had an issue with those people over there. It's our job."

"I'm almost two miles from that neighborhood."

"It's actually closer to a mile, but who's counting?" Karen said wryly.

"If you're so damn far away, why the animosity?" Riley said.

He jerked his body as he repositioned his chair, avoiding eye contact. "They bring down our property values."

Riley reached into her shoulder bag and produced a picture of the khaki jacket. "Do you recognize this?"

He gave the photo a cursory glance. "No."

Karen leaned toward him. "Take another look, Frank. Because strands of your hair are all over it."

"How do you know what strands of my hair look like?" His eyes darted between them. "I barely have hair." He gave a faint laugh as if making a cute joke about his receding gray hairline.

Karen greeted this with an impatient glare. "We have hair samples from the jacket. They match your DNA."

He sat up abruptly as if someone had slapped his face. He gave the photo a long, hard look.

"How'd ya know it's my DNA? Could be anyone." His voice quivered. A light bead of perspiration rested above his upper lip.

"Well, apparently, Frank, you did a DNA test through Ancestry and Me. Your DNA is now in a database," Karen said.

He flexed his fingers, cracking his knuckles. His pudgy face turned beet red.

Karen remembered the whole saga of the Ancestry and Me gift. It angered him then and now caused him to virtually explode.

"We've matched it with fibers on this jacket," she told him in an even tone. "Now do you recognize this jacket?"

"What a dumb gift." His voice roared through the house.

"Christ, Frank. Can we stay focused for one minute?" Karen's voice rose with her elevating irritation. "Do you recognize this jacket?"

"Yeah. It was part of a load I took to the Salvation Army."

"Then how come you said you didn't recognize it when I showed you the picture?" Riley asked.

"Wasn't stained that way when I got rid of it."

Karen took a deep breath. "Have a receipt for your donation?"

He shook his head.

The tedious questioning went on and on. Frank stated he had no receipt because he just dropped the bags off at the local drop box. The best timeline he could give was something around two weeks prior to the murder.

A request was made for Frank to come to the station to give an official statement and sign it. While they waited for him to get ready, Karen and Riley batted around the idea of obtaining search warrants for Frank's home and the interior of his car.

"I think it's way too early for that," Riley said. "We don't have anything close to PC."

The single probable cause they had was a bloody jacket that had been tied to Frank. But they had nothing to tie Frank to the victim or the scene. Ideally, they would search for traces of blood in his car or a shoe to match their partial print in his house, but they had nothing to show that his car was in the vicinity of Hillside that night to grant the warrant.

The questioning at the station began with his whereabouts the night of the murder. He confirmed he was at the bar until around midnight. His alibi left him vulnerable since he departed the bar alone and arrived home to an empty house. No one to corroborate his story.

"Frank, you said you never go over near Hillside, yet the drop box you used was less than a half mile from that street." Karen gauged his response.

He shrugged.

Karen leaned toward him, giving him a hard stare. "There are video cameras at streetlights and at gas stations."

"Frank, right now you're not alibied." Riley watched for his reaction.

The only reaction was that of an annoyed, angry man.

Without justification, they couldn't hold Frank any longer. He signed his statement and was driven home.

Retreating to her office, Karen glanced at her watch. *Ali. Probably on her way to the bar.* A queasy sensation rumbled through her stomach. She wondered if Ali's nerves were as frazzled as hers.

"Thoughts on Frank's story," Riley said. "If we have a video that captures the drop box area, we could see if someone rummaged through the bags and took the jacket."

Karen looked up at Riley, acknowledging the promise in that approach. *Why didn't I think of that?*

"With the homicide, he could've parked on the main street and walked through the backyards," Riley said. "The yards to the right of Bobby's are open. I don't recall one of those neighbors having a backyard fence."

"You really think Frank's our guy?"

"I don't. Still…need to rule it out." Riley looked at her notes.

"Okay, so our perp approached Cliff from a backyard without a fence. We know they didn't walk down the street."

"And either Frank was wearing the jacket, or the perp grabbed it where Cliff left it on the fence." Riley looked skeptical.

Karen ruminated on the possibilities and missing pieces. "Someone grabbed it off the fence. Intentionally used it to cover themselves." She paused. "We can eliminate Vince."

"Probably Frank, as well." Riley stared across the office.

"Which brings me to Keith," Karen said. "He's a definite possible and never returned any of my calls. I've stopped by his house five times at all different times of the day."

"Avoiding you?"

"Feels that way, which makes him even more suspicious," Karen said. "He's young. Could've parked on another street, walked through the wooded area, or hopped a neighbor's fence."

"He'll be an easy check, coming from Jersey. Bridge cameras and E-ZPass will flag when he crossed the river," Riley said.

"Presuming he has E-ZPass." Karen referred to the toll transponder that most residents had in their cars for the local bridges and toll roads.

She shot a quick glance at her watch. After seven. *I need to meet Ali. Can't tell Riley I need to make a personal call.*

"Joey?" Riley threw out. "He's also young. Could just park on the main street and walk through the fenceless yards."

"Maybe." Karen frowned as she looked at her notes. "I'm getting more and more uncomfortable with Keith. He supposedly had a fair amount of anger toward Cliff."

"I'm still uncomfortable with Kenny and Doyle," Riley said.

"We can push on them next week." Karen turned her wrist and looked down. 7:15. *Should I still go? Maybe just apologize next week and say I got caught up with work.*

Riley was staring at her.

Can't tell her I have a date. She never talks about personal stuff. Karen shook away her mental distraction. "Sorry. I was supposed to be someplace at seven."

"Go. We'll get back at this next week," Riley said. "All we've got is a lot of conjecture and a little circumstantial evidence. We'll have plenty to check starting Monday."

They parted at 7:20 with Karen's nerves running rampant. *Just go. Decide what to do when you get there.*

In the parking lot of the Stewart James, Karen sat, wondering if she was ready for this. She stared straight ahead. Trying to shake her anxiety, she pulled an envelope from the passenger side visor—a letter she had received two days ago but avoided opening. As her stomach roiled with nervous energy over Ali, she engaged in one last delay tactic. Opening the letter from Miles, she read the first line:

Hey Sweetie, How is my favorite person? I miss you!

CHAPTER EIGHTEEN

Why am I forcing myself to read this? Karen stared at the letter, the words blurring. Ali's tender face and glowing smile flashed through her mind. It was time to push aside her anxiety and stop delaying. She tossed the note onto the passenger side floorboard, keenly aware that 7:35 was well beyond "fashionably late." With a determined nod, she hopped out and headed toward the entrance.

Grasping the bulky iron handle of the thick wooden door, a patron pushed from the inside and rushed toward her. Karen found herself face-to-face with Ali.

"I'm so sorry. I got caught up in an interrogation," Karen blurted.

"I just figured you weren't coming." Ali's tone was flippant. They stood frozen in the doorway. "Figured you stood me up."

"I don't stand people up." Direct and firm, Karen met Ali's deep-blue eyes.

"Well, I don't know you." A crisp response.

That caught Karen's attention. It was clear: Ali wasn't going to play the coy game as Tam had. She had botched her first impression with Ali.

"I'm really sorry. Please…let me buy you a beer." Karen knew it would require a concerted effort to mop up the mess she'd made.

Ali snorted. "I just downed two." Her gaze held firm, her tone unyielding. "Why didn't you just call, or text, to let me know you were running late?"

Because I'm an ass. "I wasn't thinking. I'm really sorry." She hadn't called because she feared Riley's reaction. Ali deserved better.

Ali sighed and pivoted toward the doorway.

Sitting at the bar in the center of the room, Karen took a long swallow of her beer. "I haven't been out on a…with someone, in a long time."

Ali chuckled. "A date?"

Karen fidgeted, avoiding eye contact.

"No need to be shy. I was hella nervous waiting for you. It's been a long time for me, too. And I probably wouldn't have come to this particular bar for a date."

Christ, I don't even know where any gay bars are. "I'm sorry. I only know the local pubs."

"It's fine. I was excited to see you…to get to know you." A smile crept over her face.

Karen gazed at Ali's soft face, the gentle curves of her jawline. She fidgeted, unsure how to make conversation.

"You had my number. Why didn't you just call or text?" Ali's voice was soft. "Figured you changed your mind." Ali focused on her bottle with a trancelike stare.

"No. I really wanted to see you." *C'mon, Capp! Don't sabotage this.*

"Just my own shit." Ali gave a shy smile.

As the conversation morphed, Ali let down her guard. Her infectious smile was back, and Karen saw her come to life as she shared her work as a professional artist—a world completely foreign to Karen. She allowed Ali to take control. It felt nice. Karen was always the one steering the ship, but she felt safe with Ali.

"I've always been immersed in artistic communities," Ali said. "I don't even know anyone in law enforcement."

"Well, now ya do." Karen smiled. "How does it feel knowing I'm involved in a murder investigation the whole town's talking about?"

Ali's smile faded.

"I'm sorry. Did that make you uncomfortable?"

"A little."

The bar became crowded and noisy, so they headed to the parking lot to finish their conversation. A light, drama-free conversation—a gift for Karen. Leaning against Karen's car, they both laughed and relived the events of last Sunday.

"Oh my God," Ali said. "When you hit the pedal and all the water and clay went flying…I did everything I could not to completely lose it."

"Thanks for reminding me." Karen playfully rolled her eyes.

"It was cute. Every beginner does it. You just did it in a monumental way."

"Well, my parents always said, when I do something, I do it at full speed."

Their laughter danced across the parking lot. It was an effortless laughter that Karen hadn't experienced with someone she'd just met and felt drawn to.

"Hey, what are you doing this weekend?" Ali asked. "I'm having some friends over for dinner tomorrow."

"Oh no. Tomorrow is Halloween. I always help my parents pass out candy to all the little gremlins."

"No worries. Rain check?"

She even makes it easy to say no. How refreshing. "Absolutely. Just need you to understand…things are really hectic right now. I never know how my day or week is going to go. Just the nature of my job."

"All good. Call me when it's good for you. My schedule is always flexible. We'll grab hoagies or steaks and just hang at my house. I'm a few blocks from the police station."

Karen felt a warm sensation rise to her chest. Her head felt like it was floating in the clouds. "You got it." Her voice came out soft, almost husky. She cleared her throat.

Karen's phone vibrated. A text from Riley. "I'm sorry. I really have to take this."

"No problem." Ali smiled. "Call me." She reached over and gave Karen a gentle hug good night.

Ali turned back. "You do still have my number, right?"

Karen felt her face flush. She smiled and nodded. "I do."

Karen vaguely remembered the drive home. She was basking in a new feeling. One of happiness and contentment. She felt a burst of excitement. Excitement laced with a tinge of fear. An arousal she couldn't explain. But most of all, she felt content.

Weekends always flew by when Karen was knee-deep in a case. On Monday, it was back to the grind and testing Frank's alibi. Video footage showed Frank dropping off three full bags of items, leaving them on the asphalt in front of the bin, but nothing to corroborate the jacket having been placed in those donation bags as he claimed. Frank still wasn't in the clear.

In the middle of the Frank debacle, the dirt sample from Joey's shoes came back from the lab. Lime. No mysterious kaolinite or ultisol and no silicon dioxide. In her office, Karen threw her jacket on a hook and felt her body collapse on her chair in frustration.

"What now, boss?" Riley said.

"Finish scanning the videos of the donation box?"

She and Riley hunkered down in Karen's office. The sky began to darken with storm clouds rolling in outside the lone window. The two sat, scanning hours of video. Finally, they caught a man walking up to the bags Frank left outside the bin. The unidentified man, disheveled and in dirt-stained clothes, looked around before beginning to pull out a variety of items. He grabbed a pair of shoes and walked away, leaving articles of clothing scattered on the asphalt. Still no jacket.

A bleary-eyed Karen popped on the fluorescent light in her office as the room darkened.

"Wanna finish this up tomorrow?" Riley said, getting up to leave.

Karen chucked her pen at the computer screen and sat back as the video footage continued to play. She, too, was ready to give up. At that moment, she spotted something.

"Hold on…check this out," she called to Riley.

She noted the same hobbling gait she remembered from the first day she met Cliff. As the man came into full view, she confirmed. It was Cliff. He pillaged through the bags stacked next to the donation bin. Within minutes, he pulled out a khaki jacket, unfolded it, and tried it on. He grabbed a handful of other items and walked away wearing the jacket.

"Frank's story checks out," Karen said. "Not sure if I'm happy or more frustrated."

"At least we know we can cross him off our list," Riley said. "Okay, we've identified all the hair fibers on the jacket. So how could someone else have worn that jacket and not shed any hair during a violent stabbing?"

"Maybe the perp wore something over his head, like a hoodie." Karen's face lit up. "Maybe he was bald or shaved his head. Keith has a shaved head."

She grabbed her jacket from the hook. "That bastard's been avoiding me. I'll pursue him from Jersey to Timbuktu if I have to." She headed out the door. "I'll touch base when I have something."

While she drove across the bridge to New Jersey, questions surfaced. Why had Keith been so persistent in avoiding her? What were he and Cliff arguing about?

Instead of heading back to Keith's house for the sixth time, she drove straight to his work site. Like Frank, Keith worked for a delivery service. Unlike Frank, he drove large trucks and made deliveries throughout the tri-state area. She stopped at the dispatch facility for MJD Trucking in Vineland, New Jersey.

The modest dispatch office reeked of cigarette smoke, making her sinuses ache. She grabbed the first driver she saw and flashed her badge.

"I'm looking for Keith Stephenson. A driver," she said.

The pot-bellied, stout man wore a flannel shirt with buttons stretched to their limit. He walked Karen over to a clipboard with a list of the day's routes and drivers.

"Right here." The man pointed with a stubby, grease-stained index finger. "These three stops…that's where he's headed today."

Punching the address for Manahawkin, New Jersey into her GPS, she groaned. Over an hour to the first stop. Just as she hopped on the highway, her phone chimed. Tam. *Ugh.* It went to voice mail. After a brief stint on the Atlantic City Expressway, she merged onto the Garden State Parkway for the remainder of the drive. Winding her way through small Atlantic Ocean beach towns with sparkling waterways and pine forestlands, she continued north. The coastline sat to her right, mostly obscured by vegetation and occasional small-town businesses. She felt her body relax with the scenic nature of the drive.

She was startled by the ring of her cell phone and glanced at it with an unexpected sense of excitement. The caller ID: Miles Stillwell. She let it go to voice mail. *What the hell is wrong with me? A month ago, I would have crashed my car to answer a call from him.*

Then it hit her. She recalled how she felt after she finally finished reading his letter. His level of self-absorption became apparent as he announced his return just after the new year. She rolled her eyes. *Yup…no need to rush back in time for the holidays on my account.* He also made the assumption that he was welcome to stay at her house. *Selfish ass.* Still, for whatever reason, she refused to sever ties with him.

In the meantime, the call she hoped for eluded her.

Karen hit Manahawkin by noon. No Keith. An hour and a half to the next location on major highways south to Claymont, Delaware, and finally, a relatively local stop, in Millville, New Jersey, by almost four. One by one, the same answer: No one had seen Keith Stephenson.

Furious, Karen headed back to the trucking headquarters demanding to speak with the warehouse manager. She was greeted by a middle-aged man in respectable business attire. He stood solemn and listened with patience.

"Detective, I truly apologize. The routes were established before the start of the day. Before anyone knew."

"Knew? Knew what?"

"Keith called out sick this morning."

Oh, for fuck's sake. She rolled her eyes in exasperation.

It was almost 4:30 when she saw a message from Riley on her phone. *Probably wants to know what the hell I've accomplished.* Also, two more text messages from Tam, "needing to talk." Her patience with Tam and her incessant attempts at communication was running thin.

"Thank God," she muttered, noting a white sedan sitting in the gravel driveway as she pulled up to the house in Salem.

A couple of firm raps on the front door brought a tall, muscular man with a shaved head to the door.

Karen pulled out her badge. "Keith Stephenson?"

His pale, chiseled face studied hers. He nodded.

"I'm here to ask you some questions about your brother."

"Cliff?"

"Do you have *another* brother?"

"No," he muttered, standing in the doorway. "He's a greedy ass. Was." His voice snapped as he looked away.

Not exactly the response she was expecting. The hair began to rise on the back of her neck. "Greedy? He was homeless."

"Yeah, well, he had it coming. Left Salem for some big-ass job," he said. "Left me here to take care of my ma…by myself."

Now it started to make sense. Cliff went to Pennsylvania to work at a refinery. Keith stayed in Salem and took care of their mother, who had been in the nursing home for the last decade. *What about the sister? She moved away, too. Is he pissed at her, too?*

"Fuckin' job blew up. All of a sudden, he wants back. Like I'm supposed to save his ass."

Karen could predict what was coming next.

"Told him to go fuck himself."

With the contentious nature of the brothers' relationship, Karen felt further questioning warranted an official visit to the station with Riley present.

"Keith, we really need your help. Would you be willing to come in, answer some questions, and give us an official statement about what you know?"

Silence.

"Keith, an official statement…that's recorded…it protects you."

He grimaced.

She stood on the porch, holding her eyes firm on him, employing her favorite tactic—silence.

"I don't guarantee nothin'. And I can't make it 'til next Monday."

She nodded. "That's fine." It wasn't, but she opted to back off and let him have a few days. With Riley by her side, she felt confident they would yield better results than if she tried to pry answers out of him now on his own turf. She contemplated conducting the interview in his house. *Probably have to sit on that mattress in the living room.* A shiver radiated through her torso. Just the thought of it skeeved her out.

On the drive home, thoughts of Ali crept in—the same feelings of excitement and fear. Even though she hadn't heard from her, it didn't put a damper on her feelings. She did, however, receive a welcomed and unexpected surprise later that night. A call from Caiden.

After superficial chitchat, Karen felt an urge to test-drive the topic of Ali with her daughter. Rambling through how she met Ali, she spoke of how kind Ali was.

"We went out for drinks. Had a really nice connection." Karen felt the smile pop on her face. "We don't have a lot in common, but conversation was fun. Easy." She shared how she wanted to spend more time with her. She could almost hear Caiden smiling through the phone.

Karen mentioned the letter Miles had sent. Her words were met with silence. She circled back to Ali.

"What's wrong with me?" Karen asked. "Am I that desperate for a relationship that I need to be with a woman?"

"Whoa, Mom…what's wrong with being interested in a woman?" Caiden sounded personally offended. "Some of my best friends are lesbian, and they're fire."

Karen chuckled at her Gen-Z daughter's vocabulary but then found herself tensing at hearing the word lesbian. *Am I now a lesbian because I enjoy spending time with Ali?*

"I know, sweetie. I'm just trying to figure out why one minute I think about being alone and Miles returning, and the next there's a woman I hardly know and I can't get her off my mind."

"I say, eighty-six Miles and go for Ali."

Karen laughed. "You haven't even met her."

"No. But I haven't heard your voice sound this upbeat for a long time." Caiden paused. "I like it, Mom. It's great."

Karen shook her head. Her daughter knew her all too well. Caiden was picking up on something while Karen was battling confusion and trying to push it away.

"Just go with it, Mom. Quit trying to rationalize everything. You do enough of that at work."

Caiden had a point. But Karen didn't know how to go with her feelings, especially when her feelings fell contrary to everything she had always known. Her whole life had been spent establishing goals and going after them with fervor—and following convention, doing what was expected.

Caiden was of a generation much more open-minded and welcoming of all people. She never got caught up in societal rules and prejudices. Karen took pride in her daughter's progressive attitude but had her own norms and expectation demons to battle. Societal rules *had* to be followed. Only now, in her forties, had she started to rethink all those restrictions.

Before heading home from work the next day, Karen gave Ali a call. Since Ali lived blocks from the police station, Karen figured she could stop by under the guise of "being in the neighborhood." The perfect excuse. The call went to voice mail.

Shit. The perfect plan—ruined. She left a casual I-was-in-the-neighborhood message. Ten minutes later, pulling into her driveway, her caller ID lit up. Ali Barnes. An enormous wave of emotions and adrenaline crashed over her.

CHAPTER NINETEEN

"Sorry I missed your call. I was cleaning up at the studio," Ali said. "Still at work?"

"Nah. Just pulled into my driveway." *Ugh. Why did I say that?*

"Is it that far to drive back?"

Her direct manner caught Karen off guard. It was as if Ali was goading Karen with her faux reason to stop by. *I'm a forty-four-year-old woman…why do I need an excuse?*

Ali's voice was light and upbeat. "How about we meet for dinner? We can find a place in between. Fair?"

Karen would have driven to the moon and back to see Ali. She really didn't need her to make things fair.

"How about Zac's? I haven't had a burger from there in ages."

"There's no alcohol at Zac's," Karen jokingly complained.

"You'll survive." Ali giggled. "We can come back to my place and have a drink afterward. Sound good?"

It sounded amazing. Zac's at 6:30 and drinks at Ali's afterward.

At home, Karen locked up her firearm and threw down a beer to calm her nerves while pondering what to wear. She hadn't been on a date in ages, and never with someone of the same sex. Half her closet lay stacked on her bed by the time she settled for a pair of jeans and a hooded V-neck sweater.

Karen was the first to arrive at Zac's, making sure to be prompt this time. Moments later, Ali scooted past the line of customers, walking up in jeans, a sweatshirt, and a pair of white Converse Chucks.

As before, they fell into effortless conversation, each with a sloppy burger, lots of napkins, and a bin of fries between them.

"How's the case going?" Ali took a bite of her burger, juice and patty oozing out the back end.

"I really can't talk about it. Hopefully, we'll make an arrest soon." Karen looked down at her tray. *Actually, we have no reason to hope that. We're not any closer.* It bothered her that she couldn't be honest about the case with Ali, but that was protocol. Her pat response would have to suffice.

"I honestly don't need to talk about the case." Ali smiled. "I guess I'm just curious about what your days are like. Where do you even begin when you have such a difficult case like this?"

Jesus. How refreshing. Karen met Ali's enchanting blue eyes. She walked through the evidence collection procedure and the types of evidence they look for.

"Everything you can imagine gets collected…and scrutinized. We'll literally vacuum the area around a victim to look for minute traces of evidence."

Ali's eyes went from oval to round.

"We examine the position of the body and the extent to which it has started to develop a stiffness, called rigor mortis. We examine bloodstains and patterns in which the blood spatters—"

"Okay, that's good. Let's just eat."

Karen chuckled. She remembered her sister-in-law, a nurse, talking about types of diarrhea one night…over dinner. Bloodstains and spatter were likely outside the purview of Ali, the artist.

"Perhaps we should talk about how clay spatters." Karen shot her a grin.

Like a huge pin to burst a carefree bubble, Frank Ryanard walked in. Karen spotted him before he noticed her. She prayed he would think better than to initiate an altercation. He scowled when he finally saw her.

"Listen, Ali. I just need to prepare you. There's someone—"

"What the hell are you doing here? Don't you have a job to do?" Frank yelled, causing patrons to stop and stare. The restaurant went silent. "Don't you have a murder to solve? Or are you still pointing fingers at innocent people, like me?"

Karen took a deep breath. *Well, Ali wants to know what my job is like. She's got a front-row seat.* "Just doing my job, Frank. Why don't you go enjoy your dinner?" Karen kept a stone face.

"Your job? We still have a fucking murderer out there and you're busy making up shit about me."

"Frank, I'm going to ask nicely—"

"*Fuck you!*"

"You can have a beef with me, but right now you're ruining everyone else's dinner. Is that really what you want to do?"

"Instead of sitting here and snuggling up to your girlfriend, why aren't you out finding the real killer? Fucking dyke."

She'd heard homophobic banter in the police department throughout her career, but it was the first time she'd experienced, firsthand, the negative and derogatory comments directed at people in the gay and lesbian community. Normally, she'd be the one standing up for the person being harassed. But now, she was fending off the poisonous arrows of hatred. Karen took a deep breath, but before she could respond, a diner stood up.

"Frank…go away. No one wants to hear your crap," the young man said.

"Fuck you," Frank snapped.

Another man, twice Frank's size, stood up. "Shut it, Frank. If you can't respect law enforcement, you don't belong here." He took a step toward Frank, saying to Karen, "We got your back."

Karen nodded her gratitude and looked over at Ali, who never flinched, continuing to matter-of-factly snack on the basket of fries.

Ali's smile widened. "So, you're my girlfriend now? Okay!"

Karen couldn't help but laugh and shake her head. *Ali handled that like a champ.* Then the depressing realization: *She's probably had plenty of experience with hatred and bigotry.* A rush of sadness draped over her like a weighted blanket.

Frank retreated and stormed out.

Ali tapped on the Formica-topped table to signal Karen to sit back down.

"I'm sorry," Karen said in a hushed voice.

Ali waved a hand at her. "That's nothing. Look, he's the one who's miserable. Not me. Why should I let him bother me?"

Karen felt caught in Ali's calming, beautiful eyes. "How do you not let it bother you?"

"He was attacking one aspect—my sexuality." She grabbed a fry and popped it in her mouth. "I'm not just my sexuality. I'm so much more. A lot more." She wiped her hands on a napkin. "I'm a good friend…an outstanding potter…a loving daughter. I'm an upstanding citizen." She looked directly at Karen. "I'm multifaceted. And I won't allow him, or anyone, to define me by just one facet…a facet he doesn't even understand or accept. He's the one who's limited. I won't let his hate and labels limit me."

Karen sat, flabbergasted. Awestruck. She had never heard anyone articulate this concept so eloquently. She felt a slow smile emerge as she marveled at Ali and her strength. *Supposedly I'm the big, tough cop, yet she's the one that's got her shit together.* She felt proud of Ali. Proud to be sitting across the table from this amazing woman and sharing her evening. *Caiden would love her. They'd be like two peas in a morally righteous pod.*

"Still up for coming over?" Ali asked.

"Absolutely." Karen couldn't say it fast enough.

Ali lived in the section of town known for artists, a neighborhood from a time gone by with streets named after trees, simple homes, and sidewalks paved with brick. The quaint, shoebox-sized homes were perfect for the meager income of a small-town artist.

Karen followed Ali to her house on Mulberry Street, noting how close it was to the station and a mere five minutes from her own house. Yet Ali's neighborhood felt completely different from hers, like something straight out of *Mayberry RFD* and with neighbors who all looked out for each other.

There wasn't much to the teeny bungalow. A hallway behind the living room led to the bedroom and bathroom. French doors with paned glass, just off the living room, led to an area with a potter's wheel and several shelves filled with spectacular pieces of completed pottery. All totaled, the house was a mere eight hundred square feet.

From the front door, they entered the living room. Ali threw her jacket in the hall closet just to the left and hustled to the kitchen.

"Try this…it's excellent." Ali handed Karen a bottle of Victory Summer Love Ale from a local microbrewery.

"Yeah, I like Victory. Thank you."

Ali sat on the couch with a glass of cabernet and tapped on the spot next to her.

"I'm sorry about what happened earlier—" Karen said.

"This isn't my first rodeo. I don't let that stuff bother me. Waste of time."

"I admire that about you. It takes a lot of courage to be authentic in a world filled with ignorant people and hate."

"I have a choice. Be authentic and be happy, or live the life that others think I should live and be miserable. To me, it's a no-brainer."

Be authentic and be happy…it's a no-brainer. It seemed so hard to conceive that happiness could be attained without following certain standards, rules, constructs. *But what if those standards don't line up with your authenticity?*

"Karen?" Ali called out, pulling Karen out of a faraway trance.

"Sorry. I was just thinking about what you said."

As Ali went on to share aspects of her life, Karen felt her body settle into the couch, enjoying the simplicity of the conversation.

"I grew up in Hudson, New York," Ali told her. "Things are far less progressive there than they are here. When I was twelve, my father died, so my grandparents stepped in to help my mom."

"How did you handle that? Losing your father."

"I felt the loss, but I think I was too young to get it. It wasn't like we were all that close."

Karen began to sense that this very strong and independent woman also had weak spots and fears.

"When I turned seventeen, my mom told me I was adopted. I finally understood why I didn't look like anyone else." She let out a brief laugh. "I felt loved, but also like I didn't belong." Ali took a sip of her wine. "After I went off to college, I figured out my sexuality. I dated. But no matter how good the relationships were or how many friends I had, I always felt I lacked something."

Karen realized she hadn't even touched her beer. She finally picked up the icy bottle.

"It was as if I wasn't good enough…wasn't wanted. As if I didn't matter."

How could this amazing woman feel like she didn't matter? "But why? Did someone say something to make you feel that way?"

"Nope. It was all in my head." Ali took another sip and put her glass down. "I got into a relationship. Got hurt real bad when she left. I was a mess. I was such a mess that a friend urged me to try therapy."

Karen fought back an eye roll. She had a less-than-positive attitude toward psychotherapy.

"Therapy was okay, but what I ended up learning about myself was super helpful."

Karen finally took a swig of beer. The cool liquid washed over the sadness she felt building in her throat.

"My adoption had created those issues. Not consciously, but subconsciously. My first connection was to my birth mother, who gave me up." She went on to explain how research showed that adopted kids carried that initial loss with them throughout their lives. "Feeling not wanted, or that I don't matter…it's as if those would have been things I would have verbalized at birth…if I was able to."

Ali's self-awareness floored Karen. She began to feel small in front of Ali's transparency.

"The long and short of it is, I have a lot of fears about not being good enough for someone to stay. I have fears that if I let someone in, they'll go away. It's like a perpetual tape playing in my head. I have to fight hard to turn off that tape recorder." Ali looked down at her glass of wine. "Consequently, I don't open up my heart easily."

Christ, I'm not sure I'm ready to be this forthcoming with her. Karen gathered her thoughts. "Do you know who your birth parents are?"

Ali let out a muffled laugh. "I found my birth mother through DNA testing, but when I reached out to her, she refused to have anything to do with me."

Karen was horrified. *How could a mother bring a child into the world and not want to be a part of their life?* The concept absolutely baffled her. She bit her tongue. "That must have been awful," she finally said, wincing and shaking her head.

Ali shrugged. "It was a gut punch at first, but then I looked at where I would have been…where my birth mother lived…what her life was like. I knew I had a much better life with my mother, even without my father."

"Do you remember your father?" Karen was still astounded by Ali's composure.

"Some stuff. But I mostly remember he wasn't around much. He worked a lot and was out of town."

Karen found herself counting her blessings. She had always appreciated her large, close-knit family.

Ali shifted the conversation. "So…tell me about your family. Did you always live here?"

"Born and raised. I have one absolutely amazing daughter who just got a full scholarship to the Fashion Institute of Technology in

New York." *Definitely boasting.* "My parents live down the street from me and are very active and independent. Sometimes I think their lives are busier than mine." She chuckled.

Ali smiled. "I have friends whose parents live just down the street from them, too. That seems to be a common thing here."

"It's not that way everywhere?"

"Not where I come from." Ali smiled at her. "Your daughter sounds amazing. I'm sure you're super proud of her."

Karen smiled back and nodded. "My parents are a wild combination of Italian and Jewish. I think that's where I get my assertiveness."

"You're Jewish?"

"I'm not really anything. I don't get into religious dogma. But my mom is Italian Catholic, so I was raised Catholic. Catholic upbringing with a touch of Yiddish here and there."

Ali shifted in her seat. "You have a daughter but haven't told me about a husband."

"Divorced. I'd like to blame it all on him for not being supportive of my ambitions, but I know we both played a role."

Karen found herself unexpectedly opening up about her failed marriage and the numerous poor relationship decisions that followed. She avoided the whole topic of Miles.

"You've never been with a woman," Ali stated, not a question.

Karen felt an uncomfortable sensation rise inside. "No."

"So…where did that come from, what you did at the studio?"

"I have no fucking idea." Karen let out a nervous laugh before realizing it wasn't a joke to Ali.

Ali looked injured.

"What I mean…" She floundered, grasping for words. "I don't know where it came from. But I felt something very powerful. Not sure how to describe it." Karen felt exposed. She felt her face flush as she bit her bottom lip. "I can't really explain how I felt or how I'm feeling. It's all so new to me." She tried to assure Ali that this wasn't a cruel game but felt like she was failing miserably.

"I get it." Ali's voice was soft. "What do you want, Karen…with me?"

What the hell do I say? Karen fumbled to gather her thoughts and understand the intense feelings brewing inside. "I don't know. I know I feel something powerful when I'm with you. I know I love our conversations." She looked down and ran her fingers along her sweating beer bottle. "I know what I want in a relationship, and I know I haven't been able to find it." She looked up at Ali. "Am I making any sense? I feel like I'm rambling now."

Ali gave a compassionate smile. "I'm enjoying getting to know you, too. I have no agenda." She reached over and placed a hand on Karen's wrist.

Karen felt a surge of warmth radiate from her wrist up her arm. A charged sensation. Exhilarating.

"Let's just continue to get to know each other. If this feels like something you'd like to pursue on an intimate level, you let me know." She looked into Karen's eyes as if gauging her reaction. "I'm not going to push this one way or another."

Karen sat, immobile. *What a difference from Tam. Quite frankly, what a difference from the men I've dated.*

"Sounds perfect," Karen said. Gratitude welled up inside. Gratitude for Ali's kindness and patience. "Ali, I need to be honest with you. There's a man I've been dating. He's always out of town and I'm not sure it's what I want anymore." She felt herself choking on her words. "I know it's not what I'm looking for. But having a daughter…I just need to proceed cautiously. What I do know is that I'm very happy when I'm with you."

Karen saw Ali noticeably swallow hard and look down. She seemed to force a smile as she looked back up. But then her smile widened as she met Karen's eyes.

"I'm very happy when I'm with you, too," Ali said with a quick nod.

Around midnight, Ali walked Karen to her car and finished the evening with a peck on the cheek and a hug. Karen felt her heart catch as those soft lips touched her cheek. A flood of warmth ran through her.

During the quick drive home, she found herself luxuriating in thoughts of Ali and their night together. So simple. Fun. Easy conversation. No expectations. Yet something felt alluring…almost forbidden. *Be authentic and be happy…it's a no-brainer.* Those words punctuated the evening, replaying over and over in her head.

CHAPTER TWENTY

Karen hit the next morning surprisingly chipper and eager to determine the next direction for the investigation. She and Riley were back to the drawing board.

"We've ruled out Frank and Joey," Karen said. "So now where do we go?"

"Not all cases get solved. You have no idea how tall the stack is for unsolved homicides."

Karen shot Riley a disapproving glance. "We still have Keith. We'll talk with him next week," she said.

In the meantime, Karen spent the rest of the afternoon scanning traffic and neighborhood footage to ease the waiting time for Keith.

The leaves were falling as the first week of November neared an end. Nights had grown colder, it was dark by five p.m., and her house was empty. She decided to phone Ali and offer to bring over dinner.

"Anything in particular?" Karen asked.

"Surprise me."

Karen picked up a grilled panini, a quart of broccoli cheddar soup, a large Greek salad, a chicken pot pie, and a quiche. *Surely this should cover all the bases.*

At the front door, Ali snorted, looking at the bags and bags of food. "Are we feeding the neighborhood?"

Karen shrugged. "It's my Jewish half." She walked past Ali and into the kitchen.

With a bottle of wine between them, they picked away at dinner and, before long, were lost in conversation—for hours. Effortless.

The conversation veered back to relationships, with each going through a silly list of people they had dated and their dating follies. Karen couldn't help but mention Tam and how Tam pushed her boundaries.

"Oh. I thought you two were together. You were squabbling like an old married couple."

Karen rolled her eyes. "Nah. I think she was interested, but I never felt a connection."

"How'd you two meet?"

"She's the daughter of a man I arrested a decade ago. She lived in New York the last fourteen years, so she's more of a stranger than a native in town." Karen paused, wondering how much more to share, but felt a need to clarify. "I was trying to be a friend."

Karen explained how Tam worked as an artist in New York City but found it too expensive to live there. She hesitated. Those were Tam's words. Her research yielded a slightly different story.

"It took her fourteen years to realize that?" Ali laughed.

"I think she did well for a period of time. She owns a Mini Cooper. I don't even make enough for that."

"A Mini? I don't make that much either. It's also very impractical. How does she drive her pieces to art festivals? Is there even any room in a Mini to pick up boxes of clay?"

Ali sounded either skeptical or jealous, Karen couldn't tell which. "What kind of car do you drive?" Karen worked to change the subject.

"A Les-baru." Ali let out an uncharacteristic belly laugh.

"A what?"

"A Les-baru. A Subaru Outback. It seems to be all the rage with lesbians these days." Ali couldn't stop giggling.

"Oh my God, you're just like my mother," Karen said through her laughter. "She gets going and can't stop."

When their laughter finally ceased, Ali pointed out aspects of Tam's story that didn't quite match up. She asked about Tam's employment status and where she got money to cover her pottery expenses, let alone her car.

"How can she afford a studio membership?" Ali's tone was sharp.

"She needs a membership?"

"She shouldn't have been in there if she's not a member. Without a membership, neither of you were allowed in the studio that Sunday. And she left both of your wheels a mess. Really uncool."

Karen felt her frustration grow. "Ya know, I really don't see Tam anymore."

Ali seemed to read the mood change and shifted subjects. She was curious about what motivated Karen through the hurdles and roadblocks of her career.

"How do you do it? A male-dominated, often sexist, very homophobic environment."

Talking about her job was in Karen's comfort zone, but she pondered her response. She reflected on previous conversations with Riley about her experiences as a woman of color in law enforcement, dealing with sexism and racism. Always feeling a need to go beyond the basic requirements. Thoughts of Brennan flashed before her and her fears of being a strong—perceived as masculine—woman and, at the same time, unable to secure a heterosexual relationship.

"I love what I do. I love seeking justice for those who've been harmed," she said in a quiet voice.

"I admire that." Ali sat back against the worn sofa cushions and took a deep breath. "You're a strong, determined, exceptional woman."

Karen allowed herself a smile. Compliments. Something she struggled with. Something she was unaccustomed to, at least from someone she had feelings for.

Karen deflected the praise. "What's your biggest fear, Ali?"

Ali looked away and drew in a long breath. "Being intimate with someone."

Karen looked at her, stunned.

"Being intimate with someone and having them see my body."

As a middle-aged woman who had already gone through the childbearing process, Karen could relate. She had seen her body change over the years. Still, Ali's words surprised her. Ali appeared incredibly fit and toned.

"Your body? You have a fabulous body." Karen almost choked on her words the minute they came out.

Ali gave a nervous smile. "About two years ago. I was diagnosed with cancer."

Karen couldn't prevent a gasp.

"Breast. We caught it early, but I had a lumpectomy. I have a nasty, ugly scar on my left breast."

Karen wrapped an arm around Ali's shoulders, marveling at her resilience.

Ali gave a brisk swipe at the tears that escaped down her cheek. "I haven't been intimate since the surgery."

"Your choice?" Karen asked gently. "Or have you just not met the right person yet?"

"A little of both, I suppose." Ali sat up as if gathering herself. "Haven't put myself out there, but I've also pushed people away."

"Oh, no, no, no," Karen joked. "Pushing people away is *my* trademark."

Ali broke into a soft laugh. "No, you don't own the market on that."

Karen smiled, gazing into Ali's deep-blue eyes.

"It's all about being willing to take a chance…to let someone in," Ali said. "That's super hard for me."

"I think you're hella brave. Truly." Karen was still gazing into Ali's eyes. "Your scar is like a medal of resilience and strength. And if someone can't handle that, they're not worth your time."

Ali gave a weak smile. "I guess I've needed to hear those words. Probably for years. Most of my friends avoid the topic. With the diagnosis, I kinda established a live-life-to-the-fullest mentality."

Karen couldn't help but think Ali was the perfect tonic for her cautious, career-driven approach. They had both come into each other's lives with personal issues and life scars, and were a symbiotic support system of sorts for one another.

"What about you? What's your biggest fear?" Ali probed. "And stop with the tough cop, stoic act."

"It's just not a simple answer."

"I know I look like a dumb artist, but I really can handle complex things."

"I think it's me that can't handle complex."

Ali sat patiently. Karen's hallmark tactic of silence.

Karen stumbled over her words. "Look, Ali, all of this…this stuff going on in my life. I haven't sorted through it."

"Okay. Let's start with the 'stuff.' What are you referring to?"

Karen shared her parents' close marriage and how she couldn't imagine either of them being without the other. The type of relationship she had been exposed to her whole life was the one she had always longed for.

"I've often wondered whether I would ever have that comfort… that support…that happiness." Karen paused, trying to figure out where she was going and how to broach the main issue she needed to explain. She took a deep breath. "I've always dated men. That's what I thought I was supposed to do. It's what I saw my entire life." She reached for the half-empty bottle and refilled both their wineglasses. "Got married, started a family…" Her voice faded off. "I have a wonderful daughter, so no regrets. But successful relationships have eluded me."

"So, what's your fear? Finding one that works?"

Karen started to protest but caught herself. "I don't think that's it, but I guess I'm not sure."

Ali watched her.

How can I tell her? The dichotomy of feeling an attraction to Ali and wanting to spend time with her but fearing the lesbian label. Karen fidgeted with her wineglass, repeatedly repositioning herself on the couch as she struggled to find words.

"Ali, I really am open-minded. I have no problem with alternative lifestyles. I…I—"

"You're just uncomfortable with it for you…right?"

"God, that sounds so incredibly stupid." *Not to mention, Caiden would kill me.* "But, yeah…I think I'm afraid of going down that road." She looked at Ali, tears resting on her lower lids. "Does that make any sense?"

Ali smiled and touched her shoulder. "Of course it does. All of us that've come out have gone through it to one degree or another. Personally, I can't even imagine considering it in my forties."

Karen smirked. "Are you saying I'm too old to come out? I'm over the hill?"

Ali's smile widened. "I'm saying, I think it gets harder, especially when you've already established your life and lifestyle. But…it's never too late. And if it brings you happiness, I think that's all that matters."

God, Caiden would absolutely love this woman. "My biggest fear is…" Karen paused and took a deep breath. This was going to be the bravest thing she had done in a long time. "It's that people will stop accepting me, stop loving me if I…get together with a woman."

Ali nodded. "If people toss you aside…if they disregard all the things they love and admire about you now…then they never really loved or respected you in the first place."

Karen suddenly felt a wave of exhaustion. She didn't want to abruptly pull away from Ali, but she knew she needed to get out of there. Her head needed to sort through the mountain of feelings building up inside. That mountain was hovering on the edge of becoming a landslide.

"Thank you, Ali. I suppose I just need to sit with this a bit…let it all sink in." Karen paused as her head spun. She floundered, struggling to find words to share her appreciation for Ali's soothing words. Her voice softened as she fought back her emotions. "Thank you." She couldn't seem to articulate anything beyond those two words.

At the door of the teeny house, she turned to Ali. And in a terrifying moment for her, she allowed her vulnerable side to show. "Ali. You could have a million scars. You'd still be just as beautiful outside as you are inside."

Ali fought back tears and rewarded Karen with a heartfelt embrace.

Karen met Ali's ocean-blue eyes. A fear seared through her as an underlying excitement fought to emerge. Her eyes drifted down to Ali's mouth. Soft, gentle, sensual. A tender embrace moved to a short, but passionate, kiss goodnight.

Karen wanted to race out the door and run all the way home. She wanted to stay, embraced in Ali's warm arms, and feel the tenderness of her kiss. During the five-minute drive home, her head felt like it was going to explode. She needed the solitude of her living room. *Christ, there's irony. I've been hating the emptiness of that room. Now I can't wait to escape to it.*

She replayed her hesitation with Ali—her unwillingness to accept her attraction to her simply because she was a woman. She recoiled, thinking about her words and her hesitation. *Will she even want to see me again?* She needed to sit still, alone, and sort through it all. Everything she had known and trusted her entire life…it all felt like it was unraveling before her. *What do you want, Karen?*

CHAPTER TWENTY-ONE

By the start of the week, two pleasant surprises arrived for Karen: a text from Ali inviting her to the studio's Pottery Holiday Exhibit on Friday evening, and Keith actually showing up for his interview. Karen rushed to text Ali back, leaving Keith waiting in the interview room.

Would love to. Please be flexible. Investigation could pull me away.

Ali responded with a thumbs-up.

Keith sat on a wooden chair, leaning his elbows firmly on the metal table, hands clasped. He didn't appear nervous. Just uncomfortable. Karen had already obtained evidence that Keith was, in fact, in Pennsylvania on the night of the murder. The key rested with tying Keith to the crime scene and what he would reveal.

"Keith, as you know, Detective Riley and I are investigating the death of your brother," Karen said without preamble.

He didn't respond or make eye contact.

"Can you tell us why you were engaged in an argument with your brother…a few months ago?"

Keith glanced from one detective to the other. "Ma gave me money to give to him. Shoulda kept it. Cost me five bucks just to cross the bridge to bring it to him." He sat back in his chair, dangling his right arm on the table. "I was pissed. Had to drive over here just to save his sorry ass."

"Do you recall coming over here on October ninth?" Karen leaned in toward him.

"Fuck if I know. What was that…a Thursday, a Friday?"

"Friday."

Keith was silent, squirming in his chair. Then his face shaded red. "Ah, man." His tone seemed almost embarrassed. "Went to Grimaldi's with a few friends. Picked up this hot chick at the bar. Went back to her place…did each other in my back seat."

Karen controlled her eye roll. "Can you tell me who you were with…in your…back seat."

"A guy named Jack Doyle," Keith said. "His daughter. Meghan. She's fuckin' hot." He cackled.

Oh, good Lord. Of all the daughters for him to have sex with. "How often do you go over to Jack Doyle's place?"

"Shit…never. And I ain't never gone back. He caught me all over her. Fucking threatened me with a knife."

Karen and Riley looked at each other.

"What kind of knife?" Riley asked casually.

"Fuck. I don't know. A big-ass, sharp one. I don't know one knife from the next."

All of a sudden, it was like a lightbulb went off in Keith's brain. "Shit. Doyle's pressing charges against me, ain't he? His daughter totally consented—"

Karen cut him off. "He's not pressing charges." She stared at him for a moment. "What did you do next?"

"Pulled up my pants and drove home."

Riley scribbled notes on a notepad. They could circle back to the Grimaldi's bartenders again to check Keith's story, but more importantly, they needed to have a little chat with Doyle.

"You have any proof as to when you got home. Ring camera? Someone you spoke to—"

"I don't got no camera, and everyone in the area was asleep. House lights were all out." Keith gave her a blank stare, resting his hands and scuffed-up knuckles on the table.

Karen knew she could always verify the time he crossed the bridge back into New Jersey. She shifted the topic. "You never called me when I left my card on your door…numerous times. You never stopped by to identify your brother's body. Why was that?"

As angry and belligerent as Keith sounded when he spoke of Cliff, Karen's question stopped him in his tracks. He stared at her. And as hard as he appeared to fight it, his eyes began to well up.

"I'm not good at that shit." He looked up to the ceiling vent as if trying to gather himself and hide his emotions. "I never been good at it. Ever since my old man died."

Karen scooted a Kleenex box across the table to him.

"I knew something would eventually happen. Can't stay safe on the streets."

"Do you have any idea who might want to hurt him?" Riley asked.

"Nah. People liked him. Pissed me off." His eyes drifted. He stared at the two-way mirror with a long silence. "Shoulda let him come home. Not much family left, ya know."

Karen nodded. "Okay, Keith. That's it…for now. We'll have a statement for you to sign. If you think of anything else, will you give us a call?" She handed him another business card and escorted him out.

"Do you believe Doyle threatened him with a knife?" Karen asked Riley.

"Believe it's possible? Absolutely. But did it happen?"

Karen surveyed her stack of notes, feeling her eyes gloss over. "Just seems too coincidental that this whole 'threatened by a man with a knife' thing happens the same night Cliff is brutally murdered…with a knife."

"And likely within the same time frame in question."

"Guess we know what the rest of our week is going to entail." Karen gave a weary, but hopeful, smile.

Karen knew pursuing Doyle was going to be a chore and a maze of craziness. For the remainder of the week, he and Kenny were out of the house. Neither of them returned her calls. With other cases landing on her desk, the Friday Holiday Exhibit seemed tenuous. She begrudgingly shot a text to Ali Thursday evening and apologized in advance.

Ali promptly tapped back, *No worries. A few friends are coming over for a drink. Stop by if you can.*

In her driveway after a long Friday and work week, she shot Ali a quick text apologizing for missing the exhibit. No response.

Karen eased her tired body up the walkway. She felt the familiar empty house dread. A half hour later, she heard the ping of a return text. *Feel free to come by.*

The sound of that incoming text was music to her ears. Even through her exhaustion, she felt a renewed sense of energy. The perfect stimulant for a long, emotional, and challenging week.

Karen grabbed a bottle of wine and headed over to the little bungalow. Street parking was crowded—typical for a Friday night—so she had to park a few blocks away. With the front door open when she arrived, Karen let herself in through the storm door. Ali appeared from the kitchen where the group was gathered.

"Hey. Glad you made it." Ali smiled and waved Karen toward the back of the house. "Let me introduce you to my friends."

She introduced Dagney, a sculpture artist at the studio, and Roberto, an oil painter. Karen had never been around so many artists…ever. Roberto's wide smile stood out against his dark skin. Heavyset, with black tight curly hair and thick, soft lips, his smile lit up his face.

Dagney was exactly what Karen envisioned an artist to look like: jet-black hair with a long streak of blond down the left side. She was also incredibly thin. Quiet and reserved, she seemed to feel awkward and uncomfortable with Karen.

Karen pulled Ali aside and tipped her head in the direction of Dagney. "Old girlfriend?"

Ali gave a hearty laugh. "Not even close. Best friend."

As the artists began talking about the exhibit, an awkward discomfort flooded over Karen. She had nothing in common with these people—nothing to even add to the conversation. Wanting terribly to spend time with Ali, she tried to make the best of it and join in the chatter where she could—which was minimal. Ali made sure to explain things to Karen to help her feel included. And while Karen appreciated Ali's consideration, she was tense, her smile forced. She didn't belong.

For the first time, she felt out of place around Ali. Not even that Sunday at the studio, when she totally botched her attempt at pottery, did she feel this alienated. She was having second thoughts about coming over.

Roberto was the first to leave, and Karen saw it as her opening to head out. There was no point in belaboring the evening and hoping for something that wasn't there. She was hurting and wanted to get out—to be alone.

Karen said good night to the two remaining women. A wounded look came over Ali's face. Karen knew that on some level Ali cared for her, at least enough to help her feel included. But something was missing. As Karen headed for the door, Ali jumped up.

"Let me walk you to your car," she said.

Hurt and feeling a disconnect that ran through every pore in her body, Karen scoffed. "I'm a cop. I'll be fine."

Ali cocked her head, as if confused or hurt. "I know you'll be fine." She made unwavering eye contact with Karen. "I'll walk you to your car."

It was the first time they had been alone all night. They walked the couple blocks toward Karen's car in silence.

Ali broke the void. "I'm sorry if this wasn't your gig tonight."

Karen plodded along beside her, voiceless. Battling her emotions, she finally spoke. "The evening. It was for you and your friends. I should've stayed home." Her voice was a dejected whisper.

"No." Ali became animated. "I'm glad you came. I really wanted to see you."

Ali showed her cards. And Karen realized she had misinterpreted every one of Ali's actions. Ali was being open and honest. Now, would she be able to let Ali in, or would she push her away? She didn't have that answer yet.

Arriving at her car, Karen turned to Ali with a soft smile. "Thank you. Thank you for your openness and honesty. I appreciate it." She could feel tears building in the back of her throat.

They stood, silent, in front of the row of quaint homes, all with fresh fallen leaves neatly raked in piles at the curb. Most of the trees were bare now. In a month, winter would be upon them.

"Listen, Thanksgiving is in a couple of weeks. I don't know what you usually do, but my entire family comes to my house. We do a huge dinner and get-together." Karen toiled over what to say next. *Stop being chicken.* "Would you like to come over? I'd really like for you to meet my family."

"Yeah. Yeah, I'd really like that."

You would? "Great. I'll be in touch sometime next week." She put her arm around Ali's shoulder, drawing her near. It was the first time she initiated a kiss, with intent. The rush, the exhilaration—it was foreign to her, but it felt amazing.

As Ali turned to walk back home, Karen called to her, "Oh. I sort of need to prepare you. My family is kind of loud and boisterous."

Ali giggled. "All good. Good night."

CHAPTER TWENTY-TWO

The first thing Monday morning, Karen and Riley were hot on Jack Doyle's trail. By the time they were finished grilling Doyle, Keith's story appeared to match up—at least the part about his soiree with Doyle's daughter. Whether Keith drove straight home after the altercation or took a detour had yet to be verified. His E-ZPass records only confirmed the time he arrived in Pennsylvania, as the toll was only assessed in one direction. Bridge cameras would need to be accessed for the return information.

After chatting with Doyle, they sat in Karen's car in front of his house. "Doyle's pissed at Keith. Think he went after Cliff to get back at Keith?"

Riley shook her head. "Doyle plays innocent, saying he was joking with Keith. Then he turns stupid. Can't remember what knife he grabbed. Can't recall if it was in the kitchen or another part of the house. I mean, c'mon, Capp. The guy's hiding something."

"Agreed."

"The space of time between Keith leaving here and arriving home is critical," Riley said.

"You think Keith confronted his brother after the altercation?"

"Could have. May have had a fair amount of alcohol in his system."

"I was at Keith's house. Doesn't look like he's got the income for an expensive knife."

"Capp, don't drive off. Let's sit here. See what Doyle does next."

They sat. For fifteen minutes.

"I have an idea," Karen said.

She grabbed the photo of the murder weapon and walked back to Doyle's door. No answer. Glancing at the windows to the side of the door, she noticed the curtains were still.

An uneasy feeling grew. Reaching down with her right thumb, she disengaged the locking mechanism on her holster. Riley followed Karen, keeping a clear visual. Karen slinked around the house to the back deck. With each step, her foot landed softly on the dead brush to avoid making a sound. When she cleared the hedges on the side of the house, the muffled sound of voices penetrated the still air.

Doyle and Kenny were on the deck, both with cigarettes. She could hear their hushed murmurs as she eased her way around the corner, dodging overgrown weeds that lay dead from the fall chill.

"Yo, Doyle." Karen stood at the corner of the house, hand firmly on her firearm.

Riley kept her distance but made sure to keep a visual on the two men.

"Ever own an Ek Commando Presentation Knife?" She held up the photo in her hand.

Doyle's face shriveled. "I'm no knife collector. I got no idea what kind of knife that is."

He had a brochure for a knife show. His buddy is a knife collector. She stepped onto the deck and plopped the photo on the weathered boards of the wooden table. "Here. Recognize this knife?"

Doyle squinted and stared blankly at the picture. She glanced at Kenny and noted his face growing pale, his demeanor quiet. He sat hunched over, elbows on the splintering table, avoiding eye contact. She pushed the picture between the two men. Kenny looked away.

"Jack?" Karen waited for a response.

"No. Never had a knife like that. Here—" He strutted inside and returned with a large butcher knife. "This is the damn knife I pointed at him."

Karen held her glare. *That was a bit too easy. How come he played dumb a short time ago?* "Kenny? Does that knife look familiar to you?" She pointed to the picture.

He sat, muted.

"Have you seen that kind of knife here?"

"No." His voice snapped, garbled as if a pile of emotions were sitting in his throat. "I mean, I seen those kinds of knives before. They're expensive. But haven't seen one like that lately."

Lately? Karen shot Riley a look, then stared down at Kenny. His answer didn't match his visceral reaction. *Mr. Talkative…full of information. Can't make eye contact.*

He finally looked up at her. It was the first time she saw a softness in his eyes.

"Detective, youse know I can't have nothin' like that. It'd violate my parole. I ain't goin' back."

She leaned down, her mouth inches from his ear, and spoke in something just above a whisper. "All ya gotta do, Kenny, is stay clean." Her gaze fixated on him.

His hazel eyes met her stare with equal intensity. He nodded.

"Neither of you make any plans to go anywhere. This isn't resolved." Karen prepared to leave, relocking her firearm.

She paused, squinting, calculating if she was missing something.

Back at the car, she turned to Riley. "Doyle looked at the picture. No emotion. Kenny, on the other hand—he's hiding something."

"But he recognized that type of knife."

"Exactly. What's he hiding?"

Case progress crawled. The forensic geology report on the bandana led nowhere. Another hopeful piece of evidence turned dead end. Creating an additional challenge, it was a busy preholiday week with the usual uptick in larceny and robbery cases. Riley was also getting pulled back to deal with county cases.

Adding to her stress, Karen's parents were heading to Florida following the Thanksgiving family gathering. As much as she wanted to see Ali after work, she needed to spend time with her parents before they left. It had been a long time since she had to juggle family with personal and work commitments.

On Thursday night, Karen made plans to stop by Ali's. She picked up a couple of hoagies, a six-pack of Yuengling, and a bottle of wine. The two picked up right where they left off when they'd last been alone together.

"I told my daughter, Caiden, about you. She's looking forward to meeting you." Karen glanced at Ali. "I hope that was okay."

Ali smiled. "Of course." She took a sip of her wine. "Dag thinks you're great."

"She does? She seemed kind of uncomfortable with me."

"That's just Dag. She's guarded where I'm concerned. She doesn't want to see me hurt." Ali grinned. "But she saw how I felt when I was around you. She supports our..." Ali paused. "Our...connection."

"I don't give a shit what we call it. I just really enjoy spending time with you. You brighten up my days...my weeks."

"Ditto."

Like all the other nights, they got lost in conversation. Now, a gentle look or touch of a hand or thigh was mixed in. Ali put her arm around Karen's shoulders, drew her close, and gently stroked her hair.

Melted butter. She felt like melted butter in Ali's arms. So wonderful, yet terrifying. She lifted her head from Ali's shoulder and met her ink-blue eyes. Their lips met, soft and tender.

"You okay?" Ali asked after the first kisses settled.

Karen felt a plethora of emotions, one being fear. *Should I just go with this? It feels so amazing.* Instead of staying in the moment, she attempted to add levity—a diversion—to decrease the building intensity. "It's so nice to kiss soft lips without all that nasty, rough facial hair."

But Ali had asked Karen a serious and honest question. She was waiting for an equally honest answer.

Karen read Ali's body language. "I'm okay."

"I'm not going to push this if you're uncomfortable. You're too important to me. I don't want to frighten you away."

Unlike Karen's other intimate experiences, Ali wasn't only interested in physical or sexual intimacy. Ali was showing Karen she cared about her and cared about how she felt. Karen had longed for this type of connection. Now, it was right in front of her, but in what she had deemed the "wrong package." She forced herself to relax in Ali's arms without responding. The two sat embraced.

A loud crash vibrated from the front of Ali's house.

"Fuck, that sounded like my car." Ali jumped up and bolted toward the door.

"No. Don't go out there. I'll check your car. You stay in here." Karen reached toward her holster, an automatic reaction. But her firearm was locked in her trunk. "Shit," she muttered.

Karen opened the front door, slow and deliberate, and proceeded into the front yard. Sure enough, a brick was sitting on the ground behind Ali's car parked in front of her house. The entire back window had been shattered, leaving a web-like pattern in the glass. At the sound of screeching tires, Karen hustled to the edge of the street. A car sped past her and continued down the street. She couldn't make out the license plate, only that it was from out of state. A small red vehicle.

"Goddamn it," she said under her breath. She knew exactly who was racing away in that car—the same person who threw the brick.

Karen picked up the brick and set it off to the side before walking into the house to a frightened Ali. This was a clear case of vandalism. The protocol was to call it in to the station. But she decided to handle the matter herself. *Better to leave my officers out of this.* The sheer thought of her colleagues getting wind of anything in her personal life made her stomach tense.

"This shit never happens here," Ali said.

"It's probably just neighborhood kids. It's the holidays. Happens a lot around this time of year." Karen worked to put Ali's mind at ease. "You have insurance, right?"

Ali nodded.

Deep down, Karen knew she was likely the cause of what just happened. She instructed Ali to stay inside and keep the doors locked.

"I'm gonna drive around the neighborhood. See if I can find anything." She paused. *You should just call it in. Let one of the officers make a report and patrol the area.* Her inner conscience gnawed at her. She was going against professional protocol. Everything about her, about who she was—her conviction for doing the job right—told her to call it in. But all of that seemed to evaporate with the fears of her personal life being revealed, spotlighted.

Karen knew where she was headed, and it wasn't a drive around the neighborhood. "I'll be back, okay?" she said in a soft, composed tone.

Ali nodded. Karen kissed her on the forehead, then headed to her car.

Bobby answered Karen's knocks on the front door, clearly several beers into his evening.

"Hey, Bob." Her anger and emotions had left her slightly out of breath. "Is Tam here?"

"Haven't seen her all night. Got home from work around four. Don't know where she is." Bobby's speech slurred.

Karen nodded. "Have her call me when she gets in, okay?"

She headed back to her car. *You're playing a game, Tam. Okay. Two can play at this.* She parked around the corner and waited. *Ya gotta come home at some point. Circle by Ali's again…you'll see my car is gone. You'll head back here.* She waited. Her thoughts were interrupted by static on the police radio. Officers were responding to a call at 514 Mulberry. At first, Karen assumed Ali had decided to call the police and report the vandalism. She would probably need that for insurance. What came next shattered those thoughts. Officers were responding to a potential home invasion.

"You fool. You goddamn fool," she shouted into her dashboard. "Why did you leave her alone?" She started the car and raced across town. "You fucking idiot. Why didn't you just call it in and stay with Ali?"

She called Ali's cell. It went to voice mail. She tried over and over. *Where is she? What the hell happened?* Her mind raced. *Damn it. What the hell were you thinking?*

Another call. No answer. She struggled to harness emotions racing out of control. Redial. Voice mail.

CHAPTER TWENTY-THREE

The ten-minute drive across town to Ali's felt like an eternity. Turning onto Mulberry, she spotted the flashing lights of squad cars two blocks away.

Pulling up to the house, crime scene tape was already in place and the front door was sprawled open. She retrieved her firearm and bolted up the walkway.

Officer Roberts met her at the door. "Got a call from a neighbor. Homeowner was inside and heard someone trying to open her windows and doors. She called her neighbor, who called us."

"Was the door open when you got here?" Karen's heart was still racing.

"No, ma'am. The neighbor opened it for us. He had a key. We checked the house. No one's inside."

Where did she go? I told her to stay put. She entered the teeny bungalow, gun drawn down. At eight hundred square feet, there were few rooms to check. Easing her way past the living room, she entered the kitchen. Empty.

Heading down the dimly lit hall, she paused at the bathroom, peering behind the door before yanking the shower curtain back.

Nothing. Proceeding to the end of the hall, she pivoted into the bedroom. Ali's bag lay on top of the bed, undisturbed. She felt the hairs on her neck prickle as she moved toward the bedroom closet. Firearm positioned, she pried the door open. Nothing. Scanning the bedroom, everything was in complete order. No signs of a struggle. She stood statuesque, listening. An eerie stillness filled the air.

Heading back to the living room, fear began to set in. Futilely, she called out Ali's name, a guttural sound emerging from deep in her throat. Pausing in the living room, she glanced toward the front door. Ali was impeccable, yet an article of clothing was caught in the entryway closet door. Slowly, cautiously, she approached, raising her firearm. She braced herself, preparing to grab the door handle when she heard a muted creak.

Positioning her revolver, she stood firm, feeling an intensity envelop her entire body. The door inched open, revealing a petrified Ali crouched down with tears cascading down her cheeks—Karen's gun pointed directly at her face.

Karen lowered her firearm, feeling a breath of relief fill her lungs. "Oh my God, come here." She knelt, feeling Ali shudder as she wrapped her in her arms and stroked her hair.

"Okay. You're okay. You're safe."

Karen brought Ali to the couch and looked into her eyes. Her gaze slid lower, resting on her lips—the lips she had already envisioned kissing.

Two officers appeared in the doorway as Ali gathered her composure. Karen abruptly pushed her thoughts away, afraid she would do something that might embarrass both of them.

Karen motioned to Roberts, who pulled a notepad from his breast pocket and knelt in front of Ali.

"Ali." Karen's voice was like a gentle river. "Can you tell us what happened?"

Ali caught her breath and put on a stoic face. "About five minutes after Karen left—"

Roberts looked up. "You were here?"

Karen shot him a hard look.

Roberts looked back down, astutely aware a boundary had been reached.

"Go on, Ali." Karen gently encouraged her.

"I heard the doorknobs jiggle…a figure walked by my front window. Another shadow walked by the windows in my side yard. I called my neighbor. He said someone was at my back door." Ali's voice shook. "I didn't know where to go, so I hid in the closet."

"Did you hear anyone enter your house?" Roberts asked.

"Yes, shortly after I heard the sirens. I stayed as quiet as I could."

Officer Collins entered the house. "Detective, there are no signs of forced entry. We can try for fingerprints," she said.

Karen nodded.

"We did get a good footprint near the front window," she continued. "We'll get a plaster mold, some pictures, and document."

"Thank you."

The tension in the room settled. Karen directed the officers to finish up. They could check for additional fingerprints the next day. She would stay with "the homeowner" and make sure she was okay. The officers walked out with Karen following.

"We'll do a thorough patrol of the area," Roberts said.

Karen patted him on the shoulder and walked back into the house. She sat down next to Ali, draping her arm around her. "Not to make light of a scary situation, but I thought I was the one that was supposed to be hiding in the closet."

Ali let out a giggle.

"Seriously. I'm so sorry I left. But I'm not going anywhere now. I'll be here with you all night…I promise."

Holding Ali close, she studied her enchanting blue eyes…her soft, supple lips. Those lips. So inviting. She recalled the fear that seared through every inch of her body when she heard the call come in. The jolt she experienced arriving to find the front door ajar. The unrelenting relief when she discovered Ali, safe. At that moment, she realized just how much Ali meant to her.

Karen felt the tension in Ali's body gradually recede. Soon, she nodded off. With Ali physically relaxing, Karen let go as well. Leaning her head onto the back of the couch, she felt her eyes close. Moments later, she dozed off.

Karen awakened to all the lights in the house still blaring bright. She squinted. Ali was asleep in her arms. *This isn't the most ideal position to sleep in.* She tried to reposition her arm and get the circulation back into it.

Ali's groggy eyes popped open. "What time is it?"

Karen shrugged. "C'mon."

Standing, she held her hand out to Ali. Half asleep, Ali followed directions and allowed Karen to lead her down the hall and into the bedroom.

Karen knew that fear had a unique way of making people respond in ways they normally wouldn't, as did the feeling of genuine love. These two emotions were about to collide. Driven by her fear of losing Ali, Karen was confronted with the deep feelings for her that had evolved. This newfound clarity—a lightbulb moment—pushed Karen beyond the brick wall she had built around her heart, allowing her defenses to melt away.

She wanted to show Ali she was willing to pull off her shoes and walk through the hot coals of her demons to get to her. From the ashes of her fears rose the realization that this was the love she had been searching for. It didn't come in the package she had expected nor the one that society defined. But it was her definition of what she had longed for.

Her head felt light as she stood at the edge of a proverbial cliff. *Take a chance. See what's here.* With a deep breath, she leaped. Drawing Ali near, she pressed her lips into hers, feeling a surge of passion she had never experienced before.

Standing at the side of the bed, she reached up and began to unbutton Ali's flannel shirt. As Ali's shirt drifted off her shoulders, Karen felt her tense. She reached around and unfastened Ali's bra. The lacy black garment slid off her shoulders and hit the floor.

Glancing up, Karen saw the look on Ali's face. Apprehension? Fear? She cupped the bottom of Ali's scarred left breast. Gently, she placed her lips on the scar.

"You're beautiful. Just the way you are."

A tear tumbled down Ali's still face.

Karen removed her belt, with holster and firearm, setting it on a chair across the room. She felt Ali's eyes follow her every move. Karen then allowed Ali to undress her. A shiver ran down her back feeling Ali's gentle movements. Ali took Karen's hand, and together they slid under the sheets.

"You know I have no clue what I'm doing."

Ali smiled. A coy, sexy smile. "You know more than you think."

Karen's grin felt euphoric.

"You know what feels good to you, right?"

Karen gave a slow nod.

"Then you're halfway to knowing how to please me." She looked deep into Karen's eyes as if looking into her very soul. A look that seemed to intuitively say she knew she would need to be gentle and careful, that she would need to watch for signs of discomfort—physical or emotional. "Don't worry. I'll take the lead."

So much for being a tough, strong cop. Karen couldn't fight back the grin that was emerging on her face. She moaned at the mere thought of kissing Ali. Leaning toward her, she noted Ali's ragged breathing, her pulse pounding rapidly in her throat. Karen closed her eyes as she moved toward Ali's lips.

The sound of a cell phone shattered the moment. Karen pulled away almost guiltily and shot upright, recognizing the ringtone. "I'm so sorry. Let me grab this." She snatched her phone off the chair and pranced into the living room.

Officer Roberts filled her in on their surveillance of the neighborhood, asking if she wanted a patrol car to stay outside the house overnight. *Oh God, no. That would be a fiasco.*

"All good, Roberts. Everything is secure." Karen shuffled back to the bedroom, standing awkwardly at the foot of the bed and wondering if she could recapture the mood.

Ali reached out and put her hand on Karen's thigh. Immediately, Karen found herself fighting to stifle a moan. Ali's touch felt warm—no, hot, as if burning her skin. Clearing her throat to explain the phone call, she was startled by the huskiness in her voice.

Ali giggled as she pulled Karen back onto the bed. Karen found herself melting with each stroke of Ali's gentle touch. A slow letting go—utter relaxation—utter exhilaration. A tingling excitement rose inside her, and then euphoria.

Karen had only experienced male sexual partners, and Ali's gentle touch was vastly different from the firm, almost rough, hands she knew. Her body responded, coming alive with sensations foreign to her. It was like every sensation vibrated through each nerve ending and out the pores of her skin. *This feels so right.*

The experience was unlike anything Karen had ever been exposed to, as if her body was melting into Ali's. The tenderness of Ali's kiss. Ali's soothing touch. Nothing had felt like this, and she found herself feeling faint.

"This is what love feels like," Karen whispered.

"What?"

"Nothing."

For the first time in her adult life, she felt love—not lust, not just a turn-on, not just a building wetness with little release—but a touch and a tenderness that said *love* and a release that led to ecstasy.

"You've turned me to mush," Karen murmured. "Melted Jell-O and brown bananas." *That's how she makes me feel. I'm utterly helpless.*

Sunlight peeked through the bare trees outside and the bedroom curtains inside. Karen worked to untangle herself from Ali's embrace and slink out of bed without disturbing her. She tiptoed across the room, pulled up her slacks, and threw on her unbuttoned shirt before looking up to see Ali's eyes wide open.

"Good morning, you," Karen said, smiling, walking back and sitting on the edge of the bed. She reached over and stroked Ali's tousled hair.

"You're up early. You okay?" Ali asked.

"I'm great. How are you?"

"You're leaving…"

"I have to get to work," Karen whispered. "Believe me, if I could, I'd stay in bed with you all day." She leaned down and gave Ali a soft kiss. "Go back to sleep. I'll call you later today, okay?"

"Do you want me to make you some coffee?" Ali rolled onto her back.

"No…I'm good. Go back to sleep."

She pulled the covers up over Ali's shoulders and brushed her fingers through Ali's hair.

"Are your colleagues going to notice you're wearing the same clothes?" Ali gave a sheepish smile.

Karen grinned. "It'll give 'em something to gossip about."

Karen headed to her car relishing her last moments with Ali. With barely four hours of sleep under her belt, she felt amazingly rejuvenated. A relaxed lightness. A feeling that had been missing for years. No, decades.

Driving to the station, Karen replayed the night before in her mind. She was astounded by the equal give-and-take. Nothing had been one-sided. The desire to please one another…she hadn't experienced that with anyone…ever. One word came to mind. Content.

The station was barely a two-minute drive from Ali's. *How convenient.* She knew her whimsical mood would soon be tested. Additional interviews with Doyle, Kenny, and Keith were on the docket. The path to finding anything meaningful would be a grind. Her other task was to address the evening before with Tam.

After Riley arrived, they constructed a game plan. Along with a nagging feeling about Kenny, Karen felt a gnawing discomfort with Doyle. She reminded Riley about the brochure that fell out of his pocket.

"Yeah. He's all stupid when we question him about a knife, yet he attends knife shows." Riley shook her head.

"At this point, Kenny and Doyle are alibiing each other. If we catch Doyle on a traffic cam after confronting Keith, neither of their alibis hold up."

Before heading out, Karen grabbed Officer Perkins and assigned him the tedious task of checking late-night footage on the streets around Doyle's house the early morning of the murder. She hopped into her SUV, planning to swing by Keith's house. But first, there was something that needed to be addressed.

After Ali's car window had been shattered, Karen saw the back of a red Mini Cooper speeding away. With an out-of-state plate, Karen suspected that Tam was responsible for last night's ordeal, and her gut told her Tam viewed Ali as a rival. A quick look at that footprint below Ali's window also told her it was not a six-foot prowler. She could always seek to match the footprint to one of Tam's shoes.

But Karen wasn't looking for criminal charges. She still had a soft spot for the woman. The little girl she felt sorry for growing up with so much violence...the barely adult woman who ran away from Parks Ford to find a better life...the young woman whose father she had arrested...the woman who returned only to find herself immersed in turmoil again. She admired Tam's tenacity and was impressed by her ability to make a life for herself. And even though she didn't feel a sexual attraction to Tam, she was flattered by Tam's attention and interest in her.

Tam's Mini was back in front of the house. Bobby's car was missing, so he was likely at work. She would have Tam's undivided attention—ideal for an interview. With a deep sigh, she knocked. No answer. *She's playing games. I know she's home.* She knocked again. Again, no answer. Worry crept in.

Karen gave herself a mental shake. She had to remove her personal feelings. Tam was a vandal and, potentially, a prowler. One final knock. As she turned to head down the stairs, Tam appeared—disheveled—still in pajamas and half asleep. She looked exhausted. Depressed. There was a desperate loneliness about Tam that touched Karen.

"Can I talk with you for a minute?" Karen said softly.

Tam nodded and walked out onto the front porch. Karen noted the oddity. The old Tam would have invited her in…encouraged her to have a cup of coffee. Something was off.

"Tam. I need to know where you were last night."

"I went down to Rehoboth," Tam said without hesitation, referring to Rehoboth Beach, Delaware.

"Rehoboth? You drove an hour and a half to go to Rehoboth for the night?"

"What's wrong with that?" Tam snapped at her. "Some of us don't just sit around in Parks Ford and make our work our life."

Karen stood silent, stunned. A jab that Tam intended to land squarely on Karen's jaw. It always ate at Tam that Karen focused on her work when they were together. Hardly what Karen was there to debate.

"Tam, you don't have money to stay in a hotel in Rehoboth."

"What makes you think I stayed? I went down for the night."

Rehoboth Beach had a vibrant gay and lesbian community, so Tam's story wasn't far-fetched. It would also account for why she wasn't awake at this hour. The story was plausible. Karen pulled back from plausible. She knew it was Tam at Ali's house last night.

"Tam," Karen said patiently. "I know you weren't in Rehoboth."

Tam stared at her.

"I saw your car speeding away on Mulberry last night." She waited for Tam's reaction.

Tam's stare softened. She gave Karen a sleepy, alluring smile.

Looks like the old Tam is back. Karen cleared her throat to conceal her amusement. "Why did you break Ali's car window? She didn't do anything to you."

Tam's eyes became moist before she blurted out what Karen suspected. "She took you away from me."

"She didn't take me away from anybody." Karen forced a straight face. "Ali and I are friends."

Tam looked at her, squinting.

"And, quite frankly, if you hadn't pushed me to go to the studio with you, I never would have met her," Karen said in an amused tone, hoping to lighten the mood. "So, really…this is your fault."

Karen allowed a gentle smile to emerge. *She's jealous. It's kinda cute.* She paused and returned to a serious tone.

"After you broke her window, did you try to get into her house?"

Tam looked down. "I was just trying to scare her. I wasn't gonna go inside or do anything."

Karen scrutinized Tam's face, her body language. *Would she have hurt Ali?* Karen held her stare, then internally shrugged. *Probably just youthful exuberance. Guess she's not as mature as I thought.*

"Look, I need you to leave her alone. I won't report this. But if this nonsense continues—" Her stare bore into Tam. "I'll have no other choice. Please…don't put me in that position."

"You think I'm a loser, don't you?" Tam said.

"Tam, when I first met you, you told me no one in this town thought shit about you."

Tam wrinkled her nose.

"You're wrong. A lot of people think you're very generous. You donated your pottery to our Christmas fundraiser."

Tam shrugged.

"Tam, that's a big deal. Not everyone in town does that. People are impressed."

"Are you impressed?" Tam shot her a dreamy look.

"Yes. I am impressed."

With that, Tam promised to steer clear of Ali.

Now, it was time to deal with Keith—a good hour's drive, but Karen had a mountain of pleasant thoughts to distract her.

She marveled at the feeling of contentment that enveloped her. Her usual modus operandi was to allow fear and doubt to enter her thoughts and wall off the partners with whom she had experienced intimacy. The intense desire for self-protection and an ingrained reluctance to be vulnerable made her unwilling and unable to enter into a full, open-hearted relationship with anyone. Something felt different with Ali.

Karen recalled how safe she felt with Ali. She relished the communication and gentleness with which Ali proceeded, always making sure that Karen felt comfortable moving forward. What a difference from past experiences.

Lost in her pleasant thoughts, she felt annoyed when her phone rang. She allowed Miles's call to go to voice mail. Her shoulders dropped as she promptly played back the message to begin processing it. Miles confirmed he would return after the new year and he looked forward to picking up where they had left off. *What the hell? You think I've put my life on hold for you?*

She took an assessment of her feelings. Did she really miss him, or was he just a tonic for her loneliness—a loneliness that had been thoroughly quelled? She cringed at the thought of him coming back so soon. For the most part, she had effectively pushed him out of her mind over the last several weeks. Then, a searing thought interrupted her rationalizing brain in overdrive. It ran through her mind all the way down to her chest.

What about Ali?

CHAPTER TWENTY-FOUR

A return call to Miles would have to wait. She craved a distraction to keep her mind off the two people vying for her attention. One person had taken care of his needs and put Karen's second, and done so on a regular basis. He would be returning assuming nothing had changed. The other person took nothing for granted. She waited patiently for Karen to be ready to take a chance and open her heart. She would likely bend over backward to make Karen happy. With her, Karen felt content—an all-consuming warmth of desire.

Weighing the cost—in both her personal and professional lives—of giving herself over to this new connection with Ali was perhaps more than she was willing to pay. She needed time to sort through that possibility, and the potential ramifications.

Unable to locate Keith, again, she slipped her card into his storm door with a scribbled note that said *Call me!*

Back at her car, a text message awaited.

Dinner tonight? I can come over to your place if you'd like.

Ali. Karen felt her chest swell with warmth as her face lit with a smile. She definitely wanted to see Ali, dinner or not.

Would love that. Just not sure what time I'll finish, Karen typed back.

No worries. Text when you get home. What do you feel like for dinner? Ali completed her text with a winky-kissy face emoji.

The warm sensation returned, rising from Karen's stomach to her chest. Again, the simultaneous panic. *Damn it, Capp. Don't start closing up on her.* She felt that familiar tug of wanting to run away from her emotions. Her mind hesitating, sick at the thought of Miles's return. Sick at the thought of Miles…period.

She could hear Judy's voice in her head: "You know you can't count on him. Why are you still giving him access to your heart?"

Hello? Karen's phone pinged with another text from Ali, pulling her out of a crashing tidal wave of thoughts.

Sorry. Really distracted right now. Rain check for tomorrow night? Karen typed.

Of course. Have a great day.

"Fuck." Karen pounded her fist on the steering wheel. "It's not fair to do this to her. She has no clue why, all of a sudden, I need space." A nauseating feeling wafted over her.

Pulling her out of her thoughts, her phone rang.

"Hey, Riley. Any luck?"

"Yup. Doyle's daughter, Meghan, said they weren't in Keith's car until around 1:30 a.m. Doyle caught them shortly after. That puts Keith squarely in the area at the time of the murder."

"And Keith wasn't at work today and isn't at his house."

"Yup." Riley's chipper response made it sound as if she had a crystal ball. "He's been sitting here at the station waiting for you to return."

Karen felt both flabbergasted and annoyed at the same time.

"Oh, one other thing," Riley said. "Cameras on the bridge put Keith's car crossing back into New Jersey around 2:42 a.m. He could have driven to Hillside, but the timing would be tight. See ya when you get here."

When Karen returned, Keith was in the interview room. He looked calm, almost bored. No signs of distress or agitation.

"Just stopped by your house. A little concerned when you weren't there." Karen said, walking into the interview room. "What's up?"

"Remembered somethin' last night." Keith sat forward, resting his elbows on the table. "That night you was asking me about. Stopped for gas right after I got back to Jersey."

He reached into his back pocket. From a loose-fitting pair of blue jeans, he pulled out a tattered leather wallet and opened it. Lint flew out and onto the table. His fingers fumbled. From inside the wallet, he produced a wrinkled receipt. "I don't have nobody who seen me at that hour. But I have this." He plopped the receipt onto the table.

Karen and Riley looked at each other, then at the receipt. Karen straightened it out, both hands ironing across the top of the paper. They leaned in to examine the time stamp: 2:48 a.m., October tenth. It was barely possible for Keith to fit into the probable timeline of the crime. But still, it was possible.

They dismissed Keith, thanking him for his honesty and for making the drive over.

"Okay. We have Doyle flashing a knife in a threatening way." Riley looked like her brain was ticking away on a computer. "And it all happened between 1:30 and two, the morning of Cliff's murder. We may be getting closer to cause for a warrant to search Doyle's house and car," Riley said, referring to the probable cause they would need for a judge to sign for a warrant.

"We're going to have to put Doyle in the vicinity of Hillside." Karen squinted, scratching her right brow.

"How far along is that officer checking the cam footage?"

"He's a rookie," Karen said with a fair amount of snark. "I'll check and see."

"If Doyle left the house, then Kenny loses his alibi," Riley said. "We can request a consensual search. Put the screws to both of them for no longer having viable alibis."

After a long, silent pause, Karen looked at Riley. "What are your thoughts about Kenny?"

"Think he'd risk going back to jail? And what would he have had against a homeless person?" Riley barely took a breath. "And if he was going to kill someone, would he really leave the person right on his own old driveway?"

All solid points. But Karen knew from her years in police work that examining motives sometimes turned up shocking reasons for violence. Something the average person would consider trivial or pointless might provide a logical rationale for a murderer.

"There's still the possibility that Kenny, or even Doyle, intended to leave the victim on Bobby's driveway. All suspicion would be on Bobby. Kenny would like nothing more than for Bobby to lose that house."

Riley gave Karen a hard stare. "Hoping to scare Bobby into leaving?"

"Riley, this is—bottom line—a simple stabbing. There were no signs of a struggle. The killer didn't stab and run. Cliff walked a good thirty feet before he collapsed. The cast-off patterns, the location where the knife was thrown, and the partial footprint all occurred at the point where Cliff collapsed."

Riley squinted at Karen as if trying to follow her rationale.

"It just seems that if this was a drunken rage against the homeless or an 'oops I'm sorry I stabbed you' type of murder, the killer would have fled right where Cliff was initially stabbed. Instead, the perp stayed with him all the way to the driveway." Karen paused, gauging Riley's response. "I think they intentionally wanted Cliff to land right where we found him."

Riley slowly nodded and pursed her lips. "Let's start with the traffic footage."

"I'll have an answer before I head home tonight."

Riley squirmed as if broaching an uncomfortable subject. "Capp, I'm gonna need to start focusing on some county cases. You okay holding things down with this for a bit?"

Karen's heart sank. Riley had not only been a huge help, but she was Karen's law enforcement rock when things got difficult. But they were at a dead end. "I understand."

Karen headed down the hall to follow up with Officer Perkins. His desk was vacant with nothing to hint at anything accomplished on the traffic footage. Annoyed and discouraged, she buried her head into traffic video feeds. Her focus blurred as her mind drifted to Ali's sweet face. Her gentle touch. Her silky, smooth skin. She could still see Ali's sleepy eyes from earlier that morning and was astonished to feel such a strong tug of desire.

Stop. You gotta get this done. She shook her head, surprised by the constant distraction of alluring thoughts. *Never felt this way with Miles.* She needed to think—time to sort through everything. She needed a long talk with Judy, although she feared what Judy might say. Would she still be the same nonjudgemental friend she had grown up with? This was beyond just "finding that artist" and getting to know her. Could Judy handle it. *Hell, can I handle it?*

Slapping her attention back to the present, a white sedan appeared on the traffic footage and caught her eye. On Willow Parkway, a quarter mile from Hillside, heading west toward Hillside. Time stamp: 2:06 a.m. That put the sedan in the vicinity right around the time Cliff was caught on the Ring camera. Karen thumbed through her notes to check the exact time. 2:13 a.m.

She zoomed in to get a closer look at the license plate. Pennsylvania vehicles only had plates in the rear, and that part of the footage was blurred. She could only make out the first two letters, but they matched the first two letters on Doyle's license plate. No other footage existed for her to determine whether he turned into the neighborhood or continued on Willow.

Where was he going at that hour? Keith's vehicle had passed through the same intersection forty-five seconds earlier. But Keith's vehicle was spotted coming off the bridge and entering into New Jersey thirty-six minutes later. She needed to check bridge cameras for Doyle's vehicle. *Did Doyle follow Keith into New Jersey? If not, where did he go…and why?*

Doyle's vehicle wasn't recorded crossing the Commodore Barry Bridge. Nor was there footage to determine where he went after continuing through Jamestown Road on Willow Parkway. She tossed around the idea of presenting the camera footage to him. Maybe it would convince him to agree to a consensual search.

Sitting back in her office chair, she smiled. *We've got a potential direction now.*

Now. Now thoughts of Ali could flood in. *I'll see her tomorrow.* That delightful thought brought a grin—a grin that reminded her of when she was a teen and had a crush. She laughed at herself and her inability to handle this new experience like a grown, middle-aged woman. A grown woman who had successfully avoided the shit she didn't want to think about, now replaced by a giddy teenager giving in to the intensity of new love.

Heading home, Karen stopped by Judy's house.

"So…" Karen prepared herself for Judy's response. "Miles called today. He'll be back right after the new year."

Judy rolled her eyes.

"I've been tossing around whether to give it one more try—"

"For what? So he can leave again? Kare…leopards don't change their spots."

Karen struggled to make sense of it herself. *Maybe it's because, with Miles, I'm still a member of the socially deemed "correct" majority.* Her mind still couldn't shake the fear of being seen as potentially unacceptable in the eyes of her town.

"Jude, remember that artist, Ali?" Karen could hear the trepidation in her voice.

"The potter?"

"Yeah. We really hit it off. I've spent a number of evenings with her. We've had some great conversations."

Judy cocked her head slightly as if knowing there was more to the story.

Karen took a deep breath. "Jude, I've developed feelings for her."

"Like you do for Miles?"

"Yes…No. No…it's different. It feels totally different." Karen scrambled, wondering how much to share.

"So, what's the problem?" Judy's tone was like velvet.

"The problem is, I don't know what to do. Jude…" Karen took a deep breath. "We slept together last night."

"*Yes!*" Judy shouted, throwing her arms up in the air. "Finally."

Karen gaped at her friend. "You're cool with that? You're okay with your best friend sleeping with a woman?"

"I'm totally okay with my best friend finding happiness again. I don't give a shit if you're gay, straight, lesbian, bisexual, transgender…I love you. I want you to be happy."

Karen sat, dumbfounded.

Judy continued, "I've seen a change in your mood since you first met her. I say go for it."

"Well, I sort of already did," Karen said matter-of-factly.

"Go for Ali and dump Miles. That'll be a hundred bucks for this therapy session."

Their laughter reverberated. Judy had never been one to pass judgment, and this evening was no different. More importantly, she reminded Karen of what was most important: her happiness. Karen had defined what she longed for, and Judy was pointing out the road signs informing Karen she had arrived. What Karen desired had arrived. Judy was also urging Karen not to drive by the destination in pursuit of something—or rather, someone—else.

Ali came over Saturday night. Karen popped open a nice bottle of wine and she and Ali made their way into the living room. So many nights Karen sat in that very room lamenting her loneliness. But tonight, a peacefulness settled in as they relaxed into conversation.

"How are you doing after Thursday night?" Ali's voice was tender.

"Good. I mean, great." *That sounded lame.*

Ali giggled. "When you didn't want to get together last night, I was a little concerned."

"No. It was just a long day. I needed some time to regroup." Karen gazed at Ali. "Everything's good." Taking a sip of her wine, she reached over and rubbed her hand on Ali's thigh. "How are *you* after Thursday night? I mean, you went through a lot of trauma before we…we…ya know—"

"Made love?" Ali smirked. "It's hard for you to say, isn't it?"

Christ, what's my problem? Why can't I say it? "I'm sorry, Ali. I'm working through this. It's all still so new to me." She peered into Ali's eyes. "Are you still up for coming here on Thanksgiving? I'd really like to have you here and I'd like for you to meet my family."

"Of course. As long as you're comfortable having me here."

"Very much so." She paused. "You never answered my question. How are you doing after your ordeal Thursday night?"

Ali shrugged. "I'll be fine." She stared off into space. "Is this what your job is like? Going into dangerous situations…requiring you to use your gun?"

"I very rarely have to draw my gun."

"Have you ever had to shoot someone?"

"Never."

Ali nodded somberly. "But you were ready to shoot at my house that night."

"I was prepared to protect myself."

"You had a gun pointing at my head." Ali's voice elevated an entire octave.

"Not *your* head," Karen said softly. "The perpetrator's head. I thought he was hiding in the closet."

"What if you made a mistake?"

Karen could hear the fear in Ali's voice. "I don't make mistakes."

Ali shot her an incredulous look, then shook her head. "That was the one moment that sticks in my mind."

"The only moment? Weren't there other moments, like, later that night?"

"Smart-ass. Of course there were. Many. I still remember you kissing my scar." She looked up at Karen with tear-filled eyes. "You have no idea how much that meant to me."

Karen wrapped her arms around Ali and drew her close. *She's so down to earth—so real. Can you imagine Miles this genuine? He'd make some stupid joke if things got too emotional.* A barely perceptible sigh escaped. *Ali just opens up her heart. She trusts me.* A surge of adrenaline shot through her chest. *Shit, she trusts me. I can't betray her.*

"So, you've conquered your worst fear, no?" A gentle smile formed on Karen's face.

"You made me feel safe. I felt loved."

She feels love. And I feel confused. "Ali, I'm struggling with understanding what I'm feeling."

"What did you feel two nights ago?"

"I felt a draw…a passion that I haven't felt for a long time." Karen caught herself. "No. I've never felt that type of passion before. There was a special connection. A tenderness." She paused, reflecting. "No…I've never felt that before."

"So what are you afraid of?"

Karen let out an exasperated sigh. "I can't tell if it's fear of the unknown or if it's fear of social repercussions."

"Social repercussions, or repercussions at work?"

"I do fear my colleagues' reaction. But I also don't know how my friends and family will handle this, either." *That's a lie. Judy already gave you her blessing. Your daughter told you how happy you sound. Do you really think Mom and Dad would have an issue? Don't they want you to be happy?*

"Don't your friends and family want you to find happiness?"

Christ, did she just read my mind? Karen paused, mulling over Ali's question.

"Don't *you* want to find happiness?" Ali repeated.

"Yes. Very much so. And it's about damn time."

"So what's the problem?"

Karen let out a snort. "I can't get out of my own fucking head and my own rules and regulations." She shook her head. "Ali, you bring me so much joy. I can't get you off my mind. It's crazy."

"Are you saying I make you crazy?" Ali said with a giggle.

"You make me feel an uncontrollable excitement. Like lightning, shooting from my chest to my…you know…"

"Your crotch?" Ali seemed to get a kick out of watching Karen struggle, watching her tortured, contorted language. Her smile faded. "Karen, you're quick to say you're in your forties and the relationship you've always longed for has eluded you. How much longer do you plan to wait?"

Great question. How much longer? Isn't it time? Isn't it okay for me to be happy, regardless of other people's opinions?

"Life is short, my dear." Ali stared at Karen. "Should I head home and let you have some time?" She paused. "Or would you like me to stay tonight?"

Karen yanked herself out of her muddled thoughts and spoke in a soft but definitive tone. "Stay with me tonight."

CHAPTER TWENTY-FIVE

The holiday week arrived with Karen immersed in petty cases popping up around town. She touched base with Riley at the sheriff's office regarding Doyle and the traffic footage.

"Think we've got enough for a warrant?" Karen asked.

"First, we have to make him a suspect. Do we have a significant reason to think he's linked?"

"Doyle argued with the victim's brother. Threatened him with a knife. And we have him on surveillance in the vicinity of the scene around the time of the murder." Karen sat back in her office chair. "That's more than enough to consider him a suspect."

"What's our cause to search his car?"

"One, he's suspected of committing the crime. Two, it was a bloody scene." Karen ticked off the pieces of her rationale. "And three, he was seen driving near that neighborhood that night, so that car would've been used. If he committed the murder, blood should be in the car." Karen mulled things over. "It's a holiday week. Whad'ya think about trying to get Doyle to consent to a search?"

"Doyle? Consent?" Riley groaned. "I'll support you, but he can always withdraw his consent at any time."

They agreed to take her chances. If Doyle refused, they could seek a warrant. The minute Karen hung up with Riley, she heard a light tap on her office door. The baby-faced rookie, Officer Perkins, stood in the doorway. She returned a stone-faced stare.

"Ma'am?" He hesitated.

"Yeah, Perkins. Whad'ya need?"

"Ma'am, I apologize for not completing the traffic cams for you. Brennan pulled me from the desk. I was in the field all day."

So like Brennan to try and fuck up my investigation. Karen gave a quick nod. "Thank you for letting me know."

"Ma'am, if you need anything today, just let me know." He shot her a tentative smile.

Karen felt her face soften. "Thank you, Perkins. I'll keep you posted."

Perkins scampered out, and Karen grabbed her jacket and headed to Doyle's.

She pulled up to the crumbling cement curb at Doyle's house to find his driveway empty, with a muddy film from a brief rainstorm the night before. No dry outline of a car. The car had been missing since at least the night before. The house looked dark. She walked up the weed-framed cement walkway and knocked, peering through the window shades for any movement or any lights.

"Not home. Went away for Thanksgiving," a neighbor said.

"Know where he went?"

"Poconos. Left yesterday." The neighbor explained that Doyle had asked him to keep an eye on the house.

"Alone?"

He glanced at the shiny emblem on her belt. "Ma'am. Detective. He left with that friend of his. That guy from jail."

Karen smirked and thanked him. Any possible search was now on hold.

Back at the station, officers busily finished up paperwork and reports. Chief Walden called to her as she passed his open door.

She cringed. With the case over six weeks old and no definitive leads, she feared he would pull the plug. "Yes, sir."

"Got word that Tammy McPherson is volunteering at our soup kitchen for Thanksgiving."

"Sir?"

"Yup. Not surprised. She donated to our Christmas fundraiser." He sat back in his chair, pushing the seat into a reclined position. "Was she always this generous when she lived here?"

"Sir, she was barely eighteen when she left. But no, I don't recall any volunteer activity."

He nodded and sat forward, leaning his elbows on his desk. "Well, we're sure glad she's back."

"Yes, sir." Karen paused in the doorway for a moment, processing her superior's comment. *Guess Tam's eager to make friends. Or impress me.* She shrugged. *Nothing wrong with that.*

The case stalled for the next few days with Doyle out of town. Karen vacillated between incredible excitement and horrific nervousness about Thanksgiving. Caiden arrived home Wednesday night, and she and Karen sat up until two in the morning catching up on her life and how Ali's influence had changed her outlook. On Thursday, Karen's parents arrived by early afternoon, with siblings, siblings-in-law, and a few nieces and nephews following soon after.

A blend of Jewish and Italian families equated to large, loud gatherings. Had Ali ever been exposed to the noise and chaos of such a family get-together? How would her family react to Ali? *They'll want to know who she is...how I met her. How will they handle it? How will I handle it?*

By two o'clock, the house was full. Most everyone was gathered in the living room, with Karen's brother and his two sons downstairs in the family room watching a football game. The house was bursting with laughter and robust conversation. Scents of a marinated roasting turkey mixed in with the rich aroma of a pumpkin pie. Amidst the smells and sounds, the doorbell rang.

Nobody rang the doorbell—they just walked in. Karen poked her head outside the kitchen to see Caiden scurrying to the door. As the door sprung open, she caught sight of Ali standing in the doorway holding a bottle of wine, statuesque. Karen felt a surge of warmth run through her chest and an uncontrollable smile form, gazing at Ali in a pair of crisply pressed black slacks, a black sweater over a white turtleneck, and a stylish pair of black suede ankle boots. A gold chain accentuated the neckline of the sweater. *Wow! She looks stunning.*

"You must be Ali," Caiden said with a huge smile, taking her hand and pulling her into the house.

"Thank you," Ali said, her eyes wide with a nervous half-smile. "You're Caiden?"

Caiden nodded, her auburn curls bouncing with each nod. "My mom told me all about you. It's so cool to finally meet you." She waved Ali toward the kitchen. "Can I get you a drink?"

"Oh…" Ali handed Caiden the bottle of wine. "Happy Thanksgiving. And yes, I'd love a glass of whatever is open."

Caiden smiled and headed to the kitchen with Ali following. Juggling items on the stove and the last few dishes going into the oven, Karen stopped and gave Ali a gentle embrace. She had never seen Ali in anything other than jeans and a sweatshirt or flannel shirt—or a clay apron. Ali looked stunning. Breathtaking.

"Mom, Ali brought this for you." Caiden handed her mother the wine.

"It's for everyone," Ali said.

Karen smiled. "Thanks, Al. I told you…you didn't need to bring anything." She noted an uneasiness in Ali's body language that she had never seen before. "You okay?"

Ali gave a half-smile. "A little nervous."

"Here." Caiden handed Ali a glass of wine. "This will help."

Karen watched as Caiden marched Ali into the living room and, in one fell swoop, introduced her to every single person. She didn't refer to her as Karen's girlfriend or even Karen's friend. Just "This is Ali," as if everyone understood who she was.

Ali had only been in this room once before, and at that time she and Karen were engaged in a quiet intimate conversation. The room felt dramatically different now. The clamor of dishes in the kitchen was outmatched by the loud, boisterous conversation of family members, combined with periodic bursts of laughter.

"Free steak dinner if you can repeat all our names," Karen's father, Larry, challenged her.

Everyone laughed, and Ali jumped right in and gave it a try.

Karen watched as Ali sat listening to old family stories and jokes as hors d'oeuvres were passed from person to person in an almost frantic fashion.

News got out that Larry had just joined the town's volunteer fire department, even though he was well over seventy years old. Ali's eyes became wide.

"Oh, it's not like it sounds. I volunteered to help them build their Santa float for the Christmas parade. You know, the one that goes through the neighborhoods. They asked me to be their Santa this year."

Caiden almost choked on her drink. "Oh yeah, Pop-pop, that would've been great. The first Jewish Santa Claus in Parks Ford."

Karen laughed, overhearing the story. She kept a watchful eye from the kitchen, but Ali seemed to be holding her own.

"Did my mom tell you that when Nana gets laughing, she can't stop?" Caiden said.

Ali smiled. "I remember hearing something about that."

Karen poked her head out of the kitchen. "When I was ten, Dad was driving us all to Washington, DC to see the sights. My mom was hysterical over a joke that happened a full twenty minutes earlier."

Ali giggled while Larry's belly bounced with each chuckle.

She went on to explain that her mother couldn't stop laughing long enough to ask a hot dog vendor if the long line before them was the line to the White House.

The whole room roared.

"I heard you taught my mom how to do pottery," Caiden said.

Ali giggled.

"Was she good?" Karen's sister asked.

Ali paused as if contemplating how to answer. "She tried super hard. When she started the wheel…she hit the pedal full bore—just floored it. Wet clay and water flew everywhere."

The living room erupted.

"It was the sound of a beginner…every seasoned potter knows it well." Ali quickly added, "It was so cute. She was really trying her best."

Karen's mind drifted. The moment their eyes met. Pulling her thoughts back to the present, she yelled from the kitchen, "Thanks, Al. Get everyone laughing at my expense." She glanced out to see Caiden beaming.

Minutes later, Karen walked into the living room. "All right, everyone. Dinner's ready."

"Mom. Where do you want Ali to sit?" Caiden asked.

"Next to me." Karen never hesitated, bringing a grin to Ali's face.

Ali fit right. And when the evening ended, Karen finally enjoyed some quiet, albeit exhausted, time with her. Caiden bowed out, giving her mother time. Karen felt that same incredible feeling with Ali as their first intimate night together: content, a feeling she had never felt in any other relationship. Her house and her heart were full. As Thanksgiving came to a close, Karen walked Ali to the door and kissed her good night.

"I'm going to be spending the weekend with Caiden," Karen told her. "But I'd like to see you Monday."

Ali grinned. "Should I pencil you in on my calendar?"

"No. You should write it in with a Sharpie." Karen smiled and gazed into Ali's eyes. She caressed her face and felt desire surge within her.

"Caiden is wonderful," Ali said. "Enjoy this time with her. I'll see you soon enough."

Ali took hold of Karen's cheeks and gently kissed her lips, finishing with a tap of her index finger on the tip of Karen's nose—Ali's hallmark display of affection.

Almost nine hours after arriving, Ali headed out the door. Karen felt an unexpected sadness descend on her. *Why has it taken me so long to find this?* She shook her head. *Better late than never, I suppose.*

The holiday weekend flew by, and before Karen knew it, Caiden was headed back to New York and she was headed into the station. As things in her personal life were on a mind-boggling ascent, the case had flatlined.

On Monday morning, Doyle was back in her crosshairs. This time his car was back in the driveway. A positive start. She actually relished this "knock and talk."

Doyle scowled, yanking open the door with pugnacious force.

"Got a couple of questions." Karen stood on the porch with a wide stance. The aroma of bacon flooded her nostrils. "October tenth, after your altercation with the man that was with your daughter…"

His gaze flicked upward.

"After he drove away, you got in your car and headed west on Willow Parkway. Want to tell me where you were headed?"

Doyle stared at her.

"Well?" Her glare bore into him.

Doyle tugged at the ribbed collar of his shirt. "Headed out for a drink."

"At two a.m.? Where the hell did you think you'd find a drink at that hour?" *Dumbass.* Karen stared at his belligerent face as he plunged his hands into his pockets. "I'll ask you again, where were you headed at that hour?"

Doyle's eyes dodged hers. He fumbled, pulling a cigarette from his front shirt pocket, tossing the extinguished match on the walkway.

Karen noted the Grimaldi's matchbook and pointed at it. "Pick up a lot of matchbooks?"

"Sometimes. Haven't been there in a while."

Karen stared. "Any chance I can get an answer to my original question, or do I need to bring you into the station?"

"I don't got to answer your questions." Doyle's tone was filled with contempt.

"Here's the deal. October tenth, you left here just after two a.m. You were spotted in the vicinity of a vicious stabbing. You'd just threatened a man with a knife before you left." Karen's tone was even. "Right now, you and Kenny don't have an alibi. Right now, we have probable cause to search your home and your vehicle." *A lie.* "It would behoove you to level with me."

He stood, blank-faced, staring into the street, and gave an exaggerated sigh. "I was trying to follow that bastard that was with my daughter."

"Here's the problem with that. That man, Keith, was on video crossing the bridge into New Jersey. If you were following him, how come your vehicle wasn't on the same video?"

"Lost him. Little fucker got away."

"So, you don't have anything to substantiate your claim of following him." A statement, not a question. "Would it surprise you to hear that we're investigating a crime committed against that man's—that 'little fucker's'—brother?"

Doyle's eyes became wide, then darted.

"And now, neither you nor Kenny have an alibi for that night." Karen held a firm stare. "You're kinda up a creek…don't ya think?"

Karen continued to box him in. Consent to the search to clear himself, or she would leverage every tool available to make him a primary suspect. Despite unreasonable—and ridiculous at times—protest, Doyle finally consented.

"Go ahead," he snarled. "Search my car, search the house. You won't find a goddamn thing."

The forensics team was summoned. His car was the motorized version of *Hoarders*. In searching for traces of blood or fibers from Cliff's body, the forensics team had to make their way past old Coke cans, burger wrappers, and knife magazines. With the condition of his car alone, this had the potential of taking an entire day. All Karen could do was sit and wait. Wait and hope.

By three o'clock, the search was complete. The team returned with a boatload of evidence bags. Nothing glaringly remarkable was noted. Casts of Doyle's two pairs of tennis shoes were taken, and soil samples were taken from the shoes themselves. Doyle would have had to park near the crime scene and walk through yards. If the soil came back as a match, they were a step closer. If his shoes came close to the bloody partial print, they were a mile closer. If. *If.*

Unfinished reports sat in baskets on her desk. She had little interest in working on them.

A voice mail blinked on her phone. A simple message: "Still coming over tonight? Call me when you get this."

Call her, you moron. It's not her fault this case has you down. Karen batted her cell phone around on her desk with her index finger. It was the lowest she had felt in her investigator role. She was letting Cliff down…letting his mother down…letting the town down. *And, damn it, Brennan will gloat.* She shook her head.

Ali. Call her back.

As depressed as Karen felt leaving the station, a lightness embraced her when Ali answered her door. The simplicity of a hello kiss sent her emotions soaring. The joy of light and easy small talk was a relief.

"Caiden asked me for your number," Karen said, watching Ali grab drinks in the kitchen. "Hope it was okay to give it to her."

"Of course." Ali handed Karen a beer, her wet fingers lingering on Karen's.

Ali recounted Thanksgiving and her time with Karen's family. "I've craved that kind of family my entire life. The stories. The laughter."

Karen chuckled. "Yeah. My family loves get-togethers."

"They were so warm and welcoming. I was an only child. Most of my life revolved around my mom and her parents. A small family with tons of issues." Ali took a sip of wine. "Your parents. They seem like such a perfect couple."

"Married for forty-five years. I love watching their adoration for one another." She smiled externally, but internally she felt a touch of melancholy. "My parents have such a simple life yet manage to fill it up with all sorts of wacky things. Like Dad volunteering with the fire department." She shook her head. "This Santa Claus invite fell perfectly in line with their other antics."

Karen paused and looked around Ali's house, realizing it was the epitome of simplicity. Nothing overdone. Nothing focused on impressing others or living up to certain expectations. *Wish I could be like that.*

"Should I ask how the investigation is going?" Ali said in a tentative tone.

"No." An unintentionally curt response.

"No, because you can't talk about it?"

"No, because there's nothing to talk about." Karen played with her beer bottle. She rested her head on the sofa cushion and gazed up at the ceiling.

Karen explained how the case had ground to a virtual halt. How all the leads hadn't yielded results. How after seven weeks of investigating, she only had dead ends to show for it.

"What if it was someone outside of town?" Ali said. "How would you ever be able to find a killer if they don't even live around here?"

Karen found Ali's naivete refreshing. She explained the principles that guided an investigation and the different techniques and theories, including Locard's exchange principle.

"In every murder, the theory is that the perpetrator will leave something behind and take something with them. The key is identifying the evidence and making the connection. So we look for strands of hair. Sweat. Fingerprints." She paused. "Shoe prints."

Ali's face was blank. Karen couldn't tell if Ali was lost, disinterested, or both.

"You got a little squeamish the last time I talked about blood, so I'll leave that part out." A gentle smile appeared.

Karen explained how they check house cameras and even traffic footage. "Usually, in cases like this, the victim knows their attacker."

"How are you so sure?"

"The sheer nature of a stab wound. You have to get close to your victim. Versus a gunshot wound that can be much more random. No one heard the victim call for help or scream…he didn't have defensive wounds."

"What do you mean?"

"Okay," Karen said. "Imagine someone you don't know is coming at you with a knife. What would you do?"

"Run."

Karen chuckled. "And our victim wasn't stabbed in the back. So how did the attacker stab him in his upper abdomen if the victim ran?"

Ali wrinkled her forehead. "What if the attacker came up from behind and reached around?"

"Okay," Karen continued. Calm. Methodical. "If someone surprises you and comes up from behind…what would you do?"

Ali thought for a moment, then said, "Try to push him away. Defend myself."

"Exactly. And if he has a knife, when you try to do that, you would get cuts on your hands and forearms. Those are called defensive wounds."

Ali's face lit up as if the light bulb illuminated her brain. "I get it."

"Now, suppose I'm walking down the street with a knife… concealed. You know me. Would you run?"

Ali giggled. "No."

"Right. And you likely would have no reason to put up your hands or arms in defense because you wouldn't be expecting me to attack you."

Ali slowly nodded, putting all the pieces together.

"So, it's hard to imagine it would be someone without a connection to Parks Ford and, most likely, a connection to our victim. The only saving grace is that it's an isolated incident," Karen said. "If the killer strikes again, this town will have my head on a stake."

"You'll find the killer."

"The case is almost two months old. The longer it goes, the lower the probability."

"You can still do it," Ali said with a hopeful lilt. "C'mon. How many cases have you not solved?"

"Murder cases?"

"Yeah."

"None," Karen said as Ali lit up with a prideful smile. "Because there haven't been any. We've never had a murder like this in this town." Karen paused for a moment and steadied her emotions. "It's why I've been working with a county detective and the county's forensics team." She felt like adding "because I'm in over my head" but held back, protecting her ego.

"Okay. So you're not the only one that's stumped. He can't figure it out, either."

"She."

Ali gave a look of amusement. "A woman? Your partner is a woman?" Ali flashed a coy smile. "That's so…so…Cagney and Lacey-ish. Rizzoli and Isles."

Karen chuckled before returning to a sobering thought. *Both Riley and I have failed.*

"For what it's worth, I still think you're awesome." Ali turned to Karen's face.

As Karen stared straight ahead, Ali leaned over and stroked her cheek. The gentle touch sent a tingle down Karen's face to her neck, then chest. As emotionally dispirited as she was, she couldn't fight back a smile.

Karen turned and focused on Ali's face. "Let's talk about your profession for a while, okay?"

Ali beamed. "It's a dirty hobby. I can't ever dress nice like you."

"Dressing nice is overrated." Karen grinned.

"Maybe so." Ali shrugged. "That's why I wear an apron. I just wipe clay off my hands right onto the apron. It's messy." Ali shot Karen a playful smile. "I'm sure you haven't forgotten that part."

Ali went on to explain the intricacies of pottery, the various tools, and clay choices. Foreign to Karen, just like homicide investigations were foreign to Ali.

"I thought clay was just dirt," Karen said. "How could there be so many choices?"

"Actually, it is only dirt. And some potters will even dig their own."

"So, I can go out in my backyard and get a shovel full of clay?" Karen said, amused.

"You can if you dig deep enough." Ali sat up, eager to share her knowledge. "Have you ever dug a hole and seen the dirt turn a different color the further down you go?"

"Yeah."

"That dirt—the different colored dirt—that's clay."

"What was in the bag that Tam brought the day we met?"

"Store bought. Specifically manufactured to have a certain color and properties to behave a certain way when you throw it." Ali was in her element, her tone buoyant. "Manufactured clay already has other stuff added, like silica and ball clay. Ball clay gives the clay plasticity and strength…you can do more without it collapsing."

Karen gazed at Ali. *She's so cute. Look how excited she gets talking about her craft.* A smile crept onto her face. *She knows her shit, too.* "Are there clays specific to Pennsylvania, or New Jersey?"

"I don't know about New Jersey, but the creeks in this area have clay that's very high in iron content. So they're more red. Down in Delaware, there are areas with whiter clay. It all depends on how the sediment settles over time, which is what leads to clay forming."

"Sounds like a lot of work, to me."

"At least it's not potentially life-threatening," Ali said with a grin. "Potters don't have to carry a weapon."

Karen let out a snort.

"But we do have to develop a fair amount of upper-body strength. I'll bet I could hold my own with you."

"Oh, you do, huh?"

"Uh-huh," Ali said. "You don't have to lug twenty-five-pound bags of clay around all day. Or use your upper body to center fifteen pounds of it on a wheel. All you tried to center the other day was about a pound and a half—"

"I'm not disputing you're strong…or talented…or know your craft." She shot her an amiable smile. "I just never thought of artists as being strong. Athletes, yes. But artists?"

Ali rolled her eyes.

"But, after dinner, if you'd like to wrestle it out—"

"You're cray," Ali said, laughing. "You have no idea what you're getting yourself into."

Karen felt a warm sensation run through her chest. *Ahhh…the newness…the wanting to be playful…the banter…the feeling of excitement.* She stifled a moan, instead letting out a relaxed sigh.

"Don't I?"

CHAPTER TWENTY-SIX

Tuesday morning, Karen detoured home to change clothes before heading to the station. She felt relaxed, almost blissful, heading to work with a mountain of unknowns awaiting her.

The station had a calm and peaceful feel to it. No one called out with a pressing issue. No phone messages from the dispatch as she walked by. There were also no messages on her desk or a flashing light on her phone when she entered her office. *Shit.*

Dribs and drabs of phone calls and emails came through over the next two hours. Then a call from Trace. Her shoulders sagged as she hung up the phone. Nothing. Absolutely nothing to connect Doyle to the crime scene. The investigation had officially gone cold. She futilely tossed her pen across the desk and stared at reports for petty cases requiring completion.

Breaking her trance, Chief Walden appeared in the doorway. "I need an update," he said. "Where are we with the Stephenson case?"

She felt her heart sink as she headed to his office. Walden leaned back in his padded chair and motioned for her to sit. She sat on the edge of the chair, wiping moist palms on her slacks.

When she finished her report, Walden pursed his lips. "Consider the case unsolved. If something new appears, we can reconvene and discuss."

Karen sat up as if to protest but left the words in her mouth when Walden held up his hand.

"If you have time and something to pursue, that's fine. But I will not authorize overtime for this investigation from this point forward. Understood?"

"Anything else, sir?" Her voice was practically a whisper.

"Just your final report."

Nothing to show for everything we pursued. A killer's gotten off. Damn it. "Yes, sir." Her words were barely audible.

As Christmas neared, Karen learned that Ali would be heading to her mother's house in New York for the holidays through the first week of January. It would be the first time since they went more than a couple of days without seeing each other.

"My family is far from tolerant, otherwise I'd ask you to join." Ali looked into Karen's eyes as if trying to read her reaction.

"All good. I understand."

"How 'bout we go away together. We can have our own Christmas?" Ali's blue eyes sparkled.

"What do you have in mind?"

"I'll surprise you. I'll just tell you what to pack."

A surprise. No planning. No preparing. The antithesis of Karen's style.

When the big day arrived, Karen hopped into Ali's car and they headed north on Interstate 95.

"North. New York City?" Karen guessed.

"Nope." Ali turned to the east, over the Ben Franklin Bridge and into New Jersey.

"Hmm. The Jersey Shore?"

"Nope." Ali threw on holiday music for entertainment.

After twenty minutes, she turned west onto the Betsy Ross Bridge, reentering Pennsylvania.

"What the hell. Do you know where you're going?"

Ali giggled.

"Ugh. You're too much." Karen found a perpetual smile glued to her face.

Ali got back onto Interstate 95 heading north and eventually exited, winding along River Road. They passed through pint-sized towns established back in the eighteenth century and eventually into Washington Crossing.

"Three guesses what happened here," Ali blurted out, giggling.

Karen couldn't contain the joy she felt inside. Overflowing. She reached across the middle console and landed a kiss on Ali's cheek, gently brushing back the hair from her face. Ali glanced over with a dreamy smile.

Just past Washington Crossing, they arrived on Main Street in the quaint town of New Hope, Pennsylvania.

"Wanna stop for lunch before we continue on?" Ali said.

"How much further?"

"Not much," Ali said playfully.

"Let's just get there. I want to get out of this car and wrap my arms around you."

"Just your arms?"

"For now," Karen said with a coy smile.

Within two minutes, Ali pulled into the gravel horseshoe-shaped lot of a remote bed-and-breakfast. Beyond the lot sat a white wooden colonial structure with a wraparound porch. A handful of rockers positioned on the porch served to frame the entrance. In the distance, a leisurely creek and open meadow surrounded the structure. The only sounds beyond tires rolling on gravel were a few playful squirrels scrambling on the side of a large oak tree and the babbling water flowing from a nearby fountain. Serene and peaceful.

Ali put the car in park.

"Is this part of the game, or are we here?" *The minute I trust her, she's gonna say "psych" and put the car in reverse.*

Ali reached over, kissing Karen gently on the lips. "We're here. Really. My holiday gift to you."

Ali's playful nature was like an elixir for a detective immersed in a life of rules and regulations—where following the social order was demanded. Spontaneity, just letting go, relaxing, and not analyzing everything…it was a treat that Karen clumsily tried to enjoy. Ali often gently pushed Karen's boundaries, urging her to let down her guard. This trip would be no different.

"New Hope has a great gay and lesbian community. I figured it might put you a little more at ease. We can be out together without you having to worry."

Shame descended upon Karen. *Why do I get so wigged out over us?* She mustered up a meager "Thank you."

After checking in, they got situated in a teeny room with a queen-sized bed on one wall and an old claw-foot tub butted up next to a porcelain sink on the opposite wall. The solitary window overlooked a garden that, at that time of year, only boasted dead branches and a few trees without leaves.

"I wanna take a hot bath in that tub and look out at the chilly weather," Karen said.

Ali smiled. "I brought some candles and some Baileys. Perfect for that hot bath."

They walked along the Delaware River, tightly packaged in parkas with wool scarves draped around their necks. From the banks of the river, they made their way up to the main road of the late-eighteenth-century town. Ali reached for Karen's hand. Alarm seared through every nerve ending in Karen's body. Slowly, with effort, she tossed aside the trepidation of Ali's public display of affection and settled into the peace of her tender touch.

As Karen explored the sights, glancing at people on the street and the early bar-goers seated outside with their drinks under blazing heaters, she quickly became aware that no one cared about her and Ali holding hands. No one found it odd or disgusting. She felt her eyes get moist as her external armor began to melt away.

"Let's grab lunch in this part of town," Ali said. "Tonight, I thought I'd take you to the local microbrewery."

She notices everything about me. "You know me so well." *I take her for granted. Never even got her a Christmas gift. I really need to do that.*

During dinner at the Triumph Brewery, Karen tried various craft beers while Ali queried her about each one. After dinner, they sat by the fireplace in the guest area at the inn. No schedule. No agenda.

"I'm a little uncomfortable making love in that little room of ours," Karen whispered to Ali.

Ali giggled.

"What's so funny? Those walls are paper thin."

"You mean you can't be quiet?"

"No." Karen shot Ali a look of incredulity. "You do things to me… you make me moan." She paused. "No, I can't be quiet…and it's all your fault."

Ali beamed. "I'll put a pillow over your head when you start to climax." Ali seemed to be enjoying the playful, sexual banter.

The innkeepers walked in. *Two gay men. Awesome.*

"Hello, ladies," one said. "Enjoying your evening?"

"Very much so. Your place is just delightful," Ali said.

"Fabulous. Well, you both enjoy. If either of you need anything, just let us know."

Karen thanked them for their hospitality. This space. This environment. She felt safe. She felt loved.

The sheets on the bed were chilly—the sort of cool when the room is warm and you first pull back the covers on a winter night.

"You'll need to keep me warm," Ali said.

"Don't I always?" A playful smile rose on Karen's face. Her mind flashed back to their first night, curling up behind Ali after they made love. The soft curves of Ali's body. The smell of her skin.

"I didn't fall for a tough cop to keep me safe. I needed one to keep me warm," Ali said, unbuttoning Karen's shirt.

Caressing Karen's back, Ali moved her hands forward. Karen's stomach quivered. Ali's hands slowly descended to the front of Karen's button-up jeans, leisurely, methodically unbuttoning each button. Karen could feel desire surge inside as she helped Ali complete the process.

"Why can't you just wear jeans with a zipper?" Ali spouted playfully.

"To give you a challenge. You're gonna need to work for me."

The look on Ali's face told Karen this was going to be a long and immensely pleasurable night. Ali would take her time. She would, indeed, "work" to please Karen. And Karen knew it. Karen craved it.

The next morning, the two lingered in the inn's dining room after other guests had left the breakfast table. They sipped mugs of steaming coffee while gazing out the enormous dining room window to the gloomy outdoors and a vast meadow with the last of the Canadian Geese milling around before taking off for the winter. The smell of homemade cinnamon buns still hung in the air.

"Penny for your thoughts." Ali's voice floated like a feather.

Karen smiled. "It's gonna cost you more than that." She looked up over the rim of her mug to catch Ali's reaction.

Ali raised her eyebrows, adding an amused smile.

"It just amazes me how easily I've let go of my…not sadness, but…I guess, deep disappointment about the case," Karen said. "You really have a way of pulling me out of bad places."

Ali placed her hand on Karen's thigh. "It looks like a storm is coming. Let's get a little shopping done before the weather gets bad."

As the wind picked up and the billowing slate clouds ushered in the start of the storm, Karen and Ali made their way into a handful of unique shops back on Main Street.

"Look," Ali said, holding up a handcrafted wicker basket with an array of artsy adornments. "Caiden would love this."

Karen grinned. "You know my daughter?"

"No. I just know this would be her sort of thing." Ali's tone sounded defensive.

"That was a statement," Karen said. "You *know* my daughter. I think it's sweet. It's cute." *That's actually a perfect gift for Caiden. I could fill it with things from Parks Ford that she could take to New York.* She shook her head. *The two of them truly are similar.*

Karen purchased the basket for Caiden and found a few other items for her parents. They dashed into the next store, dodging drops of wet snow. Handcrafted leather goods. Karen eyed the business-sized leather bags but couldn't justify buying a new one when her current one was still in good shape. Ali was like a kid in a lollipop store, rushing from one item to the next, wide-eyed. She picked up a shoulder bag—the size that would hold a wallet and cell phone. Ali put it on her shoulder and smiled. She turned over the price tag, then slipped it off her shoulder and placed it back on the rack.

"You don't like it?" Karen asked.

Ali smirked. "I love it. I can't afford it."

"It looks good on you."

"I really can't justify spending that much." Ali walked on to the next rack.

Karen turned the price tag. One hundred and twenty dollars—for a small shoulder bag. She hadn't even looked at the price tags for the larger ones she had considered. *Of course she can't afford it. She just spent a fortune on this weekend.* Karen slipped the shoulder bag off the rack. As Ali made her way to the back of the store, she tiptoed to the clerk at the front.

"I'll pick it up when she's not looking."

He dashed off with a knowing smile. Just in time. Ali called Karen to come to the back to look at something. *Uh-oh. Did she find something she loves more?*

They finished up at the leather goods store before hustling on to the next shop. The periodic frozen precipitation had morphed into a consistent snowfall, with the wind whipping flakes across the streets. Patio bar-goers had all gone inside. Main Street was virtually deserted. Karen and Ali hustled down the street, bags with prized possessions in hand. It was their last day at the inn, so they dashed back to the warmth of their room and that inviting claw-foot tub.

Karen filled the tub with steaming water while Ali lit some pine-scented candles. Through the fogged edges of the window, they watched snow gracefully tumble from the sky. Ali pulled out the bottle of Baileys Irish Cream and gathered two glasses.

"Before you do that." Karen took Ali's hand. "You went out of your way to make this an incredible Christmas celebration together." She pulled a medium-sized bag from her larger bag of purchases. "Merry Christmas." She handed the bag to Ali. "I couldn't wrap it."

Ali gazed at the insignia on the bag with immediate recognition. Her jaw dropped. Frantically, she pulled open the bag, pushing aside piles of tissue paper.

"Oh my God," she cried out. "I can't believe you did this."

Karen found her eyes getting moist as she watched Ali's emotions illuminate.

"This is too expensive. I can't accept this."

Karen fought the urge to roll her eyes. "No…it's not. You've done so much for me. It's the least I could do."

Ali threw her arms around Karen's shoulders, first hugging her, then kissing her face. She leaned back and looked firmly into Karen's eyes. "You're amazing, Detective Cappelletti."

Karen chuckled.

"I can't wait to sink into that hot bath with you and show you my appreciation."

Damn it. She gets me every time…just the mere suggestion of intimacy. "I'm glad you like it. It'll look wonderful on your shoulder."

Ali giggled with joy. She grabbed the bottom of Karen's turtleneck, drawing her near. "Do you want to get undressed and get in the tub, or should I do that for you?"

"Is that a question or a statement?"

Ali didn't answer. She pulled Karen's turtleneck off with as much speed and grace as she unsnapped her bra. The bra fell to the floor as Ali nuzzled up against Karen's neck. Her hands never paused, reaching for the buttons on Karen's jeans. Karen felt a torrent of warmth flood through her chest.

Moments later, after a sensual mutual undressing, Ali handed Karen a glass of Baileys and joined her in the tub. She sank into Karen's wet chest.

This. Is. Amazing.

They headed home on clear roads with the surrounding landscape draped in fresh snow. Ali wrapped Karen's hand tightly within hers, and they passed the hour-long drive home singing Christmas carols and laughing at each other's poor efforts at holding a tune.

Even though Christmas was in two days, it felt like a wonderful white Christmas morning. Karen cherished each minute of their last day together. The next morning, Ali would be on the road and gone for two weeks. She winced at the thought.

The first Monday after the new year, Karen arrived home from work. Something was different. Off. The garbage can she took out that morning was no longer at the curb. A light was on in the back of the house. She was meticulous about turning off lights before leaving.

When she opened the front door, she realized her alarm system had been disabled. She unclipped her sidearm. Taking a step into the entryway, she caught sight of a shadow toward the back of the house. A moment later, the figure appeared from the kitchen.

"Jesus Christ, Miles. You scared the shit out of me."

He grinned. "I parked down the street. Wanted to surprise you."

Somehow, she had managed to push this day out of her thoughts. She smelled the rich aromas of a pot roast cooking. *What the hell? He never cooked dinner for me before.* In the dining room, a dozen red roses were centered on the table. *Oh my God. Who is this man?*

She fought tears forming in her eyes, not sure if they were tears of joy or tears of confusion and sadness.

In every life, there are roads with forks; some lead to happiness, while others lead to heartache. Karen recognized she was now at that fork, with absolutely no idea which way to go.

CHAPTER TWENTY-SEVEN

Miles wrapped his arms around Karen and kissed her neck, nuzzling his razor-stubbled face against her cheek. A surge of dread ran down her spine.

She stood rigid, not responding. "You made dinner?" she asked, shifting the subject.

"It was the least I could do. Great way to start our first night back together."

Karen squirmed out of his arms. "I'm sorry. I'm really tired and preoccupied." She forced a smile. "Let me go change."

Entering her bedroom, she found Miles's bags crowding the top of her bed. *Just comes in and takes over. So Miles.* She scowled. Glancing at her closet, she suddenly remembered the clothes Ali had left there. Hastily, she pushed them to the back of the closet. *Hiding my relationship…again. Christ. Nothing has changed.*

Miles entered a moment later. As Karen pulled off her belt and began to unbutton her slacks, he forced her up against the bedroom wall, hands groping at her shirt. He was like an octopus, hands and arms all over her.

"Miles." She heard her annoyance.

"What? You don't want this?" His face wrinkled with wide-eyed astonishment.

Karen fumbled. "I—I don't know." The words felt as if they were forced out between her teeth. She put her hand on his chest. "Maybe…not so…" She grappled. "Barbaric." In that moment, she realized she'd grown accustomed to a different kind of intimacy. A softness. A tenderness. A gentle and sensual touch that bordered on teasing delight. Intimacy had become a sharing of deep feelings, not just an act of lust.

"What's going on? Am I being forced to sleep in the guest room? After all these months?" His face contorted with a quizzical look.

Karen paused, feeling cornered. Her mind raced. "No." She hesitated, cautiously calculating her next words. "No. I'll sleep in the guest room."

He threw up his hands and backed out of the bedroom.

Why do I feel the need to give in? What about my needs?

Karen returned to the kitchen in sweatpants and a sweatshirt. "The roses are beautiful. Thank you."

Standing behind him, she envisioned herself wrapping her arms around his waist and kissing the back of his neck. Habit. It's what she'd done every evening when she came home when he was in town. Pure habit, with little emotional intent or desire. With a shake of her head, she consciously broke the old pattern.

"How long will you be here for?" *Hopefully, two days.* She felt an inner chuckle at the thought.

"Don't have anything lined up. Who knows? Maybe you'll convince me to stay." He grinned. "Let's talk about the future in a few weeks, okay?"

Karen stared at him, numb.

Falling asleep that night in her guest room, she thought about being out in the town with Miles—feeling safe, not feeling judged. A comforting thought. She had been brave in public with Ali but could relax with Miles. Being with him would be safe.

Then, there was the thought of intimacy with him. No desire—not with him. What she'd experienced with Ali left her longing for something completely different. It left her longing for Ali.

The next morning, Miles brought her coffee in bed. Karen couldn't help but chuckle. *He's really trying hard.* Still, there was a void. The warm and sensual connection that enveloped her when Ali brought her coffee was absent. Or maybe it was her feelings for him, in general, that were absent.

Karen headed to the station, leaving Miles to unpack his bags. *It's not like I can just kick him to the curb…can I?* With work missing anything to hold her attention, her mind kept drifting to Miles. She struggled to differentiate between the man she once hoped he would be and the man he appeared to be now. After six months, she wasn't sure who he was. And she wasn't sure what it was that drew her to him.

Ali, on the other hand, was everything she had always desired in a relationship. At the same time, it was not a relationship she felt comfortable expressing openly or in public. As her mind churned between the person with whom she felt empty and the person who filled her with joy—coupled with what she deemed as society's expectations as a roadblock to that joy—the workday dragged along at a snail's pace.

When Karen returned home, Miles announced that he had made a reservation for dinner at La Cannelle. "You up for it?"

Karen smiled. The local restaurant was an old favorite of theirs. "Sure. That sounds great."

She hadn't been to La Cannelle since Miles left. They were seated at a table for two by the window, removed from the kitchen and larger crowds. The scents of truffled potatoes, roasted asparagus, and braised short ribs filled her nostrils. The two caught up on their months apart, and Karen heard all about the city of Paducah. Miles always returned with fantastic stories. At times, it made Karen crave an experience outside of Parks Ford, except for the fact that her life, family, and everything she had worked for was in this town. Miles had always been a natural at conversation.

"Any thoughts about how long you'll stay?"

Miles grinned. "I went down to Riddle Hospital today. Checking on jobs locally."

"Seriously?"

Miles had always struggled with Parks Ford. He was an outsider. She often tried to convince him that if he just stuck around, he would become a cherished "local." Now, he appeared to be considering it.

He chuckled. "Don't look so shocked."

"C'mon, Miles. We've been down this road a gazillion times. You've never wanted to get a job here."

"Well. Maybe I've changed."

Judy's words flashed through her mind. *People don't change.* Her eyes dropped to her salad, forcing a smile. "That would be awesome." She fought to believe her own words.

The days passed, blending into mush. Karen began to lower her emotional walls. Still, she couldn't fathom sharing intimacy with Miles. *I'm not sure I could ever do it again with him. I need time.* Time. Time to determine whether she needed to follow social convention or relax and go with her heart. Could she ever be as relaxed in public with Ali as she was with Miles…or any person of the opposite sex, for that matter? She stayed hunkered in her guest room every night, keeping a healthy distance from any potential intimacy with Miles.

Before she knew it, the eighth of January rolled around—a day Karen absolutely dreaded. Ali was returning home. Time had expired. She needed to make a decision.

"I'll be working late tonight. Won't be home until at least nine," Karen said as she left for work. A blatant lie. She needed time alone. Time to make sense of what she wanted—to weigh her options—to make a decision.

Can I trust him to stay? I know Ali will. Her stomach tightened. She envisioned her and Ali out to dinner at La Cannelle. *Everyone would stare. They'd talk. But not with Miles.*

At the end of the day, she sat at her desk, spinning a pencil in her fingers. Her thoughts drifted off to intimacy with Ali. She felt an ache emerge. *It's different with her.* She pictured herself tolerating Miles. *Tolerating intimacy.* She shook her head. *Is it worth it?*

Karen stared out the window to the darkened streets—the streetlamps on poles beginning to light up. A periodic snow flurry drifted by. She thought about her career. Envisioned next year's holiday party with Miles on her arm, all the other women, jealous. *I could never bring Ali.* A sudden sadness poured over her.

Maybe Ali will be willing to stay friends. She flashed back to their long evenings and amazing conversations. It was something she had craved for so long. *So easy with her. Effortless.* Conversations with Miles never rose above the superficial level and were most often a prerequisite to sex. *Always an agenda. Miles "quid pro quo" Stillwell.* Ali never made demands or pushed anything on her that she didn't desire.

Karen sat back in her chair, her fingers steepled on the desk in front of her. She could all but feel her hands run along the soft curves of Ali's body, the softness of her face.

What do women get from men? Her answer followed rapidly. *Social acceptance.* She stared straight ahead. *Why does that matter? Who cares what people think? Shouldn't love be enough?* As much as she knew the correct answer, she couldn't sink into it and feel at ease. Every woman she knew was attracted to men. *Why isn't it okay if I'm not—if I prefer a woman?* She shook her head as if shaking herself back to reality. *Because it's just not, Capp.*

Social acceptance. Is it worth the sacrifice?

CHAPTER TWENTY-EIGHT

Karen arrived at Ali's bungalow just shy of seven. The yard was barren from the winter frost. She recalled the first time she strolled to her door, the smell of the jasmine blooming outside the front window hitting her nostrils. Karen caught Ali peering out from behind the blinds as she came up the walkway.

The door swung open, Ali scampering out and pulling Karen inside. "I've missed you so much." She plastered her lips firmly onto Karen's.

Karen felt a tentative smile form on her face.

"I brought you a few little gifts from my hometown." Ali looked like she was ready to burst with joy and excitement.

Spread on the table were magnets, trinkets, and a couple of homemade Christmas ornaments, the tissue paper they were wrapped in piled to the side. *This woman is amazing*. She loved this woman. She would never intentionally do anything to hurt her. And she knew Ali felt the same.

"You're a sight for sore eyes," Ali said. "These last two weeks felt like a year."

Karen chuckled softly. *What am I doing?*

"Let's do something amazing to start the new year. A chance to push out the old and usher in a wonderful new year together."

Those magnificent eyes. Those soft lips. Karen looked down and said nothing.

"What's wrong?"

Tears filled Karen's eyes. "Ali, the man I told you about..." She swallowed hard. "He's back in town." Karen struggled, feeling as if each word was fighting a tug-of-war with her tongue. "Ali, you mean the world to me." Tears balanced precariously on her lower lids.

Ali sat on the couch. Silent. Calm. Stoic. Her eyes were moist, but her emotions were held in check.

"I just need time," Karen said through tears. Her stomach roiled. "Time to figure out what I need...what I'm feeling."

"You haven't figured out how you feel...for me?" Ali's face wrinkled with annoyance. "What, exactly, do you need to figure out?"

Karen cringed at the ire in Ali's voice. The only sound in the room was a faint buzz from the refrigerator. Seconds ticked. An uncomfortable quiet.

Karen stood, heartbroken. But she had no answer. *She's right. What the hell is my problem?* "Maybe we can be friends," Karen said, breaking the stillness.

"No. That ship has sailed." Ali jerked a hand to her cheek and whisked away a tear. "Goddamn straight women. What was I...an experiment? Your little game? What the hell was I thinking? I should have known."

"I love you," she whispered. "Please know, I love you."

As Ali looked down, Karen turned to leave. She had no idea whether she should kiss Ali or instruct Ali to smack her upside the head. Should she take the little gifts innocently laid out on the kitchen counter with love? *Would that be rude? Would it be hurtful to leave them behind?* The last thing Karen wanted to do was hurt this woman any more than she already had.

Karen carefully rewrapped the gifts. Bending down, she kissed Ali on her head. At the door, she turned back one last time. Their eyes locked. She pushed herself to walk out. The *thunk* of the door closing had the sound of finality. She glanced at Ali through the window, watching her face crumble into her hands. She felt disgusted. She felt her own heart breaking. *All those feelings of not being good enough, not being wanted... You fucking asshole.*

Karen needed time to regroup. Time to push away the knot in her throat. Time for the swelling nausea in her gut to dissipate.

She drove directly to her parents' deserted house. The emptiness fit her mood. Trees outside were naked, with the coldest months upon them. Just like awaiting the return of spring, Karen would be in a holding pattern—figuring out what she wanted, what she needed.

The still, barren outside and the quiet emptiness inside summed up everything she felt. It was as if she was cradled in a safe womb, staring out at the cold, desolate exterior. In her closed, chrysalis state, she felt an overwhelming sadness envelop her. *Why do I always fuck up relationships?* Ali's words about "straight women" haunted her.

She sat in darkness in the kitchen, a solitary light above the stove the only illumination. What had she just done? *Will she take me back after I get my head out of my ass?* An overpowering queasiness poured over her.

She left the safe and comforting womb of her parents' house. It was time to head home. Time to face a man she wasn't sure she wanted to talk to. Hell, she wasn't even sure she wanted to see him. It was time to sort through her issues.

"Ali's right," she said to herself as she closed the door to her parents' house. "What *are* you trying to figure out? If you can be yourself…in public?"

She shook her head.

"You're such a fucking coward, Capp."

For the first time in a long time, she wished her house was empty. The thought of Miles being there and wanting her attention nauseated her. *I just need some time to myself.*

At home, the only lights on were the hall light and the light in her bedroom. *Fuck. He's still awake.* At the top of the steps, she turned to the left, avoiding her bedroom and, once again, heading to the guest room. Closing the door behind her, thoughts of Ali flooded in. The image of how she must have destroyed her felt like a twenty-pound weight sitting on her chest. She wished she could do something. Wave a magic wand. Help Ali feel better. Deep down, she knew she needed to stay away. To figure things out. *Does she know how much I love her?*

Lying on her back, she stared at the darkened ceiling. Wide awake, she replayed what she had just done. The look on Ali's face. *Why is it so hard for me to accept our relationship?* She thought about her and Ali bundling up and heading into Philadelphia to watch the ice skaters at Penn's Landing. Her mind drifted back to the evenings when she'd escape work and head to Ali's. A smile popped on her lips.

Tossing and turning in bed, she felt a longing for the nights of intense and passionate intimacy with Ali. A searing warmth rose into her chest as an ache built between her legs. *I never felt anything like this for Miles.* She sighed. *Why can't I just accept that…he's not what I want?*

The next week of long nights, tossing and turning while the man she no longer had an interest in slept in her bed, annoyed her. Miles continued to push for physical closeness, which only made Karen recoil further. She missed the warmth of Ali beside her.

Work did nothing to quell the churning in her stomach as the battle between her head and heart roiled. Having Ali back in town—and enjoying long conversations again—could have eased the drudgery of quiet days at the station and the frozen stillness that always set in when January arrived. But Karen couldn't get out of her own way, out of the way of her antiquated rules.

She gazed at the phone on her office desk. For days, she'd thought about calling Ali but dreaded her potential response. It was time to be strong. She clicked on Ali's name, panic searing through her chest. Voice mail. The first several rounds, she opted to hang up. Finally, after her fourth call, Karen left a brief message through tears building in the back of her throat:

"Hey, sweetie. You've been on my mind. I just wanted to say hi and check in."

Deep down, what she really longed for was to hear Ali's voice—hear her positive and reassuring tone, hear her tell Karen that she loved her and would be waiting for her as soon as Karen was ready. *You're living a pipe dream. She's probably avoiding your calls.* Karen felt a suffocating sadness fall over her.

The rest of January left a cold emptiness. Karen felt no desire to be close to Miles and worked through a host of scenarios for ending their relationship—if she could even call it that. Her mind played back the hurt on Ali's face over and over.

Late at night on the second night in February, Karen lay in bed wide awake reviewing the news Miles had sprung on her earlier that evening. He had found the ideal place for his next assignment: Cedars-Sinai Medical Center, in Los Angeles. Warm weather. Green grass, even in February. Beaches. Sunshine. She recalled feeling a sudden sense of relief. He would be leaving soon.

Lying on her side, staring out the darkened window, she replayed their conversation.

"Why don't you come with me?" he had said, illuminating the key difference with this assignment. He was asking her to join him.

"Miles. My life is here." She had struggled to stay nonconfrontational.

California was alluring for Karen, but also frightening. Parks Ford was home. A permanent home. Her life and career were here. Her parents were here. Siblings and extended family nearby. Caiden was only a two-hour drive away. Everything she had worked so hard for—it was all right here in Parks Ford. And even though she hadn't resolved the conflict between her rules and her desires, Ali was in Parks Ford.

Miles had let out a frustrated laugh. "You know I don't belong here." He stared at her with a half-smile as if no answers were necessary. He preferred being an outsider elsewhere rather than right there in dinky Parks Ford.

The evening had ended with a grand thud. In bed, her mind churned away. Maybe she needed to sacrifice her love with Ali and give it a go with Miles. Then there was the stalled case—Cliff's murder. Maybe it was all a sign to move on. Maybe she needed to make a drastic change.

A tear slid from one eye, then the other. This was her home. He was suggesting she give it up for him. Her family was close-knit. *He can't understand that. His family's broken.* Tears welled at the thought of all the pieces of her life that would be fractured.

Karen was still awake when the darkened sky yielded to gray. She recalled how Miles tried to persuade her to join him in California. How he pushed to have her give up her life and follow him wherever he chose to take assignments. It was that last part that stuck with her.

It wasn't about him starting a new life with her, it was about her following him all over the country. Following his agenda. It wasn't about him giving up something to be with her. It never had been. It was always about what she had to give up for him. Whether it meant waiting for him to return or giving up everything she worked for and everything she loved. Miles had never made sacrifices for her, and he never would. He would never change. *Are you gonna sacrifice everything just for social acceptance?*

In her kitchen, she felt an emotional moat beginning to form around her heart. She grabbed her mug of coffee. A searing revelation hit her. *Get real, Capp. You don't even love him.* Love. The mere word brought Ali's lips into her mind.

In her living room, she sat staring out her bay window, the clouds outside painting the street in gloom. Winter chill whipped through the brittle, arthritic tree branches. In January and February, when the excitement and fanfare of the holidays died down, people huddled in their homes. Life outside was dormant. A particularly difficult time for those battling depression. Thoughts of Ali flooded in.

Sitting in the calm of her haven, nursing her coffee, she fumbled through her thoughts. *You had everything you wanted with Ali. She put you first. With her, you felt love.* An instant sense of resolve permeated her mind. *You don't love him. You're not in love with him. Stop this nonsense.* Ali's tender face flashed before her.

A vibration interrupted her thoughts. Miles had left his cell phone on the coffee table. The screen of his phone illuminated. A message from Brenda.

Brenda. Who the fuck is Brenda? She peeked at the message.

Miss you, honey. Can't wait to see you soon. The message was capped off with a kissy emoji.

She shook her head. *Of course he's been cheating on you, you moron.* The realization slapped her across the face: she was just a safe harbor as he bounced around with other jobs and other women. *Shoulda booted him out weeks ago. Why did you put Ali on hold for this loser? Why do you always fuck up relationships?*

Slamming her empty mug on the coffee table, she considered waking him up and telling him all about Ali. How wonderful she felt. And then telling him to get the hell out. *Wait 'til you get home.*

With the investigation on life support and her love life in the toilet, she headed to work. Once again, she pulled out the homicide case files.

Sifting through photos from the crime scene for the umpteenth time, two pieces of evidence ate at her: the bandana and the partial footprint. The bandana sat three feet from Cliff's bloody footprints. It had to belong to the perpetrator. The bloody partial footprint contained no defining features. No tread, no brand stamps, no wear marks. Not enough of the shoe was present to match the size.

She picked up her phone and left a succinct message. "Riley. If you've got some time today, I want to show you something. Need your thoughts."

Fifteen minutes later, Riley arrived at her office, tapping on the door.

"Brought you a gift." Riley handed her a warm paper cup.

Karen mustered up a smile. "You're too good to me."

She pulled out the photos from the crime scene and handed them to Riley. "Look at the path of the bloodstains. We identified Cliff's footprints from the point where he was stabbed all the way to the driveway where he was found."

Riley nodded.

"But here." She pointed to the partial shoe print across from where Cliff was found. "The partial. It's not back where he was initially stabbed. But right here, where he landed and died."

Again, Riley nodded.

"The print was made in fresh blood, so it has to belong to the perp. He was with Cliff all the way up to the driveway."

Riley squinted as if trying to follow Karen's line of thinking.

"Why didn't he take off right away? Why did he stick around with Cliff until he fell over?"

Riley shot her a blank stare. "I thought we already went down this road."

"Yes. But wouldn't Cliff have screamed for help? It's as if the person pushed or encouraged him to keep walking. As if Cliff trusted the person. Doesn't make sense."

"No. And when it doesn't make sense, it means we're missing something."

"Any chance we can get forensics to give the shoe print another try? ID the brand, maybe an approximate size. Anything."

"I'll try, but not sure what an approximate size will yield," Riley said.

"There are two pieces of evidence that still have loose ends. The partial shoe print and the bandana. What are we missing?"

"The bandana. We know about ultisol, but where is kaolinite found, again?" Riley asked.

"The biggest area is in the southeastern states. Georgia." Karen recalled her earlier research on the extraction process used to obtain kaolinite.

"Our perp didn't come all the way from Georgia. Where else?"

Officer Mott appeared in the doorway. "Detective. Kenny McPherson is here. He said he needs to talk to you. Urgent."

"Put him in the interview room," Karen said. She looked at Riley. "Thoughts?"

"Let's go find out. If we're lucky, he mines kaolinite."

Karen half-smiled. *Kaolinite is mined? I thought it was extracted. We're looking for someone that works in mines?*

When they entered the ten-by-ten room, they found the scruffy man completely frazzled and disheveled. His clothes were streaked with dirt, his forehead dripping with sweat, and his boots saturated with water and mud.

"What's up, Kenny?" Karen asked.

His torso shook. "I just went back to the house to get something I left there..."

Karen shot Riley a blank look. "Something you left at the Hillside house? From ten years ago?"

"Yeah, I know. Just hear me out. I had a floor safe. Stashed money there. Every week I got paid." Kenny shot them a guarded glance. "I only came for my money."

"How much money?"

"Four...five thousand. I had other stuff in the safe, but I can't touch that shit. Just came for my money. I swear." His eyes seemed to be pleading. "I'm trying to get my life together."

"What else was in that safe, Kenny? What is it you can't touch?" Riley asked.

He squirmed in his chair. Continuing to avoid eye contact, he looked straight into the space between both detectives. "A knife collection. Four really expensive display knives. I hid 'em there so they'd be safe."

Karen shot Riley a quick glance. "What kind of knives?"

"The kind youse showed me and Doyle that day." Kenny's eyes were bulging as if ready to bounce out of his face. "Four Ek Commandos."

Karen swallowed hard. She and Riley glanced at each other.

"One's gone." Panic flooded his face. "I swear, I swear, I didn't touch 'em. I had nothin' to do with those knives. I came for my money."

"When was the last time you saw those knives, Kenny?" Karen asked.

"Ten fucking years ago, I swear." Kenny's eyes were pleading. "Here—" He held out his hand.

Cradled in his pudgy, sweating hand was a medium-sized key, clutched so hard it had left an imprint. "It's the key to the safe. Go see for yourselves."

Karen took the key and placed it on the metal table. *Why's he telling us this? We would've never known about those knives. Is he trying to point the finger at Bobby?*

"Where was this key when you were in prison?" Riley asked.

"Behind that large picture in the living room. Bobby…he changed a lot of shit…but that day I stopped by…that picture was still there." He paused. "I didn't break in or nothin'. My daughter, she leaves the back door open."

Oh, Tam. You fool.

"I didn't tell ya before because I knew what you'd think. I don't wanna go back to prison. I just wanted to get my money and move on." He looked down at the metal table. "I heard Bobby come home…I ran out the back. I knew he'd call ya…say I broke in. I didn't break in. I came to tell you what happened before you came after me."

Karen was silent. She studied Kenny's face for any cracks in his demeanor.

"Bobby never called anyone at the station. He didn't report seeing you in the house."

Kenny's eyes were fixed. He looked mentally numb, almost paralyzed by the revelation. "He didn't call youse?"

Karen shook her head. "Did you get your money?"

"No," Kenny cried out as if in agony. "It was gone. Everything I saved. Fuckin' gone."

"Kenny, who else knew where the key and safe were?"

"No one."

"How 'bout Doyle? Did he have a copy of the key or know where it was?"

He shook his head.

"Maybe you told him one drunken night."

"No."

"How about your wife? Did she know where the key was?" Riley asked.

"No fucking way. She woulda killed me if she knew I was hiding money from her." Kenny started to ramble. "Always bitched I never had enough money. Thought I pissed it all away…gettin' hammered. But I didn't. I kept from it her."

Loving husband. Karen fought a frown. *Poor woman. Married to such an asshole. Not like I had a gem, though.*

"Did you tell anyone about this key and the safe while you were in prison?" Riley asked.

"No one."

"Okay, Kenny. We've got your statement. Give us a chance to address this, okay?"

He nodded, then dropped his head. "I don't want to back to jail. I don't want to go back."

Karen had Officer Mott lead Kenny out and returned to her office where Riley was waiting.

"Ri, Bobby's the only one that's lived there the entire time. Tam left before Kenny was carted off."

"So you think Kenny's bullshitting us and this is his way to get back at Bobby?"

"Only way we'll know is to question Bobby. Wonder why he didn't report Kenny being at the house."

Riley shrugged. "Head over there now?"

Karen took a deep breath. She knew if they found something, their work would take them into the night. She needed to resolve the issue with Miles—get it off her chest. She needed a clear head. "I need to stop by my house real quick. How 'bout we reconvene at Hillside at 3:30?"

Riley's dark eyes felt like they were peering into Karen's soul. "You okay?"

"Yeah. Just something I need to handle."

"You know you can always talk if you need to."

How could she? Riley had always been tight-lipped when it came to her personal life. Hell, she didn't even know if she was married or had a partner. She knew nothing about her personal belief system or relationship history. "Thanks. I'll keep that in mind."

"Let's meet back here. We'll go over together," Riley said.

The sky outside was painted in shades of gray with billowing white clouds dropping a mistlike rain. The gloom of the day matched Karen's mood as she neared her driveway. Miles's car was gone. The house had a cold and empty feel.

She looked for a note from him on the kitchen table. Nothing. In the bedroom, all of his belongings had vanished. Everything. Gone.

She threw open the sliding door of the closet. All his clothes, gone. Except for the shirt—the one that was Karen's favorite, the one that she clung to when he would go away on assignments. She yanked the shirt down with one swift tug, leaving the thin metal hanger swinging wildly before flying off the rod and tumbling to the ground.

She marched down the stairs and threw the shirt into a corner. Grabbing his tall white mug with remnants of leftover coffee, she emptied the liquid into the sink, spun around, and hurled the vessel into the same corner, smashing it to pieces.

The black arms of the silver clock on the wall ticked to 2:55 p.m. Time to push aside Miles and all her other poor choices. Time to refocus on the case. Time to reconvene with Riley.

CHAPTER TWENTY-NINE

Driving to the station, the spitting rain of the gloomy, miserable day finally yielded to a few rays of sunshine. Karen struggled to home in on the case with her normally laser-sharp attention. *Is it really possible Bobby never touched that large picture…for ten years? Never discovered the key? But, even if he found it, would he have known what it belonged to?*

Riley stood just inside the station's glass doors and jogged out when Karen's car pulled up.

"Thoughts about Kenny's story?" Riley asked.

"Why would he tell us something that would incriminate himself?" Karen said.

"Maybe he's covering for Doyle."

"Bobby's lived there for the last ten years…ample opportunity to find the key…probably the safe, too."

"Not necessarily," Riley said. "We moved a lot when I was a kid, but there was one house we stayed in for six years. There was a floor safe in the hall closet. We never would've found it if there hadn't been a flood that led to the floorboards being pulled up."

Karen drove through town, lost in her thoughts.

Riley looked at Karen, waiting for a comment. She broke the silence. "What are your thoughts about Tam? She's kinda...odd, don't you think?"

Karen mentally rolled her eyes. *This is the shit Miles was talking about. If you're not part of the community, people ostracize you.* "C'mon, Riley. She would have to know where the key and safe were. She only moved back a couple weeks before the murder. Unless she knew about them before she left. You, yourself, said it took your family six years to discover a floor safe." Karen paused, fighting to keep her protective mechanisms for Tam in check. "If Tam knew where the key and safe were, then surely Bobby and Marianne knew, too. So, technically, all three are possibles. This is assuming Kenny's story is true."

Riley stared out the window, cold drops of water blurring the view, while Karen navigated through the early rush traffic.

"If Kenny's story checks out, we can try and grab prints off the picture frame, floorboards, and safe," Riley said.

They rolled up to Bobby's house. Karen felt herself relax, noting Tam's car was absent. The intermittent rain had finally allowed a few peeks of sunshine to struggle through. Bobby opened the door before they even hit the first porch step.

Wasting no time, Karen jumped in. "Bobby, do you know what this key goes to?"

He studied it, then shrugged. "Nope. It's too small to fit anything." He reached for his ring of keys hanging by the front door. "See, this one is to the house...this one, my car...the rest are work keys. That key is too small."

"How long has that picture been there?" Karen pointed to the lone picture encompassing half of the living room wall.

"Long as I can remember." He gazed at the antiquelike framed picture. "My mom loved that painting. A gift from her parents. One of the only things she left behind that I didn't get rid of."

Bobby appeared as the pillar of honesty and decency. A good guy who cared about his mother and her belongings. Karen glanced at Riley, who remained quiet.

Karen signaled for him to follow her. She put her hand on the pantry door. "May I?"

He half shrugged, half nodded. Karen donned gloves. Kneeling, she removed a remnant piece of carpet on the pantry floor, then pulled away two loose floorboards. They came up effortlessly. She looked up at Bobby. He stared at the floor in dumbstruck amazement. Karen removed the last floorboard, revealing a red metal door to a floor safe and a hefty silver handle.

"What the…" Bobby looked stunned.

Karen inserted the key—a perfect fit. Grasping a corner of the handle, careful to avoid as much contact with her gloved hand as possible, she turned it counterclockwise and lifted the thick cover.

At the bottom of the safe rested only a display box with three knives and a space for the fourth. Riley snapped a few pictures.

"How long has this been here?" Karen's voice was soft and neutral.

"I have no idea." He seemed genuinely astonished. "Didn't even *know* it was there." He fell back against the kitchen wall and threw his head back. "That's why he was here."

Karen played dumb. "Who, Bobby?"

"*Damn it!*" He paced in the tiny kitchen. "My father was here when I got home today."

"Why didn't you call the police?" Riley asked.

"Because fucking Tam must've left the back door unlocked again. Caught him running out the door and through everyone's backyards." Bobby paused. "Nothing was missing. Nothing was damaged. I didn't have the heart…he'd violate his parole." He looked dejected and exhausted.

"Bob, I need officers to come down and check for fingerprints, okay?" Karen said.

He nodded.

Riley summoned a team to obtain prints while Karen secured Bobby's official consent. Within fifteen minutes, officers arrived. The key areas would be the picture frame, the pantry floorboards, and the safe.

Karen cautiously pulled the aging framed painting off the wall with gloved hands. Dust flew everywhere.

Bobby winced. "Why do you have to touch that picture?"

She turned it around. At the bottom, attached to the back of the wooden frame, was a small nail protruding out. She directed the officers to grab prints in that location.

"This is where we believe the key was hanging. We have to check for prints here," Karen said. "We'll be very careful with the picture."

Karen stepped out onto the covered porch, relieved that Tam and her drama were absent. The chilly rain had cleared. The air had warmed a bit as the sun reached the front of the house. She loped down the creaking porch steps when Tam bolted around the corner from the driveway and shot for the front door.

Speak of the devil. "Hey," Karen called out in a casual tone.

Tam scooted right by her, up the steps, and through the front door, leaving a mud trail behind. Shaking her head, Karen turned back around to head to the car. She reached for her sunglasses, squinting from the glare of the sun. Then she froze. In slow motion, she pivoted back around to the steps and Tam's path to the door. The sun. The muddy footprints. She stood staring at Tam's footprints. Pulling out her phone, she snapped a series of photos.

She jogged back to the car where Riley was waiting.

"What?" Riley asked, looking at Karen's face.

"When we interviewed Tam, she told us she came outside early the morning of the murder because it was quiet and she could enjoy her coffee in the sun. Look." Karen pointed to the porch. "The porch faces the west. The sun was brightest on the porch when we arrived today, at 3:45. There wouldn't have been morning sun. Not at the time she said she walked out."

Riley's face froze, expressionless.

"Just now, she ran by me. Left these shoe prints." She showed Riley her phone. "Maybe we can use the shoe prints we do have identification for and match it with our partial print."

Riley looked skeptical. "Capp, the partial has no defining marks."

"Maybe we bring Tam in…lead her to believe we're able to make a match. See what happens."

"Worth a try."

"Call the station. We need all hands on deck." Karen accelerated away from the curb, causing Riley's head to fly back against the headrest.

"Let's get us there in one piece, 'kay?"

With that, Karen punched the accelerator with authority. They zipped back through town, tires slapping through the puddles of water on the pockmarked roads.

CHAPTER THIRTY

At the station, Officer Roberts placed the thin Mulberry file on Karen's desk. Inside was a clear photograph of a solid shoe print outside of Ali's house and identification of the shoe as a K-Swiss court shoe, size nine. Karen already knew the shoe belonged to Tam; she had addressed the issue earlier. Since Tam never bothered Ali again, Karen considered that chapter closed. But now a new possibility revealed itself. Would that shoe print match the partial from the crime scene?

Karen noted inconsistencies in Tam's story but still couldn't see Tam as a killer nor understand why she would hurt Cliff. Forensics compared all three prints: the partial from the crime scene, the ones from Ali's house, and the ones she just captured.

"Ma'am, there's just not enough," the forensic technician said regarding the partial print. "Nothing to define it. Certainly nothing that would hold up in court."

"Without that...doubt we can obtain a search warrant for those shoes," Riley said.

"Why not? We're looking for shoes that have no tread. No identifying marks." Karen rubbed her forehead. *What are we missing?*

"We can still bring her in. Question her. Make her think we've got the goods."

Riley nodded while Karen summoned an officer to bring Tam in.

In her office, Karen sat alone, reflecting on her Internet search of Tam. Tam had said she lived in New York City, but in actuality, she had lived in a plethora of nearby cities. Five different locations in fourteen years—not a crazy number considering she was a young adult branching out on her own. Now, she dove into the National Incident-Based Reporting System for each location.

Her search was interrupted by the mild-mannered Officer Roberts.

"KC, we have Tammy McPherson in interrogation when you're ready."

Karen viewed Tam through the one-way mirror, leaning back in a wooden chair, seemingly bored, or annoyed, or both. Inside the room, Tam was framed by soft blue walls, her legs stretched out in front of her. She raised her arms over her head as if to stretch.

"Do you know why you're here?" Karen began in a soft, measured tone.

"You couldn't wait to see me." Tam lowered her arms and rolled her eyes.

Karen pulled out the picture of the shoe print from Ali's yard and placed it on the table in front of Tam.

"We have this shoe print from 514 Mulberry Street," Karen said with a deadpan, no-nonsense stare. "Do you want to tell us anything?"

Tam snorted. "Are you fucking kidding me? I already admitted to that. You told me you weren't going to report it." Tam sat up and slid her hands into the pockets of her jeans.

Karen took a deep breath, centering herself. The game had begun.

"You knew I was jealous over your relationship with Ali…You're still with her, right?"

Karen took a brief, inconspicuous glance at Riley, who sat motionless, her stare on Tam.

Riley broke the silence. "This isn't about Ali. It's about you. *Your* shoe print."

Tam shot Riley an acid glare and wrinkled her nose.

What happened to that charming, charismatic person I first met? "Look, Tam, all it will take is a search warrant to find those shoes. Be a lot easier for you if you just come clean."

Tam let out a deep-in-her-throat laugh. "I already came clean. You don't remember? I told you I was there that night. I was playing with Ali cuz she stole you from me. You told me as long as I left her alone, you'd let it go. Remember?" Tam finished her declaration with a soft, insinuating smile.

Christ, who's standing outside watching this? Karen's decision to speak directly with Tam and not report the incident went against department policy. Right now, that was water under the bridge. *Don't flinch. She thinks she's got you.*

"Perhaps, for the record, you could go back over the details of where you were that night and what you did at Ali's," Riley said.

Riley. My lifeline.

Tam willingly repeated every detail she had copped to the morning after the incident, sprinkling in new tantalizing details.

"I was driving by and saw some teens walking down the street. Then I saw your car." She looked at Karen. "It was parked in front of Ali's house…again." Tam smiled with apparent satisfaction. "But I never saw them throw the brick. When I circled back around, they were gone."

Karen remained silent, watching her.

"I saw you get in your car and leave, so I figured you weren't gonna spend the night with her." Tam's face wrinkled with a wide grin. "That's when I figured I'd play a little game with Ali. Freak her out a bit."

Karen challenged her. "How did you know they threw a brick?"

Tam's eyes squinted. "I saw it on the ground by her car window."

"Impossible. I picked up that brick and put it aside before I left. Wanna try again?"

Tam's face became mottled. She looked down. "Okay, so I threw the brick. Big deal. You want me to pay for the damage?"

"Vandalism is a crime, Tam," Riley said, her tone harsh.

"So is prowling," Karen added.

Tam smirked. "You arresting me for that? Sure seems a little late. Wasn't that, like, three months ago?"

With Tam calling their bluff, Karen decided it was time to go all out. "Thank you for being so honest and forthcoming. And I appreciate that you've stayed away from Ali."

Tam flashed one of her classic infectious smiles. Previously drawn in by those, Karen felt her rational detective-based mind return.

Removed from the tangled web of fabricated truths, she felt an odd buffer from Tam's insidious ploys.

She continued, "We know it was you at 514 Mulberry that night. We know it was your shoe print there. But what I don't understand is why your shoe print is also…here." She pulled out the crime scene pictures and pointed to the partial print.

Tam glared at her, then sat back, reverting to feigning boredom. Karen stared at Tam while Riley looked down at her notepad. They were both banking on Tam not knowing that they had no proof. If she figured that out, she'd call their bluff and the plan would be toast.

"What makes you think that's mine?" Tam was defiant.

"They're identical to the footprints in these other two photos, which I know are yours." Karen pulled out the pictures of Tam's footprints on the porch steps from less than an hour prior.

"I don't know if that footprint is mine." Tam pointed to the crime scene photo. "I told you, I walked out that morning and saw the man lying on our driveway. I walked over to see if he was asleep."

"What did you do then?" Karen probed.

"He was just lying there. Still. Couldn't tell if he was breathing, so I got closer. Checked for a pulse." Tam seemed to be starting to relax. "That's probably when I got too close and stepped in blood."

Tam sat up and leaned over the table, examining the photo. She pointed at the direction of the shoe print and the path of the blood, claiming it was a logical direction to go in if she was checking on the body.

The footprint was a solid three feet from where the body was lying. If Tam had gotten that close to Cliff's body and stepped in blood, she would have left a different type of print: one of a shoe stepping in blood that had already dried to a gelatinous state versus one that had stepped in fresh blood. Karen knew Tam was lying and proceeded with caution.

"Okay…got it," Karen said as if to affirm Tam's explanation. "How did you check for his pulse?"

"Huh?" Tam wrinkled her nose. "Whad'ya mean?"

"Well, there are lots of places to check a pulse." Karen looked at Riley. "You could do the carotid, the radial, the groin area, behind the knee, on top of the foot, inside the arm—"

"Yeah…inside the arm."

"He had on a long-sleeved shirt," Riley said.

Tam stared at Karen as if hoping she would come to her rescue. Silence. She continued staring before blurting out an answer. "I remember now, I just felt him…to see if he was warm."

"Your footprint is here." Karen pointed to the print three feet from the body. "Unless you have extremely long arms, how could you reach the body at all to see if he was warm?"

Tam tightened her jaw and stared at Karen.

"Tam, when we spoke to you that day…when your mind was fresh…you said you were here." Karen pointed to the area about three feet above Cliff's head. "The footprint is on the exact opposite side…also about three feet away. How could you be in both places?"

"Oh. Well then obviously that's not my shoe."

"So, you're telling us that if we get a search warrant for your house, we won't find shoes that match that?" Riley asked.

"We've got forensics working now to match that print with your shoe print at Ali's," Karen said, pointing to the bloody print. "Tam. It's only a matter of time."

"You can't match those. There aren't any marks on this one." Tam's eyes gleamed as she pointed to the bloody shoe print.

"It's just a rough photo, Tam. The ones with forensics have much finer detail."

"There's nothing there." Her declaration was made with such certainty that Riley and Karen peered at each other.

"Information about the shoe print was never made public. How would you know if marks were found or not?" Karen's gentle tone had evaporated.

"I was there, remember?"

"And you examined the bloody footprint on your way to checking the body?" Karen shook her head with amusement.

Silence. Karen sensed Tam was reaching for her lifeline, her way out—what she had learned in every one of her previous altercations with people she'd conned. It was no longer about winning over Karen. It was only about survival. Nothing else.

"You can't prove anything," Tam fired back, shooting Karen a cold hard stare.

"But you just admitted that you stepped there." Karen pointed to the picture.

"No. I said I checked to see if he was warm and I *may have* stepped in blood." Daggers flew from Tam's mouth. "You're a fucking detective. Pay attention. Stop putting words in my mouth." A frosty chill blew across the table.

"Ahh, I apologize. I thought you told me those *were* your footprints," Karen said.

Tam sneered. "You got nothing on me."

Karen kept her cool and spoke in an even, steady tone. "We didn't bring you here to make accusations, Tam. We just needed you to help us understand—"

"You got nothin'." Tam enunciated each word. "If you're gonna charge me, do it. Otherwise, I'm outta here."

Tam stood and marched to the door, waiting for someone to open it. Karen did and followed her out.

"Roberts, can you give her a ride home?" Karen said. "Thank you for your time, Tam."

Tam gave Officer Roberts a bright smile, then bounded out the door of the station.

Karen grabbed Roberts by the arm and whispered, "Once you drop her, stay nearby. Let us know if anything looks unusual…if she looks like she's skipping out."

Karen retreated to her office. She dove back into the NIBRS databases and checked the places Tam had previously lived. One by one, in each location, Tam had been accused of crimes by the person she was living with. Each time, Tam got off because there was insufficient evidence to bring charges. *Goddamn it. This is her gig. She's got it down pat.*

Larceny in Manhattan, just shy of a year ago. Not enough evidence to charge her. In Hoboken, four years ago, Tam was the subject of an investigation for theft with a woman claiming to be her partner pressing charges. Teaneck, New Jersey. A fabricated story about having cancer that falsely enticed people to donate money to help pay her bills. When she got caught, she moved to Hackensack.

The individuals making the accusations—some were women, some men. *Is she bi?* Karen internally rolled her eyes at herself. *No, you idiot. She just goes after whoever she thinks she can con, male or female. And you were next up on her bingo card.*

Karen felt disgusted. Emotionally sick. *I'm an investigator…how did I not see it?* She'd protected Tam after the incident at Ali's, telling the responding officers that she couldn't get a license plate number. Riley had pointed out Tam's over-the-top friendliness early on.

Karen had brushed it off. Ali pointed out that Tam used the art studio facilities but wasn't a member. Tam was dead broke but drove a Mini Cooper and donated high-end ceramic items to the police auction. Everyone else picked up on the red flags while Karen defended her.

Karen shook her head. *I let my emotions get caught up…I felt bad for her…and she took full advantage.*

She remembered Tam's disdainful comment about the victim, that he was "just a homeless person." *Utter disregard for humanity, and I let it slide.*

An urgent call came in from Roberts. Tam had thrown a large duffel bag into her Mini and was headed east, in the direction of the Commodore Barry Bridge. Soon, she would be out of town and out of their jurisdiction. If she got on the bridge, it would be mere minutes before she was in New Jersey. Tam could go north and be in New York in under two hours. She could go south to Delaware and be in Maryland twenty minutes later. While Karen worked to secure evidence, Tam could buy herself a lot of time.

Karen stepped into the hall. "Riley, call in the state troopers. Tam is headed for the Commodore Barry. We gotta stop her on this side of the state line."

Riley was talking to Chief Walden. Both silently shifted their eyes to her.

"We need an emergency search warrant for her house…and her car," she said to Chief Walden.

"We need probable cause," Walden said with raised eyebrows.

"She admitted to her footprints at the Mulberry house. We need to find those shoes."

"So, you want to bring her in for prowling?" Walden said.

Then it hit her. *That's exactly what we should do.* She scrambled. Time was of the essence. One false move or error and she would send a potential cold-blooded killer walking.

"She admitted to the prowler incident." Karen spoke with conviction. "She drove her car there. We've got PC to search her house and car." Her head spun. *Slow down, Capp. Think. Carefully.*

"Riley…where are we at?" Karen snapped as the clock ticked and Walden looked on.

"Troopers are on it. What are they stopping her for?"

"Charges of vandalism and attempted home invasion." Her eyes met Riley's, searching for her colleague's calm affirmation.

Riley gave a solemn nod.

Bringing Tam in for the prowler incident would buy them time. Time to finish with the fingerprinting. Time to secure warrants and search her bedroom and car. Time. Karen just needed more time.

And now, the waiting game. Would Tam make it across the state line? Would she try to outrun the state troopers?

CHAPTER THIRTY-ONE

After securing the warrant, Karen sat rigid in her hushed office, awaiting the outcome of the pursuit. She sat in disbelief.

I opened up to her. I protected her. She froze. *I let her kiss me.* The last thought nauseated her. It had never bothered her before. She'd felt flattered. Now, the realization—it was all a con game. *No wonder I'm single. I trust totally screwed-up people.* Her mind flitted off to Ali, the one healthy person she had become involved with, and she had pushed her away. Tears welled up. She felt battered by demands and emotions.

"First Miles. Then Tam. Christ, Cappelletti, could you be more stupid?" she muttered. Then it hit her. *Yes…and you were.*

She pulled out the evidence file and looked up the information on the bandana. Soil, traces of silicon dioxide, and kaolinite. *You idiot! How did you miss that?*

"Riley," she called out.

Riley popped her head around the corner.

"The bandana. We thought the silicon dioxide was related to glass. It wasn't glass. It's an ingredient in clay."

"Look." She pointed at her computer screen. "The other name for kaolinite is kaolin, or ball clay. A potter I know told me ball clay and silica are the main ingredients in white clay. Tam works with clay."

"We can't prove that bandana is Tam's, though."

"No, but if my head wasn't so far up my ass, I would've seen it sooner." She pounded her fist on her desktop. "Shit. Ali told me… potters have solid upper body strength. Tam could have easily thrown that knife. It was all right there. I totally missed it."

Karen couldn't quite go so far as to acknowledge a harder truth: Tam was a sociopath. An expert. She was crafty. People outside of Tam's sphere of influence saw everything that was "off," but Karen was already entangled in the web of lies.

"Don't be so hard on yourself," Riley said. "We both missed it."

"She told us she went out front that morning because she wanted to enjoy the sun. The sun was on the opposite side of the house at that hour."

Riley closed her eyes and nodded when her phone rang. Moments later, she hung up and looked at Karen. "State troopers stopped Tam. On the bridge. She pulled over willingly. Played the coy, innocent game."

Of course. It's all about the con.

"Officers took her into custody. She's on her way here, spittin' mad." Riley couldn't help but chuckle. "Car's being towed. They've got her duffel bag."

Fingerprints on the safe and picture frame had already been determined as Kenny's. Now, the house was being searched for shoes to match the prints at Ali's, as well as a half-dollar-sized ceramic wind chime that went missing from outside Ali's home that night.

Riley hesitated before sharing her worst fears. "You know, Capp… we're only assuming those bloody footprints are hers. We could be totally off base."

"Riley. She knew the shoe print had no tread. She knew she left nothing that could identify her." Karen pointed to her computer screen. "Look at her history. She gets caught, but there's never enough evidence to bring charges and she gets off."

"Why hurt Cliff?" Riley said.

"Why hurt anyone?" Karen reflected back to Tam's comment. "To Tam, he was 'just a fucking homeless guy.' He was disposable."

"Think she and her dad were in on it together? Frame Bobby, her father gets the house, and Tam lives there free and clear? After all, so much evidence kept pointing to Bobby," Riley said.

Karen squinted, considering the scheme. It certainly was possible.

Riley continued, "Tam couldn't care less about her brother. The only person Tam cares about is herself."

Karen turned to catch a state trooper squad car pull up outside her window. She gave explicit instructions: have Tam wait in the interview room and give her whatever she wanted to eat or drink.

Her office phone rang. She stared beyond the lip of her desk, replacing the receiver as if moving in slow motion. "They found a pair of shoes in her duffel bag. They have a definite tread, but it also had a sticky residue."

Riley looked puzzled.

Karen held up her finger. "A wad of used duct tape was found in the back of her bedroom closet. I'm having both tested for blood."

"Match the shoe outline to the partial print and the residue on the shoes to the duct tape…" Riley thought out loud.

"Uh-huh," Karen said with a bobblehead-like nod.

Karen periodically glanced at Tam in the interview room. One minute, Tam sat staring at the ceiling, and the next, she acted like a caged animal, seething and ranting as she paced, screaming at the one-way mirror, stating she was being mistreated.

The sky outside had morphed into a deep indigo blue, just shy of the seven p.m. hour, when word came that something of significance had been recovered from Tam's car. Wedged between the cushions of her back seat was a pair of used medical exam gloves turned inside out. They were bagged and whisked off for examination. Forensic analysis would be completed within a couple of hours.

Tam was given a Coke. And the cheesesteak she asked for. And another Coke. Minutes ticked by.

Tam sat silent for over two hours, her arms crossed in front of her chest, maintaining an icy stare. Her tousled blond hair wisped in the air as the room's ducts blew warmth into the room.

"She looks pissed," Karen said.

Riley nodded. "Sociopaths usually do when they're caught and cornered."

"You knew all along."

"I saw the warning signs."

Karen entered the interview room and sat across from Tam. "We have officers searching your car and your home." She paused, assessing Tam's reaction. "Is there anything you want to share with us?"

"There's nothing important in my room. You know. You've been in there." Tam smiled. "All I had in my car was a duffel bag with some clothes. Big deal."

"Where were you headed tonight?" Riley asked.

"Going away for a bit. Not sure where. I just needed to get away." Her voice was soft, like it was bathed in honey.

"Ya know, something always made me curious. How did you afford a Mini when you couldn't even afford to live on your own?" Karen asked.

"I couldn't afford to live in New York City, asshole. Two totally different things."

"But you don't work here, so how can you maintain that car? Those are expensive to maintain, aren't they, Riley?"

Karen turned to her colleague.

"You said you were a potter, or, um, a ceramicist. Yet you never got a membership to the art studio. You don't have equipment at home."

"It's none of your fucking business what I do," Tam said.

"It might explain why thousands of dollars were missing from the floor safe at the house."

Tam became still. Her face grew pale—a physiological response she couldn't avoid or conceal. "Did Bobby tell you about the safe?"

"You think he would have left all that money there if he knew about it?" Riley said. "He was desperate for money to keep the house from foreclosure."

After a faint tap on the door, Officer Roberts tiptoed in and handed Karen a sheet of paper. Karen sensed her eyes were the only thing moving in the room. Dispassionately, she handed it to Riley.

In one slow, measured movement, she looked up and spoke. "Tam, is there anything you'd like to tell us?"

Tam squinted as if trying to assess whether Karen had something or was bluffing. She sat still, emotionless.

"Now would be the time," Riley said, placing the paper upside down on the table.

Tam glanced at it, her body rigid. "I got nothin'." There was a brief pause. "And you got nothin'."

"Do potters use medical exam gloves?" Karen asked.

"Sometimes." Tam sounded nervous.

"Ahh. That explains why we found a pair of used exam gloves tucked in the back seat of your car."

"Those probably weren't mine. Maybe your girlfriend put them there. Maybe you put them there. Maybe you're both trying to frame me for something."

"The gloves have your DNA on them."

Tam let out a nervous laugh. "You don't have my DNA."

"Yeah…yeah, we do. Remember all those sodas you drank? The napkins you used?"

Tam sat, reticent.

"On the gloves were traces of blood. Blood that matched that poor man who was lying dead on your driveway."

"Those gloves had his blood on them because I reached down to check him, remember?" Tam smiled at Riley. "Maybe you should help her, Detective Riley. She seems too incompetent, or maybe too old to remember information from all of a few hours ago."

Ouch. It wasn't the incompetent part. The age thing was a low blow.

"Tam…the blood on the victim had dried all those hours after he died," Karen said. "It's documented in the original report. Forensics confirmed it along with confirming the time of death. So, your footprint was made several hours earlier. The blood on the gloves… hours earlier, too." Karen looked at Riley.

In the silence that followed, Karen summoned Roberts before reading Tam her Miranda rights. Roberts's hands trembled as he placed the handcuffs on a stunned Tam.

"Do you understand your rights?" Karen asked.

Suddenly, Tam shouted, "Why don't you understand? I had to do this. It was the only way. I needed to get your attention. I needed for us to have a chance. But you blew it."

"What the hell are you talking about?"

"I tried to get you to see me…to get to know me. All you had to do was give me a chance. Give us a chance. This never would have happened if you let me in when we first met."

Karen and Riley stood silently.

"Everything I did was for us. And now you're trying to make me the liar. But I'm the one that was fighting for our relationship. You threw it all away." Tam barely blinked. "Why don't you understand that? Why can't you support that—support me?" Tam's tone held a blissful innocence. "We could have had a great life together."

For Karen, it felt like the moment froze. Time stretched, encompassing the enormity of what Tam was revealing. She felt chilled by the icy premeditation of this homicide and the unconscionable explanation.

Karen felt viscerally ill. She gestured to Roberts, who led Tam away, the faint trace of her musk dissipating on her way out.

Karen slogged back to her office as if sleepwalking. Riley popped her head in.

"I don't get it, Ri. Why didn't she just throw the shoes away?"

"Sociopaths often feel invincible. She probably thought she was smarter than all of us," Riley said. "You heard her in interrogation… commenting that the shoe prints left no marks. She felt she covered her tracks."

"I still can't believe she would take a person's life, just to get my attention…to get me to be with her."

"For a sociopath, people are disposable…just props to get what they want and need. Like you said, she saw Cliff as disposable. He was a means to her ends."

"I didn't see it. I didn't see the warning signs." For Karen, the comment pertained to more than just Tam.

"Don't beat yourself up. The first time I dealt with a sociopath, I fell for every ounce of deception." Riley gave her a reassuring smile. "Once you've dealt with a sociopath, you'll never forget it. Capp, trust me. You'll never be duped again."

After Riley's calm presence vanished, Karen fought through her astonishment and her emotions. Her report would have to wait until the next morning. She needed to get away from what she had just witnessed. There would be plenty of time to debrief with Riley and file her report the next day.

Karen's parents' house was lit up like a Christmas tree on the otherwise darkened street. She drove past her house and into her parents' driveway. Walking up to the front door, Karen felt as if she were carrying a two-hundred-pound backpack. The door was unlocked, odd for that hour. Her mother's voice echoed from the top of the stairs, the lights assaulted her eyes. She looked past her parents to Judy, who sat in the kitchen.

"What's going on?" Judy's voice was soft and guarded as she studied Karen's face.

Karen shook her head and muttered, "I was a fool…an absolute fool. How could I have been so blind?"

Everyone stared, dumbfounded. Karen just shook her head. She had zero emotional energy remaining to explain the horrific day she had just endured. She just needed to decompress, in a safe environment. To feel loved.

"Have you eaten? We have leftovers." Stella tugged the refrigerator door open.

Karen shook her head.

"A beer?" Stella pushed.

"Maybe, like…five hundred." Karen grimaced.

She sat quietly as Judy made small talk and her parents shared stories about Florida. Karen nodded, numb.

After finishing her second beer, Karen stood. "I need to get home. I'll fill you all in later. Right now, I just need to shut down my mind." *I need to shut down my heart.*

CHAPTER THIRTY-TWO

The next morning, Karen awoke weighed down by the enormity of the previous day. Her hopes and dreams had been annihilated—trampled on and crushed. The previous twenty-four hours replayed in her mind like credits scrolling at the end of a movie. A cold-blooded killer had duped her. She had been outed at work. Her fears caused her to push away the woman she loved.

Scenes played out, over and over. Tam took a man's life in hopes of attracting her attention. She suffered a guilt that wasn't hers to own. Tam had taken a man's life and now was destroying Karen's, from the inside out.

And then there was Miles. She allowed herself to be conned by him—to be used by him—missing all the warning signs. *You're a goddamn detective. You're supposed to see through lies.* While she realized he was merely a bracer for her loneliness, she couldn't shake the thought that she had actually considered allowing him back into her life simply to not feel judged and ostracized.

And Ali. Poor Ali. She devastated a woman who had always been true and honest. Ali fit, like that missing puzzle piece that falls into place once you find it. She had thrown it all away out of fear of societal repercussions. *You don't deserve to be loved by someone like her. Hell, you don't even deserve to be a detective.*

The revelations swung like a lead wrecking ball, heavy and powerful. Yet the emotions behind them landed flat. Holed up in her living room, she felt herself crumbling. She needed to pull back. She needed time away. Later that day, with reports complete, she requested a leave of absence.

For southeastern Pennsylvania, February was the snowiest month, leaving a quiet stillness and a deep, damp cold in its wake. The winter chill outside paralleled Karen's heart inside—existing in a frozen hibernation. Karen collapsed into her own personal winter, literally and figuratively. Cocooned in her living room, she spent hours simply existing.

Memories of Miles were corrosive. Replaying her time with Ali—gut-wrenchingly painful. A depression, metallic and hard, invaded her and took possession.

After two weeks, Judy stopped by without an invite. Karen's once impeccable living room—ordered and picked up—now sat in disarray. Unopened mail piled in heaps on the coffee table. Plates of half-eaten food and empty beer bottles scattered about.

Karen confided in Judy in a manner akin to emptying the garbage. Everything poured out and in no particular order. It all smelled rancid.

"How could I have been so blind? She was a sociopathic killer."

"Her expertise is lying. But you put her away. You solved the case."

"I missed the clues. I bought into the lies. And I'm a detective." Karen closed her eyes tight as if to vanquish the memories. "She came across as so goddamn sincere."

"You know what they say…sincerity is the province of the effective liar."

Karen slammed her fist into the back cushion of the sofa. "And the one fucking person that was good for me…I chased her away."

"Why don't you talk with her? Be open. Honest," Judy prodded. "The only way out is through. Confront your pain to get to the other side."

She knew Judy was right. She needed to step through the muck herself, a journey she wasn't feeling strong enough to make.

Karen hibernated in her living room, most days never getting out of her flannel pajamas. Each day blended into the next. She was adrift on a never-ending ocean of despair with no land in sight.

When March finally rolled around, it arrived with a massive nor'easter barreling up the East Coast and dumping a foot of snow. It was just one more reason to isolate herself. She gazed out the window the morning after the storm. A beautiful white blanket covered the neighborhood. *Like putting a tux on a pig.*

A handful of neighbors gathered at the end of the street, bundled up, steam flowing from their mouths into the biting, pure air. They began clearing all the walkways. A ritual, neighbors helping each other. Karen would normally be out there, too. Instead, she grabbed the throw on the back of the sofa, wrapped herself like a burrito, and reclined out of sight. Her eyes closed as she drifted off into a mindless daydream of thoughts.

Days grew longer and a touch warmer. Judy prodded Karen to get out and do something…anything. To no avail. Karen had no interest in being social, or being anything, for that matter. Her sleek physique hollowed out and her face became gaunt as her weight plummeted. The dark circles under her eyes matched her disheveled hair. At this point, she just pulled it back into a ponytail and ignored it. Unpaid bills piled up along with the unopened mail. Mugs and plates that never made it to the sink accumulated on the countertop or coffee table along with leftover containers.

Judy paid another visit. "What can I do for you?"

"Nothing. Just need time."

"It's been six weeks!" Judy shrieked.

"Didn't know there was a stopwatch running," Karen said with a long sigh.

"Please tell me this isn't about Miles."

Karen smirked. "I thought I adored being with him."

"You adored being with him in public. You adored the concept of him. You didn't adore *him*." Judy's voice held a parental tone.

Deep down, Karen knew Miles was just a tonic to fend off feared assumptions about her sexuality.

"Jude, you don't get it. I'm a total fuckup. My personal life… my professional life. I've fucked it all up. I can't even show my face outside this house."

"You're wrong. Nobody's judging you."

Karen vigorously shook her head.

"You think people have any idea what happened with Tam? All they know is you found the killer and she's behind bars."

"It's not just that, Jude. I can't hold a relationship. And worse, Tam outed me and now everyone knows I got involved with a woman."

"Oh, brother. A sociopathic liar said things about your sexuality." Judy rolled her eyes. "Who cares, anyway? It's your personal life. No one else's business."

"You're kidding, right?" Karen threw Judy a look of sarcasm.

"The people that love you want you to be happy. Ali made you happy, and that's all that mattered to us."

"Jude. This town isn't ready for their detective to be a fucking dyke."

Judy cleared her throat. "I know you're new at this, but I believe the correct word is lesbian."

Karen finally grinned. "Do you remember when our town manager was forced to resign? The rumors about him being gay?"

"Geez, Kare. That was ages ago."

"Yeah. And it was a big deal."

"Things have changed a lot since then. And it was also never proven. He resigned on his own terms."

"He was *forced* to resign. And the guy that went after him was none other than Officer Dan Brennan." Karen paused. "If you think Brennan hasn't gotten wind of my relationship with Ali, you're crazy. He's probably spending my time on leave scheming to take my position."

"The way I recall it, the town manager chose to resign due to Brennan's accusations," Judy said. "The whole town was up in arms. Everyone loved Gus Matthews. They were pissed at what Brennan did."

Karen remembered the town gossip back then. Gossip in her department was slathered with homophobia. It took almost three years to die down. Judy reminded her that it was just a handful of hateful people.

"Kare, this town loves you. Everyone loved Gus, too. Remember how they tried to push him to rescind his resignation? No one gave a shit whether he was gay or straight."

Karen stared at Judy.

"Why don't you give Caiden a call?" Judy's voice pierced the silence. "She'll be an elixir for you."

Karen knew Caiden would see right through a faux-happy voice on the phone. Better to just work through her issues before talking to her.

As it turned out, Caiden beat her to the punch, calling her just a few days later.

"Mom...what the *hell* is going on?"

"Nothing."

"Cut the crap, Mom. Judy told me something's up."

Walled-off emotions bubbled to the surface. Karen found herself sharing the whole sordid mess with her daughter, including the internal issues she had yet to resolve.

Caiden groaned after hearing that her mother had pushed Ali away. "Have you reached out to her?"

"I hurt her. I'm pretty sure she wants nothing to do with me."

"Mom. She loved you."

"Loved. Past tense."

More than a heartbreak, this was something deeper for Karen. It was as if she was searching for something and, at the same time, trying to outrun something else. She felt suffocated by a terrifying self-revelation—her uncanny penchant for being drawn to all that was wrong for her and, at the same time, the desperate need to follow social convention.

"Ya know, Mom, when I was a kid, you sacrificed your marriage for the sake of your career. Maybe it's time to do the opposite. Accept a loving relationship with Ali and screw your career."

"I'm not worried about my career." Karen's chest tightened as she spoke.

"Really?"

"Hon, it's about my actions. I made a bad mistake. I can't expect her to forgive me."

"Mom...she's not like that. Just talk with her."

"I'm sure she's moved on by now." Deep down, a different reality was seeping in—the reality that she didn't deserve someone like Ali.

March came to a close, and with it, the snow shovels were put away. Spring was around the corner. Karen persisted in hibernating. Even the early buds on the trees did little to lift her out of the darkness. With her return to work a couple of weeks away, she wasn't sure she'd be welcomed back, let alone be returning as the town's detective.

Spring beckoned, a beautiful and welcoming time of year. Brown lawns greened again. Stunning white blossoms filled the dogwoods and cherry trees in the neighborhood like cotton balls dotting the landscape. Early spring brought an earthy scent of damp soil along with the perennial sight of cheerful daffodils and the delightful scent of blooming hyacinths.

Trees transformed from their cachectic, desolate state to a burst of abundant green. The handful of people out in their yards came armed with ice picks, breaking through the frozen soil to add flowers to their gardens. That always amazed Karen. If they just waited another few weeks, the ground would soften.

The thawing of the winter brought people back outside. Streets filled with dog walkers. Kids played in the yards again. But Karen's heart still was encased in ice. She knew she needed to emerge from her burrow. Caiden was also scheduled to return home for the summer—the only thing Karen looked forward to. The house had fallen into chaos. Her yard was an overgrown disaster. A mountain of work to do and little energy or desire to take it on.

Neighborhood yards sparkled with bright flowers and meticulously edged lawns. Karen's glared like blinding headlights. A handful of neighbors gathered, as they did to shovel snow in the winter, and organized a yard cleanup at her house. The sense of community—something she loved about Parks Ford—warmed her heart, perhaps even thawing it a bit.

She gazed at her mowed yard and mulched flower beds. Bunches of petunias and pansies lined her walkway. The stagnant, deep chill began to melt.

With her return to work now just a week away, she refocused and began to let go of the corrosive guilt she once felt. It wasn't her fault that Tam had a personality disorder. It certainly wasn't her fault she chose to kill a man just to get Karen's attention. As sick as it made her feel, she had to let it go. But the person who had given her the love she longed for…it was this that she struggled with the most.

Sun splintered through the foliage. The air was clear and temperatures mild—a beautiful spring day, a time to be outside enjoying the weather. Around ten on Saturday morning, Judy helped herself through Karen's front door, arriving in a low-cut tank top and flowing skirt. Karen, still in pajamas, was sipping coffee on the back deck.

"Okay, girlfriend, it's time to get back to living. You've had enough time and space," Judy said, walking onto the deck.

After they both returned back inside, Karen glanced at Judy.

"What…are you freakin' going on a date at this hour?" Half-awake, she looked Judy up and down.

"Kare, it's time." Judy pointed to the mounds of dirty clothes on the floor and the pile of papers littering the coffee table. She glanced at one particular item—a flyer—and pointed to it. "You should go to that art festival. The weather's terrific today."

Karen cowered, envisioning being social when her safe little cocoon worked just fine. But the art festival? A knot twisted in her stomach. "No way in hell I'm gonna take a chance of running into Ali…in public. Have her tell me about the new person in her life… how she's so happy…how I was such a fool," Karen rambled, then took a deep breath. "I don't think I can see her. Pretty sure she doesn't want to see me."

"You don't know that."

Karen realized how her emotions had become governed by her feelings for Ali. She reflected back to the night Ali's car had been vandalized by Tam and how she dreaded calling in her officers because of what they might think. It went against protocol and it went against everything she stood for. What she did back then—to protect Tam from legal action, she had told herself…hell, to protect herself from being revealed—it wasn't who she was. She may stretch the rules occasionally, but she didn't break protocol. She wasn't that kind of person.

Yet her terror over revealing her sexuality ruled her. Fears had led her to break protocol. Then they caused her to push Ali away. How could a relationship be good if it caused her to go against everything she stood for? How could the two coexist?

Karen shook her head. Right now, her biggest angst was over the possibility of laying her weary eyes on Ali. *How will I react? How painful will it be? What if I fall apart at the sight of her?*

"So, what are your plans for the day?" Judy asked.

Karen half raised one shoulder and looked away.

"You need to get out…out of pajamas and into the world. We're not gonna have this weather much longer." Judy paused. "If you won't go to the festival, why don't you join me at Ryan's T-ball game?" she said, referring to her nephew. "It's just down the street at Hamilton Park."

"I don't know."

"Kare, it's easy. Just cheer for the kids when they do something good. Starts at noon. Ryan will be thrilled to see you."

Karen felt a smile emerge. *Ryan's a good kid. And he always enjoys asking police questions.* "Okay. I'll be there."

Relief flooded Judy's face like she had just moved the Rock of Gibraltar. With her commitment to Judy, Karen would finally venture into her wonderful little town and become a part of it again.

Starting the shower, she realized it was indeed time to emerge.

CHAPTER THIRTY-THREE

Karen hopped into the steaming shower. Throwing her head back into the beads of water, it felt as if she were rinsing away months of emotional debris. Showered and dried, she threw on a pair of jeans and a V-neck T-shirt.

She caught her reflection in the steam-framed mirror as she ran a brush through her hair, frowning at the gray strands popping up around the edges. *This will have to do.* She had no one and no need to impress—getting out in public was impressive in and of itself.

Hamilton Park was an easy five-minute drive from her house. She rolled down her window, allowing a cool spring breeze to run through her hair. Driving through familiar streets and neighborhoods, an unexpected sense of joy filled her soul. Her head fell back onto the headrest as her shoulders lowered. Kids played in yards while adults yakked over chain-link fences and hedges. The hum of power yard tools punctuated the atmosphere after the silent winter. The town was alive again.

Karen glanced at her watch. 11:55. With the park only minutes away, she decided to relish the sights and sounds of spring, driving around a bit longer. She wound around various neighborhood streets as if lost in a pleasurable maze. Town residents waved to her. It brought a smile to a face that ached to feel joy again. At a stop sign, a man called out, "Great job, Detective." *Ugh, if he only knew.* She smiled and nodded, the recognition bolstering her spirits.

Driving around, she felt her heart coming back to life. Her soul blossoming. The essence of fresh-cut grass filled her senses. After a quick glance at her watch, she pulled into a gravel lot and stared straight ahead. Her first social outing. For a split second, she considered driving back home. With a deep breath, she reached for the door handle. She could do this.

Her foot crunched into the gravel. Children played tag in the foreground. Their joyful voices and laughter brought a smile to her tense face. She gazed beyond them, focusing on the space in the distance.

Standing in utter disbelief, she gasped at the vast number of artisan tents lined up, row after row. After a deep, affirming sigh, she made her way to the main area of the art festival. Central Park was right in the middle of the business district and the only location in town big enough to host such a popular, well-attended event.

She strolled down a row of vendor tents, marveling that all these artists spent so much time and energy making things that she couldn't imagine owning. *Who needs a wall hanging made out of sea glass?* The next aisle. *Why buy a picture of a sunset, when you can take one with your phone?* Next aisle. *Who on earth would wear jewelry made of feathers and beads?* She paused. *Judy. Judy would probably wear that.*

Standing at the top of a new aisle, she scanned the tents.

Pottery. The back of a blond artist's head. She would know that head anywhere. *The only way out is through*. The words played over and over in her mind as she strode down the row. With every step, her stomach, then chest, felt like they were caught in a vise grip. She couldn't tell if each step represented a step closer to slaying the dragon of her fears or a step closer to the guillotine.

At some point, she was going to have to confront Ali. She couldn't exist in this small town, looking over her shoulder, fearful of running into her. Arriving at the front of Ali's booth, she stood frozen.

Ali pivoted to greet her as if she were a customer, with a wide, welcoming smile plastered on her face. The smile turned to wide-eyed surprise. Her face tensed.

"Hi, Karen. How are you?" Ali's voice was soft and quivered as if forcing back emotions.

Karen began to feel an excited discomfort. A strange, unsettling longing. "Good." *Liar.* "How are you, Al?" She struggled to keep her gaze focused on Ali. Looking away, she perused Ali's pottery display. "These bowls…they're beautiful—"

Ali responded to Karen's question at the same time. Just like the first day they met, nervously stumbling over their words and talking over one another. They both stopped talking and smiled. Ali wasn't throwing daggers, as Karen had expected.

"It's good to see you." Karen found herself choosing her words carefully. "Anyone…new in your life?" *God, I can't believe I just asked that.* Self-annoyance bristled through her.

Ali smiled. "No. No one new. Not dating. Not even looking, for that matter." Ali's pinched expression preceded a question that seemed to be eating at her. "So, are you and Miles back together?"

"No. No Miles. I wanted more." She stared into Ali's sweet blue eyes. "I wanted better."

Karen felt a lump forming in her throat. A touch of a sting came to her eyes as the first moisture began to well up.

"I just figured when I didn't hear from you—"

Karen felt a wave of nausea wash over her. *Caiden was right. I should've reached out.* "He's gone. And I'm not welcoming him back."

Ali rolled her eyes, but Karen could see tears beginning to form.

"Ali. I'm sorry. I'm so, so sorry." For the first time in a long time, maybe her life, she dropped her guard and said exactly what she felt. "I was scared, Ali."

"And now you're not?" Ali's tone was a lash.

Karen couldn't tell whether Ali's words were coming from a place of anger or pain. *Aren't those two emotions the same?* "I finally realized I had a choice. Grow a pair, or live an inauthentic life."

Ali stared as if she expected more—expected something else.

"I've had this time to figure out what I was so afraid of…that led me to push you away."

"And?" Ali's tone was challenging.

"Society's rules." Karen paused. "You're the first and only person I've ever truly loved. And now…as long as it takes…I'm going to work to get you back. As long as it takes."

"You can't just put the raindrops back in the cloud."

Karen felt a glimmer of a hopeful smile form. "How 'bout putting them back in the rainbow?"

Ali's ire—the way her face turned red and the freckles bounced off her cheeks when she got mad—was something Karen always thought was so cute. She swallowed the smile that was forming. *Not the time, Capp.*

"Excuse me," Ali said in a curt tone as she turned to help two customers who entered her booth. Her drawn face lit up with a sudden I-need-to-pretend-I'm-happy smile.

With Ali distracted, Karen made her way to the back table of Ali's wares. There it was. The mug. That tall coffee mug with soft yellow tones and blue falling down from the rim. It was the one Karen first laid eyes on when she went back to find Ali at the studio. She admired it. Loved it. Ali had offered it, but Karen had felt uncomfortable and turned it down. She never forgot about that mug, and over the last several months, she'd wished she had kept it—something of Ali's to hold on to.

The couple finished browsing and left, leaving Ali with the inevitable—having to face Karen. Ali squared her shoulders and turned around.

"Why didn't you stop me?" Karen's voice was soft, almost trembling. "Why didn't you knock some sense into me? Tell me I was a fucking fool?"

Ali swiped at a tear that escaped down her cheek. "That wasn't my job."

"I love you."

Ali snorted. "Just figured that out?"

"I figured it out a while ago. Just wasn't sure how to approach you."

Ali's face filled with hurt as she shook her head.

"Straight women. Forbidden fruit…so enticing, isn't it?" Ali scolded. "You think you can waltz in, get your kicks, fuck up my life, and say you're sorry as you head back to your safe world."

Karen felt her face deflate. *She has every right to feel that.* A pit in her stomach began to swell. Looking up at Ali, she handed her two twenty-dollar bills.

"What's that for?"

Karen's other hand held up the yellow-and-blue mug. She let it go when they first met, she wasn't letting it go this time. She had no idea if there was hope for anything with Ali, but with that mug, she knew she would always have a part of her.

Ali waved her hand at the bills. "Just take it."

"No," Karen insisted. "You work hard at your craft. This is your business." She thrust the bills toward Ali.

Ali begrudgingly took the money. "Here. Let me at least wrap it for you."

"Nope. I'm good." Karen heard the lilt in her voice, something that had been missing for months.

She turned to walk out and stopped. *Sometimes you have to run the risk of exposing how you feel.* She looked Ali square in the eyes. "As long as it takes."

Grabbing ahold of Ali's shoulders, she pushed her lips firmly into Ali's, opening her mouth to steal an intimate, and very public, kiss.

Karen pivoted and walked away. A mile-wide grin. The shame that had held her back so many times before…she pushed through it. She survived. No one pointed or glared at her. Nobody even seemed to notice.

She hustled to her car. Almost one o'clock. She had made a promise to Judy, never imagining she would be diverted by an unexpected bolt of courage. In her car, her head felt light again. She felt a sense of joy again.

She felt like Karen again.

CHAPTER THIRTY-FOUR

Karen arrived at Hamilton Park to find the game practically over. She jogged to the teeny set of metal bleachers, hearing the *tink* of a ball hitting a bat followed by an intimate crowd cheering. She could see the bottom of Judy's skirt through the bleacher steps, blowing in the breeze.

"Where the hell have you been?" Judy spoke in just above a whisper. "I was getting worried."

"Sorry. Took a detour."

"You okay?"

Karen felt a smile unconsciously form on her face. "I needed to purchase a mug…at the art festival."

Judy's eyebrows popped. "The art festival?"

"We'll talk later." She felt her chest swell. Deep down in her gut, she knew things were going to be all right. She had faced her demons, put herself out to Ali completely and without reservation. Whatever happened at this point was meant to be. She accepted that. For the first time in months, she felt gratitude to be alive.

At home, the stark realization of how much she had let things go slapped her in the face. She crunched across the debris on the living room floor, picking up stacks of dishes that needed washing. She gazed at piles of laundry and shook her head at the disheveled mounds of papers and bills needing to be sifted through and discarded.

Caiden would be appalled. Hell, I'm appalled. "Actually, Caiden would be alarmed," she muttered.

There was so much to do. She would be back to work in less than a week. No one from the station had contacted her. Her chief hadn't called to tell her she'd been demoted or that Brennan was now the town's investigator. Consciously, she put anxiety-laden thoughts about work on the back burner and began preparing for Caiden.

Karen's parents were planning a party for Caiden at her house with all of Caiden's favorite local foods: cheesesteaks from Michael's and crab fries from Chickie's and Pete's. She knew the extended family would also be stopping by. The garbage dump of a house needed a major overhaul and pronto.

In a crescendo of excitement, it hit her: her baby was coming home. The angst over Tam dissipated. Anger and self-loathing over Miles—gone. She missed Ali—terribly—but in a few short days, her house would no longer be empty.

From the front window, Karen could see Caiden's beige Camry pull onto Summit Road and into the driveway of her childhood home. She was back in Parks Ford. Within minutes, the entire family stood in the front yard, waiting for Caiden to come around the four-foot privet hedges separating the driveway from the front walkway.

Caiden left her bags in the car and pranced around the hedges, beaming. She ran up the walkway and wrapped her arms around her grandparents, embracing Karen next with what felt like an endless hug. Tearful emotions formed in the back of Karen's throat. *My little baby. All grown up.*

After the initial front yard reunion, the family retreated into the house.

"I'll be right in, Mom. Gonna grab my bags." Caiden trotted down to her car.

Karen stood in her sloping front yard. She heard Caiden pop her trunk, then the *clunk* of what sounded like a large bag hitting the driveway. The trunk door slammed. She waited for Caiden to reemerge. Nothing.

"Oh my God," Caiden yelled from the driveway. "I'm so glad you did. Come on inside. We're having a big party."

Who the hell is she talking to?

Karen came around the edge of the hedges as Caiden picked up her oversized duffel bag and reached for Ali's hand.

Karen froze, staring, unsure what to say.

Ali, too, stood frozen. It was as if time froze, as well. All three women, motionless and silent. Karen's stare was fixed on Ali. As the gentle breeze blew wisps of blond hair across Ali's face, she didn't move, not even to brush the strands away.

Karen squinted. "What are—"

"I texted her when I got across the bridge," Caiden said. "I wanted to see her when I got home."

Karen walked over to Ali. Pulling her near, she wrapped her in a gentle embrace, feeling the sting of emerging tears in her eyes.

"I've missed you," she whispered into Ali's ear.

Caiden slung her duffel bag over her shoulder and scooted up the walkway. Karen pried herself away and met Ali's blue eyes. They, too, glistened with moisture.

"What's going on?" Karen whispered.

A tear rolled down Ali's cheek.

Karen read Ali's facial expression as one of pain and apprehension. She knew she couldn't change what had happened, only vow to never allow it to happen again. But promises were only words. She would have to show Ali—prove to her—that she could be trusted. And that would take time. *As long as it takes.*

Karen held out her hand. Ali hesitated. Biting her bottom lip, she took Karen's hand. Together, they sauntered up the walkway toward the front door. Halfway up, Karen threw her arm around Ali, drawing her close and landing a quick kiss on the side of her head. *God, I love this woman.*

Larry pushed open the storm door and stepped aside. The rebirth of spring was complete. The house was full again.

Bella Books
Happy Endings Live Here
P.O. Box 10543
Tallahassee, FL 32302
Phone: (800) 729-4992
BellaBooks.com

More Titles from Bella Books

Jones – Gerri Hill
978-1-64247-598-2 | 260 pages | Mystery
One weekend getaway, six friends, and a deadly secret that will wash away everything they thought they knew.

Merry Weihnachten – E. J. Noyes
978-1-64247-610-1 | 292 pages | Romance
Christmas traditions aren't the only things getting mixed up when these two hearts collide beneath the mistletoe.

Sweet Home Alabarden Park – TJ O'Shea
978-1-64247-570-8 | 362 pages | Romance
She came to restore a royal estate—she never expected to rebuild her heart.

Dr. Margaret Morgan – Christy Hadfield
978-1-64247-628-6 | 286 pages | Romance
Facing the professor on campus everyone hates is terrifying—but falling for her might be even worse.

Overtime – Tracey Richardson
978-1-64247-630-9 | 278 pages | Romance
A charming romance about second chances, found family, and scoring the goal that matters most.

The Big Guilt – Renée J. Lukas
978-1-64247-657-6 | 206 pages | Romance
What if the one who got away became the one you can't have?

www.ingramcontent.com/pod-product-compliance
Lightning Source LLC
Jackson TN
JSHW020226120925
90865JS00002B/3

* 9 7 8 1 6 4 2 4 7 6 9 4 1 *